GALLOWS HUMOUR

LEVITY BROWN

CONTENTS

NOT NEARLY A WEEK

Under a mantle of ebony hair, Solomon Monday prodded his birth certificate across the desk to the impassive Crookshank who, very slowly, picked it up. There was an icy silence as the solicitor studied the document behind his horn-rimmed glasses, keeping the recipient of Gallows Humour in suspense.

But this was how Crookshank preferred to do business, with the lowest tricks played against a backdrop of the highest stakes. For the entire fidget over his client's death, Crookshank had recognized certain Monday hallmarks - a man of entirely different calibre. His nature was such that he had the capacity to take on a challenging role with an ability to energise and deliver. And that's what Crookshank needed the most, someone to deliver. It was Monday or a throbbing bag of gloom above him.

'Our occupations are not so dissimilar.' Crookshank returned the document. 'As you would check the validity of a story, so I must check the validity of a claim. Did your mother ever mention Gallows Humour?'

Monday raised his head and slowly shook it, his dark eyes implacable as those of the big predatory cats. 'Were you aware she died last year?'

'My deep sympathies go with you. Just to set the record straight, this has nothing to do with your mother's estate.'

'So would you care to switch on my lights?'

Crookshank pushed back his chair, stood in a moment of contemplation and quietly laughed. There was greater meaning to those words, as no doubt Monday would soon discover. 'I think we should by-pass the coffee and 'switch on your lights' in the car. Come. All will be explained on the way.'

The tall Monday spilled out of his seat and followed the squeaky leather soles that frequented the corridors of a dusty old law firm. The mention of his mother brought back the picture of her face, bloated and pale, the smell of soil and flesh, and the stumbling words of the vicar. Those were the memories he carried with him; the unspoken words buried down deep into a valley of stone.

Outside to the opening lustre of a private car park, Monday sniffed the air to the afternoon sky fading towards early dusk and crawled into the front of a black BMW, sinking heavily into a leather seat. With the quiet Crookshank at the wheel, the motor joined the city traffic inching along at a speed somewhere between that of a turkey and a worm.

'The property,' Crookshank began, 'was constructed as a courthouse during the mid-part of the eighteenth century. In those days, the entire population of Norfolk was agricultural and uncultivated and, of course, the most ignorant as well as the most degraded came that way to be hung. When the judiciary transferred all cases to the assizes in Norwich, Judge Culver Week took title to the property and converted the building into his residence.' A quick glance to his side, and Crookshank added, 'It would appear he also had a sense of the macabre and called his estate Gallows Humour.'

'Am I related in some way to this Week character?'

'Indeed you are, Mr Monday, indeed you are - on your father's side. Let me explain. Week had six children by different women, whores to be precise. He could not offer paternity to the world so each child was registered with a surname corresponding to the day of their birth, not necessarily in the same year, you understand. However, the children were sufficiently provided for and one could say Week had almost completed his week.'

Blinking rapidly with comical astonishment, Monday bent his thoughts to the matter at hand as this solicitor's strategy began to unfold. 'Who put you up to this? Mike? No, strike that. It had to be Harry.'

'There are good reasons why there has been no emergence of Week's private life and those reasons will become clear if you can widen your thoughts. The facts of the matter are, Week had six children and their births were registered quite legitimately. He placed Gallows Humour in Trust, which, until recently, was managed by Jeremy Sunday for sixty-two years, a good man but a little behind the times. Believe it or not, you are now the beneficiary of Gallows Humour. Monday naturally follows Sunday if you get my drift.'

And that was the problem. Monday was unable to get the drift, that moment, that afternoon, and why such names had never been mentioned before. If this was a wind-up, then Crookshank was certainly playing his part with accustomed ease.

'Let's cut to the chase, Mr Monday. You're an intelligent man in your prime, you haven't worked for some months and your future hangs in the balance. So, what I'm offering you is a second chance in life. The estate is yours, not to sell but to manage at the Trust's expense. Should you fail to take up the offer, you forfeit control of Gallows Humour. No changing your mind, now or in the future. It would be offered to the next in line.'

'Tuesday, I suppose,' he said as if to himself. His mind was in some far-off unseen world as he tracked the open countryside skirting along the A47. It appeared to him that Norfolk was like a pancake, flat with an odd rising hump of benign dominance.

'When you consider security of tenure,' Crookshank went on, convincing, soothing, 'no financial worries, and all legitimate expenses paid, this is an opportunity to take seriously. Of course it does require an element of responsibility, though it will not preclude you from continuing your line of work; reignite your political mind, if you so wish. Or perhaps something interesting can be done with the estate, say, lose a little round the waist. One can do a lot with fifty acres if they have the will and imagination.'

Fifty acres sounded impressive enough but what could Monday do with it? Anyway, it would be like owning part interest in a business that he could neither sell nor let. But regardless of all that, he had become tired of deadlines, tired of peddling faster in order to stand still and another consideration was Britain. Economic contraction, rising unemployment, the addiction to borrowing huge sums from more self-disciplined countries, and the ascent to notoriety of more and more members of the feckless underclass, all indicated a nation on the slide.

'Not sure what I could do with the land other than admire the view,' Monday finally spoke. 'Besides, I don't see this as a country at all; just a bankrupted and balkanised domain under the direction of Washington in the West and Brussels in the East.'

'Are you thinking of moving abroad?'

'Not really.'

'Well then, now is a good time to exchange your pessimistic pencil for an optimistic packet of seeds.'

Any gratitude Monday might have felt for this piece of advice was exhausted by the time the motor pulled softly between huge rusty wrought iron gates which, when shut, baptised the name Gallows Humour.

The uncomfortable cruise down a potholed drive was dwarfed by trees, their green glow casting tall shadows until their canopies unwrapped like sweet paper to reveal a daunting edifice rising up from manicured lawns. Chimney stacks and a bell tower protruded from moss-flaked tiles, square sash windows bucked against flaking white paint and long tongues of broad-leafed ivy crept round corners like jagged ominous cracks. It was the approximation of Pandora's Box nuzzling in a cloud of green smoke.

Immersed in the scene, the only negative was a hint of nervousness, but then that was to be expected. Yank Monday out of his fashionable London apartment and thrust him before an antiquated building hiding a cocktail of mischief inside, he stuttered a few times.

'Come along, Mr Monday.' Crookshank jumped out of the motor. 'Let me introduce you to Palfrey.'

On the front steps under a dilapidated porch, the resident butler looked more like a sentry, black shoes shining brighter than his face. Palfrey answered a few benign questions, much lighter fare than what had been served up before, and then a small trickle of masonry powder fell from the ceiling. Another detail, another manifestation and Monday looked up.

'Not to worry,' Crookshank said. 'Palfrey, I am taking Mr Monday to the bell tower. Make a nice pot of tea, there's a good fellow.'

New imperatives crowded in as Monday strode the marbled grandeurs of an ancient hall led by the energetic Crookshank. The solicitor's feet exerted a wide flight of polished oak stairs that expressed a better opinion to the surrounding walls. The possibility of the place falling down could bring out the politician in any man.

'Did you say Jeremy Sunday lived here for sixty-two years?'

'As our bodies grow old so do our houses. Come along, Mr Monday, this way.'

Almost lost among the confusion, the solicitor's voice soon became audible when, from a narrow staircase, Monday finally stepped into a swoop of fresh air under a one chime bell. Here, his horizons opened up to a far more generous vista, deep in leafy levitation. To the east lay the drive from whence they came, to the south a patchwork of oaks, to the west a settled lake of floating white lilies, and to the north, taller and more compact trees oozing over a shallow hill like thick green lava. For the next few moments, he stood in the midst of endless possibilities in favour of games in the sun and games in the moon. If nothing else, it gave rise to the hope there might be a future in his otherwise woeful life.

Shrugging off his jacket, he sent a meaningful look at Crookshank. 'What would my position be if I made a thriving business here? How is my investment protected?'

'If we are talking about monetary investment, the Trust would provide it, as it provides for all running expenses. Palfrey is a man of many talents, is fully conversant with the workings of the Trust, and will assist you.'

'And any profits I make? Who has that?'

'Naturally the Trust will benefit. Yet there is no reason why you cannot pay yourself a salary commensurate with your achievements.' Crookshank could afford to be generous. 'No different from a banker's bonus.'

Monday listened to the drifting sounds of the birds on the water, to the noise echoes about the treetops by the green woodpecker hammering at bark in search of small insects and grubs, and somehow it felt more real than anything he had ever known. Perhaps he had been too negative, perhaps too quick to criticise for what now appeared to be an excellent opportunity. It gave way to the notion that the environment could be a product of him rather than him be a product of the environment. When he looked back to express his views, Crookshank's head was disappearing down below.

In the same flurry of energy, the solicitor returned to his motor and hung on the driver's door. 'It may be a good idea to stay overnight,' he called out to Monday as he came into view. 'Think things through. Palfrey will show you the rest of the house, see to your needs and answer any questions that come to mind. Let me know your thoughts tomorrow morning.'

Naturally, Monday could sense the urgency and stood on the front steps beside Palfrey, gazing at the wake of dust coiling behind the motor's wheels, and froze the image of being left behind. Secretly, the idea of getting away from Angela was not altogether unappealing. He swung his jacket to the back of him, adopting a slightly different posture.

'Tea is served on the veranda, sir. I do hope you like cucumber sandwiches.'

'Cucumber sandwiches?'

'We must start our diet sometime, sir.'

If Monday was honest with himself, there had been nothing of late to stir him from the doldrums. He loosened his tie, rolled up his shirt sleeves and fell into step. 'Tell me about Jeremy Sunday. What did he do all day?'

'Twiddled his thumbs and spent your inheritance.'

'Has it all gone?'

'It was a joke, sir. I shall try harder next time.'

Monday smiled. 'Crookshank informed me you did all the paperwork around here.'

'Most assuredly, I am the forever obliging all-rounder at your service, six days a week. Saturday is my day off. Peace and tranquillity for an old codger who likes to watch the Canaries play.'

'Canaries?'

'Norwich City Football team.'

'Ah yes, the major shareholder is Delia Smith.'

'Her cooking has not improved their performance.'

The butler had taken Monday through the central core of the building, out to the rear garden, where stood a set of wrought iron furniture padded to a high degree. Crustless sandwiches cut into squares and curling at the corners, accompanied by watercress and tomatoes, were so arranged on a blue and white plate as though to transform them into a trance of memory rather than an appetising supper.

'I do hope we can get along, sir,' Palfrey said, pouring anaemic tea from a chipped Dresden coffee pot. 'Life was a little slow with Mr Sunday. But there again, he was on his way to heaven.'

'Tell me about yourself.' Monday waved him to sit. 'How long have you been here?'

Palfrey removed his white gloves, pushed his fingers into the thick white strands of his hair, then let them fall into his black suited lap. 'I came at a time when one could sit next to a child without being suspected a paedophile. My wife, though I wish her dead, left me for another man after emptying my bank account. Here, I have security of tenure for the rest of my life and have served Gallows Humour for sixteen years to the best of my ability.' There was a belligerent pause before he added, 'Now it is your turn, sir.'

'Ah, well, I have come at a time when sitting next to a woman constitutes sexual harassment. My girlfriend Angela prefers to swan in my London flat, hoping my modest ambitions will exceed her expectations. Here, I have been offered security of tenure for the rest of my life and have a muddle-headed business concept that might not be served to the best of my ability.'

'Then welcome to the club, sir. May I enquire as to what business you had in mind?'

'Crookshank informs me I am entitled to dip into the Trust, in which case, I thought of creating an adventure playground. Swing through the trees and act the idiot with a paintballing gun.'

'Most certainly, there is an element of hooliganism in us all, sir. However, had you not considered a market aimed at imbeciles who like to dress up in combat trousers and go on a serious hunt?'

'Serious hunt?'

'How fast can you run, sir?'

Monday rocked with raucous laughter. But why not? Why not be the hunted, turn the game around, quick on his heels, traps to ensnare the hunters. Disregarding his out-of-condition body, the adrenaline rush alone would be worth something.

'I like it,' he admitted. 'And the name is apt. Hang the clients up by their ankles, hey, Palfrey.'

'Perhaps we should re-install the gallows to lend the atmosphere.'

Now there was a thought. 'Do you know where they were built?'

'Not fifty yards from where we sit.' The well-informed butler stamped a foot hard down on timber, a thudding sound to make his point. 'Solid oak,' he declared, 'straight from the gallows. Judge Week had this platform constructed so he could reminisce about the poor souls he let hang.'

This brought Monday to a sudden standstill in his thoughts. Indeed, Week sounded a very macabre character. 'So,' he said, shaking himself out of it, 'should I manage to thwart the enemy, do you know any after-supper tales to soothe their defeat?'

'There is one which I find particularly amusing.'

'Then fire away. I'm all ears.'

Palfrey cleared his throat and began in utmost fervour. 'The most curious experience that ever befell the local vicar was over a woman of 40. This poor creature had not even the instinctive disinclination for her fate that the dumb animal feels on the threshold of the slaughterhouse. The night before her hanging, she sent for him. It had been a pouring day, as most November days in Norfolk are, sir. To those who knew the circumstance of the case, she was scarcely an object of pity, for the murder she had committed was a most brutal and appalling one, but it was impossible to behold her without sharing her wretchedness. She was standing under the barred blank window with her eyes fixed upon the gallows, listening apparently to the splash of the storm, but she turned quickly round as the vicar came in.'

He gave a little cough and emulated the tone of a woman's voice. '*Vicar, is it true I am to be hanged tomorrow?* It was not easy to reply to such a question, so the vicar only inclined his head gravely. *Will you grant me a favour?* The vicar told her that anything that lay in his power would be done. *Well, tomorrow will be wet. Now, never in all my life has it happened to me to walk under a silk umbrella. Will you let me do it just this once?* He gave her, of course, the required assurance, and her warders reported afterwards that she went to bed in good spirits and passed an excellent night. Her first words on being awakened in the morning were to inquire if it rained, and on being informed that it did, she expressed her satisfaction. The rest of the sad ceremony seemed to interest her very little, but never would the vicar forget how her dull hard face brightened up at the sight of the new silk umbrella that was presented to her. She held it over her head to the gallows foot with a hand which, if it trembled at all, did so with conscious pride.'

Monday sat back and crossed his legs in a mask of astonishment. From the butler's performance, he gathered Palfrey was educated, fluent and glib, a hidden gem that could work in his favour. 'You execute a story very well, Palfrey.'

'Thank you, sir. I am not without experience. My parents were thespians of sorts, mostly played at the London Palladium alongside the likes of Norman Wisdom and Bob Monkhouse.'

'Bob Monkhouse?'

'Not of your era, sir. I never rated him as a comedian, more suited to hosting shows. And you, sir, I understand you write political slots.'

'Did do, Palfrey, did do. Contrary to popular belief, a man of my age should be climbing the ambitious rungs of the media ladder; instead, I just want to jump off and seek terra firma. Admittedly, I was wavering, the usual thing, like how do I get my girlfriend to pay the bills, then lo and behold this came along. I tell you, I thought this was a wind-up. Is it a wind-up? No, strike that, you wouldn't tell me if it was, would you?'

'I may look like a clockwork toy, sir, but I can assure you the only person who has the key is you. Would you like a tour of the house?'

Standing in agreement, Monday arched his back and soon found himself returned to the central core of the building, the main hall with its formidable staircase rising up to secret doors, as yet unknown. Rather than head that way, Palfrey whooshed open a pair of twin oak doors to courtroom furnishings. Here, it was like walking into the physical period of past jurisdiction, easy to visualise rank upon rank of hobbling boots, nodding caps and furious faces as Judge Culver Week brought down his gavel to restore law and order.

'Why has this area remained unconverted?'

'History,' Palfrey explained, 'to be remembered with a buzzing in the ears, to be revisited when the mind is strong. Here is the tangible evidence the building was constructed as a courthouse.'

'I see,' but did Monday really see? 'It has a conservation order.'

'One could say that, sir. Shall we continue with the tour?'

'Lead on, my man. Do we have central heating?'

'We do, sir. The vents in the floors provide hot air from a wood boiler in the basement, installed by the previous Mr Friday.'

'You mean Mr Sunday.'

'Prior to Mr Sunday, there was Mr Friday.'

Monday stopped mid-way. 'Crookshank never mentioned a return to a new Week.'

'There would have to be others, sir. Mr Sunday was not immortal.'

'Yes, I realise that, of course I do, now you mention it. So how many came on board?'

Palfrey clutched at his throat, head tipped back, mouth gaping, staring at the intricate plaster work on the ceiling like a tourist in the Sistine Chapel, which in turn made Monday look up as if the answer was there.

'It rather works on a rotational basis,' Palfrey finally said, recommencing the tour of the ground floor. 'The first to come on board was, quite rightly in my opinion, Nathanial Sunday, for he was the first day of the week. That would be in 1840 when Judge Week passed away. When Sunday departed, it automatically transferred to the next willing Monday, and so forth, until we arrive back at the next Sunday to do it all over again.'

'But no Saturday,' Monday flippantly added.

'Even God had a day a rest.'

'We must agree to disagree on that one, Palfrey. So where are we?'

'Judges' chamber, sir. It was said in the twilight years of Week's life, he would sit in that chair, hunched over his desk, looking at his work. And there he died with a pen in hand but no work.'

'No work?'

'He had retired, sir.'

Monday was unimpressed with this modest-sized room, in which had been gathered a lifetime of trophies, including some oddments of cracked china, a bust of the man himself, and a feeling there were ghosts in the furniture, ghosts in the walls and ghosts in the floors. But elsewhere his eyes appreciated the antiquities caressing the accommodation, the monolithic fireplaces, niches and silences, barely stained by the encounters of family life and mourned for its lack of contemporary living.

So Monday had to ask, 'Why no electricity?'

'Mr Sunday thought he ought to leave it a generation or two to see if it catches on.'

'Did he ever marry?'

'Like the seven dwarfs, he was far too busy doing nothing, sir.' A door opened wide. 'Here we have the gentleman's library where he spent most of his time researching his past with a port bottle.'

There was nothing to dislike about the smell of old paper and leather, cluttered lines of history waltzing across polished oak shelves and the traditional hollow globe of the world that flipped up England to reveal a brandy or two. If Monday had the money and space, minus Angela, his London apartment would similarly be representative.

'I, too, will execute my duties with a malt. Is there enough in the kitty to extend this far?'

'At current levels of interest rates, an hour will buy you a crate, sir.'

'Are we talking millions?'

'Indeed we are, sir.' Palfrey indicated to the books of trade and commerce, of profit and loss and all such matters concerning the Trust. 'If nothing else, Mr Sunday was extremely good at choosing the right commodities and increased the portfolio substantially. He often reminded me, when it came to rock bottom, there were two ingredients people are forced to buy…food and water.'

'How right he was, Palfrey. The Chinese are buying up land in Africa to harvest food for their people. And in ten years' time, our population will grow to seventy million. Can you believe that? Seventy million on this tiny island? Where on earth shall we put them?'

'Not here, sir. Trees are considered more valuable than people and there is the paradox, for without trees there would be no people. Shall we move on?'

The basement, once an area exclusively for the condemned, had been converted for domesticity. There was a large kitchen with an old-fashioned range, a wine store, a washhouse, a boiler room chugging heat by wood, and Palfrey's accommodation. The inner hall felt damp and smelt musky even in summer, and the ceilings were low with very little natural light squeezing through the original barred windows.

'I suppose,' Monday said with a vague chill linked to his ancestral past, 'this is where a condemned prisoner would look out and see the gallows.' He craned his head round and stared back at Palfrey, bringing stilton to the table. 'If I remember correctly, there are no windows in your quarters.'

'That is because they are to the front of the building, sir. It would have been unseemly for the condemned to observe the advocates arriving at court. Would sir prefer cheese and grapes with a glass of port before bedtime?'

A far better option than cucumber sandwiches, he thought. 'So, let me see. There's no electricity, no gas, but there is a telephone in case of emergencies. How fortunate. What did he think about television?'

'Mr Sunday felt the BBC was undeserving of its licence fee, preferred to read the paper instead, or listen to the radio until the batteries went dead. He rather enjoyed your interpretation of the Labour Government.'

'So, he knew of me?'

'Oh yes, sir, as did Mr Crookshank. Both knew a day would come when Gallows Humour might rest at your fashionable feet.'

'My mother was the true philosopher, Palfrey. Before she died, she told me a person needs a change, to find new experiences. Without change, something sleeps inside us, so here I am, the sleeper must awaken.'

'How did she die, sir?'

Monday's heart grew heavy with recollection and regret. It was something he cared not to talk about, and simply said out of politeness, 'cancer of the breast,' trusting Palfrey would leave it at that.

And he did. 'Shall we proceed to the bedrooms?'

These rooms were the same, the way their doors all spilled along dull corridors, all interiors bearing striking similarities as though someone had ordered a mountain of blue striped wallpaper and matching tiles in suspect en-suites. But still, Monday thought, open this one and it might be different.

But what he actually discovered to be different was his suitcase and laptop resting on a four-poster bed.

'How did my things get here?'

'I removed them from the boot of the car, sir.'

'And how did they get in there?'

'Norfolk is renowned for its village mentality. Shall I unpack?'

As the shadowy little smile came and went on Palfrey's face, Monday nodded, unaccustomed to the attention he was given, though indeed, was now enjoying. Overall, the property was certainly not his desired choice, and it made him feel he was in a place a little to the left of the twenty-first century.

So, with the blue striped curtains drawn closed, candles casting ominous shadows, and the cheese and port on its way, Monday settled down at his laptop, wearing his rimless spectacles, scrolling through electoral rolls. There were a number of Sundays, plenty of Mondays, and, of course, loads of Fridays linked with Robinson Crusoe. In between, there were Shrove Tuesdays and Ash Wednesdays, certainly no ordinary Thursdays. He veered off on a slightly different track, punching in *Gallows Humour* that appeared to be restricted to a realm that left no trace in history.

When Palfrey walked in with a tray, Monday looked up from his laptop. A question burnt on his lips but said, in an unthinking way. 'Do you know if there are any days left in the Week?'

'Well, sir, discounting Sunday and today, there are five.'

'Ask a damn silly question and get a damn silly answer. I was referring to Week's bloodline. I don't seem to be getting much luck in tracing them.'

'In those days, young children dropped dead like chickens, their diseases not well understood. However, families were large enough to compensate the successive invasions of diphtheria, whooping cough, pleurisy-'

'Yes, yes, I get the message, Palfrey.'

'May I remind you to blow out the candles?'

'Why? Are we short on them?'

'No, sir, we are short on fire extinguishers. Good night, sir.'

Glancing once more at the laptop, Monday waved Palfrey good night and decided to give it a rest. What difference would it make? Apart from draining the battery dry, his search would be out of curiosity, not out of necessity.

He kicked off his shoes that told of battles won and lost, reclined against the pillows at the head of a creaky bedstead and watched bare flames play eerie shadows on the walls. But he was unable to help himself and further exerted his instinct for intrigue while distant thunder shook the sky. Was he consciously denying Lady Luck had landed in his lap, or was there something fundamentally odd about Gallows Humour?

Five minutes later, with a glass of port in his hand, he parted the curtains and watched as the sky lit up. Forked lightning afforded a brief glimpse of the lake, gardens and trees like a picture book that drew a familiar scene. He turned away and walked to the laptop as though it was impossible to let go of his nagging discontentment. Punching a few keys into Google, a page came up on Judge Culver Week.

Far from being the maverick of tradition, the Judge was a skilled player of politics with a strict punishing hand. But what was of immeasurably greater importance was what he did before rulings. He made the accused in the dock sign a register, whether by a cross or a dirty thumb print and those decreed guilty by a jury of influential men, Week doodled a hangman's noose. The register, a small leather brown book which was humorously titled Week's Work, never left his side and was so thick that his small hands could not close round it.

Monday thought most of this was legend or rumour but knew even legend and rumour usually had some basis in reality. He grabbed his mobile off the bedside cabinet and contacted Michael Kern, a friendship accrued from university days.

'Mike, it's Sol,' Monday said when the writer picked up. 'Can we talk?'

'Hang on a mo.'

Monday lit a cigarette and dropped back into silence. He heard muffled voices, a closed door and guessed right away his friend was adding another notch to his gun.

'Okay, all clear. How did you make out?'

'Still in Norfolk, sitting on a four-poster bed, drinking port under a roof of historical importance, all mine for the rest of my life once I sign up.'

'You're shitting me!'

'I shit you not. Crookshank picked me up from the hotel, never said a damn word, drove me to his gold-plated offices, examined my birth certificate and spilled a bizarre story about an ancestor widening the waters of his gene pool.' Then Monday related the legend of Judge Culver Week, the children he sired, his extraordinary requirements, and the extraordinary estate called Gallows Humour. 'The cells were under the courthouse,' he continued more wearily now and reclined back on the pillows, looking up at the discomforting cracks and stains on the ceiling. 'Palfrey is up to scratch on its history, whereas I got the feeling Crookshank was attempting to separate himself from the property.'

'Odd, wouldn't you say he squirrelled your luggage?'

'It seems to be a common practice around here. Logically, it made sense. He saved me the cost of a night's hotel.'

'What are you going to do about Angela?' Trust Kern to give him a clearer view of basic truths. 'You know she contacted George, put you up for the political slot.'

'I'll handle it.'

'Like you handled her moving in? Look, I know sex plays a pivotal role between couples, but it's the pound signs which give her a climax. She'll have multiple organisms when she hears about your inheritance. She telephoned earlier, asked why you switched off your mobile.'

'I never switched it off.'

'Okay, so what does this impoverished writer say if she rings again?'

Monday was unconcerned. 'Mike, what are you doing over the next few days?'

'Not a lot.'

'Then get your arse down here. Take the underground to Liverpool Street and the fast track to Norwich. All expenses paid, what do you say?' There was a long pause and Monday asked, whilst stifling a yawn, 'Is it the girl in your bed?'

'I only met her six hours ago. No, Sol, I was thinking of doing away with my latest crap and concentrate on this Week character. Do you think that butler could supply enough ammo?'

SIGN UP FOR THE LONG HAUL

Last night, Monday had glided away under the surface of sleep like a whale in tropical seas then emerged to a day full of paradise, the storm having passed over rowdy without so much as disturbing his dreams.

He swept back the covers, pulled up the window and breathed deep of autumn air so that he could sense the weather and the life to come. There was no inclination to investigate further the operatic flavour of Week's life or his bloodline, which currently remained void in the pages of the world-wide web.

As the hot water made its leisurely pursuit through the ramble of furred pipes, he braced for cold water passing beyond the antiquated shower head. After a quick swill down, he dried himself off and dressed again in the same navy blue suit and yellow shirt as yesterday, leaving the red tie wrapped round a hanger. Now, taking a look at himself in the wardrobe mirror, he decided against wearing the suit jacket thus exposing his burgeoning waistline.

'Solomon Monday,' he talked frankly at his profiled reflection, 'we should do something about this.' But at a deeper level he appealed to his weaker side and breathed in. 'Oh yes,' he said smiling, 'much better.'

Buoyed by an energy and optimism attributable to his new-leaf frame of mind, he waltzed out of his bedroom, went down the main flight of stairs, swung into the dining room where there he took the back stairs toward a kitchen from which breakfast would hopefully emerge. Yet scarcely had he stepped one foot through the door, a small-framed body, pinched of colour with silver hair wispily tied up in a bun intruded upon him.

'What hev we here,' said she with a flavoursome twinge of mischief. 'Solomon Monday no doubt, come fer his breakfast.'

'And you must be the cook.' After a well noted shake of the head, he guessed again. 'Palfrey's bit on the side?'

Doolally let out a shriek of laughter, and flames threw up around a warm copper kettle lodged on the stove. 'Pay no heed,' she told him, waving the incident away. 'If yew hear broken crockery that's me, Doolally, crashing the plates in the sink.' Then suddenly she took on a worried frown. 'Hev yew signed up yet?'

'No, but-'

'Then I shouldn't be here, talking to yew. I best be off.'

'And miss my illustrious company?'

There was something about her which intrigued Monday. Not least the absence of two front teeth, sharp little veins crackled around her playful eyes. The grey dress was buttoned to her neck with sweeping tattered threads to her feet and she was compounded equally of curiosity and cheek.

'Hev yew got a wife?'

'Are you proposing?'

'I could teach yew a thing or two.'

'Is that so?'

'What yew need is a young gal that isn't as shallow as a puddle.'

Obviously referring to Angela, Monday reckoned she heard and saw through keyholes, and switched his attention to the kettle that had sighed its way to a boil. When he looked back, she was gone. But she was the beginning of wisdom chipping away at his principles. So, while the kitchen remained mostly in shadow, he made treacle coffee and burnt toast then later telephoned Crookshank from the library.

'Mr Monday.' Crookshank came on the line. 'Have we come to a decision?'

'I certainly have, which rather brings me to the issue if you cancelled my hotel booking.'

'Do you wish to leave?'

'No, I wish to stay.'

'Then what is the fuss all about?'

Monday opened his mouth to speak then closed it, trapped in his own argument.

'Tell Palfrey,' Crookshank went on. 'He will know what to do.'

'Do you know the name of the dish washer?'

'Hotpoint, I believe. Good luck, Mr Monday.'

Looking at the receiver with a furrowed brow, it occurred to Monday that Crookshank took the world without worry or chastisement, that his ceaseless duties were shuffled in a mutinous rush upon a dry sense of humour.

After dropping the telephone onto its cradle, he leaned back in the desk chair and lit a cigarette, allowed his eyes to travel up the wall in front of him and roam across a painting. To the untutored eye it probably represented a country scene of no significant value but to him, he recognized it as a genuine Constable that was sold to an unknown buyer at Sotheby's auction house four years ago. Now his journalistic mind began to work again. He snatched open a drawer, scrambled around for some paper, picked up a pen and scribbled a note. How many days in the week are left? It looked odd so he drew a line through days and wrote bloodlines. Then he folded the paper, leaned to one side and shoved it in his trouser-suit pocket. There it would remain until another query popped up.

Bearing in mind last night's conversation with Kern, he dialled Angela's mobile with his fleshy bottom lip coursed over his top uncertain what her reaction might be. When she picked up, he said, 'I'm still in Norfolk.'

To which she replied, 'What did you get?'

'A future.'

Instead of a belligerent response to conflict with his views of which he was geared to convey, the line went dead. Not sure whether he was disappointed or relieved, he looked round when the butler walked in.

'Good morning, sir.' Palfrey placed a cup of tea on the desk and a plate of ginger nut biscuits. 'Did you sleep well?'

'I did, Palfrey. I most certainly did and I remembered to blow out the candles.' He pushed back the chair and stood up in a relatively good frame of mind. 'Who is the dish washer? No, strike that. Who is the woman that claims to be doolally?'

'As she informed, sir. We tend to drop the formalities.'

'Exactly how many people work here?'

'It depends, sir. They come and go when the need arises. Perhaps it would be a good idea to introduce yourself to whomever you bump into.'

'Mmmm,' Monday grunted, stirring his tea. If there had been doubts before, blown away under misapprehension, they were certainly gliding back in. 'Crookshank slips my luggage in his boot without any meaningful dialogue except to say I am a descendant of a man who fathered six illegitimate children registered Sunday to Friday. Since Saturday is the God of Agriculture who ruled the earth during the age of happiness and virtue, I am wondering if Judge Week put his pecker away on that day. Setting aside the absurdity, I stand in front of an intelligent man who takes a very relaxed view towards unreliable staff notwithstanding the dysfunctional dish washer called Doolally. Now, I don't know exactly why Jeremy Sunday would want to live a century behind the times but there should be some changes around here, not least the introduction of electricity in order to recharge my batteries.'

And all the while Palfrey's concentration powers showed in his expression; his mouth was slightly open and his tongue poked out between his teeth.

'Perhaps you can enlighten me further,' Monday continued picking up a ginger nut. 'Or am I to assume Norfolk is entirely cut-off from the outside world?'

'Oh, how right you are, sir. Norfolk has always been a forgotten part of England. Not even the motorway is duelled completely, and we only have half a ring-road. But we do know the way to a man's stomach.'

'Damn, you're right. This is the best ginger nut I've ever tasted.'

'Are we ready to sign up for the long haul, sir?'

'Go for it.'

The pivot point had been reached, the critical instant for which every beneficiary had signed up to. Palfrey removed a red leather-bound volume from the top shelf, Gallows Humour embossed in gold on the spine. He laid it on the desk, opened to a blank page whereupon a pen was taken from the inkstand, dipped in the ink-well and handed to Monday.

But Monday was far from happy. 'What's this?'

'A blank page, sir.'

'Yes, I can see that, but why?'

'Tradition, sir. As Judge Week required inmates to sign in then so too must his beneficiaries do the same in order to gain access to the Trust.'

'And that's it? No terms of employment?'

'Sir, Gallows Humour is not employing you. It only requires your heart in the running of its estate.'

Beginning to see the humour of it, Monday smiled resignedly, bent down, signed and dated his signature. At the point of returning the pen to the ink stand, the front door knocked loudly, twice. Palfrey went to answer leaving Monday to leaf into the memory of the pages where he discovered an abundant of past signatories dating back from 1840 when Nathanial Sunday first signed, taken over by Arthur Monday five years later. As he continued to scan the many signatories, he was making mental notes of the short durations between each one with the exception of Jeremy Sunday who lived at Gallows Humour for sixty-two years. That was an encouraging sign.

So, when Palfrey came into the room, Monday, whose suspicions were growing incrementally looked up and asked, 'Were these beneficiaries old when they came on board?'

'Sir, may we dispense with the history lesson for now? A gentleman roams in these woods. I took the liberty of asking him to give you advice on your new venture.'

'Who is he?'

'Mr Woods of Treetop Games, though he is known as Woody.'

'And exactly where shall I find this Woody?'

'Follow the worn track by the lake, sir. It will take you to the oaks.'

For now, scepticism could wait. Monday walked on and the sun climbed, the autumn wind barely registering. He smelt the crushed freshness of greenery beneath his feet and kicked freely between the long grasses beyond the manicured lawns. The lake was a haven for insects buzzing above sprouting lilies whose cool white petals fanned murky waters too deep to paddle. Typically, he noticed a rowing boat tied to a peg but unusually something else much larger covered by tarpaulin banked under a weeping willow tree. Had time not been of the essence he would have investigated further.

Upon reaching a jungle of shrubbery, the worn path ended and there, just beyond the first thickness of oaks was a giant of a man, smoking a pipe. His arms were tattooed in every quarter, his breaches held up by braces and he waved in the shadows with a whiskered smile.

'Woody at your service,' he boomed in a deep barrel voice.

'Solomon Monday.' They shook hands vigorously.

'Now tell me, Solomon Monday what do yew hev in mind?'

'A few years back I went to an adventure park somewhere in Hampshire, forget the name. Anyway, we chugged around on quad bikes, did a spot of paint balling and drove a Chieftain. I liked the tank, got boring after a while but the paint balling was fun. The drawback, the scope of our perimeters was limited, which made it easy to spot the enemy. When I saw the extent of these woods, I thought this has potential for paint balling then Palfrey suggested an even better idea. Why not boys with toys become the hunters and I become the hunted. So, what I need is to lay a few traps, something to keep them on their toes, and perhaps a few other things, like swinging from tree to tree.'

'Mums don't take too kindly to having their kids break a leg.'

'You misunderstand. I want to tap into a niche market, men looking to play dangerous games, well not that dangerous but enough risk to give them a good run for their money.'

With the stem of the pipe clutched firm between his teeth, Woody ambled on without looking up, his mind in obvious overdrive. 'I can rig perilous traps for leg stretching, hazardous traps to knock them out or terrifying traps to wet their pants.'

'Terrifying sounds good. What does that entail?'

'Ever heard of Russian Roulette?' Woody laughed heartedly and smacked Monday fondly on the back. 'I be messing with yew, lad. I can rig safe traps to stop them from catching yew. But what fun is that? Yew hev the advantage, so the joke is on them and that won't be good fer business.'

Monday nodded, another doubt added to a sea of concern. 'So, just do what the competition does, paint balling and tree-walks.'

'These oaks are spread too thinly to be any use as tree-walks but over to the north the trees fight for light that's why they're tall, a good place for young uns to learn what life's all about, the struggles and hardships.'

'Not sure I want screaming kids on this land.'

'Screaming kids hev screaming parents. If there's a place to knock them out at night, parents will pay. On the forest floor is the hardest place to survive, the canopy over there is so thick it's hard to get any sunlight through. But plants on the forest floor need not be passive. If the light doesn't come to them, they must go to the light and climb another plant to use as scaffolding but they won't get any higher unless they can hold on tight. That's how kids are, just the same and they like to climb the trees to get to the light. Fer every metre they climb, the light gets a little stronger. Other plants hev a different strategy to find light and that's what the oaks can do fer yew. Let kids go on a treasure trail and find what creeps on the forest floor.'

'And supervision? Insurance? Health and Safety? How long is a piece of string where kids are concerned?'

'I can supply all that and make it safe as houses. Close down fer winter, like the oaks, the trees go to sleep without their blanket of leaves. If yew can't make money six months of the year, then yew need your head examining.'

Monday looked at Woody. His settled face suggested a man of bottom, a man who had seen it all. 'Okay, let's veer in that-'

Suddenly a distant shout gave rise to the obvious. Thief!

Too jittery to continue with the business at hand, Monday made a bolt for the house. Impulse required no sense. By the time his fourteen-stone body leapt the steps and pushed through the hall, there was no doubt someone had visited. Scattered about, broken crockery lay discarded on the marbled floor and from within the courtroom a struggling visitor shouting and banging on the door.

'Let me out you silly cow!' To the turn of a key, Michael Kern was exposed, a blue-eyed red-faced shaggy animal with a fondness for paisley and snakeskin shoes. 'Who's the batty woman?'

'Doolally.'

'You can say that again. One minute I'm on the front step, next I'm looking at plates heading my way.'

'She thought you were a thief, an easy mistake.'

'Hey! Do I look like a thief?'

Monday could tell by the set of Kern's shoulders he was annoyed and momentarily squeezed his eyes shut trying to quiet the pounding in his head. 'How did she manage to lock you in the courtroom?'

'Now that is a very good question,' Kern replied picking up bits of crockery. 'Let me see. Perhaps it was the plate that cracked my nuts or the threat to disembowel me.' He paused, his manner now tranquil, a charmer living in a charmless life. 'Why are you out of breath?'

'I ran all the way.'

'Not like the damn train service. Where shall I put this?'

'Leave it for Doolally to clear up.' Monday walked on. 'Come on, I want to show you my library.'

Their conversation was functional as they headed toward the library, brief discussions about the deplorable train service, a passing enquiry about Angela, her capacity to create histrionics, and the efficient Palfrey who lived down below.

Kern squirmed out of his leather patched jacket, flung it across a chair, rolled up his paisley shirt sleeves and eventually came circumspectly to the point. 'So it's all legal then?'

'Yup,' Monday said, placing his feet on the desk and his hands behind his head, though not relaxed enough to totally erase that distant stirring alarm. 'Mike, there's a whisky bottle and glasses in the globe.'

'By the way, don't bother to cover my expenses. I spoke to my agent. Maggie loved the idea. Gallows Humour...how's that for a title?'

'You're not turning this place into a gothic horror.'

'Hey, it'll be good for business. Boredom is a far greater threat than the turn of an unsolved mystery.'

Professionally, Kern was confident. Surefooted, arrogant even. Monday had seen him wring concessions from agents that made his efforts appear like a damp squib.

'Look, the way I see it, the book comes out in six months, yeah? The publicity alone would save you a fortune.'

'I have a fortune.'

'Not your fortune,' Kern reminded passing over a drink. 'Can you write yourself a cheque to the Bahamas or a yacht on the Med? No, apart from being staffed by odd balls in this antediluvian property, your duty is to manage the estate, not spend it.'

'Thank you for that belligerent response to my otherwise hopeful self. I am not looking to be a pirate on the high seas or get laid under a banana tree. Have you ever come across a situation like this?'

'Hell, people do funny things when their loaded. I knew a chap once who gave his entire fortune away to a midget. Why a midget, because he looked up to him.' Kern laughed, perching on the arm of a leather armchair looking at Monday whose expression was fixed in assumed indifference. 'Okay, why the long face?'

Monday sprang to his feet, removed a volume off the bookshelf and passed it to Kern who, with a puzzled expression, slowly flipped through the pages. It was one of those immutable facts of signing on for the long haul, the bizarre wishes of a senile Judge.

'Why sign blank pages?' Kern asked.

'That is not the right question. What you should be asking is why so many signatories? The first to sign up was Nathanial Sunday in 1840, that's the year Week died. Apart from my predecessor, everyone who came on board never stayed long.'

'How do you think they left?'

'Logic dictates they took up the offer well past their prime but that strikes me too coincidental. And you know my feelings about coincidences. If we are to assume they took over the estate in their prime, then why leave? Look at this place, Mike.' Monday motioned to the painting on the wall. 'It has money crawling all over it. So that leads on to another question. Did they leave vertical or horizontal, the latter is hard to imagine. Not even the Queen can cover up so many deaths. So I'm back to asking the same question, why did they serve a short period?'

Kern returned the book to its spot on the shelf and knocked back his scotch. 'Okay, here's a good theory. They never left voluntarily but were kicked off the estate for thieving.'

'Why do it? Why bite the hand that feeds you? In those days jobs such as this were virtually unheard. A large house on a large estate, tenure for life, no restrictions, everything paid for. Damn, Crookshank had me so confused I never asked the right questions. I never even asked to see a copy of Week's Will.' The last line he said more to himself than to Kern. Was it staring him in the face? He picked up his reading glasses and traced a finger along the leather spines of well used ledgers. 'Here,' he said, weighting Kern down. 'You look through the accounts and see if you can find any anomalies to back up your theory.'

Without further word, Monday left the library and made his way to the basement. There he rapped twice on Palfrey's door without an answer.

'I shan't apologize.' Doolally surprised him. 'He should hev waited to be invited.'

'I invited him.'

'See,' she said with eyes wide open, 'this is how it works. Yew tell the butler who comes to stay. He tells the cook, the cook tells me and I tell the chamber maid who then tells everyone else so they can be on their best behaviour. Hev, we got that?'

'And where are these people?' Monday irritated. 'All I see is you and Palfrey.'

'That's because there hasn't been much call for their services, hev they now?'

He stood staring down in mutual fascination. A second later he heard a noise in the kitchen and trod quickly along the damp corridor. But if he had stayed, if he had found the courage to poke around in the dank corners, to let his eyes see into the gloom and the shadows, he would have found a lot more.

Palfrey, who was stirring a simmering pot on the stove, turned when Monday walked in. 'Everything is under control, sir. Mr Kern's suitcase has been placed in the room next to yours. I thought cream of mushroom soup, followed by roast beef and a dry red, finished off with apple pie and cream.'

Monday breathed deep of hunger, lingered over the mushroom soup and smiled. 'It smells wonderful.'

'The table will be laid at six. Meanwhile, to keep the tummy from rumbling I made a pot of tea and a plate of sandwiches.'

'Not cucumber, I hope.'

'Sir, I cannot be cruel two days running.'

'Palfrey, do we have a copy of Week's Will, details of the Trust and all that?'

'Is there a problem?'

Monday hesitated, uncertain whether to speak his thoughts, if it were wrong to involve an innocent in his cause. 'I was curious...after all, I am a descendent of Week and thought it would be interesting to delve into the chap's mind. Do you have a copy of his Will?'

'Would you like me to get it?'

'No, just tell me where it is.'

'In the Ming vase precariously balanced on the drawing room table.'

'Surely it should be kept in a safe.'

'We have Doolally, sir.'

Shaking his head in wonderment, Monday picked up the tray full of goodies and walked on thinking it was a strange thing to do but then he started to feel relaxed about the whole thing, the way sometimes a new person in an unfamiliar place can feel when they meet a friend.

In the drawing room, he placed the tray on the table and foraged in the vase whose glueless seams suddenly came tumbling apart, pieces skating across a polished surface. There was no excuse for lack of diligence when Palfrey had clearly given warning.

'What hev yew done!' Doolally scorned.

'Err, it just fell apart.'

'Of course it would, I heven't got round to gluing it back.'

'And who broke it in the first place?'

'Widdle worries, who broke it first. It wus mended and yew broke it last.'

Monday tried to keep a straight face and picked up the tray. 'If you have nothing better to do than mess around with a broken vase, I suggest you piece it together using glue this time.' Not that she approved of this. There was nothing he could do about her, except to smile at the things she said. 'Mike, we shall be dining at six.' He kicked the library door shut. 'Can you last that long on a ham sandwich?'

'Sure, no problem. What's that?'

'The Will. It was in a Ming vase that broke on contact.'

'Say that again?'

'It was already broken but pieced together without glue. Actually, come to think about it that was a clever thing to do.' He chuckled at the thought as he passed over a cup of tea. 'I told Doolally to piece it back together again with glue this time, not that I can see her doing it. She's impervious to authority, importing moreover a kind of outrageous view so inspired that it remains unanswerable. So where are we at?'

'So far there's diddlysquat. Entries for general maintenance, etcetera, etcetera but nothing untoward. The interest on the money was accruing faster than it was spent.'

'Okay, keep at it.'

Monday slipped into a leather seat with a ham sandwich and the Will on his lap He was familiar to some degree with legal jargon, the document being composed of all that which Crookshank had mentioned, and more. Sexual behaviour was usually the life blood of gossip. The story of Week's affairs and the subsequent births of his children was the sort of thing that would make the rounds regardless of his wife's noble acceptance. But here was proof that Week did claim paternity for each child and their constraints to the Trust.

By six, silence in the library was suddenly broken by the rattling noise of the dinner gong as if the intemperate sound laid a curse upon them. Kern closed the books and asked for the bathroom whereupon Monday obliged then dropped back into thought as he wandered on. He was no longer thinking of the Trust but another something else just as mysterious and tackled Palfrey who was at the cutlery drawer counting out the spoons.

'Palfrey, where do the servants sleep?'

'I had not the mind to ask, sir.'

'Ah, so they're local, live nearby. I never saw any cars in the drive. Come to think about it, do we have transport. I presume there is a car.'

'We have a Rolls Royce Phantom, sir, to the north side of the house. A little past its prime but so are we all.'

'I ran from the woods to the house realizing I was out of condition. If I am to be the hunted, my only hope of escape is to climb up a tree and keep out of sight. By the way, who broke the vase in the drawing room?'

'You did, sir.'

'No, before me, who broke it?'

Abruptly, Kern walked in rubbing his hands. 'Good evening, Palfrey. I see my case turned up.'

'Things never go far in this house, sir.'

'Solomon tells me you're good at story telling. How about joining us?'

'Yes, sit down, Palfrey and relax.' Monday struck out a chair but the butler remained unmoving. 'Mike has written a couple of inconsequential books so now he has it in mind to write a consequential one about Judge Week.'

'A very ambitious plan, if I may be so bold as to say, sir.'

Kern nodded as though he understood completely. 'Everyone has a skeleton in the cupboard, hey Palfrey?'

'Sir, we have a whole bloody cemetery.' Palfrey addressed Monday. 'I find it rather unsettling to eat with one's employer, besides which I do have other duties to perform. If you will excuse me, gentlemen, please enjoy your meal.'

Monday had this strange sensation that Palfrey had aged in the last five seconds, and that the lines formerly confined to his neck had migrated up to the sides of his eyes. A dull nervous something throbbed in his stomach, a feeling he worked hard to quell. 'We made him feel uncomfortable. After all, he was employed as a butler not a dinner pal.'

'With a face like that, I don't think so. Let's assume, for argument's sake, that these guys signed up round about your age, discovered the place was haunted and left pretty sharpish.'

'Mike,' Monday said picking up his soup spoon, 'if you ever have an idea, warn me first. I don't want to die of shock.'

'Hey, I have yet to hear your contribution.'

Between them they covered a number of dubious equations. From cooking the books to murder and conspiracy, if nothing else it roused and summoned the imaginations like clay lumps falling on an empty coffin. But not everything conspired against them, not when they tasted the cook's apple pie.

'Don't eat it all,' Kern balked stuffing his face.

'I'm taller than you.'

'You're fatter than me.'

Monday conceded and brought out a packet of cigarettes, went forward to the patio doors and opened them wide. He cupped his hands around the flare of a match then held it up to let the wind extinguish the flame. 'So, what did you glean from the accounts?'

'When Week died, he left the house and twenty grand, not bad going in those days. As each beneficiary came on board they took modest gambles, some paid off. The third Tuesday invested heavily in the armaments trade, which really thickened the portfolio. There are no records of any big payouts, none that cannot be identified. If a scam has been going on, then search me. I couldn't find any evidence. What did you make of the Will?'

'Week wanted his Sunday child to be the first to manage the estate, thereafter it worked on a rotational basis. There are only two ways for the next to come on board. Either upon death or given up freely by pen to the other.'

'Huh?'

'It's a stupid clause. One passes the pen to the other so they can sign in the register. Remember what I told you last night, how Week made the prisoners sign in. This whole damn place is weird and Week was the one to start it all off. It's almost as if he planned the whole thing, you know, sire a number of kids from different women, keeps it under wraps then obtains the courthouse when the assizes moved to Norwich. In effect, he has ensured his bloodline never runs dry.'

'Are we to assume his wife was unable to have children or are we to assume he was mentally unbalanced?'

Monday brought out a piece of paper from his pocket that reminded what troubled him most. 'I can't get my head around this, Mike. How many bloodlines are left? Do we assume there are others and if so, do they know about this place? It stands to reason families would gossip. In my case, I never knew my Father. And Mother certainly never mentioned it. Yet Crookshank asked if she had mentioned it to me, which suggests she might have known.'

Kern came to his side. 'Jeremy Sunday certainly knocked a lot of Week's ancestors on the head, including your father.'

'Which brings us back to the same question, why would they leave? Okay, Jeremy never left. So why give all this up, even if it's held in Trust? No, I can't draw upon the Trust to live under a banana tree but I can make use of this land, draw a sizeable salary for my efforts, no mortgage, no outgoings, everything paid for, the occasional trip abroad, a new motor. I always fancied a Jensen and a 4x4 for the wife.'

'Are you thinking of marrying Angela?'

'You must be joking. To marry Angela would be a tragedy in itself. One day, providing I find the right woman, I shall get married and take the kids to the zoo.'

'Right, just send the list to Father Christmas. Solomon Monday with his head in the clouds has forgotten women are fully liberated. My agent and Angela are two of the millions who roam like foxes in a field of randy rams. Apple pies and zoos are for the sad bastards of which you are slowly becoming one. Before Hilda died you were the voice of sense and reason, exposing the liberal parasites and how the Labour Government was a temple for apocalyptic visionaries. You have walked into the dark side of redemption, my man.'

Monday shrugged. 'Oh, I prefer to see it as the promise of redemption. Tragic irony or poetic justice, the world is on the brink of terrifying possibilities and a column of news is not going to stop the progress of disasters.' He paused to weigh up his vistas, the lowering sun falling into the lake that stood between two woods, parted like forbidden love. The trees moved in the wind with a dry roaring that brought strange oaths and odours of a world which was now the limit of his horizons. He looked back at Kern and contemplated him fondly. 'It's strange, I can't explain it but I rather like it here. Sure, it needs some updating but I feel it's me, whatever that means. Perhaps my reporter's nose has forgotten how to smell a good thing. What say we empty the malt and listen to some music? I think I saw a radio in the kitchen.'

That night with a pale moon rising they dozed on the patio, lay with their bodies to the night sky, ashtrays and cushions spread across the grass, a radio operated by batteries mounted on the wrought iron table alongside an empty bottle of malt. There they were, out in the open among sleepless owls and badgers, with their intoxicated breaths drifting upon an autumn breeze. Meanwhile Palfrey had covered them with a blanket, propped pillows under their heads and settled down to his own in the basement.

Once in a while Monday was gently roused to a sound amplified by sleep, then words broke and went floating away. He stirred and lifted his eyes, glimpsed at Kern with his mouth wide open catching some stars. Warned by some hooting owls, he wrapped the blanket round his shoulders and sat to the night that was growing more secret and late, and reached the less cynical conclusion Gallows Humour was like a box of mixed chocolates, some to savour in the mouth, others to spit out. Then his wandering attention reeled in a distant scene, illusions perhaps. He blinked at smudges, shapes emerging until the apparitions stayed, solidified into an assorted clump of human beings lining up at the gallows. What was this trickery, this resplendent ability to mimic human fragility?

Soon they were gone. No pause or rewind, no image enhancement of that moment.

'Will yew look after us, Solomon Monday?'

And he heard himself say, 'Am I not the moon to watch over you.'

A toothless smile, Doolally fed her fingers through the strength of his where he felt a small surge of knowledge, a clearer view of Gallows Humour which to him offered infinite possibilities of horror.

A CHANGE OF HEART

As midnight passed and the early hours of Wednesday progressed towards dawn, Monday woke half-crippled.

From damp wood planking, he groaned to his feet and stared ahead as he stretched his back, his fingers curling tightly above his head. How different the views looked again, the trees and lake steaming with mist and bird song carving its way towards the house. But it was only when he glanced at the rousing and yawning Kern with his hair stuck up like a bottlebrush, the whole thing crept back, the visions and the fixed belief it was no dream. What he now felt was the fear of his own oblivion.

'Mike, I saw dead people!'

'Good for you...any chance of a cuppa?'

Without giving himself time to think too long, Monday swept a hand over his face, took a deep breath and said, 'Follow me, stay close and don't make a sound.'

Nerves could conjure illusion from the air. For no other reason, Kern stuck close to his friend who proceeded in cautious fashion, gauging his surrounds with impending doom. Not a word was spoken between them, not even when the kettle hissed to the boil and used as a teapot. For Monday, he just wanted a quick in and out, up the back stairs and into the library where he stupidly believed this room offered greater protection than anywhere else in the house.

'Why do you think Jeremy Sunday stayed in this room?' Monday said harshly as Kern closed the door. 'It's out of bounds, that's why.'

'Am I entitled to speak?' The nod gave permission. 'Jesus, Sol! What the hell has got into you?'

'This place is haunted.'

'I thought we discounted that concept.'

'Well, its back on the agenda.'

'How so?'

'I saw dead people last night, that's how.'

Kern, with large blue eyes of an extraordinary diversity of expression, poured out the tea as silent as the grave. It seemed to him that Monday had been away a year and returned a different man. 'Okeydokey,' he said passing over a cup, 'so how about this, that you had a nightmare due in no uncertain terms to our conversation last night, triggered off by a half bottle of whisky. I too had a nightmare, dreamt my agent was ripping me off.'

But Monday had prepared himself to be defensive, argumentative even, to have to listen to criticism and not be crushed by it. 'This is not what it seems, Mike. I saw dead people and Doolally was one of them. I can't explain what she is but she is what she is and that's a bad thing. I can't explain what she does but she does what she does, and that's scary. She made them appear, lining up at the gallows, thieves and murderers.' And talking about it made it seem even more frightening. The cup shook in its saucer while his other hand shook clutching at his throat with the thought of a rope tied round his neck. 'I think she wants to hang me too.'

'Why?'

'Because I am a descendant of Week, that's why! She probably hung the others, buried their bodies in the woods. Yes, that has to be it. Palfrey said this whole bloody place was a cemetery and my God didn't we see his face change.'

'Sol, can we take stock?' Kern lit two cigarettes and passed one over. 'This is a new environment for you, for me even. After Hilda died, you-'

'It wasn't a dream!' Monday irritated and placed his cup on the desk, now padding the room. 'Everything adds up. The way Crookshank sneaked my luggage in the boot of his car, got me here, only said what was necessary to whet my appetite, same too for Palfrey.' The little things, insignificant at the time but now full of meaning, came into mind. 'Yes, that's the number one rule in a reporter's life. Ask the right questions. Do the staff live in, that's what I should have asked. Instead, I assumed. I assumed because it suited me, because I was presented with a pot of gold. Here is everything to tempt a man from his senses, security for life when there is no security not unless you're a hard bastard and kick others down. Nothing comes free in life, nothing.'

'So let me get this straight. This Doolally woman is dead, right?'

'Right.'

'So why did I see her?'

'How do I know? I'm into politics not physic phenomena.'

'And Palfrey? I mean if you're saying she's dead then maybe he's dead too and that being the case he certainly serves up a great meal.'

'Doolally mentioned a cook. It was her that served up the meal.'

'So is the cook a ghost too?'

Monday met his brows. 'You're taking the piss.'

'No, seriously, Sol. Convince me, because I'm standing here looking at a man that's lost his marbles. Ever since Hilda died you've been back-peddling instead of getting on with your life. First you shack up with Angela, then you quit your job then you disappear for-'

'I never disappeared!' Monday growled on that touchy subject. 'I was doing a piece on Brown.'

'Well I never read it.'

'It never got taken up by Harry.'

'Angela thought you were making it up.'

'Angela, Angela, I am sick to death of Angela.'

'Right, err, so you're sick to death of Angela. That's good, that's a good start. But now you have a great place, money in the bank, your road to freedom and what happens? You come up with a bizarre plan to turn the woods into some sort of playground for nutters then try to convince me dead people want to hang you.'

'So you think my business concept was crap?'

'Would you just stop pacing the damn room and listen to me?' Furiously, Kern swung Monday round to face him, choosing his words. 'You have a profession and you're good at it. The money was good. You could carry on doing it from here but suddenly you want to bury your head in the sand.'

'Not from here I don't.'

'Fair enough,' Kern simply said and sat on the arm of a chair. 'I don't see dead people, Sol. And if Doolally is what you say she is then Palfrey is holding on to the biggest scoop in history. Give me four days, minimum three to get the full story. You can sleep here. Yes, we can both sleep in here and make box office money.'

'This is not a damn game where you can dial 999 for an exorcist. She threw plates at you for Christ's sake and locked you in the courtroom. And how did she do that, Mike? Tell me how it was possible for a woman of her size to do all that, man-handle a twelve stone bloke?' Monday watched those blue puppy-dog eyes stare blankly under a mass of dishevelled hair. 'Ah see, point made. You cannot remember a damn thing, can you? She invaded your mind as surely as she invaded mine.'

'Okay, I give you that one, yeah? But look at it logically. Jeremy Sunday survived sixty-two years and the others survived more than a week.'

'But they never survived long, did they?'

'So why wasn't Jeremy Sunday hung?'

'Look, you can stay to find out but I'm leaving.'

'But you signed on for the long haul, Sol.' Kern was trying every excuse he could think of. His book deal was in jeopardy. 'If there is something unearthly going on, then whatever you signed had greater meaning than a blank page.'

The door moved by some unseen measure. They held their breath in attitude of painful attention and then chugs of air breathed out in relief when Palfrey came into view.

'Sir, you have stumbled upon a tragic story and now like it or not you are lost in it. You can walk away but Gallows Humour will hold on to your heart.'

The world seemed more than upset and Monday began to feel trapped. He dropped his cigarette into a half-full cup of cold tea and sat at the desk, his expression instantly distressing. 'Explain your meaning as succinctly as possible so I am left in no doubt.'

'The difference between primates and ourselves is that we have social and anatomical baggage. For example, the sea squirt. This little chap is a motile hunter in its larval form and therefore needs a brain. However, once it has found a suitable niche to which it can anchor itself to become sessile, it no longer needs to think, so it eats its own energetically burdensome brain. Brains are great consumers of energy, and it is a good idea to get rid of your brain when you discover you have no further need of it.'

A nerve tugged beside the eye of Monday. 'So, I will be forced to eat my brain?'

'Not unless you are sea squirt.'

'Do you think this is funny?'

'You asked me to elaborate succinctly, sir.' Palfrey dared to move closer, absorbed so rapidly into Monday's plight. 'What I am trying to convey, sir without entering into the paranormal is that your basic instincts will override your compassion. You will feel no remorse, no sympathy, no love or hate. You will do what is necessary to do regardless of consequences in order to survive. Your very meaningful heart, metaphorically speaking of course, will be held by those you broke your promise to.'

'In effect,' Kern added to make light of the situation whilst removing that book in contention off the shelf, 'you will become a very rich heartless bastard.'

Burying his head in his hands with a groan, this was a nightmare Monday wanted to wake up from. It would appear Gallows Humour was a far easier mistress to enter than she was to leave. 'How can all this be possible? There are no such things as ghosts, not one recorded sighting.

This is the damn twenty-first century, and no-one has ever queried or suspected Gallows Humour...I don't buy into this, I can't see-'

'If you will permit me-'

'No, Palfrey!' Monday angered. 'I will not permit you! I just want to leave the same way I came in. There has to be a solution or I shall put a torch to Gallows Humour then we shall see who has my heart.'

'Then pass the pen to Tuesday, sir.'

'Is there a Tuesday?'

'Mr Crookshank has the entire list of Week's bloodline, keeps his eye on everyone. I give my assurances you will not be pestered while you stay here.'

Kern shoved the book under Monday's nose, along with a magnifying glass. 'Take a look at this, Sol. You signed away your heart, yeah? The writing is so small that not even a near sighted person could read.' Now Kern was snatching every opportunity he could. 'The others,' he said to Palfrey, 'they did the same thing, passed the buck to the next sop. Why did they leave it a few years before doing so?'

'I am sorry, sir. I take my instructions from the master of the house. If he wishes an explanation, he must ask me himself.'

'Mike, leave it alone. The less I know the better I shall feel about duping the bloke. Palfrey, am I right in thinking this library is out of bounds from dead people? A yes or no will suffice.'

'Yes, sir.'

'Is it my duty to ring Crookshank? Yes or no will suffice.'

'Yes, sir.'

'Then make us a fresh pot of tea.'

'I'll go with him.' Kern stared at Monday for a long time, the telling and receiving translated into a cold silence before he mustered the energy to follow Palfrey.

A knot had already formed in Monday's gut as he just sat there looking at the telephone thinking about Crookshank and his devious nature. Why would Crookshank think he could pull the wool over his eyes, hope for the best and trust such a peculiar arrangement would be acceptable? But he was a Monday, and Monday followed Sunday.

He picked up the receiver and dialled. While waiting to be connected he looped the telephone wire around his finger, the spirals hugging tight between his knuckles.

'Mr Monday, what can I do for you?'

'I saw dead people.'

There was a long pause before Crookshank replied. 'What do you want, Mr Monday?'

'Get Tuesday here, pronto. I don't care how you do it but do it fast or this is news in Saturday's papers. Do I make myself clear?'

'As transparent as those residing at Gallows Humour.'

'What do you get out of all this? Does it give you a hard on or what?'

Crookshank's surly voice rattled in defence. 'It may interest you to know, that I take it upon myself to execute my legal duties as did my predecessors and as far back when Judge Week hired a Crookshank to be honoured bound by his wishes. This holds no surprise when in contrast to your father. Goodbye, Mr Monday.'

As much as he wanted to comprehend Crookshank's meaning, Monday steeled away from that thought and considered it was best in not knowing. But what did he already know? He most certainly recognized the truth had been cleverly told to be the biggest lie of all. Why do I need to sign a blank page, no terms of employment? Answer from Palfrey, it only requires your heart in the running of its estate. Now Monday viewed Palfrey in a sharp and unforgiving light and watched him lay the tray down on the desk, his anger climbed, bitter and vengeful.

'They have no quarrel with you do they, Palfrey, conceal the truth as Crookshank's lackey, play your part, get me here and get out with a nice little handshake.'

'You are fighting against your natural instincts to widdle out the truth against a moral dilemma, sir. Try not to feel too bad about the situation. Soon you will be leaving and no doubt return to a political desk which is just as chaotic as here. Will there be anything else?'

'Yes. One thing and I do not want it circumvented. Since my Father's name is not in the register, Crookshank intimated he had something to do with Gallows Humour.'

'Charles Monday was a reprobate, sir. Every happy moment of his life came from lying. He showed to be a friend to Mr Sunday when in truth he was a thief and a swindler. Do you wish me to go on?'

'Does it get worse?'

'It depends which way you look at it. For my part, I say good riddance to the man.' Palfrey laid a friendly hand on Monday's arm but the offer was fiercely rejected. 'He was found hanging from a branch in these woods.'

'Christ!'

'And now you want to know if your mother knew.'

'Am I that easy to read?'

'Like newsprint, sir.'

Suddenly there was an almighty crash, the sound of china chinking and clinking to the floor. There was muffled yelping and shouting, demonstration of contempt for what Monday had done. Doolally had heard the news.

Palfrey withdrew and left Monday to his torn and crippled thoughts. On the one hand, guilt stuck fast in his head for what he was about to do, especially now with the knowledge of his father's reputation. On the other hand, he was afraid of the unknown, something he could not possibly have imagined had happened all the same. He was absolutely at this moment in the horrors, fearing from the idling here, that the phantoms, especially Doolally would ruin all his dreams, which had been currently on the verge of ruination anyway.

After toast and tea, two friends strolled around the grounds as if they had nothing on their minds but leisurely pleasure. With their hands in their pockets, they admired the lake and talked about politics but the only thing Monday could think about was dead people. He had to keep telling himself that none of this was real, however vivid it may have seemed, none of it was real.

'When do you think they come out to play?' Kern asked.

'Drop it, Mike.'

'You know, you're not really giving this a fair whack, Sol.'

'You never saw them. I did. My Father was hung in these woods.'

Kern swung him round, concern written on his features. 'This puts a different light on the matter. If Week's bloodline has been systematically popped off then you're condemning a man to death.'

'So, you would condemn me?'

'No, Sol. I'm saying you should find out what's really going on.'

'I know exactly what's going on. Jeremy Sunday sold his soul to the devil. The others refused, so they hung them. They hung my Father because he probably knew the truth, tried to blackmail Sunday.' Monday walked on in a northerly direction, stifling the acid pang of remorse. 'I should never have asked you to come here. I put your life in jeopardy. Try publishing that book and you're a dead man. You must leave, Mike.'

'Leave? I'm sticking right by your side, Sol. That's what mates do. How do you intend to play it? Give the man a handshake and say you're leaving all this behind because you won the lottery?'

'I shall think of something.'

'Well, you better make it convincing.' Kern squinted at a distance scene. 'Who's the hairy monster in the woods?'

'That's Woody from Treetop Games.'

With a sketch book in his hand, Woody closed the gap between them. 'I made my pricing and some drawings, thought yew would like to see what I hev in mind.'

'Woody, this is my colleague, Michael Kern.'

'Hell, you're a big sod,' Kern said shaking his hand.

'True, I do block a lot of sun.' They enjoyed the joke. 'Now here,' he told Monday passing over some drawings, 'is how I see these trees. Tell me what yew think?'

Aside all else, Monday was struck by a magical tree kingdom high in the sky. Therein consisting golden-planked walkways among branches, stairways to heaven that mysteriously led to a maze of chambers that looked like coconut huts. If Robinson Crusoe really existed, then surely this expressed all that an island should be in magic, design and eccentricity.

Quietly he looked up from the drawing and into the eyes of a visionary. 'Kids would never want to go home.'

'I take it yew be looking at my design with kindness. It's not cheap but worth every penny.'

'May I keep these?'

'Course yew can.' Woody touched his forelock. 'I be off now on another job.'

As Woody slipped away, Monday regarded the drawings again, perfectly content to linger in this world of make-believe, muddled-headed though it might be.

'I thought you were going in for paint balling,' Kern said.

'I am. I was. Woody suggested these taller trees could work for screaming kids with screaming parents.' He rolled up the drawings with an idea coming to life. 'This may work in my favour. I could genuinely tell the chap it was my intention to do this, but that my girlfriend hated the idea and rather than lose her I am willing to give it all up and go back to London and take the political slot George is offering.'

'And when he asks why not sit back and live off the Trust, what excuse can you give?'

'That's easy. Angela hates Norfolk. Even I hate Norfolk.'

'You liked it yesterday.'

Monday laughed quietly of fear and wiped the rough side of his cheeks with the palm of his hand. 'Let's finish the tour.'

They walked along the edge of the forest that snaked round the side of the house, stopping to admire the Rolls, its highly polished chrome and running boards. Just then a motor appeared from the long drive and hooted, tinted windows and gleaming hubcaps with loud music booming from inside. They watched a brief flare of flame illuminating Angela as a long cigarette was lit behind the darkened glass.

'Did you tell her where to come?' Monday asked and Kern looked apologetic. 'Oh for Christ's sake, Mike, what I am supposed to do now?'

'Hey, she's your girlfriend, remember. With any luck they might hang her instead.'

Long-legged Angela wearing a belt for a skirt climbed out of a silver Mercedes. She was sexy, bubble, toil and trouble. Short cut blond, false lashes, and a powder-keg of make-up, she approached with wide open arms and plonked a bright red-lip imprint on Monday's cheek.

'Sweetie,' she said in her sing-song voice, 'you look absolutely washed out.'

'Why did you come?' As if he never knew.

'Mere details, sweetie.'

Monday and Kern shot a despairing glance at each other, picked up their feet and followed the clicking stilettos into the hall where Palfrey stood like a frozen penguin, his eyes painfully working over an emancipated tarantula.

'Does he move or he is a wax work dummy?'

There was a brief moment of silence before it became apparent that chastisement was required by Monday. 'Angela, try to behave. This is Palfrey, the resident butler and in charge of the staff.'

Angela walked around Palfrey, sizing him up with amusement as though she wanted to test his devoted service to Gallows Humour. 'My luggage is in the car,' she told him. 'Put it in sir's bedroom and make sure the cook is aware I have grapefruit for breakfast, no sugar and black coffee followed by pure orange juice and a bowl of muesli with half-fat milk.' She turned to Monday. 'I stopped off at some horrible eating place in Thetford. God, this place is flat, not a hill in sight. Where do we go from here?'

'The library will be safe.' Oops, a slip of the tongue.

'Angela!' Kern came to the rescue. 'You must see the lake.'

'Our very own lake!' she squealed in delight.

Monday noted *our* as opposed to *your*, knew from long experience never to say too much where money was concerned and judging by the thin smile played on Kern's face, he knew it too. Feeling disinclined to follow, he twizzled on his heels and headed upstairs in pursuit of Palfrey but he should have known better.

'How long is she staying?' Doolally asked.

Monday jumped out of his skin, vaulted over a banister and rushed to the library, closed himself in with his back to the door, panting heavily. Then he double blinked at the desk chair quietly taking a trip across the room.

'We hev to talk, Solomon Monday.'

'I don't do talk, not to dead people.'

'Yew had such lovely plans fer the woods now yew want to leave it all behind and shack up with that tart. Yew be making a big-'

'Doolally!' Palfrey shouted climbing through the window. 'Get back to your station.'

'But I needs to talk to him.'

'Assist Flour in the kitchen.' Palfrey straightened his composure. 'Sir, I must apologize. It will not happen again.'

'You said this room was out of bounds.'

'No, sir, you assumed it to be out of bounds. I could only answer with a yes or no. To answer in the negative would infer I had no control over the staff.'

'But you have no control over Doolally and just look at me.' Quivering hands thrust forward. 'I'm a nervous wreck.'

Palfrey poured a single malt and gulped the lot in one go. It would seem he had problems of his own. 'Notwithstanding the reason why you require leaving, the emancipated tarantula will insist upon staying to protect her interests and spin a web of confusion when Tuesday arrives. Alternatively, you can use her arrival to your advantage, actually propose, tell her you are selling the estate for an exorbitant amount and climb into her car ten seconds after Tuesday has signed the register.'

'So I jump out of the frying pan into the fire?'

'A fire that can easily be dowsed, sir.'

Monday pulled out a packet of cigarettes and sat on the edge of the desk, forming a different perspective about Palfrey. 'They don't bother you, do they, Palfrey. I mean, you seem to communicate with them as though it's an everyday occurrence like eating a sandwich.' He blew smoke in the butler's direction to get a reaction of which there was none. 'Are you one of them?'

'It is rather late in the day for explanations, sir. The wheels are in motion and fate has unkindly sent you a hurdle. It will take me fifteen minutes to travel to the nearest jewellery shop, purchase a diamond large enough to keep the spider occupied while you do the deal.'

'Mmmm, let me see if I can make a correct assumption. You don't require my signature because in truth Crookshank is the sole Trustee.'

'Well done, sir.'

Monday's thoughts about this spun into question how Crookshank might work a fiddle. It seemed to him it was likely that this solicitor had made certain dubious arrangements with local businesspeople. 'So how does it work?' Monday asked. 'The cost of the article is inflated, say by twenty per cent then Crookshank pockets the difference. Is that why you contacted Treetop Games?'

Palfrey walked to the door and gave an equally robust response. 'The hand of God balancing our lives, our punishments merely deferred.'

Monday poured himself a drink and went onto the patio through the library window. It was peaceful, no doubt about that. Kern and Angela were at the edge of the lake and he wondered how easy it would be to break off the engagement. He remembered how she wormed herself into his apartment. First it was the odd pair of shoes then the dresses in his wardrobe but the moment her toothbrush appeared next to his he knew he had made a terrible mistake and that getting rid of Angela would be like getting rid of squatters.

When the alcohol had worked its way into his system rendering Dutch courage, Monday sprang into action and went upstairs, had a shave and a shower, and prepared himself for the charade. But it was one thing to do something in theory, another to do it in practice. He just wanted to get it over with, the whole damn sorry business. Looking in the wardrobe mirror, adjusting his tie, another reflection came slowly into view and his face began to work, one eyelid twitched uncontrollably.

'Now yew listen to me.' Doolally cautioned him. 'Do this and yew'll regret it.'

'No!' Monday angered, wagging his finger. 'You listen to me! I will not stand for your flagrant disregard for my privacy or be intimidated by your threats. I am still master of the house and you will stay in the kitchen or haunt to regret it!'

'Sweetie?' Angela called from behind. 'Who are you talking to?'

'Eh? Hem, err, myself.'

'Yourself?'

'Yes, I was, err, hum, you look rather lovely.' He nervously pointed to the bed. 'Look, we have a four poster.' Angela appeared unimpressed, looking round for her luggage so Monday continued, 'I am selling this place.'

'Why?'

'I want to take up George's offer at The Times and buy a flat near Mayfair.' He had her attention now. 'It would be convenient for you and for me. We could sell my flat or let it out, whatever. The thing is, when this chap comes down, I shall be very busy doing the deal so you best make yourself scarce.'

'Bliss,' she said folding into his arms. 'You know me, sweetie.'

And that was the problem, he knew her too well. She had a spendthrift nature, a compulsive shopper coupled with promiscuity, one who opened her senses to physical pleasure and produced a certain sexual besottedness in her behaviour. Whilst that may have suited rampant males with more than their fair share of testosterone, Monday found it at times distasteful. There was no warmth and intimacy suggesting some residual tenderness, at least not on her part.

'Sir, cocktails are now being served in the drawing room. Mr Kern has requested dinner at eight and the cook wishes to know if madam consumes meat.'

Angela answered. 'Madam prefers lemon sole, with a side salad.' Then her expression hardened. 'Where is my luggage? Did I not specifically tell you to put it in here?'

'All bedrooms look the same, an easy mistake,' Monday interjected, knowing where this road would lead. 'I shall go with Palfrey to ensure your requirements are met. See you in the drawing room.' Closing Angela in to put on half a pound of makeup, he said to Palfrey as they moved on, 'Did you get it?'

'I gave it to Mr Kern.'

'Good, Palfrey. Is everything in order?'

'Indeed it is, sir. You handled Doolally extremely well, if I may say so. Will you require a sleeping draft on the lemon sole?'

The wonders of Palfrey, he thought. It required a nod to which he duly gave and went his merrily way not even thinking about her when he reached the drawing room. But there he brooded darkly in his seat, occasionally massaging his temples when the throbbing pain of guilt threatened to engulf him. He was about to propose to a woman he disliked intensely, conspired to knock her out with a sleeping draft, after which he was going to dupe an innocent man into taking his place, and then, who knows what, a hanging? He could hardly look at Kern, let alone Angela when she walked in. The hair on his forearms had come erect and prickled electrically, for he had just stared into his soul.

Be that as it may, he outlined the details of the sale as much as could be said and passed over the ring like one would pass over a piece of carrot cake. Angela, who wore nothing under the pale blue blouse was itching with ambition and accepted the proposal with her bosoms bouncing elastically. In the background, Kern groaned softly in his throat, comprehending at last the book deal was on its way out.

But was Angela really satisfied? 'Sweetie,' she said to Monday over the dinner table, 'how much would you get if the land had planning permission to build loads of houses?'

'The trees have a preservation order,' he concluded and realized it was not the most sparkling conversational gambit, but his wits seemed to have deserted him.

'See,' Kern said cutting into red meat. 'Sol just wants to take a bloody good offer, get out while the going is good, yeah? It's not as if he was left any cash. And what with the country in debt for the next forty years, it gives Sol a-'

Impatiently, Angela lifted her hand to stop him. Her skin was tanned in contrast to the silver white diamond sparkling on her finger. 'Tell him, sweetie, tell him what you told me. This country has a shortage of housing. Why we have a pile of immigrants lining up to buy houses.'

'Sol was referring to wealthy Russians buying up London. Who the hell wants to pay top whack and live in Norfolk?' Kern had hit upon the one argument that might stop her.

Monday saw her thinking about it carefully, and he sighed silently with relief when she shrugged and popped a piece of lemon sole in her mouth. He was, after all, a Monday, waiting for Tuesday on a terrible Wednesday praying Thursday would be a better day

ANOTHER CHANGE OF HEART

'What if this whole thing is a set-up?'

As if Monday was confused enough, at breakfast, with Angela still in bed he stared vacantly into his empty coffee cup. 'I thought that was already established.'

'No, you miss the point.' Kern thought he had everything figured out. 'Remember that film called The Game with Michael Douglas?' He paused for confirmation but Monday was in a world of his own. 'His brother, forget the name, turned up on the scene and gave him a birthday present from this firm called The Game. Anyway, the long and the short of it, Douglas was put through the mill, defrauded of his fortune, sent round the bend by this mysterious woman, shot his brother and jumped from a tower block.'

Monday shifted his troubled dark eyes. 'I suppose there's a point to all this?'

'That was the game, Sol. He landed safely ninety flights down, shocked, yes but still he was alive and taken to his birthday party. The whole thing was a set-up, yeah? Actors played their parts and his brother was in on it. Douglas was so fixated on making money he had no time for his family. Can you see where I'm taking this? By the mere inference of this place being called Gallows Humour is a dead giveaway. Crookshank, Palfrey and this Doolally woman are actors, like in the film. This could be a test, yeah?'

Monday sat back in his navy suit, folded his arms and thought it was worth a shot. 'Okay, how did I see dead people?'

'You were given a drug, like they slipped a sleeping draft to Angela. I bet they never figured her turning up.'

'And you?'

'Easy, hypnosis...I walked in the front door and was met by a therapist or whatever putting me under, telling me what to do.'

'And Doolally appearing in the mirror, how was that accomplished?'

'You can easily create illusions. Magicians do it all the time.' Kern wiped his mouth with a serviette, anxious to put his view across. 'Come on, Sol get your brain in gear. Maybe this Jeremy was your grandfather, really a Monday, yeah? And let's assume you're not the only one to inherit his fortune but gives you first shot at it, to test your mettle. It all adds up. He uses his solicitor who's like a priest, yeah? The history of Judge Week is the basis for the story line. Take that page you signed. Who really signs a blank page to gain access to a Trust, yeah?'

'You forget the page was worded.'

'Hell, it was all part of the drama. They knew you would look more closely.'

Monday was warming to the scenario. 'And Palfrey, he's too damn intelligent to be a butler.'

'Unerringly spot on, my man, and don't forget he's good at story telling. As you said, you never found any names on the Electoral Roles for Tuesday, Wednesday or Thursday. Fridays were loads. Mondays were in Hull and Sundays less than a hundred. So where are these descendants of Week?'

Slowly nodding his head, the whole thing seemed far more acceptable than the unacceptable world of ghosts. 'If this Jeremy is my Grandfather, then where does my Father fit into all this?'

'Hey, what if this Jeremy was your father, yeah? Maybe he wants to make up for things...leaving your mother in the lurch and all that? Didn't Crookshank ask if Hilda knew about Gallows Humour?'

Before Monday was able to respond happily to this, a disturbing sound like a thudding crash came from outside but it seemed that distance could not take the fierce edge away from the noise.

'They have this place bugged,' Kern whispered across the table. 'Don't rise to the bait. They're trying to steer you off course.'

'What do you suggest I do?' Monday whispered back.

'Don't pass the pen.'

Palfrey walked in and they straightened. 'Sir, we have a problem. The taxi driver crashed into a travelling Mercedes.'

Monday stood, adjusted his shirt cuffs and fell into step like he was striding onto a stage, so sure was he that Kern had hit upon the one thing that made sense. 'Who was driving Angela's car?'

'Charlie, sir. He mistook the gear change from first to third.'

'And why did this Charlie need to use it?'

'It was parked inconveniently. He wanted to create a good impression for our guest.'

'Has Tuesday arrived?'

'A little shaken but not stirred.'

She wore a simple dress of printed cotton on her final journey, the flat leather sandals were new and her soft auburn hair fell over her shoulders like apple peelings. There was nothing sensational about her body, just a lovely curving shape that reminded Monday there were women who could wear their desirable carriage without influence of magazines. Standing with her back towards him, she was talking to the disgruntled driver leaning against the damaged grill to his taxi. When the driver spotted Monday, he straightened and their eyes met.

'Solomon Monday.' He held out his hand. 'I expect you could do with a nice cup of tea. Palfrey will sort things out.'

And just as they began to walk away, a tap on his shoulder and Monday turned to a smile. She was so naturally balanced with nature, he wondered if heaven had sent an angel.

'Miss Izabo Tuesday,' she said, 'at your service.'

He shook her hand and, in that moment, he felt his past and future rolled into one. 'Sorry for the mix up, I expected a Mr Tuesday.'

'Not a very good start, is it?'

'Have you travelled far?'

'Amalfi, near Napoli.'

'Were you born in Italy?'

'No, I was born in Somerset where the cider apples grow.'

'Funny you were not on any Electorate Role.'

'Why should I be? I live in Italy.'

'And how convenient, Miss Tuesday.' Monday had made his point. She was good, he thought, her acting was good and the choice was excellent. 'Palfrey, take Miss Tuesday to the dining room, make her feel comfortable. I need a word with the driver.'

'Yes, sir.'

When they were out of earshot, Monday brought out his wallet, sifted a five-pound note and flagged it under the driver's nose. 'This,' he said, 'is yours to a simple question. Did your current passenger direct you to this house?'

'No.' The driver went to grab it but the note was held back. 'I knew where to come.'

'So you know about this place?'

'That's another question.'

Monday looked into the eyes enquiringly, handed over the five pound note, then dug deep into his wallet again bringing out two twenty-pound notes. 'What is this worth?'

'When the gallows closed down, it was handed over to a man called Judge Week, a nasty piece of work. He used to make the prisoners sign in then he'd hang 'em.'

'That much I know from the web.'

'Did you know that after he died the gates were closed, out of bounds to the public until the last bloke who lived here opened them up?'

'Go on, I'm listening.'

'Betty Cross remembers that day. She was serving behind her old man's counter when this bloke walked in, said his name was Jeremy Sunday and that he'd like his papers delivered right to his door.'

'And this Betty Cross, does she still run the paper shop?'

'Her daughter runs it now but she's still there. Cross Newsagents, a mile down the road right next to the filling station. Her youngest son runs the fruit and vegetable shop; the oldest one runs the garage. She got very friendly with the bloke, used to have tea and cucumber sandwiches served by that butler. Then something funny went on. She never said what but she stopped coming.'

'Is there anything else?'

'The usual rumours,' the driver begrudgingly acknowledged. 'Orgies, witchcraft, hangings...err, hum, lots of rumours about hangings...long before my time. Two lads went missing about fifteen years ago...some say they went to burgle the house. The police were called but nothing came of it. Oh, and something else, there was an old geezer found in the woods one winter, a vagrant frozen against a tree. The coroner said he died from the cold but the papers mentioned something about a rope tied round his foot.'

'Have there been any rumours of Week's descendants?'

'Like what?'

'Well did he have any children, illegitimate children?'

'You're asking the wrong chap, mate. That goes way beyond me. Anyway, rubbers weren't invented in those days. Strange he was a Sunday, you're a Monday and that woman called herself Tuesday.'

'Perhaps someone is pulling your leg.' Monday passed over the forty pounds and asked, 'Can you take me to the newsagents?'

Monday felt if he could follow this up, get some proof then he was on his way to establish the truth. It also gave him the opportunity to get out of the house and keep his mind focused rather than confused.

And it all became normal, everyday occurrences, laughing boys standing at the bus stop, terrace cottages lined up in rows, a girl with a hair-band flattening her hair and all things sung constant in an ordinary hamlet too small to be a town yet large enough to serve its community with everyday things.

When the taxi drove onto the garage forecourt, Monday got out and walked over to the newsagents. Inside he asked a well-rounded woman for the Daily Express and then waited for the shop to run empty of customers before he said, 'Excuse me, I am looking for a Betty Cross. I understand she lives here. Are you her daughter by any chance?'

'Me? No, luv. I help out on half day closing. Her daughter goes to the city on Thursdays. If you walk round the back of the garage, you'll see a little bungalow. That's where Betty lives now.'

Monday picked his way to the rear of the garage, ventured through a white wooden gate and knocked on a bright blue door. No-one answered so he rapped a little harder. The door opened to the smell of boiled cabbage, a buckle of skin folding below each eye, tightly curled hair like a pelt of a white terrier.

'Mrs Betty Cross?'

'Are you selling?'

He could see the expectation she had in her eyes, not knowing what he would say but knowing he would surely say something to get his foot in the door. 'Betty,' he said to make it less formal. 'My name is Sol. I live up the road, have done since Monday and perhaps by tonight or tomorrow I shall be leaving or staying because it depends entirely upon your help.'

'Oh, that sounds dire. You better come in then.'

It was small accommodation, ordered and tidy, wing backed armchairs in the living room arranged to suit the television. There were photographs on the dresser, a life story waltzing across the varnished wood and it suddenly occurred to Monday what was really missing at Gallows Humour. He picked one up, a wedding photograph, he in a soldier's uniform, her with small white flowers trailing down a white silk dress.

'Is this your husband?'

'Dead now, long time ago. I live with my daughter. Her husband died in Iran last year.'

There was common interest and he seized upon it. 'My Mother died last year from cancer. I understand the pain of losing a loved one.' He looked back. 'This is going to sound strange but can you tell me why you stopped seeing Jeremy Sunday?'

'Are you living at Gallows Humour?'

'I am.'

She sat down rather awkwardly. 'Oh my,' she said with a dismal face. 'If you'd asked me that when my son-in-law was alive, I would've showed you the door but things change, and we still live on. Would you like a cup of tea?'

Monday shook his head, pulled his trousers up slightly at the knees and sat down on a protruding spring sprouting from the sofa. 'I have a taxi waiting to take me back.'

'You should learn to use your feet around these parts.'

'I was told you used to have tea with Jeremy Sunday.'

'Oh, he was such a lovely, lovely man but he wasn't quite the ticket, had a weight of worry on his shoulders.' She shifted her portly frame, adjusting the half flattened cushion to her back. 'After my husband died, we struck up a lovely friendship. It never lasted that long...no, it never lasted that long. A year I knew him proper, if you know what I mean then one day, oh, this must be about nine years ago now, I shall never forget it. Palfrey picked me up in the Rolls. I did like being driven in the Rolls. It made me feel like the Queen of England. When I got out, there he was standing on the steps under that canopy, waving me in from the dark, all excited he was. He took hold of my hand and pulled me into that courtroom. Betty, he said, here's proof, come and have a look at this. What proof, I said. Why, he said, proof Judge Week visits this place. Get away with you, I said and laughed it off.'

She paused in the difficulty of her words and Monday wondered if he should speak.

'Sol,' she said, 'I was never more frightened in all my life. I swear as God is my witness, I saw Judge Week in a long-eared wig banging down hard on his bench and pointing to a prisoner in the dock. I ran out of that house screaming my head off. Palfrey tried to calm me but I pushed him away and ran as fast as my feet would carry me.'

'So they were ghosts?'

'Oh they were ghosts all right, no mistaking that. My daughter never believed me. Her husband, he was going down there to knock seven bells out of Jeremy and that's when I changed my story and said I made it all up. I never took him seriously, never in all my while did I believe that place was haunted. Poor, poor man, living in a dismal place with those terrible things going on...I don't know why he stayed. I telephoned him a few days later, on the quiet if you see what I mean. I was ever so worried. Jeremy, I said, move out of that place and come live in the bungalow behind the garage. It was empty then, needed doing up. He cried down that telephone. He was that upset. I never spoke to him since. I went to his funeral and that was a sad day. There was Palfrey and Hugh Crookshank, a very nice man. He dealt with my son-in-law's estate. I felt guilty...I never believed him and when I did, I abandoned him. Oh, that was a sad day.'

'When was the funeral?'

'Two weeks ago.'

'Do you think there were others looking on?' He felt his own words sticking in his throat for her story sounded believable.

'It was sunny.' She folded her hands into a pious box and settled her eyes on the ceiling. 'Oh yes, Lord it was sunny that day but I never felt so cold.' Her eyes touched upon his. 'Mind you, I feel the cold anyway so that doesn't say a lot. You can't stay there, my dear man. You have to leave or you'll suffer the same way. Jeremy was handsome in his day when he moved in, had a nice head of hair, not a grey strand in sight. I was young, still at school, had my eye on him I can tell you.'

'When you had tea with him and apart from Palfrey did you see anyone else?'

'Well, there was this woman called Doolally. She was just as daft as Jeremy. She drew up a chair and sat watching us eat our cucumber sandwiches telling him off for burping. And then a young pretty girl came in, her face was covered in white dust. Palfrey called her Flour, spelt like the flour you use for cakes. She was the cook. I know he had others working for him but I never saw them.'

'Did they appear more than odd to you?'

'Look, dear. Lots of folk around here are odd. Even my youngest is odd. He spends a gallon of petrol to get cheaper cauliflowers to sell in his shop when he could quite easily pay less and get them from the farmer opposite. He says the cauliflowers he gets are tighter, whatever that means and customers know about these things. I say a cauliflower is a cauliflower.'

'Did Jeremy ever tell you about the history of Judge Week?'

'He said he was a man who tried to do the right thing and give a home to lost souls. I said, what lost souls and he said those he hung by mistake. I never paid any attention, not for one moment did I believe him. Not until that night. Are you related to him?'

'Who, Jeremy or Week?'

'Don't mind me, dear. Either one will do.'

'In a roundabout way I suppose both. Personally, I never met Jeremy or any member related to the Week bloodline. Hugh Crookshank informed me I was next in line to inherit Gallows Humour, the very reason I am down here. How well do you know Hugh Crookshank?'

'He lives in this village, that big old rectory opposite the Three Feathers. That's been in his family for generations. I asked him. By Jeremy's graveside, I asked him if he knew Gallows Humour was haunted but he said it was all gossip. I was inclined to tell him about my experience but who would believe me. Do you believe me?'

He told the only answer he could muster. 'Unfortunately, I do, Betty. Do you think Palfrey is a ghost?'

'Palfrey a ghost,' she said in utter amazement. 'If he's a ghost I'll eat my pension book. I remember when he first arrived at Gallows Humour, be about sixteen years ago. I was still running the shop when he came in and introduced himself. Very polite and posh he was. He's been a good friend around these parts, likes to help out now and then. The two I saw in that courtroom, weren't like anything I'd ever seen...and that's the truth.'

Monday had gleaned enough information to throw his friend's theory out the window. He stood. 'I thank you very much, Betty. You have been a great help.'

'If you ever need someone to talk to, you come and see me.'

At the door she waved him goodbye and without looking back, he jumped into the taxi, and thought to himself, it's dog eat dog, do this right and it's someone else's problem.

Life was too short to be miserable.

Moving swiftly on, he struck out of the taxi and into the dining room where he caught the steamy glare of Angela.

'Where have you been?' she demanded.

'I ran out of cigarettes. Where is Miss Tuesday?'

Kern answered. 'Palfrey is showing her the lake.'

'Sol, I want answers.' Angela voiced harshly, prodding her polished nail on the table. 'Miss Freckle Face mentioned this was her inheritance.'

'Sweetheart, you misunderstood.' He smiled and wondered how long he would have to hold that inviting gesture before he got lockjaw. 'She is from Italy, did she tell you? No? Well, there you are. Buying houses in Italy is considered an inheritance.'

'And my car? Who's going to pay for the damage?'

'No, problem, all arranged.' He bent down and pecked her on the cheek. 'I must see to Miss Tuesday so we can get out with a bundle of readies.' Then he brought out his visa card thinking sod the consequences. 'Mike, why don't you take Angela to the city, lots of lovely shops with pretty dresses.'

She snatched it out of his hand and bolted through the door so quickly it raised a troublesome draft.

'Mike,' Monday said on a more serious note. 'I have solid evidence this place is haunted. Just keep Angela occupied to give me some space with Tuesday.'

A wave of sweat broke out on his forehead and Monday considered he would be walking a tightrope. Worse, he would be bankrupt at this rate. With a chance to recover his composure, he strolled on with an upward glance. True enough, there was Palfrey doing his duty by the lake, gesturing with his hands at the magnificent parting of the woods. Monday beckoned him over so they would meet halfway.

'Where do we stand, Palfrey?'

'In the same spot when you first arrived. May I suggest a little boat trip?'

'No need, Angela's gone shopping with my credit card.'

'I do hope you have a limit.'

Monday glanced beyond Palfrey and suddenly there were no limits. 'I suppose a little trip might not go amiss.' He walked on. 'Miss Tuesday,' he called out, 'once again my apologies. I thought we could take a short trip on the lake, have a quick conversation in private.'

'There's coincidence for you,' she said. 'Palfrey suggested the same thing.'

He immediately set about slipping the loop from a peg in the ground then jumped into the rowing boat offering his hand for support. She was ballerina light on her feet, almost weightless and sat demurely with her knees together and her hands in her lap. He tried not to stare but the eyes… Yes, her eyes were like sapphires and found them splendid, something unspoken but real.

'So, what do you think to the place so far?'

'Truly beautiful, truly, truly,' she replied in Italian then translated. 'It's beautiful, Mr Monday. You must love Angela very much to give all this up. I understand she's an actress.'

'A freelance model,' he corrected. 'We met at the British Embassy. Angela's work is really based in London, as mine will be.'

'She gave me the impression I was supposed to buy this estate.'

Monday laughed nervously. 'To Angela everyone transacts. I have to be honest and mention she's not entirely blue-stocking. Did Crookshank explain I had a deadline to meet?' *Bugger, why did I say that?* 'There's a political slot to fill at The Times,' he quickly rectified his mistake. 'I was hoping to return with Angela rather than travel everyday on the train to London.'

Tuesday said nothing at first, dropping her right hand into the water, allowing her fingers to travel with the swells. 'Do you believe in fate, Mr Monday?'

'Good or bad, you bring it to your door.'

'Then how would you explain the poor soul who is killed on the road by a maniac driver?'

'Okay, so we sometimes turn a bad corner, but that is not to say fate is anything other than a bad piece of luck. What about the lottery winner losing their ticket and someone else finding it? Would you class that as fate? I would class that as one person's folly and another person's shrewdness. So how do you view fate as if I cannot guess?'

'Yes, you guess correctly. I am a fatalist, through and through. What is meant to be is meant to be, follow the yellow brick road and see where it leads.'

'Even if it works against you?'

'Life is what you make it, Mr Monday. Imagine that, though very distant, we are related.' She smiled and he found himself wanting. 'If you like, I shall sign the register and you can be on your way.'

Despite himself and his rage at Crookshank, Monday threw back his head and laughed with relief. Then she laughed, her eyes screwed up and in between there were the bursts of unfinished sentences, waving their hands for emphasis.

'I have so many plans for the house,' she went on excitedly. 'Mr Crookshank said you have an open cheque book.'

'You do, Miss Tuesday. Have you seen much of the house?'

'Yes, it does need taking into the twenty-first century. I think that would be my first order of the day, to give the house electricity.'

'What is your profession?'

'I design and construct houses, Mr Monday.'

'So, you're an architect?'

'And a builder,' she replied stepping out of the boat. 'I can tile a roof as good as any though I prefer to mix up cement and lay bricks.'

'This is a joke, yes?'

'I know it's hard to imagine a woman shovelling cement but I enjoy it. Besides, it stops me from being a hypocrite on site. To be in the thick of it, you appreciate the fabric of the build, the fundamental spaces shaped from the drawing. Did you know many architects don't have a clue to the problems they create for builders? They never count the courses for the windows; never bother to consider the ergonomics of bathrooms or the difficulty they cause for plumbers.'

'Surely the architect is only following the client's wishes.'

'Now how would a client without build experience know about perps?'

He had no idea what a *perp* was other than in the language of slang for a perpetrator. And he had no intention of asking. She was Tuesday, full of grace, a well-shaped nymph walking by his side and so much smaller than he and yet she confessed to have the abilities of a man working on a building site. It just beggared belief.

'So, you build these houses in Italy?'

'No, I was taking a very long break. Mama is Italian, most of her family live in Amalfi. My Father met her there when he was on holiday. He brought her back to Somerset and there they married.'

Strolling into the library with Tuesday behind, Monday reached for the register and said, 'This is just a formality. Did Palfrey explain there are no terms and conditions?'

'I understand I must telephone Mr Crookshank to let him know my decision.'

And standing there now, waiting, trying to be calm with a fragment loop of unease and despair, all those things rattled around inside his head like coins set loose in a tumble dryer.

'Yes,' she said down the line, her finger twirling a loch of hair and it reminded him of yesterday, how he looped the telephone cord round his knuckles venting his anger at Crookshank. 'He's here with me now. Do you wish to speak to him?' A pause and a shake of her head indicated he did not. 'Well then,' she went on. 'You must come over for tea when you have time. Thank you so much, Mr Crookshank.' Returning the telephone to its cradle she said, 'He's such a nice man.'

And she was so gullible, he thought. He wiped his face with an open hand, from forehead to chin, in an agony of indecision, torn between his conscience and survival. 'So, after you settle in, what will you do? Carry on building?'

'Not sure. Single or double plots are hard to find and they go for such a premium. I understand I should try to make money for the estate.' Then her attention was drawn to the sketches on the desk. She picked them up and went silent.

'Woody from Treetop Games came up with that for the north side. It's for screaming kids with screaming parents.'

'It's wonderful. How could anyone possibly dislike such a great idea?' She looked up. 'This may sound very rude, but how much does a reporter earn in a year?'

He could see where she was taking this. 'I hate Norfolk.'

'What is there to hate?'

'It's flat.'

'Flat?'

He motioned to the window. 'You cannot get much flatter.'

'But without it being flat there would be no lakes, no seas.'

'No waterfalls, no skiing.'

'And you need to work in London.'

'Absolutely.'

Blowing her fringe from her eyes, she said, 'Well then, shall we get on with it?'

He opened to a blank page, took the pen out of the ink stand, dipped it in the ink well and passed it over. She looked down at the pen in her hand, at the blank page, then nodded to herself and looked up at him.

'It's bizarre, isn't it?' she said. 'I get all this just for signing a blank piece of paper. Do you mind if I take up your project?'

'Not in the least. We only need to operate it six months of the year.'

'We?'

'Err, Angela and me.'

'But she has her modelling job.'

'Quite.'

'Oh look,' she said at the nib of the pen. 'The ink has dried. It needs refreshing.'

It was all too much for him. The palm of his hand thrust down on the page. 'I changed my mind,' he said swamped with a sense of guilt, and guilt was followed almost immediately by anger. 'You can look at me with those judgemental and incriminating eyes all you want but it will do you no good. I suggest you get your bags and leave.'

Monday wanted to say, forgive me, I'm tired and jumpy and there are ghosts in the walls, in the floors and in the trees waiting to make your life a misery and expected some terrible retribution to follow but nothing happened at all. The great infinite unknowable Izabo Tuesday slipped away as thick tides of blame overwhelmed him.

All the same, below stairs was an underworld of phantoms and a shoulder to cry upon. Monday walked into the murmured kitchen, acceptance now part of his creed, pulled out a chair, sat glumly at the table upon which invisible hands worked a rolling pin. With his pulse up ten beats per minute, he reasoned quite rightly it had to be the cook and took a deep breath, unsure where he fitted into this unseen world.

Palfrey slowly lowered his newspaper. It crumpled to his lap. He removed his pince-nez, placed them on the table and said among this lip of chaos, 'I take it you failed to pass the pen to Miss Tuesday?'

Monday nodded and said nothing.

With that, Palfrey pointed his finger to a shelf of pleasantries. The rolling pin stopped working and an empty glass with a bottle of rum floated to the table. Filling the glass, Monday drank it off as if it was water.

'How do you feel now?' Palfrey asked.

'Ready for another.'

'Where is she now, sir?'

'Upstairs I presume, getting her bags. But I couldn't do it, Palfrey. Not because she was a woman, a very nice one at that but it's a matter of living with your conscience.'

Palfrey stared into the younger eyes which burnt back with the same understanding, self-same mixture of fear and confusion. 'It was said that Judge Week extricated himself from duty to live a debauched life after he had gained free and simple the gallows from the Crown. The Lord of the Manor wrote a letter to The Times endorsing this view, whereas Week's inconsequential denial only reached the Parish magazine, compliments of the vicar. In it, Week claimed the estate was haunted by innocent souls who were unjustly punished by his misguided hand. From the vicar's point of view, far from being slighted Judge Week should be pitied and admired for trying to make amends.'

'So Week knew of the hauntings?'

'Indeed he did, sir. A young man of the silks and with great fortitude took Week's side and offered a radical solution to keep the property out of the Crown's domain. With the courage of his convictions, he made a strong case for Week to own the old courthouse and cells, including land of sufficient acreage to be put to good use. Can you make an intelligent guess as to whom that man might be?'

'Crookshank's ancestor.' For Monday, it was slowly coming together.

'Edmund Crookshank, a God-fearing man and a dear friend to Week. Fortuitously, Judge Week had six illegitimate children by different women and it would be them and their offspring to carry the burden of his sins. The eldest, born on a Sunday was informed of the position at the time of Week's death. He never took the claim seriously, foresaw Gallows Humour as his escape from poverty. Later, as with most of them, he discovered to his cost the story was true, stole what he could and left, only to return in wretchedness and dupe the next kin who did the same thing. The only man who took on his ancestor's burdens was Jeremy Sunday. He never married, considered he could find the solution to put these poor souls at rest. But what he discovered over time was that these poor souls were not seeking retribution upon Week's bloodline but the return of their signatures.'

'Week's Work.'

'Precisely, sir. Unfortunately, Week's Work was never found. Some say the book never existed, that it was legend, others claimed it was destroyed and for those who live around us can remember it all too well.'

'So who put the curse on the register? Week?'

'One can only speculate, sir. Perhaps Week's soul was guarding the Trust. Who really knows of these things?'

'Well,' Monday sighed, long past anyone's scope of help, 'it looks as though I have cooked my goose. Like it or not, I am here for the long haul.'

'Sir, I have lived among them for sixteen years. True, they can be a little boisterous, come and go when it suits. Doolally exceeded her station. She was tremendously excited at your decision to stay, wanted to be part of your games and acted too hastily, believed you were ready to comprehend.'

'But they are dead, Palfrey. Even now I can hardly get my head around it. How can these things happen? And my life is finished. I might as well be dead too.'

'Your life would have been finished with the tarantula, sir.'

'So, I am to become a Sunday. What did he do for comfort? Have tea and cucumber sandwiches with Betty Cross. I know I'm not ready for marriage, but I want apple pie and all that. I'm not cut out to be alone and neither am I cut out for quickies behind the bicycle shed.'

'Think of the advantages, sir. We have unpaid staff keeping the home fires burning, first class tradesmen ready to do your bidding and a new business on the horizon.'

Monday's expression darkened. 'If you think we're running a business here you're very much mistaken. We cannot have children running about while there are ghosts everywhere. I mean, have you looked at Doolally, I mean really looked?'

At that, the cook came into view. Her name was Flour and Monday understood why. She was quiet as a mouse, feather-soft in her movements, young powder-white face dressed in powder-white cotton yet redeemed from insipid vacuity by her chestnut hair and eyes.

'Does she speak?' Monday asked.

Palfrey shook his head. 'She was the worst victim of the gallows, sir. Eighteen years old, raped by nobility and her only mistake, if it can be called a mistake was to defend herself from a brutish beast. She was convicted of grievous harm, found guilty by those who licked the gentry's boots. She never spoke a word in her trial, was unable to do so. The prosecution claimed she bit out her own tongue as a source of madness. Judge Week could no more see through that lie than see through a pane of glass. Week was popular in those circles, ruled with an iron fist yet he lusted for life and women.'

'In other words, he was a hypocrite.'

'And something entirely beyond understanding in his latter days of remorse.'

In the sorrowful silence that followed Monday thought he caught a teardrop falling down the powder-white face and his throat closed. What did her youthful life have to offer except injustice and despair and all those things ruled by a despotic lord who pursued pretty skirts down the passageways.

'Sir, I have just been informed the tarantula is stepping out of her car and Mr Kern has his arms full of packages.'

'Oh Christ, what the hell am I going to do?'

'May I suggest a solution to the current problem? Miss Tuesday should remain the night. She has come a long way and needs her rest. Supper can be served in the drawing room with the tarantula, allowing Mr Kern to entertain Miss Tuesday in the dining room. He appears to have a handle on the situation and has taken a liking to Miss Tuesday.'

And somehow Monday resented that last remark. 'I like Miss Tuesday, regardless of what you may think.'

'But you have nothing to offer her, sir.'

Alone, Monday would agree.

COURTROOM DRAMA

And so, things were going pretty much according to Palfrey's plan. Tuesday slipped into a nice black dress, which could justify its expense only by its exquisite cut and the quality of the material. At the same time, Angela was pulling her stockings up tight towards the hem of a bright red outfit that offered no imagination for her admirers. Monday kept to his navy-blue suit wishing the ground would swallow him whole and Kern was combing his hair straight back gulping for a book deal. They all passed each other in the hall, fleeting exchanges as one couple went hither and the other went thither.

'Why are we dining separately?' Angela asked.

'Because we need to talk.' Monday smelt the wine stopper and poured two glasses of red. 'What I am about to tell you will come as a huge disappointment. I have decided not to sell.'

'We can get another buyer.' She misunderstood entirely and sat at the table with melodramatic gusto. 'Do we know what's on the menu? I hope it's not lemon sole. Last night it tasted like cardboard. The cook should be sacked. This morning, when I came down for breakfast, there was no muesli or orange juice.'

'Angela, do you ever stop to consider your attitude problem?'

'What attitude?'

'For instance, you speak to Palfrey like a piece of dirt and-'

'Oh, stop being pompous. That's what they get paid for. You and me, sweetie, we have brains.'

'You have no brains and mine went out of the window four days ago, probably long before then.' He swigged down his wine and poured another. 'Angela, I am keeping this place. This is where I want to live. Now it may not suit you, in fact I don't think it will suit you at all but this is my decision.'

However, it came as a surprise when she said, 'If that's what you want then fine by me…I can live here, sweetie. We need complete modernization. I know it's fun to have meals by candlelight but this is ridiculous. Have you seen that dreadful wallpaper in our bedroom? I'm sure the woman who lived here before had no taste whatsoever. And we also need to get rid of that courtroom. It's positively grotesque.'

'I rather like it.'

'It has to go.'

Monday stared moodily into his glass when Palfrey entered, wheeling a trolley, expressing lamb cutlets for Sir and fish pie for Madam who looked on in disgust and demanded something else.

'It's alright, Palfrey.' Monday swapped plates. 'She can have mine.'

'I don't eat meat!'

'Angela, shut up! Will you just shut up?' He watched the reflex stiffening of her body and waited until Palfrey had left the room before continuing. 'This house will stay as it is, no new furnishings, no expensive trimmings, no ripping apart the courtroom. Do you understand?'

'And you expect me to stay?'

'No, I expect you to leave.'

'This has to do with Miss Freckle Face, doesn't it?'

Shit, he thought, women have testicle telepathy. 'For Christ's sake, why can't you just listen for once? The estate has been left in Trust. I cannot sell it. For the rest of my life, I have to live here and manage it. The only way I could get out of my inheritance was to palm it off but I couldn't do that because the place is crawling with dead people.'

'That is just typical. Now we have dead people as your excuse to break off the engagement. Ever since Hilda died you-'

'I do wish you would leave my Mother out of our conversations. The simple truth is that I used our engagement as an excuse to convince Miss Tuesday why I wanted to leave Gallows Humour.'

Angela rushed back her chair. 'Well, we shall see what Miss Freckle Face has to say about that!'

'No!' His fist banged hard on the table and the vase which should have been glued back together simply fell apart in front of them.

Then the real argument started, the past wickedly brought up, accusations and regrets, all of it laid bare for Angela's consideration while the cockroach skittered beneath the floorboards. The knot of misery in his stomach eased a little as he lost himself in the labyrinth complexities of their relationship.

'I do not love you, Angela.'

'So why tell me,' she bawled.

'I have never told you, never. In fact, the only girl I ever told that to was my classmate in first grade.' He looked at her, saw that her eyes were full of tears, and his heart softened. Should he say a word to her, let her know there should be something left, but it occurred to him if he did, that word would mean so much, and would lead perhaps to the saying of other words. 'I'm sorry it came down to this but you should have stayed in London.' He held out his hand. 'Best you return the ring.'

'Why? So you can give it to that whore!'

'No, so I can return it to the Trust!'

Her attitude changed so dramatically. 'Sorry, sweetie, I do try, I really do.'

'Trying has nothing to do with it. We have nothing in common. I watch cricket and you turn the channel to that come dancing programme. I like drama or comedy at the theatre, sometimes opera but you never stop talking through the whole performance. And yes, I like to lie in from time to time, not a lot but it's irritating when you wake me for sex on demand. You have some sort of misguided urge to assail me. When we met you were totally different until you moved in and I never asked you to move in.'

The mood was sombre, as might be expected but a much calmer Angela took off the ring and placed it on the table. 'It was good while it lasted, sweetie,' she said rising to her feet, a tight smile barely visible. 'I'm going to toddle off and have a good soak in the bath. I take it you will be sleeping elsewhere or perhaps we can have one last bash.'

Monday made no answer, the thought was unbearable. He just stared away at the broken pieces of that vase under a luminous fragile glow. After a long, long silence she kissed him warmly on the head as though they would part company as friends, no animosity, only the vague hint of regret.

So, with the meal untouched, he settled down to the evening in his library and lit candles, two on the desk and one on the windowsill, balls of light suspended, which swelled or contracted to the sputtering wick or leaned to the moving air. He then submerged himself in notebooks, tall, short, fat or thin they surrendered the shelves and cluttered the desk. These were the closed scribbles made by Jeremy Sunday, a mass of uninformative information. There were doodles of hangmen's nooses, crossed out dates and names, question marks around tales, summary sentences, riddles and an infinite range of flat-dried daisies strung in a row. He was growing a little tougher, a little colder, and turned his attention more towards the outside world when the door rapped softly.

'Come in.'

Tuesday popped her head round the door. 'May I have a moment?'

Monday heaved himself to his feet and crushed out the cigarette. 'Miss Tuesday, I wish to apologize for my behaviour. It was uncalled for.'

'Solomon, can we dispense with the formalities?' She approached with her hands clasped to her chin, her beguiling sapphire eyes looking up to him. 'I simply couldn't believe it. One minute you were so anxious to get on with your life and next you had a change of heart.'

He opened his mouth then closed it, would give nothing away.

'In the mid-nineties it was very popular to feed hot air through vented floors. It can still be very effective, heat wise I mean, though not very soundproof.'

She heard everything, he thought. Now he struggled to find something sensible to say, confused by the rush of his emotions and watched her move slowly to an armchair. She sagged back and pressed her fingers into her closed eyelids.

'Are you alright, Miss Tuesday?'

'Just a little tired of life, like you. Please, call me Izabo.'

Monday drew up a chair, the easier to observe, to converse and painfully filled in the holes about Gallows Humour where she kept opinions to herself. They spoke little after that, but somehow their silences seemed to bring them close.

'Solomon,' she spoke movingly, 'every once and a while fate reaches out and extends its hand. It extends it for you and for me.'

'You will never be able to have a normal life. This place will consume you like it did for Jeremy Sunday.'

'I want this, I really do. There's a future for me here, a far happier one than returning to Italy.'

'Would you care to elaborate?'

'It's the same old story,' she replied but barely able to face him. 'Unrequited love and all that sorrow when you discover the man is hollow.'

'I find that hard to believe.'

'Do you?'

Suddenly he felt desire, watching the shallow rise and fall of her chest. 'Err, well, I mean you're very pretty for a builder although your head is not exactly screwed on right. So, this chap, what was he, a gigolo?'

'A gigolo, like all I deserve is a gigolo?'

'Well how am I to know?'

'You could stop guessing for a start. He started out as a handsome crusader for the forces of good but grew arrogant in the extent of his self-regard. Strange how one thinks something can last forever but it never does. I went to Italy to get away from it all and discovered further complications. If you ever want complications in a family, look to mine.'

He was so close, close to take in her smell like freshly laundered linen handkerchiefs or a new motor. For a moment he covered her hand with his own, intensely aware of their situation. To ease things away from the awkwardness, he posed an intelligent question, which never sounded that intelligent. 'Have you ever encountered the afterlife?'

Predictably, she smiled at the question. 'How can any of us be sure who we encounter in life?'

'Point taken,' he agreed. 'There is no privacy in this house. Doolally, and I dare say others, might be in this very room though Palfrey has tried to reassure me he has them under control. Truthfully, no one could ever control Doolally. She's beyond the scope of scientific explanation.'

'Was it bad for you when your mother died?'

Wow, the question came like a bolt from the blue. He puffed out his cheeks and thought for once, why not bare his soul to a stranger. Resting his elbows on his knees, head bent, he sadly said, 'When she needed me most, I wasn't there. I couldn't face losing her. Sounds trite, but I kept thinking she will be fine, she will get better but she died. And on top of that I had the fate of the Labour Government in the palm of my hands, solid evidence of corruption and the real corruption was going on in my head, hooked on drugs. I messed up on the scoop and lost my job. Not even Mike knew and we go way back. After I cleaned myself up, I realized she was the only contact I had in the real world not the world of rhetoric and Angela. Christ, she drained me. She walked into my life a week after Mother died and I would have liked to say I had someone to love, even if it meant losing them but there was Angela, never more so there was Angela right in my face as though it was my punishment.'

'I suppose you feel as though you have jumped from the frying pan into the fire.'

'Perhaps,' he sighed and looked up. 'How it was done, I don't know but why it was done I do know. Week put a curse on his bloodline. It sounds crazy, but the records show that for everyone who comes here leaves with a greater madness unless the pen is handed over to the next. I reacted to the whole thing badly but maybe, just maybe, somewhere in that pile on my desk I might find the answer. Your answer is not here, Izabo. There will be no happiness for you at Gallows Humour, only misery.'

Which brought up the rather large issue of what exactly was on his desk. She walked over and picked up a notebook, flicked some pages and looked back. 'What answer?'

'Apparently these lost souls, as Palfrey likes to call them, signed their name in a brown leather register, small but quite thick so legend has it. Jeremy Sunday claimed to have worked out that they are here to take back their signatures. But as you can see, his notes are all to cock. He refers to tales, strikes through a sentence, doodles nothing but hangmen's nooses. Personally, I think he went mad, followed the same route as Week.'

'Solomon, let me stay on, just for a while. I might be able to help you with this.'

Perhaps the mutual issues were important but something else was at work here. From the moment she entered his life, he was now in the flow of it and it scared him. 'Look,' he said. 'I've been paid my whole life to be suspicious even when there's nothing to be suspicious about. So, if anyone can make sense of this, it will be me. It doesn't seem to worry you that a bunch of dead people served up supper?'

'Why should it? I had a lovely meal this evening.'

'But they are dead, Izabo. They do things without recourse. Why do I seem to be the only one around here who takes things seriously? My Father was hung by one of them, and God knows how many others have gone the same way.' He glanced at his Omega. It was past the time of no return, his game of make believe was at an end. 'It's late,' he said going to the door. 'Thanks for the offer but no thanks. Tomorrow you must leave.'

Tuesday managed to display the right shade of indifference. 'If you change your mind let me know.' As Monday stood aside to let her pass there was a strange noise, disturbing in the glow. She looked at him, her voice barely above a whisper. 'Did you hear that?'

Monday nodded and signalled for her to stay in the library. He crept towards the drawing room, the door partly open in the shadows of the moon, and there was Angela inspecting trinkets with due consideration, systematically packing them one by one in her overnight bag, blissfully unaware that one by one they were being systematically removed. Amused, he gathered the invisible menace to be Doolally, absorbed as usual in some freakish behaviour. This was a scene worth savouring.

And when the moral warning dawned upon the track-suit thief that her bag was being emptied, Doolally materialized and all hell broke loose. She gave chase to a hysterical female shrieking its way to the hall, the oak pair of courtroom doors flung open, Angela was propelled inside, the double doors slammed shut and Doolally stood guard.

'Open the doors,' asked Monday, which had seemed a sensible enough thing to say.

'Yew believes she's outside our laws?'

Already he could hear raised voices coming from inside, the pleading shouts of Angela and felt his own intestinal fortitude weakening. On their lips was only one word and in their minds was a single thought. To punish Angela was a privilege.

The fracas had drawn the inquisitive living out in the open. With a pink quilt wrapped round his shoulders under which discretely covered a pair of candy-stripe underpants, Kern stood beside Tuesday who was looking on in her black dress, their faces holding quiet apprehension, speechless in the moment. If there were doubts before about the impact of Gallows Humour, there were certainly none now. Then Palfrey swiftly came into view, tying a cord around his tartan dressing gown.

'Palfrey,' Monday said, his exhaustion rising. 'Get Doolally to open these doors.'

'We need to talk in the library, sir.'

'Now is not the time to talk. We must get Angela out.'

'She will be perfectly safe, sir. I assure you.'

Accompanied by Palfrey and pausing only to motion for the others to follow, Monday made his way to the library, every muscle in his body under stress, his fists clenching at his sides, appalled at himself, angry that he had allowed this to happen.

'This better not be what I think it is, Palfrey.'

'Acquire the courage and reason of Mr Sunday. This is their way to seek justice for what they deem their right.

After all, this is their home, left in Trust to them. That is how they view it.' Palfrey brought out a thick manual on law, thumped the book hard on the desk. He licked his index finger and rapidly turned to page one hundred and sixty-two and pointed to clause VI. 'You can act as defence council.'

'Pardon?'

'As master of the house, you have priority to take any position.'

'And if I lose?'

Palfrey sighed. 'Sir, negativity only enhances the poorer view you take of Gallows Humour.' Again, he licked his finger and turned to page two hundred and ten. 'Sentence is passed appropriate to the crime bearing in mind mitigating circumstances.'

Monday reached for his rimless spectacles. And silence dropped down from out of the night, into this room, a catch of breath and the slow exhalation as one clause was left behind and a new one began. Finally, he stood up straight and slowly peeled off his glasses with an air of exasperation. His audience in bated breath.

'If found guilty, she is to labour here for no more than a year and no less than a month depending upon mitigating circumstances. Apart from having no mitigating circumstances whatsoever, have I got to suffer Angela's presence in this house for a year? This should have been brought to my attention before now, Palfrey. This is not on, not on at all. Angela will be a physical wreck. No, strike that. I shall be a physical wreck. This whole place will be a physical wreck. Angela has the capacity to alter men's minds and I would go so far as to say she will thrust her will against them and this place will be a living hell.'

'Are we to assume Week is the judge?' Kern asked.

Palfrey looked at Monday. 'Do you wish me to answer that, sir?'

'I think we have gone beyond that stage, Palfrey.'

'Judge Week has never presided. They take it in turns, though they rather favour the woodsman, known to you as Woody, sir.'

Monday slammed shut the book. 'This is a frigging nightmare! I must be dreaming this. What is real around here? I shook the man's hand and that seemed real. Is Mike really here? Did I meet a Miss Tuesday or was I rowing with myself on the lake. Perhaps I'm in a psychiatric ward with a bunch of nutcases or maybe I'm dead from a drug overdose.'

Kern was alerted. 'Why a drug overdose?'

'The four of us can stay here and discuss irrelevant issues,' Tuesday said quickly, 'or we can find a way to help Angela, deservedly or not to escape the clutches from that gathering.' She looked quizzically at Palfrey. 'Mr Monday needs the full low down on what exactly is going on. So far, I question what is meant by them taking it in turns? Have there been other incidents? And this book on law, how can he represent a client when clearly his case will be weakened by prosecuting council claiming conflict of interest.'

Hell, Monday thought, she had everything sussed. And all eyes went to Palfrey who was looking up at the ceiling, just as he did before when Monday arrived that afternoon asking a question that seemed too complicated to answer.

'There have been those,' Palfrey admitted, 'with dubious qualities, drawn to the side of the living, Gallows Humour acting rather like a magnet so to speak. For a good term, there were the innocent but others popped up that were guilty. How it began is left for speculation but their questionable attendance encouraged interaction for courtroom drama. They go through the motions of their own experiences, rather like a retrial and use the law books as a guide although certain aspects have been changed to suit their whims. In the case of Hodges verses Gallows Humour, he was found guilty and given a year's sentence labouring on the land. Unfortunately, he was unable to endure the torment and subsequently died of frostbite.'

'He was that chap,' Monday said. 'The taxi driver told me about, stuck fast to a tree, a vagrant, died of the cold but he wasn't a vagrant, was he, Palfrey? He was a thief.'

'Yes, sir, sadly, there have been a few incidences. However, we have the formidable Doolally, our perfect alarm system.'

'I could represent Angela,' Tuesday said bringing a blank page to the desk, pen dipped in ink and waved under Monday's nose. 'Fate has once again shown this is meant to be, Solomon. I know the perfect defence. What other options do you have?'

Monday regarded her for a moment, beautiful Izabo Tuesday in her lovely black dress but so eager to have Gallows Humour. Why? 'Mike,' he said, 'do you gain the impression she could handle herself in court?'

'I gain the impression she can handle herself full stop.'

'My thoughts entirely,' confirmed Monday.

'I made no secret of it,' she told them. 'Did I not say this was my future?'

'A very depressing future,' added Monday, 'locked in Gallows Humour.'

She let the words go by but Monday studied her look. He saw the flash in her eyes. It was there for only a second and it was not fear. Keeping the stare, he waited for the look to return. Was it confusion? Disappointment? Her eyes showed nothing now. But Monday believed he knew the look. The same look in Palfrey's eyes when the pen was handed over. What he had seen was the truth cleverly told to be the biggest lie of all.

'You know, Miss Tuesday,' Monday said reverting to formality and going to the globe of the world. 'One of the reasons why I was a good reporter was because I could sniff out a lie as a dog could sniff out a bone. Yes, I grant you, of late my mind wasn't exactly in full sync but then whose would, considering the circumstance.' He passed a drink to Kern. 'Palfrey, will you join me in a glass of whisky?'

'Don't mind if I do, sir.'

'Miss Tuesday, would you like a drink? I have whisky, port, vodka and,' he lifted a cobwebbed bottle, 'some sherry.'

'Alcohol only serves to cloud the issue,' she replied.

It was not really a question of being smart. Nothing made sense. 'Here we have an independent woman, gentlemen.' Monday went on searching for that look again. 'She claims to have a future at Gallows Humour like she claims to lay bricks as another course in life. You are an example to us all, Miss Tuesday, a mighty oak standing proud against the storm.'

'The choice is yours, Mr Monday. You can hope to defend Angela, live here for the rest of your sorrowful life and perhaps meet a woman that might share your woes. Or you can pass the pen to me with a guarantee of her acquittal?'

Monday shook his head in dismay. 'The Miss Bloody Know-it-all gives her guarantees. By comparison, you make Angela appear like a seraph.' He could see her eyes smouldering and pushed her further. 'You never hopped on a plane just on the whim of an unknown benefactor, an unknown inheritance. I know Crookshank. He would have asked to see your passport, shown you here to offer his party piece, especially when there was a lot at stake. So why was that, Miss Tuesday or should I call you by another name? Where is your passport?'

Tuesday, visibly surprised by Monday's pig-headedness, glanced at the other two held in suspense and said, 'ermm, I have no idea.'

'Ah ha!' Monday exclaimed. 'Are you flesh or are you spirit?'

'I am bankrupt, if you must know. Week's Work exists and with it the entire fortune of Gallows Humour. And only I have the answer.' It was her turn to remind him of what he had reminded her. 'You can look at me with those judgemental and incriminating eyes all you want but it will do you no good. I suggest you pack your bags and leave.'

Monday's face glowed with anger. 'Palfrey, were you aware of this?'

'Truthfully, sir, I am a little confused. It is true to say that if Week's Work is found the estate will pass without hindrance. I was hard put to wonder if that piece of information was relevant since his Work has never been found, not even by the most ardent seekers.'

'Seekers?' Kern asked.

'Prior bloodlines, so I understand, but it did them no good. Sir, allow me to convey your current position.'

'He knows his current position,' Kern intercepted, holding up his glass and using that as a pointer. 'She's got him over a barrel and knowing Sol he won't budge an inch. He would rather rot in this place than give into a blackmailer. Right, Sol?'

'Err,' Monday never sounded too sure about that but realized the tremendous leverage Tuesday held over him. 'Perhaps I would feel a lot better if this place was razed to the ground. End of problem.'

'Nor do you feel a hangman's noose round your neck.'

Another presence, a different voice, had entered the room. It had great effect as the hidden spectre remained close, talking in riddle.

'None care for those who were executed without reason. I know not the crime I commit yet two days in another has ordained it. Entries should mean something.'

Everyone looked at Palfrey for an explanation. 'Ned is referring to Monday and Tuesday at loggerheads on a Thursday. He wishes to put forward a joint venture.'

Monday glanced at Tuesday. There was a softening in her eyes and he wondered if the solution would work. 'Miss Tuesday, would you consider a joint venture?'

'I would,' she replied without hesitation. 'But how are my interests protected? Legal documents will not wash. I need to be signatory in that register and marriage is totally out of the question.'

That called for a wicked response. 'Perhaps not in bed but on paper.'

'Like your engagement to Angela,' she reminded. 'You made her give back the ring.'

'She never deserved a thirty grand ring!'

Ned intervened again. '*Two days can share the same date.*' Was there hope to remedy the situation when they were hard to sway, their minds set? '*Pass the pen to Tuesday who must sign over Monday and become two days in one.*'

They scrambled to the register. Monday got there first. With Tuesday trying to share his view through the looking glass, her intoxicating fresh linen smell ran up his nostrils, deep down into his lungs where he found himself wanting again. Being a lot shrewder than he looked and definitely inclined to torch the place in the current mood he was in, Monday confirmed the invisible Ned was right.

'Did you know about this, Palfrey?'

'Sir, I am in the midst of revelations this late hour. If the ruling is there then one must consider Judge Week had foreseen such an event.'

Monday picked up the pen, dipped it in the inkwell and handed it to Tuesday whereupon she signed not above nor below but over his signature leaving the date untouched.

'To work, gentlemen,' she said returning the pen to the ink stand. 'Angela's defence will be a simple one. Mr Monday, you will be witness for prosecuting council. Palfrey, how do I get time alone with Angela?'

'Madam forgets you are mistress to Gallows Humour.'

'Oh, so I am, how wonderful.' And that irritated Monday. Taking with her the book on law, she then advised chirpily, 'let's go gentlemen.'

'Hell,' Kern said to Monday on the sly, 'she's something, isn't she?'

'I am never going to last the distance.'

'Be resolute, sir.' Palfrey said. 'Remember, she is just a woman.'

'I tell you, Palfrey such acts could foster the appropriate response. I was genuinely impressed by her presence. Now I'm teetering on the border of killing her.' Monday strode on grinning to himself. The games of make believe were not at an end. And in a perverted sort of way it excited him.

At the courtroom doors, Doolally stood guard like a fossil in sandstone ambushed by Tuesday poised for discovery and courtroom drama.

'I wish to speak to my client.'

'Do yew now.'

'I am defence council.'

'Is that so?' Doolally refused to budge.

'It's alright,' Monday said. 'Miss Tuesday signed the register,' and then quickly added, 'on the same page. I am going to be witness for the prosecution.'

Doolally's emotions were entirely without reserve. She jumped up and down, squawking and chuckling that Solomon Monday was still in for the long haul then kicked him in the shins just to set the record straight. 'I go first as witness. It wus me that caught her thieving.'

With that the doors creaked open to a thickness in the air, the noise of wagging tongues and tight knit circles. Monday had walked into the past that smelt as pungent as the forest floor, fanatical and worn-coloured souls, bonnets and breaches, tinkers and tramps, maids and horsemen, young and old, the rousing harmony which persisted to haunt Gallows Humour.

Doolally held Monday back. 'Yew can sit with me.'

'How thrilling,' Kern said.

'Here,' she looked at him sternly, 'you're not dressed.'

'Palfrey, give Mike your dressing gown.'

'But sir, I cannot sit in my pyjamas. It would be unseemly.'

'Oh come on, Palfrey,' Kern pleaded. 'I'll swap you my underpants.'

'Really, sir, this place is slowly going downhill.'

Palfrey conceded of course, after which Doolally led them to the gallery where candles had been set apart, each in its proper order and revealing faces more by casts of darkness than by any clear light they threw. There they could look down at proceedings and watch the ranks of men and women open respectfully for Tuesday who steadily worked through the length of the courtroom, up to the far point of the Judge's Bench then quickly advanced towards Angela forlornly sitting in the dock. The hand wielding a mallet instead of a gavel belonged to a lean and straight man, a duelling scar puckered the corner of his mouth and it was his turn to be judge.

'That's Ned,' Doolally told Monday. 'He's judge this time round. Yew met Woody, he draws lovely pictures. He was hung for stealing a pie.'

'A pie?'

'Don't yew be going deaf on me, Solomon Monday. A pie is what I said.'

'I understand a lot of these people were guilty of their crimes.'

'That's true enough. This place don't belong to them but here they are and here they stay. See that woman in the bouncy hat, she belongs here. Bumble wus hung fer killing her husband but she never killed him. It was his fancy man that killed him.'

'So he was gay.'

'No, he was as sad as they come.'

Their conversation was unequal as it was unconventional. But what did he really know about Doolally? Nothing, he thought. 'What was the circumstance of your death?' He watched the reality slowly settle on her face, the wounds were old, but the scars were still very fresh in her mind.

'I wus hung fer stealing Able's cow. He wus a loathsome turd who stole me chickens. Able Soper, a man whose purse grew fat with gold prised from corpses. If ever a man needed hanging, it was him. The sky wus black that day, and my lads were praying hard through their folded hands.'

'You had sons?'

'Two fine boys, long gone now. Never sees them, none of us never sees what happens to our kin.' She laid her hand in his and it felt like a small dry flame which he could neither hold nor throw away. 'They were your age when I last saw them. Do yew want a mum?'

First, she wants to marry him, now she wants to adopt him. There was no simple answer, probably no answer at all.

When the mallet went down and the accused was asked to submit a plea to which the response was not guilty, the room gasped in complaint. Then ordered tension broke by Tuesday's protesting.

'Be careful of what you say, madam.' Ned, acting judge had been goaded enough.

'I will not.' Tuesday spat her contempt. 'My client has every right to proper judiciary proceedings.'

'These are our proceedings.'

She held up the ancient words on law. 'You use this to convenience rather than to seek justice. Why you might as well drink the blood of your enemy and become vampires for surely that is your purpose. One day you will face judgement at the pearly gates. What shall you say? That it pleased you to run amuck? Pleased you to seek revenge on the innocent?'

Woody, prosecuting council stood. 'Your client is not innocent.'

'So why have these proceedings if your mind is set like jelly in a mould? Was it not the same for you?' She pointed at the jury of men in frocked coats. 'And you, you, you.' Then she looked at Angela then looked back at the judge and smiled with a twinkle in her eye. If it never melted Ned's heart it certainly melted Monday's. 'Your honour, are we not here to be heard?'

'Very well, a plea of not guilty shall be entered into the records. Prosecuting council, you may proceed with your argument.'

The mighty Woody stood again and drew on his pipe. 'I call upon Doolally.'

Instantly Doolally was there in the witness box, picking up the bible whilst casting wilful glances at Angela. 'I swear to tell the truth, the whole truth and nothing but the truth so help me God.'

'Doolally,' Woody asked. 'Tell the court what yew saw.'

'There she wus, packed her bags, crept downstairs, put them in her fancy car and crept back in as if she had the devil inside her. Picking and choosing all the nice things Mr Sunday collected over the years.'

'But you manage to salvage the situation.'

'I surely did, Woody. Every last one wus put back.' Doolally stared at Angela, a message she did send. 'We don't need reminding of my all-seeing eye.'

'No more questions, your honour.' Woody sat down.

Tuesday stood and smiled graciously. 'Doolally, have you ever met the devil?'

'That's her there.'

The courtroom exploded into laughter. Even Monday enjoyed the joke.

Tuesday glanced salaciously at acting Judge Ned. Down came his mallet. Order was restored and she went on. 'Explain to the court what you meant when you said she had the devil inside her.'

'Why she wus acting suspicious, like she had something to hide but she wus the one doing the hiding. I was not well brought up but to be sure I know when someone has a mind to do bad.'

'So we can safely assume she was not the Angela you first met when she was invited to stay by Mr Monday?'

'What do yew mean?'

'Well, for instance, did she take her time in choosing the items?'

'Oh, she wus choosy alright, picked what she wanted to take.'

'No more questions, your honour.' Tuesday sat down.

Prosecuting council stood. 'I call upon Solomon Monday.'

By now, Monday thought he had the gist of Tuesday's case. It was obvious to him she was going to plead temporary insanity and that was a good thing. For, if it worked, Angela would go free and he would see the back of her. He deliberately failed to catch her eye as he stepped in the witness box, the proceedings taxing and comical. To his right lay the Holy Bible, knew he was expected to swear in but instead he said nothing and waited.

'You must swear an oath to tell the truth.' Ned reminded.

'Your honour, I do swear to tell the truth.'

'Then place your hand on the word of God and swear to tell the truth.'

Monday held up the Bible. 'I am reminded this bears significance among you when clearly this bears no significance to me.'

There was puzzlement, rebellious murmuring among the assembled.

'You must swear on the word of God.' Ned insisted.

Tuesday stood. 'Your honour, if I may. Mr Monday has given his heart to Gallows Humour. It would not act in his interests if he lied.' She sat down.

'Miss Tuesday has reminded us all,' said Ned. 'Carry on, Woody.'

'Thank yew, your honour. Mr Monday, in your own words what did yew see the accused do?'

'She was packing items in her overnight bag.'

'And did yew give her permission to do so?'

'No.'

'Your honour, no more questions.' Woody sat down.

Tuesday stood and smiled at Monday with such girlish pleasure that his heart flipped and traded places with his stomach. 'Mr Monday,' she said so softly, 'is it fair to say you asked the accused to marry you?'

'Yes.'

'And she accepted.'

'Yes.'

'And what did you tell her before she was caught putting items in her bag?'

'That I had no intention of marrying her.'

'And did you give the reason why?'

Monday threw Angela an embarrassed half-smile. 'I told her it was the only way in order to get out of my commitment to Gallows Humour.' The moment he said it, he felt the weight of disgust crease the brows of the assembled. 'The thing-'

'Yes,' Tuesday interjected. 'Not all men can face up to their responsibilities.'

'It was not-'

'Mr Monday,' she interjected again. 'Would it not be fair to say you asked for the return of the ring?'

'Yes.'

'And did the accused comply?'

'Yes.'

'I have no more questions for this witness.' Tuesday sat down.

In those brief exchanges Monday felt Izabo Tuesday had bruised his standing among the assembled and reduced his ego to a quarter pint of milk. As he returned to his seat in the gallery the tempo increased.

Hunched over his bench with his fist supporting his chin, acting Judge Ned listened to prosecuting council confirming he had no more witnesses and thereafter Tuesday stood and called the accused to the stand.

Angela's track-suit top was flapped open to great effect to defy any man to remain unaffected. She picked up the Bible and swore herself in. 'I do solemnly swear to tell the truth, the whole truth and nothing but the truth, so help me God.'

Tuesday gave that time to register and then asked, 'Angela, let us not waste the court's time. You did put certain items in your bag. Is that not so?'

'Yes, I did.'

'And is not so you intended to take them home?'

'Yes, that was my intention.'

'Now let me ask you, why were you taking your time to survey each item before placing them in your bag...why the fastidious picking and choosing?'

'I wanted the value of the ring Sol gave to me. He promised to marry me. He broke his promise and I had the right to keep the ring.'

'Do you know the value of the articles you tried to take?'

'Not really,' Angela replied, fluttering her eyelids to jury members.

'Your honour, I have no more questions for the accused.'

Prosecuting council took his time to rise and it was then that Monday realized Tuesday had her case perfectly sewn up.

Even Woody knew this, shaking his head and confirming he had no questions for the accused, then, in summation, he said, 'Make of it as yew will but there stands a scarlet woman who wanted her cake and eat it. She couldn't hev Solomon Monday so she took what she could and hoped to make a clean getaway. It weren't enough to hev a nice place in London, not hers mind yew or that fancy car she drives. That was paid by Solomon Monday, a generous man, more generous than most. If she really loved him, she would hev understood his position, wished him well but she wished him spite, she wished for that ring along with all the other things she would hev stolen. Looking fer it, that's what she was doing. Looking for that ring, it stands out a mile. But he put it where she has no brains to look, back in the hands of Palfrey where it belonged. I rest my case.'

Tuesday stood. 'I refer to page three hundred and ten, clause II whereby it states a woman may keep the engagement ring if the pledge of marriage is not honoured by the man.' Confidently she walked to the centre of the courtroom, her hands behind her back and her head held high. 'Now, gentlemen, in your day, the penalty was greater. A man would be made to pay for his release. The problem is that my client is a model not a valuation expert. Had she known justice existed right here in this very fine courtroom then she would have sought for recompense, put her case before you and trusted your judgement. No, what she did was perhaps in your eyes a little unconventional but you must remember she was not a thief but an invited guest of Mr Monday who promised the world, offered love and marriage, spoke how Gallows Humour could be sold and with the money they could buy an apartment in Mayfair. To express his intentions, he gave her a very expensive ring, an astounding thirty thousand pounds.'

The room gasped.

'My client,' Tuesday continued, 'was not looking to take more than its value for if that were so she could have just taken the painting off the wall in the library and abscond with the most valuable article in Gallows Humour. In fact, what she did was to take silly little trinkets, one of which had no formal identification, hardly worth the effort of silver plate and put them in her bag whilst under emotional stress. Not only was she dumped like a piece of used tissue but she was confronted by Doolally who frightened her half-witless.

And let us not forget why her belief in Solomon Monday was so strong. They were living together virtually as man and wife. To find her guilty is to say to every man, go ahead, break my heart, use me like a dish rag and cast me aside when you no longer have need of me. Is that how you would treat a woman who has lived with you, asked nothing in return, washed your dirty linen and kept your bed warm? And the car, I wish to remind you is a rental car, albeit paid monthly by Solomon Monday, though nevertheless a small price to pay for her devoted services…'

My God, Monday thought as the jury was shaking their heads. 'This is not on,' he whispered to Kern. 'She's made me out to be a right bastard.'

'Well, when she puts it like that, you are.'

Doolally spoke. 'Never yew mind, yew will always have me.'

'I cannot marry you, Doolally.'

'No, but yew can watch over us, keep us safe, just like yew said.'

'I was drunk.'

'I wus dead.'

Humour had its place while conferring and decision took time. It was only when the moon had passed into the early hours of Friday the verdict was returned not guilty and subsequently the courtroom emptied of the supernatural like bubbles bursting in the air.

With Angela taking a speedy departure, daring not to look back, in a darkened room upstairs Monday turned away from the window and held the palms of his hands over his eyes for a moment. At least she was out of the equation but in exchange he had Izabo Tuesday. Now he was faced by a new struggle where he made a pact, fighting for his place in Gallows Humour.

MEETING OF MINDS

When Monday spilled from a restless bed, he squinted at his wristwatch and gathered it was either quarter past twelve or three in the afternoon. Whichever, the best part of Friday had gone and his sleep-starved mind wondered what his next move should be. At the window he stared at the low clouds watering the estate, a quiet noise burbling across the roof, and listened to the drum of rain as it suffocated the lilies on the lake.

'Hey, my man you're up.' Kern walked in as bright as a button with two mugs of coffee and a plate of buttered toast. 'I haven't been up long myself. That was a night, yeah?'

'I suppose you're pretty pleased with yourself.'

'The way I see it, if you come out on top then I can use the ammunition for my book, yeah? Happy people all round. Izabo gets to have her slice of the cake and you can twiddle your thumbs working out how to spend your money. Personally, I would be inclined to twiddle thumbs in warmer climes where the girls are less inclined to damage your ego.'

'Is Miss Know-it-all up?'

'Do I detect some animosity or perhaps a little jealousy? You have to admit she was good. She telephoned Crookshank, told him the arrangement.'

Monday reached for a slice of toast, took a bite and muffled. 'Do we know how much he knows?'

'He knows as much as she wants him to know, so Palfrey said. What you have to do is find out what she knows.'

'Since she likes to be in charge let her do all the running.' Monday tried looking at Kern again, but his eyes were focused on the lake as if something was on his mind. And he correctly guessed. 'It was a temporary hic-cup, that's all.'

'Why didn't you tell me you took drugs?'

'Why do you think?'

'So you got the sack?'

'Is this the third degree?' Monday took a gulp of lukewarm coffee. No surprise there and then headed for the bathroom. 'I was depressed just like you were depressed when your book never reached twenty thousand.' He glanced at himself in the cabinet mirror and sighed heavily. 'I look and feel like death…perhaps I signed my death warrant…perhaps I'm now slowly ebbing away into the clutches of Doolally and her tribe.'

'You know your problem,' Kern said, sharing his reflection. 'You're too wound up, always was, take everything too seriously.'

'It should be taken seriously.' Monday turned on the tap.

'Five days ago, I was walking into Crookshank's office in the belief my Father may have left a little something or even a note, anything by way of an apology. What actually happened was that I walked into a nightmare and you say I take everything too seriously. Wake up, why don't you? This is another world where dead people think their alive. They play with people's emotions. No, strike that. They condemn real people in that courtroom and have the weird notion they can overturn their own sentence. Nobody in their right mind would have accepted this post. And your book, just tell me how you intend to establish credibility? Do you think the dead will be happy to greet the media? Why they will crucify you.'

'Damn you, Sol, ride with me on this.' Kern was unsympathetic and took an opposite view. 'Okay, so it was scary and confusing at first. But it's incredible to think there is life after death, albeit a bit balmy. I did some research on the subject. Did you know when questioned half the population actually believe ghosts do exist and here is living proof. The research into physic phenomenon is huge, especially in America. This place would turn the science community on their heads, everything, right down to Darwinism.'

'And the church,' Monday said swilling his razor in warm water. 'It gives them an open door to persecute more souls. No, I don't like the way this is heading.'

'So what's your real problem? Is the thought of having loads of money and freedom less scary than the lovely Izabo wringing your balls?'

'There is something about her which doesn't ring true. How did she know the Trust money was up for grabs?'

'Perhaps she got the information from her father. He would have to be dead in order for her to be next in line. Did you know she's a fan for my literary output? So, what do you say, Sol? Can I make a move?'

'Fine by me,' but it never sounded fine when he heard himself say it.

'Thought I would take her dancing tonight, what do you think?'

'You're asking me? How the hell am I expected to know? One minute she's a builder, next a treasure hunter then a defence attorney cracking my nuts…take your pick. Who knows, you might discover she won medals for Latin American dancing.'

The unspoken meaning of this was that Kern had sensed the unease Monday radiated toward himself and Tuesday. 'Okeydokey, I'll see you downstairs.'

Moments later Monday threw down the towel and emptied his suit pockets. One cigarette left in the packet, train tickets, chewing gum and a folded piece of paper. He breathed slowly and deeply, unfolded the note and read, who is the benefactor. It was something he wrote whilst on the telephone to Crookshank, a call this solicitor made to evoke mystery and suspense, refusing to give details. But yes, he thought, who really benefits out of this sorry affair? So, he will become rich but at whose expense? Certainly at the expense of those who regard Gallows Humour their home.

Brushing his suit down, ensuring the crease of his trousers met, he hung it in the wardrobe and discovered there was not much else on the rail. He pulled out his stonewashed jeans and sweatshirt, dull colours printed on thin cotton fabric, wondering what on earth made him pack for summer when autumn was clearly established.

Taking the treads two by two and raking his hands through his mop he bumped into Palfrey who had an umbrella in his hand.

'Good afternoon, sir.'

'What's the umbrella for, Palfrey?'

'For madam, sir.'

When Izabo Tuesday came into view, she acknowledged Monday by a token dip of her head and took the umbrella. 'Thank you, Palfrey.'

'Going somewhere?' Monday asked

'Yes, I thought I would take a walk to the newsagent.'

'And you need to do it in the rain?'

'Where would the country be if we all stopped walking in the rain?'

It was that smile or maybe those freckles on her cheeks which had Monday pinned to the floor. Torn between wanting to follow her and going to the city, he asked Palfrey if the car was insured for him to drive.

'May I suggest the tailors in White Lion Street?'

'Dammit, why am I so transparent?'

'Try a spur of the moment thing, sir. It really is invigorating.'

'Right, you get me kitted out. I shall walk to the newsagents.' Monday strode off then quickly twizzled on his heels stepping backwards. 'Palfrey,' he called out, 'nothing black, something warm and bright but not too bright and tell Doolally I wish to see her when I get back.'

'Yes, sir.'

As he headed outside, Monday found himself bothered by the detail of the purchases Palfrey would make on his behalf. Details fuelled his thoughts. Just like Izabo Tuesday whose choice of words and wear were just as important and not to be misplaced or forgotten.

'Do you mind if I join you, Miss Tuesday?'

'Am I to get the third degree, Mr Monday?'

'You did rather paint me in a bad light.'

'We all make mistakes,' she said passing the umbrella to Monday. 'That's why there are rubbers on the end of pencils.'

'I think my only mistake was not telling Angela how I felt when she moved in with her toothbrush.'

'Yes, the toothbrush, a dead giveaway. All you had to do was bin it.'

'Then she would have used mine.'

'She probably used it anyway to clean the taps.'

Monday went quiet, thinking this really needed to be an important conversation. And in some deeply instinctual way he knew she was thinking that too.

'I never lied to you about my business, Mr Monday. I do build individual homes. My Father was a builder and I was a disappointment. He wanted a son, naturally, so I spent my life trying to make up for it and that is as much as I wish to say about him. I really do enjoy building homes. Of course, I do have help. It's not as if I do it all by myself. Plumbing and electrics are not my scene, and besides you have to be qualified. But that is neither here nor there. Like you, I have a new direction.'

'Yet you live in Italy.'

'My family lives in Italy. The weather is much warmer and the scenery is spectacular. It was supposed to be a sabbatical but the sabbatical extended due to family complications but what are families for other than to have complications. However, quite fortuitously fate stepped in and here I am.'

'Yes, here you are about to claim a fortune. How soon are we to see this fortune?'

With her thumb and forefinger a centimetre apart, she said, 'There is just a tiny bit missing.'

'And this tiny bit missing, do I take it you're still in the throes of working it out?'

'I cannot tell you the effort that's needed in order to fill in a blank spot. People to see, places to go, sounds very dramatic, doesn't it, but make no mistake, Mr Monday I shall not let the side down.'

'Oh, I am certain you will not, Miss Tuesday. Such tenacity, such attributes, house builder, treasure seeker, legal council, I am grateful just to be eclipsed by the long shadow of your accomplishments.'

He happily walked in her silence knowing he had won a small verbal battle. It may have left sticky trails around the edges but her quietness suggested she was in that moment now of understanding him.

At their destination, Tuesday purchased the Daily Telegraph and Monday purchased a packet of cigarettes. Then rain fell hard and heavy and cold. It changed the colour and texture of the road, polishing every surface to a dark shine. They stood in the shop entrance looking at each other, he gazing down at her, she gazing up at him before the moment was broken by a customer dashing in.

'Well,' she said brightly, 'we might as well go for it. I have a dinner date.'

Monday threw up the umbrella, felt her hand squeeze through his arm, her summery clad body clung close to his side as they walked steadily on in torrential rain.

'Are you not cold?' he asked feeling cold himself.

'The trouble living in Italy you forget the weather in England.'

'I too packed light. Is this your first time in Norfolk?'

'Is it for you?'

'We shall get nowhere if you keep answering my questions with a question.'

'You do exaggerate, only once did I answer with a question. Ask me another and see if we can make that two.'

'Ghost of promises past, what do you make of that, Miss Tuesday?'

'Ah, Week's Work, yes…when it's found, we shall release their souls. Only then can the fortune be claimed.'

'Are we looking at exorcism or a blessing?'

'What is there to bless?'

Monday went silent, the rain drumming hard on the black silk umbrella like irritable fingers as he considered the significance of her words. 'If,' he finally said, 'your assumption is correct, which I very much doubt then what is to be gained?'

'Surely that's obvious. Gallows Humour will be cleared of its hauntings. No more threatening souls or courtroom drama. That is our destiny.'

'Destiny you would put lives at risk?'

'Mr Monday, you read too many Dennis Wheatley novels.'

'A man died in the woods because of them, and God knows what other hidden incidences I care not to know.'

'They got what they deserved, no more, no less. Gallows Humour is not there to be plundered or used to line dishonest pockets. I would have preferred Angela to have laboured on land to teach her a lesson. However, there was no other recourse to take.'

'Setting aside the issue for a moment about Week's intention, the book and releasing souls are two different aspects.'

'And how have you suddenly become the expert?'

'Logic, Miss Tuesday. The innocent occupants of Gallows Humour want their signatures erased, no differently to a man seeking exoneration for a crime he did not commit.'

'But without them returning from whence they came, the terms cannot be met.'

'Crookshank runs the Trust. Crookshank holds the cards. No way can it be proved in a court of law that souls have been banished from Gallows Humour, so what on earth made you think that was part of the condition. Only by-passing Week's Work to Crookshank can the fortune be legitimately claimed. Do you know where to locate it?'

'If I tell you I might put your life at risk.'

Monday irritated and passed over the umbrella. 'Have a nice evening.'

'Oh, for goodness' sake, you will get soaked.' She rushed to catch up. 'Week etched a riddle on his desk.'

'I saw no riddle.'

'Why should you? You never knew it was there, but I can assure you it is. And remember when his Work is found, the mark of the guilty as well as the innocent shall be exposed on those pages. And the guilty do not want to be exposed, do they, Mr Monday?'

She made a good point, he thought. 'There was something in Jeremy's notes about returning the marks of the innocent.'

'Perhaps Jeremy was trying to find a way to rid the interlopers but in vanquishing them then surely we automatically vanquish the others.'

'And this little bit you failed to elucidate at the time of our agreement is that you have no idea whatsoever where to look for his Work and how you go about vanquishing lost souls.' Monday paused for an answer but got no response. 'Your resume reads like a botched builder and is still in working progress.'

'Hark at the man who lives in the gap between rhetoric and reality. You have the temerity to question my judgement when your own seems to be way off base. The obvious solution is to explore Gallows Humour from top to bottom. Week would have hidden his Work there.'

'Not necessarily. As Palfrey pointed out, others have looked without success.'

'But they were not builders.'

'So we shall live in chaos.'

'I thought we were doing that anyway. Besides which, Gallows Humour could do with an overhaul. Think of it as killing two birds with one stone.'

What irritated Monday the most was her overriding objective to have the last say in a fifty-fifty business arrangement. But this is what happens when an unstoppable force meets an immovable object.

'Before any exploration is undertaken, you will consult me first?'

'Then consider yourself consulted. Do you have the time?'

Monday looked at his watch. 'I think it's nearly six.'

'Gracious, we must get home.'

Home. It rolled off her tongue so easily that he felt for the first time in his life he had a home where a utopia of unexplored delights waited for him. Yes, there were the oddities, ghosts in the walls and the floors but as he turned into the gates, drenched from the waist down, home was no longer Pandora's Box wrapped in greenery but a mystical wonder, made all the more desirable in her presence.

'Just look at yew two.' Doolally flung towels at their faces. 'Yew'll catch your deaths of cold. Best yew warm up by a fire and hev summat to eat.'

'Not for me, Doolally. Mike is taking me dancing.'

Monday watched the third day of the week twirl round and round in the hall with her arms outstretch. She had the capacity to light up dark holes and revive old walls by her shadowy prancing. He thought it would be a physical challenge; he had not bargained for emotional turmoil.

'Yew should be taking her,' Doolally scorned. 'Her puddles aren't shallow.'

'No, they are deeper than the lake.'

'Yew can swim, can't yew?'

For once Doolally was right. 'Who among us gives a decent hair cut?'

'Ned. Mind yew he does get carried away with his shears.'

That raised such frightful images he said, 'I shall ask Palfrey.'

'Yew wanted a word?'

'I most certainly do but first let's find us a riddle.'

In Judges Chamber under candlelight Monday removed dusty items off the desk, studied the doodles and writing, the scribbles and scrawls, the everyday scratches of life. Doolally was looking too, shared the same sense of passionate undertaking, a mutual awareness based solely on sight. But finally, what Izabo Tuesday had told him was true. It was so blindingly obvious that it was so blindingly obscure. Carefully constructed between all the jottings, the riddle was there to be interpreted.

Law holds that answer which does not consist

in the marks but in the whole of the parts.

Doolally rounded the desk with breathtaking speed. Cheek to cheek bent over with Monday, so close he could smell the earth in her hair and feel the air of her giggles when she asked what it meant.

'To be honest,' he replied, 'I don't have a clue.'

'Yew blind as well as deaf, that's the clue.'

'I know that's the clue but I haven't got a clue what it means.'

'Yew mustn't worry,' she said sympathetically. 'It will give yew a headache. What yew need is a little help.'

They had always been there, somewhere in Gallows Humour, if not kitchen or garden, attic or bell tower, bedroom or library, who knows which, one by one they came into view, their sense of fashion irrefutable, for had they not lived in the past? Woody with his braces holding up his trousers, Flour with her powdered face, Ned with his duelling scar, Bumble with her bouncy hat and another, a young lad wearing a greasy smile. Six in all and allowing their moment, their patient clambering to study the find, Monday went into his own internal distance, suddenly mute, aware of their anticipation. Far from the threat he first perceived them to be, he was fascinated by their presence, drawn to their histories and plights.

'Solomon Monday, can you find our signatures?' asked Bumble, she with the bouncy hat and hung for not killing her husband.

'Why do you require them?'

Ned spoke. 'We seek merely to save our reputations. A horse thief he claimed me to be when it was my horse he stole.'

'And when your reputations are saved, what then?' Monday looked about him, the intensity of his gaze raking the room, uncertain if all the innocent were here. 'Since I have little understanding of the paranormal, I must point out that you run a risk of being taken out of the equation the moment your reputations are restored. So you must weigh the odds. What is more important, your reputations or staying here?'

'I can remember a time I walked as flesh and blood, innocent and free.' Again, it was Ned, the man with a duelling scar. 'When Judge Week forced us from our earthly bounds, we wandered aimlessly, some longer than others. For how long would he have us wander? His deathbed promise released us of our wander. Here is where we found our stations in life. We may be few in number, but we are strong at heart. Take our chances we will. Seek his Work, Solomon Monday.'

'If we go, they go,' Woody said. 'Their marks are in that book. To their destruction, to their eternal shame and damnation they struck bargains with each other. Some would hev us hide. Others would hev us reach accord with them. Sunday promised to find a way but his promises never held water. He said nothing of the riddle.'

That got Monday thinking why Jeremy Sunday kept the riddle quiet. And then there was the issue why Week, knowing they wanted their signatures, hid his Work, which begged another question, did he know? If not, then he never wrote the riddle. And if he never wrote it, who did?

'I know this might not count for much but I'm in for the long haul.' Monday picked up the candle, his face a mask of resignation and stern resolve. 'Look, whatever it takes, if his Work exists, I shall find it.'

To their delight and satisfaction, it was Doolally who excited the most, literally melting into his body and passing through him like a doorway to heaven. Such a peculiar action, that it sent an invasion of tingles down his spine, not in the least threatening but leaving him a little disorientated as the room vacated of souls.

Retreating to the kitchen, he removed his sweatshirt, kicked off his sodden shoes and left a trail of wet footprints on the floor while the air embalmed hot soups and brews. Whatever small indulgences this kitchen had to offer, it certainly warmed up Palfrey's life.

'Sir, may I suggest a short back and sides.'

'Like yours.'

'Precisely, sir.'

'No, I want a trim.' He sat down. 'Who does yours?'

'Ned, sir. I know his shears look fearful but he can trim a head as neatly as he can trim a hedge, quickly I may add.' Palfrey reached for a hand mirror. 'How is that, sir?'

Incredible. Without the feel of a nick, the sound of a snip or the sight of a hedge-cutter at work, in ten seconds flat Monday's hair had been edited to perfection and considered Ned had been born with a talent that made him unique among his kind.

'So,' Monday said grabbing his sweatshirt. 'Ned was a barber with a horse.'

'A handsome traveller,' Palfrey added. 'All the ladies loved him. Unfortunately, that was his undoing. Not that he encouraged them, but he rather fell in love with the local magistrate's daughter. Her father sought to marry her off to a London gent with a pension of £500 per annum.'

'That sounds a very trifling amount.'

'In those days it was considered a fortune.'

'Ned mentioned something about his horse being stolen.'

'He was hung for stealing the magistrate's horse, where in fact it was the magistrate that stole his horse. It was a rather confusing case because the magistrate's horse and Ned's horse were one of the same. The night before Ned planned to elope with the magistrate's daughter, the magistrate with news of this, stole Ned's horse and painted the white flash. Naturally, Ned whistled for his horse and it broke free of its tie. There ensued a chase, Ned was caught on his horse but because it did not look like his horse, he was arrested for stealing the magistrate's horse.'

'Surely the flash could have been wiped clean.'

'It was painted, sir. I think I did mention that. By the time new growth appeared, Ned had been hung.'

'And the magistrate's daughter?'

'Ned cannot remember what happened to her. I suspect she did her father's bidding, who knows. I understand that Miss Tuesday pointed you toward a riddle.'

'I cannot make head or tail of it. Why did Jeremy Sunday keep that information to himself?'

'Perhaps to delve further might find the answer.'

'She's a crafty monkey, Palfrey. She doesn't know any more than anyone else, so where does that leave me…sifting through chaos, that's where. This whole house is going to be ripped apart for that book and do you think I can stop her? She has the mindset of a wild tiger.'

'Yet a tiger can be caged, if I may be so bold as to say.' Palfrey set down a bowl of stew and crusty bread on the table. 'A man cannot think on an empty stomach.'

'Have you eaten?'

'On this occasion, may I join you?'

'Palfrey, that's the first sensible thing you have said since I got here.' He picked up a fork and spoon. 'So, are we alone?'

'For all the years I have served, I still find it difficult to establish that fact. If you stand very still, very quiet, you can feel the movement of them on your cheek. Sometimes they walk through you, mostly out of forgetfulness yet I do believe they leave a little of themselves behind…' His voice drifted before reviving. 'They have become my family these good souls, filled the voids in my life, as too for Mr Sunday when he was alive.'

'Why did he want Betty Cross to see Judge Week?'

'Oh yes, Betty Cross who saw Judge Week and a prisoner. Mr Sunday over estimated her calm exterior but then he was excited for that was the first time he had seen him.'

Monday shifted his gaze, was plainly summoning his thoughts. 'Izabo has a very calm exterior. She never batted an eyelid, not when Ned spoke up in the library, not even in court. I mean, there she was among dead people arguing the toss. Don't you think that strikes you as rather odd?'

'Perhaps she has a greater constitution than most women.'

'How many are there, Palfrey? The good ones, how many?'

'Well, that's rather debatable. Flour, Doolally, Woody, Ned and Bumble were, without doubt, the most tragic of cases in the miscarriage of justice. One other did break the law according to the edicts in those days yet his case required compassion, not indifference.'

'Six turned up to look at the riddle. So that clarifies what I thought. Is the young lad Charlie?'

'Little Charlie grows the vegetables and takes care of the Rolls. They all like to potter under the bell playing poker. To my cost I lost all the buttons off my shirt the second week upon arriving at Gallows Humour. Since then, I have reclaimed my buttons and hold one promise.'

'Promise?'

'They have nothing else to barter,' Palfrey explained. 'I had to play poker in order to get them to behave upon your arrival. Unfortunately, when it suits, Doolally ignores the promises she makes.'

Monday smiled, pointing his spoon at Palfrey. 'You know you're an exceptional man, Palfrey. How did Jeremy manage to find you?'

'I applied to an advert in the Sunday Times. Compassionate butler required with an open mind and sense of humour. The day I arrived for my interview,

I was a little like you, lost in my world of confusion. Doolally sat beside Mr Sunday and asked if I believed in a two-hundred-year-old woman whereupon I said if she existed at all I would certainly like to meet her.' Palfrey chortled into his napkin. 'I have to admit I keeled over when she vanished before my eyes but I picked myself up, brushed myself down and we started all over again.'

'I behaved deplorably, it was uncalled for and I apologize for my behaviour. I should have kept an open mind. Instead, I acted the idiot.'

'No apologies are needed. Your reactions were understandable though a little unpredictable.'

'Am I right in assuming the interlopers are increasing?'

'Unfortunately, you are correct. Mr Sunday never extrapolated how or why it happened, but it happened long before I came on the scene. Now the courtroom echoes to an entourage of interlopers rising exponentially, I think.'

'All the more reason to find Week's Work.' Monday's voice was low and grave. 'Is there anything else I should know?'

'Saturday is a recognized day of rest due to the presence of Judge Week, and one not to be concerned. It is very unlikely that you will encounter him, and if you did you would see right through him. Doolally once explained it as a black cloud with a silver lining. To know he is suspended between worlds, makes her rather happy, which does suggest if his Work is found he might possibly be delivered into the jowls of hell. One good deed is not enough to redeem a man for a lifetime of wickedness.'

'I take it you would prefer not to encounter him?'

'Your assumption is correct.'

'It's a pity I cannot talk to Week.' Monday set his bowl aside. 'That was very good. Did you make it or was it Flour?'

'My expertise stretches to cucumber sandwiches. Would you like to try her fruit cake?'

Monday patted his bulging stomach. 'I should lose a couple of stone.' But he soon changed his mind when the cake came to the table. 'Well, perhaps a small slice. I would like to ask if Week actually wrote that riddle. Consider this, Palfrey. Why would he hide his Work knowing they wanted their signatures? That would suggest Edmund Crookshank was in league with Week. But there again, Ned mentioned Week made a deathbed promise to release them of their wander, that here is where they found their stations in life, suggesting at the time of his death he set out his intentions to give them a home.' Monday relapsed into silence as he finished his fruit cake and then said, 'Explain more about the legend of Week's Work, how it releases the Trust?'

'I can only reiterate what small knowledge was told by Mr Sunday.' Palfrey allowed himself to break wind. 'It was in a past conversation some years ago in so far as the Trust would be relinquished on the proviso of handing in Week's Work. Correction, he used the word dispensing in Week's Work.'

'Dispensing suggests distribute or administer; not necessarily handing in. Do you have Crookshank's home number?'

'The number is written under the telephone.'

Monday pushed back his chair. His newfound passion for seeking the truth seemed to spring from nowhere. By the time he left the pots and pans of Gallows Humour, Palfrey had again slipped into kitchen contentment. There were so many inconsistencies and nobody could distinguish between fact and fiction, only offer hearsay. But there was no doubt that Crookshank could fill in some blanks. The biggest obstacle was getting him to talk. In the murky world of death and divorce, where loyalties never shift from the client, deceased or not, it was possible Crookshank would refuse to divulge any information if it affected the Trust.

Monday moved across the room and poured himself a whisky. The liquid trickled down his throat in trackless movements then he looked under the telephone and dialled the number.

The line picked up. 'Crookshank.'

'Monday here, we need to talk.'

'Have we changed our mind again, Mr Monday?'

'No, we are still on the register.'

'We?'

'Yes, Miss Tuesday signed on the same page.' Monday heard the breath of confusion. 'Did she not telephone you this morning?'

'Can this not wait until Monday?'

'Look! You're speaking to Monday who's had nearly a Week full.' He quickly curbed his irritation. 'I am not asking you to divulge too much, just a straight answer to a simple question. Your ancestor, Edmund Crookshank, was he aware of Judge Week hiding his book called Week's Work?'

'Why do you wish to know?'

'Miss Tuesday pointed me toward a riddle etched on Week's desk. But I am in grave doubt about that riddle or if the book really exists. For if this is true then it suggests Week hid his Work deliberately, rather like a perverse treasure hunt to keep his blood line amused.'

'Are you able to handle the truth, I wonder?'

'Do you have any idea what I've been through these past few days? And you're asking me if I can handle the truth, huh? Clarification, I need clarification before Miss Tuesday turns this place upside down and inside out.'

'Do I take it this is not to your liking?'

'No, it's not to my liking, Mr Crookshank. There are others to consider not least the increasing traffic of interlopers.'

'Very well, get Palfrey to drive you to the Three Feathers.'

'Miss Tuesday has the car.'

'I shall meet you outside the gates in ten minutes.'

Monday was surprised. Whatever he had been expecting, that had not been it.

As nightfall brought its own sounds, Monday trudged the wet sludge on the drive for his pre-arranged meeting, the last few drops of rain falling inconspicuously. There were dribbles and drips trailing off leaves like a slow exhalation of tension before the storm passed out into the city beyond.

The motor idled until Monday got in then Crookshank drove a mile up the road, the wipers gliding softly across the surface of glass as he pointed to his property. Like Gallows Humour but without its curious survivals, Crookshank's house had been in the family for seven generations. And as he mentioned in passing to clarify the position, it was not a question of mistrusting Judge Week but of supporting him.

At the Three Feathers with its black painted beams, far from a continental winery which frequented every quarter of London, it slipped into silence when Crookshank ordered two beers among nostalgic farmers, red-faced couples and hair-gelled youths.

'Is this your local?' Monday drew up a chair.

'You are a curiosity. Betty Cross is the local gossip. Her news spreads quicker than the local rag.' Crookshank held up his pint mug and legitimately smiled. 'Call me Hugh. Cheers.'

As the grumblings and mumblings reignited the pub like a veiled curtain to give them privacy, Crookshank went on. 'My ancestor was given Week's Work purely as a reminder of his duties towards Gallows Humour. There was never a question of conspiracy or trickery. It was Week's intention the estate be dispensed to the one or the other, or however many contributing to solve the problem of the six haunting Gallows Humour. Upon reflection, this was probably a bad incentive. It gave rise to a series of beneficiaries looking to the church for exorcism, or gypsies claiming they had the power to banish lost souls. They all gave up and stole what they could, some never returned and died a sorry death and some returned to hoodwink the next in line, and so forth until a good man, Jeremy Sunday took his responsibilities on board and realized that those poor souls required their marks. Jeremy had a way with them and listened to their woes, understood they wanted to be part of Gallows Humour. He allotted them duties, played harmless games, you know, the generality of family life.'

'And the book?' Monday looked at him thoughtfully, the crisp dresser with squeaky leather soles and painfully concealing a problem behind his horn-rimmed glasses. 'You don't have the book, do you?'

Crookshank leaned forward, his eyes falling to his beer. He had held onto a secret for so long, there had been times when he wondered if he had dreamt it. 'We never got off to a good start, Sol and I regret that. Given what I am about to tell you, I had grave doubts, and those doubts increased when you asked for a replacement. Has Palfrey informed you about your mother visiting Jeremy Sunday?'

Monday shook his head, surprised at this. 'He has informed me about my Father taking Jeremy for a packet full, notwithstanding he was found hanging from a branch, so I am hard put to understand why she never told me.'

'Jeremy befriended your mother, eight months pregnant, no place to go thanks to your father's abhorrent behaviour leaving her stranded without a penny to her name. There you were born. There you both lived under his watchful protection until your father re-emerged professing deep regret. Jeremy, having parted with his assumption that those souls required their signatures also informed your father the impossibility to distinguish one from the other for there, in the book were crosses and thumb prints. Your father seized upon the idea for the book to be shown to the six who would surely be able to identify their own mark. My Father was against this. Logic dictated they would not be able to do so and was ill prepared to remove the book from his safe.'

Monday was ahead. 'So, my Father scratched the riddle on a Saturday when he was sure the place was empty of onlookers, claimed it was Judge Week and presented the argument for courtroom drama. Law holds that answer which does not consist in the marks but in the whole of the parts.'

'A terrible dilemma but there was the riddle, and did it not point the way? How easy to fool the obsessed. Jeremy was convinced. My Father was convinced. Did I not tell you there is still an element of chance in life which an individual can do little about? My Father placed that book on the Judge's Bench. But nobody anticipated a six-year-old snatching it to play hide and seek. Needless to say, the book was never found, your father was punished and Jeremy, being the man that he was gave your mother a new start in life.'

Monday lowered his glass. 'I don't remember any of this.'

'You suffered a terrible shock, went into a fever for a number of days. When you woke you had no memories of the event. Your mother believed, as did Jeremy that you would one day take over Gallows Humour. After all, you had the training as a reporter, to delve into mystery with an unbiased mind.'

'My Father, what did he hope to gain?'

'He wanted the book to hold Jeremy to ransom. He had already been paid a substantial amount to leave you and your mother in peace. Unfortunately, something else happened that night. Whether it was through the death of your father or the book, either way, others who were hung at the gallows began appearing.'

'The interlopers,' Monday confirmed. 'Now I understand why they came on the scene, why Doolally and her tribe hadn't seen the riddle and why Jeremy kept it quiet. It all adds up. You mentioned I had no memories. Do I presume they were deliberately erased?'

'Anything is possible. My Father skirted the issue to a large extent and when I enquired to Jeremy after I came on board, he told me none of the six owned up to the crime. Fancy another beer?'

'I'm fine with this.'

'Sol,' Crookshank said in an almost air of frustration, 'for the sake of my son, I too wish to be free of the burden. To be told you must coerce future beneficiaries leaves a rather repugnant taste in the mouth. I seriously considered when Jeremy died to let Palfrey handle the estate, live out his time there and close the whole place down.' He shrugged. 'But there are other complications, not to mention how I dispense with the Trust. Are you sure you don't want another?'

'Okay, but make it a half.'

While Crookshank went up to the bar, Monday moved outside to an inner courtyard and lit a cigarette, trying to get his brain in gear. Did it really matter who killed his father? The deed had been done with probable good cause. But what was a six-year-old doing in the courtroom that night? Without experience of children's habits, especially that young it would seem he was allowed to roam anywhere at any time. Perhaps the ghosts were his guardians as well as his playmates?

'Pity they banned smoking.' Crookshank removed one from his gold cigarette case. 'Do you know why I love this place?' He paused to light up and the smoke blew away like a fine imprint. 'Peace and quiet, Sol. Yes, without doubt, a small piece of tranquillity in this maddening world. Paradoxically, less maddening is Gallows Humour. They never go beyond the estate. A chap told me once that lost souls stay in the familiar.'

'Does your son know about them?'

Crookshank nodded. 'Hard to keep secrets from the family not that I would wish to. Flour bakes wonderful cakes. My wife tries to copy her recipes, especially the Christmas puddings. It has always been a tradition to share Christmas at Gallows Humour. The atmosphere is unexplainable, the smell of cinnamon and nutmeg, burning candles, roaring fires in the hearths. It snowed heavily one year and the whole estate was a fairyland.'

'I would never have pegged you for a romantic, Hugh.'

'We all dream the same dreams, a little piece of happiness in a mad, mad world.'

'This will make you smile. A new coffee house opened in Oxford Street. I thought to give it a try so I ordered ham salad. The girl, pretty young thing smiled apologetically and asked me to speak in Polish, at least I think it was Polish. It made me feel ancient, behind the times though why should we make the effort to speak their language when it's our bloody country.'

'A balkanized country, remember.'

'Too late now to go back,' Monday said wryly. 'The tribe, they obviously know I lived there. Do I take it Palfrey knows too? No, strike that. It doesn't really matter. Tell me about Miss Izabo Tuesday. What do you know about her?'

Crookshank gravitated to a table and sat down on a damp bench. 'As much as I know about you but would no more divulge your personal history as I would hers. However, I will leave you with two thoughts. The first is that she is genuine to the club, and the second is that reality is not always quantifiable.'

Monday smiled and seated beside him. 'I also find it hard to imagine her on a building site mixing up cement. She made little mention about her father. And what she did say never sounded complimentary. I presume he's dead or else he would have been offered the position. How did she know about the riddle?' He looked back at Crookshank who was still glaring at him and giving nothing away. Now the intoxicating smell of subliminal life suddenly reminded him of how she advantaged her position at his expense. 'She conducted a court case and made me look a right prat. Okay, I feel deep regret and disappointment about my escapades but she never let me put my view across.'

'In the end, overcoming life's challenges is what really counts.'

'Unfortunately, I made another cock-up. They have seen the riddle, entirely my fault. If I could get my memories back, I might be able to track down Week's Work then find a way to solve the problem.'

'I have been in touch with various universities, mostly in America, dealing with the paranormal. There have been a number of catalogued events, nothing remotely as strong or as weird as Gallows Humour. These souls are barely distinguishable from humans. And they learn very quickly. Jeremy kept to his daily papers, refused to have a television not that he considered it worth the licence fee.'

Strangely, Monday was at last able to breathe freely. All the pieces fitted perfectly, the picture was there to be seen so the choice was quite easy. 'Okay, first on the agenda is to discuss this with Izabo. It will give her an opportunity to bash my ego again.'

PIECING A WEEK TOGETHER

Opening wide the wardrobe doors, the colourful choice was limitless and how Palfrey achieved it so quickly was again left for speculation. From country casuals to dinner jacket, there was an outfit for every occasion though what the occasion would be for a Saturday, Monday had no idea. He moved into the bathroom and took a long hot shower, then wrapped a towel around his waist and used another to wipe the fog off the mirror so he could shave. His eyes were red-rimmed and bloodshot and he wondered if Kern slept with Tuesday. The fear blossomed like a mushroom cloud, left clinging to a tiny shred of hope it was not the case, as if his sanity depended upon it.

When he stepped back into the bedroom, he was greeted by Kern sitting on the bed reading a newspaper. He never looked up. 'I see the stock market has taken a tumble.'

'How did it go last night?' Monday wished for the courage to ask if he slept with Tuesday.

'Great, we found a great place, dancing was great. She's a terrific mover and good conversationalist.'

Returning to the bathroom, Monday swore under his breath and went back into the bedroom, foraging in drawers for underwear. 'So,' he said, unable to forget. 'She's a good mover.'

Kern looked over his paper. 'Hey, I like the hair cut not sure about the boxer shorts and knobbly knees. And why does this place smell like a coffin?'

'Judge Week rules on a Saturday. Everyone else takes the day off. Is Izabo up?'

'I left her in bed.'

Monday's spirits quailed and said the only thing that sounded reasonable. 'Do you want breakfast?'

'I need an on-line café. My battery went dead. Yours is dead too. Damn nuisance having no electricity. Do you mind if I use the motor?'

'Why do you need to get on-line?'

'Because my dear, Watson. I have exploring to do.'

'Izabo told you about the riddle.'

'Yup, she sure did.' Kern stood and rummage in the wardrobe. 'Between you and me, I think Judge Week and Edmund Crookshank were into some pretty heavy stuff. Here, wear the brown cords. Ask yourself why they hid the book?'

Clumsily struggling into his trousers, Monday tried not to smile. If he could get Kern out of the house, he would have Tuesday all to himself. 'Nope, you got me there.'

'See, it's the Schadenfreude syndrome, you know, malicious pleasure in the misfortunes of others.' Then Kern passed over a mustard-coloured cashmere V-neck sweater. 'That goes with the cords. All you need now is a title and a horse. So, what do you say? Can I use the motor?'

'Sure.'

With a pull at his ear lobe, Kern quelled Monday's curiosity. 'Don't get me wrong, she's a great woman but she's giving me the third degree about my novel, so I thought I should just be, you know, up front about it.'

The brows met. 'Did you upset her?'

'Hey, what do you take me for? Flour was the one who was crying, flinging her arms about me. A man cannot be expected to deal with waterworks and precipitate emotional outburst. It's not in my nature. How the hell can I communicate with a mute ghost, eh? She can't even spell.' Kern dug into his pocket and passed over the note. 'She left this for me.'

'My glasses are downstairs.'

'Dear Mickle, told you she couldn't spell, can I bake you a cherry pie?'

Although Monday had yet to gain a clearer view of Kern and his exact relationship with Tuesday, he carried forward to the kitchen convinced his friend had added another notch to his gun. He could smell and taste the difference of his surrounds. Strange life existed somewhere. There were fusty odours in the walls and stuffy hydrocarbons twanging through his airways as though a creeping sickness had enveloped Gallows Humour. Now he was beginning to understand why Saturday was everyone's day off.

He made a cup of coffee and took it to the library then pulled out Jeremy Sunday's old notes where they made far more sense than two days ago. Small things tied up nicely with what Crookshank had said last night; the ambiguous marks, murky intelligence, and apparent exercises to eliminate the wicked without corrupting the good.

Approximately an hour later, he peeled off his reading glasses when Tuesday walked in. With her hair loosely hitched, jean hugging hips and a white embroidered blouse, his eyes trickled over the rich geometry of her body with a physical ache in his groins.

'Have you had breakfast?' she asked.

'I cannot operate the stove. Have you?'

'We are in the same boat, Mr Monday. Mike has left us stranded. I could make us sandwiches.'

'And take them on the gondola?' He watched her eyes dip. Whatever did she make of that remark? Considering now was not the right moment to tell her about the riddle, he picked up one of Sunday's notes and quoted verbatim. 'They cannot breathe our air, they will not change their wear, they rise from earth and live on earth but water is not there.' He looked up. 'You see, Miss Tuesday, I have discovered we can talk quite freely on the lake without being overheard.'

'But Saturday is their day off,' she argued. 'We can talk freely anywhere in the house.'

'Why waste our eating habits indoors when the scenery favours us.' He watched her move toward the window, rubbed his chin thoughtfully and anticipated her response. 'All you need is a heavy knit jumper.'

'I hope this is not a ruse to get on my good side, Mr Monday.'

'For certain it is, Miss Tuesday.'

'Right, Gondola it is and a pair of boxing gloves.'

'Good.' He matched her business-like tone. 'I will uncover the vessel and hoist a flag of truce.'

There was no doubt about it. This was going to be hard work; obviously yesterday's conversation left an indelible mark. So while Tuesday made sandwiches and a flask of tea, Monday swept back the tarpaulin and brushed off nature's debris from the black and gold gondola moored under the hanging willow tree. Amassed with silky cushions and cotton covers, it was self-evident he used to play pirates on the high seas under command of his mother. He picked up a pillow and smelt it, that same perfume she wore, weak but unmistakable. *Mother*, he spoke her name softly, *forgive me.*

Tuesday travelled through the silver grasses with a woven basket to her side while shafts of splintered sunlight brightened the red in her hair. Monday stood leaning against the vertical pole, his chin resting against his clenched hands and wondered what it would be like to make love to her; would it be sensual or erotic, would it be like floating on air or would it be somewhere between Mars and Jupiter.

'Miss Tuesday, do you know the legend of the lake?'

'I read the lake was man made, hardly a legend for such a simple feat or are you referring to why it was man made?'

At this he pushed off from the bank. 'I prefer to look upon the lake in a more romantic setting. Why is the gondola here? Perhaps Betty Cross and Jeremy Sunday ate their cucumber sandwiches on the lake shortly before making love.'

'I hardly think so. I read somewhere the gondola was made by Woody for the purpose of giving him a job.'

'Strange there should be comfort among silk cushions and perfume.'

'Perfume?'

'Yes, I thought I could detect a woman's smell.'

'Did you not see,' she said while pouring tea from the flask, 'that we are surrounded by water lilies.'

Monday thought she was good. But he was better. 'Water lilies have no smell.'

Tuesday looked up, her face composed of knowledge. 'Actually, I beg to differ. Nymphaea Caroliniana is a fragrant variety making few demands, preferring an open, sunny site and still water.' She tilted her head to one side with dazzling effect. 'Has it been a while since you rubbed up against a woman with a brain?'

Although he had to admit Angela thought a spreadsheet was a duvet, she did have streetwise credibility to keep ahead of her rivals. 'So,' he said reclining against cushions, 'did you have a nice evening?'

'My feet never touched ground. And you?'

'I studied the infamous clue, the blind leading the blind.'

'Surely it depends who wears the blinkers.' She regarded him for a moment. 'Tell me, Mr Monday. How do you view your friend's enthusiasm to expose Gallows Humour?'

'His endeavours will be thwarted, no doubt.'

'And who would thwart them?'

'Why you, Miss Tuesday,' he replied holding the cup to his lips. 'How would these poor souls fare were your friendship and concern be absent.'

'I do care,' she responded emphatically. 'I may appear disingenuous but I do care what happens.' She offered him a tormenting sandwich, and Monday waved it away. 'Oh dear,' she said as if she never banked on him disliking Marmite, 'you either love it or hate it.'

For several more moments the lives of these two continued to revolve in intimate enmity like irritated twins, linked but divided.

'What can I attempt to say about first impressions? You scoot off with the driver and Angela scoots in asking me how much I am willing to pay for Gallows Humour while Mike was jotting notes for his book deal.'

'Palfrey was supposed to be looking after you.'

'We are all susceptible to the frailties of human traits, Mr Monday. There is an irreconcilable gulf between those who are motivated to run away and live another day, and those who cherish Gallows Humour. Palfrey cannot be blamed for your arrogance which I might add was not supplanted by decency.'

'Look!' Monday irritated. 'Yes, I took drugs. Yes, I lost my job. Yes, I schemed to pass over the pen, used Angela to meet my objective. And all this pales into utter insignificance in light of the fact my Father scratched that riddle to work a scam!'

There was stillness, a bite in the air as Tuesday comprehended the magnitude of his last statement. Her hands quickly worked over her knees as if she was annoyed with herself for assuming the riddle was a clue to finding Week's Work. Eventually the obvious question was asked. 'Why did you keep this from me?'

'It was unintentional. I never knew until last night when I met up with Hugh Crookshank at the Three Feathers. Would you care to tell me how you knew about the riddle?' But Tuesday looked as though she might shoot herself rather than reply, and Monday tried to think a way round it. 'You're right, you came here and discovered I was prepared to turn you over but, in the end, I couldn't do it, so surely that must mean something. I am profusely sorry. Christ, I seem to be always saying sorry. But you kept things from me too. You could have easily told me you had been here before, maybe not right away, but you could have said when you came to see me before Angela began her thieving campaign. Had you been here before or were you told about it?'

'Oh, Solomon I am me, the whole of me wishes-' her voice trailed off dubiously, and he wondered what the parts of that whole might be. 'I cannot change circumstance nor do I wish to talk about my past.'

Monday reached for her hand, held it between both of his. 'If we can put our two intelligent heads together, we can find a solution. You were right and I was wrong. Hugh needs proof we have found the answer before the Trust can be disbanded.'

'Is the money important to you?'

'The money was never an issue. Why, I never even knew there was money to be had until you mentioned it. Look, you obviously have your reasons to be secretive but I need to know if you're willing to work with me, no hiding clues to obstruct the objective and no pulling this place apart.'

'You do realize there are tiles missing on the roof.'

'Fair enough,' he said when her hand slipped away. 'A few tiles are easy to replace. How much do you know about Gallows Humour?'

'We probably are on a par. I suppose I too should apologize for my behaviour. Though it was imperative to get Angela out of the way and, hum, dare I say enjoy a little bit of pay back.' She squeezed her eyes and blew her wispy fringe away. 'What I dislike most is a hypocrite. Women fit the bill more than men.'

'You surprise me.'

'Why? Just because I'm a woman you think I must be on their side. What you told Angela was justified. She entered your life as one thing then changed when her nails dug deep into your shoulders. How fraudulent, I must say. Angela is not exactly the kind of girlfriend a man needs when he's having an inconvenient attack of conscience.' She smiled. 'It was rather funny to see Doolally chase her across the hall. Though I doubt that will be the last you shall hear from her.'

At a moment like this Monday was beginning to understand her unorthodox sense of humour and attitude to life. 'Angela is like a bad penny. She also has my contacts in the media. Not to worry, I shall handle her.'

'What did Mr Crookshank have to say?'

'I was born here, lived with Mother and Jeremy for six years until my Father came back on the scene to try a scam for more money. Hugh's father was tricked into bringing Week's Work into the courtroom and for some unknown reason I stole it. I have no memories of that night but it was on a Saturday if that means anything. Whatever I saw or did caused me to go into a fever. Hugh's a desperate man. For his son's sake, he wants us to find the answer. The problem is two-fold. Their signatures are undated, marked by crosses or thumb prints. Should the book be destroyed, as Hugh said there's no guarantee the good go up and the bad go below, assuming there is a heaven and hell. Did you know the interlopers were increasing?'

'Yes, unfortunately I do. Perhaps something happened that night to start it all off. Maybe Week's Work coming into that courtroom was the impetus. We should probably concentrate on what we have. Do you want another cup of tea?'

He nodded and said nothing.

'Fact one,' she began as she refilled his cup. 'It's probable your memories were taken away rather than induced by trauma. If we can get them back you might be able to remember where you hid his Work. Fact two, the signatures are impossible to distinguish. Even if we showed them his Work it would be of no help because they cannot even remember their true names.'

'Yet they remember their accusers, their families.'

'I know. It's most puzzling, isn't it? Perhaps time is indicative for memories to fade for them as well as for us. After all, they have been around for nearly two centuries. Jeremy gave them silly names pertaining to their idiosyncrasies.'

'I can understand all of them except for Bumble.'

'Bumble wears a silly hat and has a big bottom but she is lovely, the complete opposite to Doolally. Where she is a true guardian of Gallows Humour, ready to obliterate uninvited guests, Bumble is nervous and disappears into cupboards. If you think there's a bee buzzing in your ear then rest assured it's her. Charlie is the only sensible name. Jeremy thought he looked like Charlie Chaplin until he realized the moustache was engine oil. Another possible fact is that you might have encountered Judge Week because Saturday is the only day his presence is felt. Why is that? What is he looking for? Does he want his Work? Or is he just keeping an eye on the place?'

Monday lit a cigarette and lazed back with his tea. 'You may have hit upon something. Hugh was adamant his ancestor and Week were genuine in their endeavours to make amends. Is it conceivable when Week died, he discovered the answer but was unable to communicate. Interestingly enough, Jeremy discovered they were quick learners and that's why he never had a television. How would you explain their ability to enter a world of substance? I shook Woody's hand and Mike claimed Flour was crying into his arms.'

'Oh, that's easy to explain. For the very reason they have come into a world of substance, they manipulate it. Why, if Flour wanted to and Mike was willing, they could make love, though theoretically it would only be superficial.'

'Okay, let's back-step to the time Week's Work came on the scene. I am inclined to agree with you. The book is placed on the Judge's Bench. It triggers a reaction. Let us assume the energy is greater when the book and Week are together-'

'That's assuming Week was there.'

'Quite. From what Palfrey has told me, and Betty Cross, Week appears anaemic, wishy-washy, more like a phantom than a human repository. Can we assume that night he might have appeared more dynamic.'

'I go along with that. Perhaps you saw him and got frightened, or maybe you saw him and thought here's another new playmate, or perhaps I am talking a load of nonsense. It would be so useful if you could remember.'

'Wait a minute!' Monday had an idea forming. 'Consider this. I'm hiding under the Judge's Bench. I take his Work. He goes in pursuit and others go in pursuit of him. I'm not a fast runner but I'm small and can hide easily. Let's say I tuck the book away, then I hear my Father shouting…no, pleading for his life. I rush outside, follow the noise and what do I see. I see Week hanging my Father. Hugh said that none of the tribe admitted to the crime. And why should they? It was a Saturday and Saturday is their day off.' Monday shot up and grabbed the pole. 'I need to go in that courtroom and figure how far a child can run, damned whether it suits Week or not.'

'Oh wonderful, I love crusades.'

Monday smiled and realized such alarms were neither threats nor prophecies but simply repetitions for Tuesday, being composed of all that had fashioned her long past.

'Unlike the Greek's speculation about the atomic nature of matter,' she said stepping onto the bank. 'We now know the nucleus of an atom has a lot of things stuffed inside it.'

'Izabo, do you by any chance have room in that brain for anything else?'

'Room for what?'

Me? 'You seem to have an extensive knowledge about almost anything.'

'Not true. I don't fill my head with soap operas nor do I have any knowledge whatsoever of cooking, movie stars, pop singers or politics.'

'Politics are my jurisdiction.'

'Well then,' she giggled, 'you have loads of room in your brain.'

He reflected she was the cause of his butterflies, the strength rising within to tackle adversity and kept secret since the moment he shook her hand and looked into those deep sapphire eyes. Whatever his fate, he had no doubt in his mind Izabo Tuesday was his apple pie and taking the kids to the zoo.

In the cold gloom of the courtroom, Monday paced and Tuesday timed, both calculating the distance of a rushing six-year-old pursued by Judge Week or someone, if not his father. Twenty seconds seemed a short duration for such a long way, out into the hall and where next?

'The dining room is exposed,' Tuesday said travelling toward the stairs. 'If you made it to here you would also be seen, so that leaves the back stairs and lots of hidey-holes.'

'Lead on Sherlock Holmes.'

In the kitchen, Tuesday poked her head round the pantry door. 'You could quite easily hide in here and nibble away at Flour's pastries. Were you always pleasantly plump?'

'No,' he lied, holding in his stomach.

Tuesday shook her head. 'Mmmm' and that sounded ominous. 'For myself, I never went in for sports, more a liking for books.'

'That would explain a Miss Know-it-all.' Touché.

She smiled. Ambushed, he smiled back and the treasure hunt was forgotten in that moment. There was challenge in her eyes and something else, something that seemed almost like desire. He could think of more suitable places to make his move. Taking two steps toward her, she shifted her feet and moved away as though to discourage false illusions. The treasure hunt was back on the menu.

'Well,' Monday said disguising his disappointment and scratching his head. 'Based on the assumption of hearing a noise, would it resonate in here?'

It was a basement, the kitchen barred windows were high and there were none in Palfrey's quarters. Why not the library? He remembered instinctively how he attached himself quickly to that room. Was it because he spent a lot of his time there as a child, watching Jeremy doodling away with a drink in his hand?

Since Tuesday now had her head stuck in the boiler room, Monday shot upstairs. In the library he looked about, the paintings, the bookshelves, the globe of the world, the cluttered line of cosy chairs, a cover to keep warm and the window ledge low enough for a child to crawl outside. He crouched low and looked under the desk, cocked an eye when he saw Tuesday beside him on all fours.

'Right,' she said. 'So you're here, with the book. Where would you put the book?'

'That's assuming I never took the book outside.'

'If you did, logic suggests you certainly never had it on you when you were found.' She scrambled to her feet. 'I suggest we remove the books from the bottom shelf.'

And so, they removed all the books from the bottom shelf and because nothing was found, they removed the books from the next shelf up assuming a little child would climb on a chair. The things one did for lost souls. It was an uneventful journey.

The telephone rang. 'Second day of the week, here,' said Monday in a flippant manner, expecting it to be Kern.

'It's George, Sol.'

'George? How did you get this number?'

'Is that any way to treat an old friend?'

'So, what's up? No strike that. It's the job, isn't it? I'm finished with reporting, George. Seriously, find someone else to fill the slot.'

'I want you to listen to something. Can you do that for me?'

'Sure, go ahead.'

…had she known justice existed right here in this very fine courtroom then she would have sought for recompense, put her case before you and trusted your judgement. No, what she did was perhaps in your eyes a little unconventional but you must remember she was not a thief but an invited guest of Mr Monday, who promised her the world, offered love and marriage, spoke of how Gallows Humour could be sold and with the money they could buy…

Monday slumped in the chair letting his mind drift into the enveloping chasms of repercussions. Gallows Humour would become a media circus for years, his life and that of others would never be the same. What started off as an exercise to teach a lesson had become something far more serious than it warrants by the sheer weight of chaos it would cause. Feared washed through him as he glanced at Tuesday, the expectation in her eyes, her lips mouthing what is the matter. A reporter working overtime can do terrible things to the human spirit.

'Clever little bitch, that Angela,' George went on. 'She dialled my number on her mobile so I could tape it. I even have some pictures of a weird looking bunch. Admittedly, they could be better. So how are we going to play this, Sol?'

'How much did you pay Angela?'

'You know I never discuss tawdry details.'

The only ace Monday had up his sleeve was playing for time. 'Tell you what, George. Before you go printing half a story, ring me back when you come up with a sum to whet my appetite.' Replacing the receiver he said, 'Angela used her mobile to record the court case.' With the distress written on her face, he stepped up in one springing movement, was tall at her side and placed a finger under her chin and raised it. 'Izabo, I am playing for time. It would be risky to print the story without my version of events.'

'Nice try, Sol. But in the end, it won't stop him from printing something and then what?' It appeared that neither Monday nor a fresh commitment of promises would alter the predicted course. She pushed away, lost in misery. 'I was so anxious to get her out of our hair I never considered she had a mobile. Now fate and its consequences rest in Angela's hands. Why must it be so hard to keep Gallows Humour out of the limelight?'

'Had I known what I know now, I would have turned her car round.'

'Why did you have to invite her?'

'I never invited her. Mike told her where he was going.'

Speaking of which, their ears pricked up to the happy sounding lungs of a whistling Kern treading loudly through the hall in his snakeskin shoes. When he appeared in the library holding on to a plastic carrier bag, his feet stepped between piles of books.

'Someone's been busy,' he said and the room fell silent. So he asked, 'What's up?'

Monday was already at the globe pouring two drinks. 'George gained a recording of the court case through Angela's mobile. He also has some pictures, soon to be known to the whole damn world.'

Kern looked decisively uneasy. 'Hell, that's a bummer.'

'Did you know what Angela was up to?'

'Not a clue, my man.'

'Strange you should tell her where to come, turning up like that.' Monday's manner was wrapped in sarcasm and veiled accusation.

'Hey! Be careful what you say. Angela was the architect of your damnation. I told you she was after your contacts, but no, you were the big I am on the scoop of the century. Never mind Joe Blog here as my book sales plummeted to an all-time low. Your favours steered in another direction. So just you remember that!' Kern glanced beyond Monday. 'Sorry, Izabo but I'm not the wicked witch of the east here. Sol and I go back years but when Angela came on the scene, she fucked up his brain.'

'My Mother's death fucked up my brain!'

'Bollocks!' Kern poked the chest, his expression framed in censure. 'You recognized your mistake and swallowed it hard. I know because I was there watching you spill your tears over Hilda's dead body. We talked about it, remember. You were upset because you never got to the hospital on time and I told you it wasn't your fault. And you accepted it like you accepted losing your cricket bat to frump face. It was when silicon tits turned up at the British Embassy dinner that got you all rat-arsed. I know that too because I was there, watching her play you like a puppet. The moment you fell between her legs you decided to stay on chapter one paying tribute to the media moguls. Angela had you wrapped round her little finger and your best friend got shoved aside. A whole year, Sol and I can count the number of times on one hand you bothered to ring me. But no, instead of talking it through about your addiction you buried your head in the sand.'

Monday searched the face for signs of weakness or misgivings. There were none. 'Yes, you're right I took drugs to escape the mental struggles. I shouldn't have done but the Brown investigation was heavy, and Mum's illness was doing my head in. If every man did the same, we would all be riding high on a plateau of love and the wheels of commerce would stop turning. But the trouble was I liked taking drugs. Sure, you say to yourself, I can stop at any time but you can't and that's when you know you're heading on a downward spiral. I couldn't face you, Mike. I skipped into a rehabilitation centre after I lost my job. And that's the truth. So call me a prick, whatever it takes to make amends, okay?'

They grinned at each other, remained unmoved, a still presence radiating calm while Tuesday returned the books to their rightful places. Women changed men, hardened them or set them apart. But here, they had no other festering words, had cleared the air and fondly embraced.

'Engage your heads, gentlemen.' Tuesday looked up from a kneeling position. 'Mike, if we get through this, I am prepared to offer you some of my half for-'

'Like hell you will.' Kern delved into the carrier bag and hunkered down to face her. 'I came up with something much better. Have a read of the outline, see what you think.'

Monday peeped inside the bag and pulled out a pastry brush. 'Well, well, well, what have we here? Are we thinking of baking a cherry pie?'

'Hey, she was crying, alright? I could hardly buy her box of chocolates.' Kern sat down at the desk and lit a cigarette. 'The way I see it, George is not printing because he needs your side, right?'

'But he will do.'

'Will he?' Kern was unsure. 'He'll be reluctant to print without some comment so ride with it, Sol. I feel pretty sure nothing was mentioned about ghosts or hauntings or some such thing to suggest weird things happen in this place.'

'Weird things do happen and Angela taped one,' said Tuesday.

'But George only has Angela's word for it.' Kern pointed out. 'Makes you wonder why Angela contacted George. I mean, how close is she to the guy? It was in the middle of the night so she must have had his home number.'

Angela and George? Monday was unable to see the picture. 'He's twice her age and a married man.'

'You think humpy dumpty is fat then use your imagination on his wife.' Kern puffed out his cheeks and Tuesday laughed. 'Angela isn't fussy when it comes to getting ahead. Anyway, there's no real proof of hauntings, yeah? The Times is not into silicon tits and stupid courtroom dramas by unknowns.'

When Kern put it like that, Monday felt more at ease.

'This is wonderful.' Tuesday passed Kern's notes to Monday. 'Mike has dropped his story and is concentrating on the judiciary system during the late eighteenth century.'

'What changed your mind?' Monday asked.

'There I was, searching the web and thinking about Flour, poor kid. Instead of lambasting the male species, she wants to bake me a pie. For what it's worth, I scrolled through other cases country wide and found some very interesting stuff. I would have liked to keep the title, Gallows Humour but that's out of the question now.'

'Izabo, is there any chance of a cup of tea and something to eat?' Monday was anxious to have some time alone with Kern and frowned at him after she left the room. 'Did you sleep with Izabo?'

Kern was unperturbed and stubbed out his cigarette. 'Why should I sleep with a woman who never stops talking about the worst day of the week? Boy, did you ruffle her feathers.'

'Did she tell you anything about herself apart from building houses?'

'Nope, not a thing and before you ask, she never even volunteered her home address. So, fill me in on the latest.'

'I went to see Hugh Crookshank last night. Bottom line, I was born here, spent the first six years of my life here with Mother. My Father was after more money so he devised a scam, scratched the riddle on Week's desk, convinced Hugh's father to part with Week's Work. Next scenario, Saturday night in the courtroom, I picked up the book, run off and apparently watched someone hang my Father, or not as may be the case.'

'So you think it's somewhere in here?'

Monday shrugged, hard put to know what to think. 'So far, we came up with zilch. Did Izabo mention anything about the guy she was involved with?'

'Okay, spill it out. What's ticking in that head of yours?'

'How did she know about that riddle? Hugh never told her, so that leaves Jeremy Sunday but it makes no sense. Jeremy wanted to keep it quiet. So we are left with two possibilities. Either her father stayed at Gallows

Humour, saw the riddle and told her, or she's been here before. Now, if she's been here before, then why wasn't I told, at least by Palfrey?'

'Sol, does it matter? So what if she's been here before.

Maybe she came here with her boyfriend, like Angela came here to fill up her purse, yeah? She saw the riddle, yeah? Suddenly it's a crusade for her and a honey pot for him. If you want my-'

The telephone interrupted their conversation and Monday picked up the line to hear Angela's clear and unremitting message. 'If you think this is the last of it you are very much mistaken. Don't think I don't know what you're up to.'

'Angela, get out of my flat.'

'Now you want to put me on the streets!'

'From what I gather you've already been working them.' He replaced the receiver and smiled at Kern. 'George is not playing ball. Come on, let's have some lunch.'

From there, they travelled to the kitchen posthaste with great expectations but had Tuesday not warned Monday of her failings?

He picked up a limp celery stick. 'Izabo, what is this?'

'Healthy eating,' she said sitting down.

'So what's the next step, find the book?' Kern asked.

'We think there's a connection between Week and his Work in so far something happened that night to wake up others. That said we also believe Week was at his strongest, hung my Father and probably erased my memories. Somehow, from the courtroom to the branch wherever he was hung, I either stopped off to hide his Work or carried on. The latter is doubtful. I must have hidden it somewhere in this house but as Hugh pointed out, none of the other beneficiaries found it.'

'You need to get into a child's head,' said Kern.

Monday grinned. 'Well, that shouldn't be too difficult for you.'

'I'll have you know I wrote a very successful children's tale. Unfortunately, Walt Disney revived Cinderella and my princess got dumped on the back shelves. No, see, little kids never go in a straight line. Even if they know where they're heading, they still veer off, a bit like dogs. You take the book, yeah? Wow, you say to yourself, I've got something great here because the grown-ups want it. But here's the rub. Grown-ups run faster than six-year-olds. So something else must have happened in that courtroom to take the scent off you, giving you time to hide the book. Can you be absolutely sure Week hung your father? If so, then it was the book which drew his skeleton from the cupboard, him who opened the gateway for others to come haunting, and probably him who hid the book down a rat hole, or some such bizarre place.'

'Perhaps,' Tuesday said, 'what we should really consider is not the net interaction between Judge Week and his Work but the more detailed interaction between their individual components in that courtroom. There may be a profound difference.'

Kern blinked. 'Hell, she sounds like Palfrey. Do you know what she's talking about?'

'Not a clue but we might get there in the end. Carry on, Izabo.'

'Try looking at the energy levels. Is it so impossible to believe his Work has a greater energy level than its maker? Putting them together is like putting cream over cream because in effect they both created each other. But the book holds the most energy because it has the marks of others before they left this world. You don't die right away, not in those days. You can die instantaneously if the neck is snapped but they never snapped necks on the gallows. It takes a while to suffocate, your legs kick out and your brain is still active, your tongue swells and your eyes bulge but still, you are in effect aware of your death for a painfully long time.'

Monday lost his appetite. 'So what you're trying to say is that we should concentrate on the book as the harbinger of all the trouble that's happening in the courtroom, per say, it might be hidden in there.'

'Yes, that's exactly what I am saying.' She smiled at Kern. 'You made me think when you said rat hole. The emptiness of space is not unlike the emptiness of an atom. Inside is the seat of an element's personality, rather like Judge Week. While the nucleus is a passive bystander merely responsible for marshalling its complement of electrons, the wisp of electrons are the participants in reaction. Ergo, his Work is in reaction and that's probably why the interlopers like to go over their trials.'

'That is not to say if we remove the book, we remove the interlopers,' Monday said.

'No, possibly not but I bet you any money you like if the book is in there and we take it beyond the estate, no additional interlopers will arrive.'

They each looked at one another, the possibility was there and suddenly they downtooled their cake forks and rushed to the courtroom. Here, there were no tactics, no finesse. On bended knees, they searched, explored and investigated every possible angle a child would pursue. Benches, on them or beneath them they clambered about, jostled in tight corners and scraped their knees.

'Was this not a good idea?' Tuesday laughed at her joke. 'It makes you wonder, if the book is really here.'

'Here's a thought,' Kern said with a concerned head popping up into view. 'We might bump into a grouchy judge.'

Monday was on his feet and slapped the dust on his cords. 'From what I gathered from Palfrey, there is nothing to be concerned.'

'Only be concerned,' Tuesday added, 'if you confront him.'

'And why would you say that?'

'Are we not dealing with an unknown element?'

Considering her question was rhetorical, Monday said nothing and moved to the gallery which would have meant an unlikely proposition for a child to take but he had to try. Rat holes, he said to himself. Virtually thirty-six hours prior he was up here looking down at proceedings, watching eloquent Tuesday defending a conniving bitch. Now he was on all fours again, tracking the edges of benches, foraging in the musty smells of gloom and sweet paper. Sweet paper? He picked up the red wrapper and held it to the ancient sunlight filtering through the tall windows, squinting at the words, Bubble Gum.

'Mike,' he called down. 'Did you bring chewing gum?'

'No, why?'

'Do we know if Palfrey likes chewing gum?'

'Not that I am aware,' Tuesday answered.

Excited, Monday processed the aisle with zeal. It has to be here, he thought. The clue was simple enough. So he continued poking around to the termination point then vaulted to the next seating bench and again went down on his knees, his flattened hand foraging deep until his fingers closed on a soft lump wedged between the wall and the bench. Instinctively knowing what it was but concerned for its fragility, he was unable to pull it free. Instead, he tried to liberate the book by exerting pressure against the bench nailed to the floor. And when that never worked, a foot to the bench wrenched it away.

The noise had brought enquiring minds to his side, first Kern then Tuesday, shaking their heads, quietly laughing and advising care. But most of Monday's attention was fixed on returning his memories, fondling and caressing an object he once held as a child. He flicked through the thickness of pages and snatched brief glimpses of marks while those around him looked on.

'Can you remember anything?' Tuesday asked.

'Not a thing, which may suggest my memories were taken. But why? What had I seen that made it so imperative not to remember?'

'Certainly the death of your father,' Kern said offering a cigarette to Monday but Tuesday took it instead. 'When has smoking been on your menu?'

'It never has. I just thought I would try one.'

Monday swiped it out of her mouth. 'Smoking is bad for your health.'

'Well really! You smoke.'

'That's because I'm starving.' Monday walked on with grinning pleasure. 'I suggest we have something to eat at the Three Feathers and discuss this with Hugh.'

Alone he advanced to the library and telephoned Crookshank, a preliminary chat without giving too much away. Then he sauntered upstairs and washed his face and hands, the reality finally dawning. He was halfway to a fortune. Moreover, close proximity to Izabo Tuesday and exposure to her views began to have an equally exciting effect.

Humming a Beetles tune all the way to the Three Feathers, Monday strolled on with an upward glance, content to linger behind Tuesday and Kern, both in deep conversation. Or rather she was in deep explanation about atoms to a shaggy dog that suggested everyone should be injected with a microchip.

'See, I look at it like this,' Kern slapped his hand on the bar. 'If I lose my memory at least I could pop into a police station and find out who I am. What's your poison?'

Tuesday picked up a menu. 'I think you should be injected with some brains.'

Monday peered over her shoulder scanning the menu. Such closeness, he could almost taste her in his mouth. 'I fancy the steak and kidney pie.'

'I fancy, now let me see, the duck…no, liver and bacon…err perhaps not. Perhaps I should have steak and chips.'

'Perhaps what you're looking for is not there.'

Slowly she turned to face him. 'Where would you suggest I look?'

His eyes teasingly veered to the chalk board. 'No, I am not there either.'

Tuesday was quick to hide it, but not quickly enough. There was a depth to her, a profundity of longing and all it needed was the right man to tap into it. And he believed he was that man.

'I recommend the steak and ale pie.'

Monday recognized Crookshank's voice and turned to greet him. 'If you have not already met face to face, may I introduce you to Miss Tuesday and this is my good friend Michael Kern.'

After shaking of hands, three ordered their meals but four sat around a corner table that taunted the knees begging for space. Monday was quite happy to rub his calves against Tuesday who seemed not to complain. Then Week's Work was laid on the table in front of Crookshank. For a while it rendered him speechless. He picked it up, fondled it and virtually went through the same motions as for Monday.

'My promise duly kept.' Crookshank uttered smoothly from smiling teeth. 'I was seventeen years old when my Father cried that day. It was to be some time later he would inform me. I cannot hope to explain my feelings. Now tell me, where did you find it?'

Monday went on to explain, leaving no detail untouched by which time the meals had arrived and Crookshank was on his second pint of beer. If nothing else, this foursome gathering had ironed all the creases and concerns that had been steadily building up from the moment Izabo Tuesday signed the register.

'Nigel Friday,' Crookshank suggested, 'is a discreet and skilful man of the cloth. I think it would be worth your while to have him on board.'

Monday glanced at Tuesday, who seemed to be playing with her steak. 'I'm not too sure exorcism is the way forward.'

'He has neither authority nor inclination for exorcism, Sol. But he does have incredible insight and it's that which we need more than ever. You may or may not have stopped the influx of interlopers. Let us hope you have, at least it gives you breathing space. May I also suggest you keep quiet about your find? Tell Palfrey by all means.'

On almost every relevant measure Kern played his cards. 'Hugh, when you have some free time, would you be able to fill me in on some background details about the judiciary system during Edmund's time.'

Tuesday clarified. 'Mike is not writing about Gallows Humour, not in the true sense.'

'Then he has his work cut out. Yes, I will lend a hand.'

Monday glanced at his watch. 'Hugh, when Week turned up that night, what time was it or thereabouts?'

'I have no idea other than it was in the middle of winter. What's on your mind?'

'To try and connect with Judge Week.' Monday paused to let that sink in. 'Look, any information I can get has to be of some help. Did Jeremy ever communicate with him?'

'Not to my knowledge and that wouldn't surprise me. He considered his ancestor's remorse came a little late in the day. I would advise against it.'

'So would I,' Tuesday said. 'If Week was the one to hang your father and take your memories, there's no telling what else he might be inclined to do.'

'It's a chance I'm willing to take. Hugh, do you know the tree from which my Father was hung?'

'Oh, this is utterly ridiculous!' Tuesday pushed back her chair. 'I am coming with you.'

'No!' Monday was adamant. 'This is my call. Mike can take you to the pictures.'

'Oh whoopee, organize my calendar why don't you. How am I supposed to sit through a film knowing your life is at risk?'

'Why, Izabo, I never knew you cared.' Monday stood to her burning cheeks and gave her a furtive wink believing every step in the dark was one step closer to her heart. 'Mike, can you cover the bill?'

Crookshank shook out of his pensive look, offered to pay the bill and accompanied Monday to the exit point. 'Sol, any sign of trouble just get out and run to the gates.'

'It stands to reason Judge Week was on my side that night. If he showed up, he could easily have found me. But did he show? That begs the question who really hung my Father. Let's say it was Doolally for argument's sake. What's going to happen when she gets her signature back? Are you getting my drift, Hugh?'

'Indeed, I do, most certainly I do. But if it was one of them, it suggests Saturday is not their day off. Highly unlikely.' Crookshank fondly tapped stubborn Monday on the arm. 'Just ensure you keep your head clear. Heroics will not impress Miss Tuesday.'

'What will?'

'Brains.'

Crookshank walked off, leaving Monday to move into the cooling air where the setting sun was slowly gliding behind trees. It had become increasingly easy in Gallows Humour to accept the strange inhabitants, their extreme humours and ignore the more perilous routes that were only talked about between friends.

The light filled the court room with a pinkish green glow and there was a strange hard silence while musty vapours seemed to curl from the floorboards up as though memories were rising from out of the dust. Nothing moved or happened, nothing happened at all except for the changing weather autumn usually brings. So Monday moved quickly into the hall, through the dining room and then down the back stairs to the kitchen. He stood there for a moment and realized he had not taken a breath since leaving the courtroom.

'Palfrey? Are you about?'

A voice came from the wine store. 'In here, sir.'

'I never gave it a thought when I told Mike he could use the motor.'

Palfrey revealed himself with a bottle of wine and cheddar cheese. His manner of dress was in contrast to what Monday had known. Wearing army boots and trousers and a woolly vest under which outlined his muscled frame, he smiled without apology. After all, it was his day off. 'This morning,' he said uncorking the wine, 'I spent my time in bed reading yesterday's news. I then indulged in a stroll to the garage where Bert Cross and I spent a leisurely afternoon tinkering with the brake pads to a Roadster XK Jaguar once owned by Sterling Moss.' He passed over a glass. 'There is no home game today, sir.'

'You never fail to amaze me, Palfrey. Cheers.'

'The house seems inordinately quiet, sir. Where are Miss Tuesday and Mr Kern?'

'Ah, good question.' Monday dragged out a chair, swung it round and straddled the seat then proceeded to tell Palfrey the latest. When he was done, and another glass later, he said, 'So you see, Palfrey, it's imperative to communicate with Week.'

'Do you wish me to stand by your side, sir?'

Monday shook his head. 'I wish you to keep safe. The problem so far, he's not there so it's doubtful anything will happen.'

No sooner mentioned when they heard a rap, rap, rap, these were the trace sounds of a gavel-strike, muffled and distant through the walls. And it confirmed only one thing. Someone was presiding at court.

Monday moved like a panther, long and smooth, flung open the doors to the light of a candle where a face appeared on the high bench, disturbing in the glow. It was the barely visible Judge Culver Week about to pass sentence on a man who was also barely visible standing in the dock wringing his hands in fearful contemplation.

'Though it is my earnest wish to temper justice with mercy, your persistent dedication to a life of crime is an abomination before God and man. I therefore sentence you to hang by the neck until you are dead.'

The condemned prisoner limped from the dock as if afflicted by the palsy, babbled incomprehensibly then vanished into the dark recesses of the night. And Monday wondered if this was the exact same scenario Betty Cross had encountered before she fled screaming from Gallows Humour. But here lay the opportunity to speak to Judge Week. Monday owed it to others and moved forward, unnerving to be in this empty courtroom, to be tiptoeing through Week's inner sanctum. Oddly, the difference between the bust portrayal and to what Monday saw, underscored the fact Week's charisma was not in his looks. Nor did it derive from physical presence. Judge Week was too small and too slight to be physically dominating, but it was when he spoke and acted that he became a person who claimed attention.

The Judge sat in silence for a while, observing Monday. 'Come here,' he said, his words insistent, hung seductive in the gloom. Monday tried to see beyond the pale surface of Week's mass and recognized those intelligent and lucid grey eyes were looking through him rather than at him. 'To whom do I address?'

'Solomon Monday.'

'Solomon Monday,' the Judge murmured. 'Am I in transitory or am I consigned to a dream?'

'Slight as we may seem to each other, I can see you as surely as you can see me. Did you take my childhood memories?'

'Yes, yes, that is so. As far as a man dare venture to guess at the very uncertain position his kin may be found. Little Solomon Monday, your face has the brightness of the moon and stole you my work for safe keeping.'

'The objective must be to return only those signatures unjustly accused. Are you able to distinguish each mark?'

'My work was but a score of plenty to assimilate the count of hangings.'

'But I forage in the dark. I need help to work it all out. Can you return my memories?'

'No man has more confidence in another than I have in you. And no man will render more justice than I.' He banged down his gavel and passed sentence. 'Your wish is my command.'

The Judge's words trailed off into an unsettled interlude. Slowly the sounds of a new day supplanted it, the tempo of the grandfather clock striking into the past and the murmur of voices behind growing louder. A scene was taking place; that of a tall dark man striking a child, his face contorted and angry and the young mite absconding before stricken again.

And suddenly Monday was no longer an on-looker, but that of himself, frightened and scared of his father whose wicked tongue echoed to the tempo of death.

'I shall kill that little bastard! Let me have him! I'll show you the back of my hand!'

As little Monday wretchedly hid under a wooden bench, he heard commotion break out. Something was wrong. He had only taken the bible, or so he had thought, and now everybody was shouting and he felt petrified at the sounds of his mother's choking screams. Then heavy censures from men mixed with his father's cursing. Little Monday was confused and shaking with guilt. The noise died away and he was curious for the crime that was spoken.

'Hang you we will, Charles Monday and damn our souls for doing so. Never shall you put a finger on your son again.' It was his mother's voice, guarding and protecting.

Lodging the book in the gap between wall and bench, little Monday scrambled to his feet and followed the unprotected sounds which betrayed his father's struggle against certain death. The condemned was kicking against the strength of two men as he was dragged along the path by a frozen lake toward the oaks, their breaths like chimney smoke.

Having tripped on his feet a few times, little Monday hid behind large crisp nettles and watched his mother fix up a noose while two others held down his father, a rambling stream of prayer and terror. The rope was pulled, the sound cutting instantly to a glottal stop, the legs of the doomed beginning their wild aerial gyration. The eyes of his mother were chill as she absorbed the scene, sweeping from Sunday and Crookshank's father holding fast to the violent shaking on the rope and to the quivering body of her husband.

To this silent, horrific night shambles where a cloud passed to cover the light of the moon, Monday was no longer a little boy lost on a Saturday night but that of his true self in an entirely different time zone. The cloud moved away and the sky lit up the gallows like a rising sun and showed the extent of the land. There were people selling their wares before a hanging commenced and where there had once been a lake there were small wooden crosses with names chalked in red. The times were hungry but active, horses pulling ploughs and only a few oaks where children swung on knotted ropes, their dirty bare legs mimicking the hangings that danced to the toll of a bell.

Monday felt a chill in the air as he stared crookedly down, the names on the crosses, each becoming clearer as he moved into the wilderness of death. A hand clutched at his ankle, gaining purchase, pulling him down. Crying out for release, he twisted but the grip tightened and he went under, the rush of water in his ears then the noise replaced by the sound of his own heartbeat slowly diminishing.

THE DARK SIDE OF THE MOON

While life was still there on the edge of death, time had left Monday's calendar. As his feverish body grew pale, he was visiting those anonymous crosses sprawling across a field of grass where bones of the dead were buried down deep. Seldom did he open his eyes, and sometimes to a row of intangible smiles and sometimes to the ceiling where a flame of a candle threw shadows like cloaks.

'Sol?' He heard his name and rolled his head to face the voice and shaded figure of Izabo Tuesday. 'Don't give in to bad dreams, my love.'

Monday would dream of her. He would feel the press of her breast on his back, the radiated warmth of her body, her hand touring his chest and stomach, turn and bring her into his arms and kiss those lips that were meant to smile, slow lingering kisses, playful kisses, little kisses in the middle of the night before he would plunge deep, the rock and thrust and the dreams of the desirable consequences, the mathematics of genealogy, the picture of swelling flesh, the stretching of skin, the shaping of limbs and fingers. All this and more lingered on as he drifted into a parcel of contentment. What is for real and what is not when living at Gallows Humour?

From that Saturday night venture to a Saturday of bird song, Monday woke dry in the mouth, deliverance miraculously gained. Paradoxically, his restored six years of childhood memories came at the expense of six days in bed. He propped himself up on his elbows focusing on the room, his mind on the tangible reality of meeting Week. For between this sleeping and waking he felt he had lived through a night of corroding darkness where occasionally a light was afforded, a door through which he was visited by messengers whose words and actions had completely escaped him.

He swept back the covers with a swaying in the head and ventured to the bathroom, drank from the tap in trackless movements then heard a friendly voice.

'Ah, welcome back, sir.' Palfrey ran a bath. 'I made a nice pot of tea.'

Failing to find the word to describe how he felt, Monday placed a comforting hand on Palfrey's arm and staggered back to bed, pulling the covers up to his chin. 'Why is it so cold, Palfrey?'

'You will feel much better after a hot bath. Come now, sir. Sit up and get hot beverage in your stomach.' Palfrey waited for Monday to obey then placed the tray on his lap. 'Did you achieve anything in your endeavours, sir?'

'I think so.' Monday smiled at the miniature white flag stuck in a crumpet. 'Who did this?'

'Miss Tuesday. She said you would understand its meaning. You have been a worry, sir. But all's well that ends well through the mist of a muddled morning.'

'Muddle morning?' Monday muffled.

'You first, sir.'

'I did meet Week but I suppose you gathered that. I had more than my memories restored. I saw Gallows Humour in its original state with the gallows in situ, a most depressing sight to say the least. I also saw a number of graves with red crosses where the lake should have been. I know it holds some meaning. Makes you wonder how that was achieved. I mean, surely coffins float.'

'Bodies would be wrapped in cloth, sir. It was Nathanial Sunday who created the lake.'

Monday's brows met when something fell past the window. 'Did you see that?'

'See what, sir?'

'Nothing, it must have been a bird. Yes, I remember now being struck by the names on the crosses, their rough edges and irregular surfaces then I was-' Monday paused when another something fell past the window. He placed the tray to one side, hopped out of bed, pulled up the sash, and poked out his head, looking down. 'I think a couple of tiles just slipped off the roof.'

'Miss Tuesday is overseeing remedial work, sir.'

'Is she on the roof?'

'Actively making us watertight and enjoying every moment.'

'She has the temerity to tell me off for dangerous exploits when clearly, she has no regard for her own safety. Where is Mike?'

There was some explaining to do.

The bathroom, warm and steamy now, vibrated to the voice of Palfrey who had taken comfort on the toilet seat.

'You appeared quite yourself in so far as any man could feel to a near drowning. Occasionally you drifted in and out of consciousness but we all felt there was something going on in your head so rather than call the doctor, we rode the storm. Presently, Mr Kern and Mr Crookshank are on their way to the Himalayas to seek out Nigel Friday.'

Monday ducked under and rinsed his hair. Re-emerging he asked the most obvious question. 'How long was I out for?'

'Today is Saturday, six days in bed, sir.'

'Wow, six days.' He smiled. 'Six days for six years. Did you know, Palfrey? Did you know I had lived here as a child?'

'Not until recently, sir.'

'And Izabo, has she ever been here before?'

Palfrey looked curiously at his shoes as if seeing them for the first time. 'Yes,' he said equably. 'And that is as much as I can say, sir. It is not for the want of being disloyal.'

'At least it clears up a few things, why she knew about the riddle. That was really niggling me. Did you know about the riddle? You know, before I came on the scene.'

'The riddle was a surprise to me as it was to you, sir. But now we know why the truth was suppressed. Had Miss Tuesday informed me or Mr Sunday, I am sure her enthusiasm would have been quelled. On the bright side, the riddle served another purpose, used as her bargaining chip.'

'Ah, but on the darker side, we have to ask ourselves if she was already aware the riddle was suspect in the first place.'

'Sir, show me a man who can fathom a woman's mind and I will show you my Victoria Cross.'

'I am impressed, a Victoria Cross.'

'So would I be if I had one.'

Monday laughed and eased himself out of the bath. Wiping the mirror with a hand towel, he startled at a face that was not his face. He looked gaunt and pale, and his temples had turned grey. 'Jesus, Palfrey, I look nearly as old as you, no offence meant.'

'None taken, sir. May I enquire if you gained knowledge of your father's executioner?'

'Judge Week hung my Father.' It was a necessary lie. 'So, when can we expect the return of Mike and Hugh?'

'They left yesterday, sir. Mr Crookshank is hoping to persuade Nigel Friday to come here. Meanwhile, he trusts you will avoid dangerous pursuits.'

To the sound of shouts there was an almighty shudder and it felt as if the roof had collapsed. Half shaven with a towel round his waste, Monday sprinted down the corridor, shot up the narrow staircase and out to the daylight under the one chime bell. Against a grey sky blackened further by dust and soot, men were shouldering a new beam into place. Elsewhere, tiles had been stripped, purloins exposed and for a while the sight rendered Monday speechless. It was the worst of scenes, the best of Tuesday's triumphs. Dirtied from head to toe with her hair tied back, her skin roughened by the rigours of work, she hopped from rafter to rafter like a kangaroo on heat. Danger held no fear.

'Miss Tuesday!' Monday called out. 'What the hell are you doing?'

She bounded toward him and stopped just short of his nose. 'What does it look like I'm doing?'

'I'm sure I need not repeat my constant desire to do anything in my power to end this madness.' Monday was showing his darker side, which might have been less painful with more tact and discretion. 'Unless you give up the idea of turning this place into a building site, I will personally lock you in a store cupboard and throw away the key.'

'Will you come in the cupboard with me?'

A smile grew on his lips. 'Are you trying to get on my good side, Miss Tuesday?'

'For certain I am, Mr Monday. This roof hasn't been touched for over two hundred years. Some timbers really, truly need replacing and those lovely corbels on the north gable wall cannot be left to crumble, tumble, can they?' She removed some shaving cream off his cheek and wiped it on his nose. 'I mean…a brick might fall on your distinguished head and where shall we be without our courageous but dim-witted Mr Monday.'

A confused swirl of pleasure whisked its way down into his body as he returned to his bedroom, although dulled resignation had replaced fervour. But it was difficult not to smile about Izabo Tuesday. She made no secret of her trade or ambitions.

'Palfrey,' he said finishing off his shave. 'Who are those men?'

'Local trade, sir, brought in especially for today.'

'Of course, it's a Saturday. This is your day off. Why are you here?'

'Sir, I need to explain recent events. Our six good souls did not vacate the house this morning. I woke to Doolally and Flour in the kitchen where they informed me Judge Week demanded their presence. Woody, Ned and Charlie are trying to be inconspicuous in a conspicuous sort of way, helping out with the workload. Further, Bumble is hiding in the boiler room.'

'And the interlopers?'

'This past week, they have been quite active with a number of breakages, courtroom agonies and screaming fits. Thankfully, they are not around today, the very reason why Miss Tuesday started on the roof. She plans to replace rotten timbers, felt and batten, thus making us watertight. Tomorrow onwards she will work alongside Woody, Ned and Charlie though I have a deep suspicion she would like you to get involved.'

Now irrevocably committed to Gallows Humour, he pulled into jeans and sweater. 'I have never worked on a roof. Shouldn't there be scaffolding?'

'Scaffolding is to the front and the north facing wall, sir. I think Miss Tuesday is hoping you will help on the drive, as will I.'

'Drive? No mention was made about the drive. Why the drive? What's wrong with the drive?'

'In winter it puddles like a quagmire.' Palfrey passed over the trainers. 'Hogging is currently being compounded into the drive then a layer of tarmac for a finished surface.'

'Right.' Monday stood. 'I see I have been presented with a fait accompli.'

Outside and beyond the scaffolding a crew was digging a wide strip of earth sweeping from the steps of the house to the trail of the drive. Monday gave them a sharp clear look and uttered not a word as he strolled in the direction of the lake. He turned back once and stared up to the roof. She too, he thought, had entered a new world of overwhelming strangeness and anything less would surely be instinctively uninspiring.

At the lake he gazed at the lily roots coiled down deep, at the spongy weeds around them. That is where he entered, a green foot under and further along to be consumed, alone in the night. What was so important about this lake apart from hiding dead bones?

'I'm undecided about whether to polish the silver or give a hand on the roof. I asked Bumble about it, and she wus no help.' With her hair loose-tangled and shedding pins, clothes shapelessly humped around her, Monday looked into those mischievous eyes that were about to upset the roots of his order. 'What wus yew doing in the lake?'

'Taking a swim.'

'Tis no good yew telling porkies. We all know yew were up to summat. And sitting in a bath won't help.' Her eyes narrowed to a disapproving tut. 'Yew weren't ready to be told. Best yew leave without knowing, says Woody.'

'But I changed my mind, Doolally.'

'Yew still weren't ready to be told. Now what's a grown man like yew want with his six-year-old memories? Not to hark back on his nappy change, that's fer sure.'

'The others, where are the others?'

Doolally sent her eyes to the lake. 'Be down there, consigned to their places.'

'But I thought water was out of bounds.'

'Who told yew that?'

'Doolally, I was sent back to a time where there was no lake, only graves with wooden crosses. Do I take it this is where you all go when you're not in the house?'

'See, this is how it works. Judge Week has the house on a Saturday and he consigns us to our places down there. Sunday to Friday we hev the house, that wus his promise. Summat happened after yew lost your memories. Others came from down there. They made pacts and bargains with others, others who claimed to hev God's holy orders and there be many of them. Down there we don't exist. Saturday be not a day fer us.'

'Yet it is today.'

'That's 'cause Judge Week blocked our path, heard him bang his gavel and make a ruling. A different point of the compass beckons, he says. Heed Monday's words, he says. Nothing about the riddle, he says nothing about that.'

'My father wrote it as a cruel joke, Doolally.'

'Pah!' she scowled with far less grace. 'No wonder it wus kept from us. Sunday always kept things from us. He never liked us knowing what wus going on in the world, said we wus not meant to. Your lovely mum liked us knowing. She read us stories. We learnt about aeroplanes taking yew up in the sky and how yew can see the stars through a periscope.'

'Telescope,' he corrected.

'What's the difference?'

'A submarine has a periscope.' He could see her bewilderment. 'A submarine is a ship built to go under water. In order for the captain to see on the surface he brings up his periscope.'

'Why would he want to live under water?'

'Because he likes fish more than humans.'

'Yew wus always one for telling porkies.'

'I was a child.'

'Pah, thass no excuse.' She slapped his bottom, and vanished.

At which point Monday's stomach gave a thunderous groan. Besieged by a new set of clues, he abruptly turned on the spot and picked his way to the kitchen whose occupants always remained the same. There, he pulled out a chair while Flour was tearing crusts off a loaf with her fingers. Truly a happy scene.

'Bread pudding,' Palfrey said reading Monday thoughts. 'Would you be taking your breakfast with Miss Tuesday?'

'I thought she was on the roof?'

'No,' she said waltzing in from the larder. 'Here I am, Miss DIY.' She sat opposite with a bacon sandwich, tomato ketchup oozing over the sides.

'Can I have one of those, Palfrey?'

'Here,' Tuesday offered. 'You can have mine, call it a peace offering.'

'Izabo, you never mentioned your enthusiasm to renovate Gallows Humour. You gave me the impression your enthusiasm was for the book. So what do I find? No strike that, you know damn well what I find. No mention of the drive. I had to find that out from Palfrey. Are we communicating here or what?'

'Well,' she said in defence, 'you go berserk at the mention of renovation. It's not as if the place is being demolished. What's your apartment like?'

He swallowed. 'At this point in time, probably trashed, knowing Angela. However, it does have its good features. There are two bedrooms, an open lounge and kitchen with views of the river. It's one of those in St. Katherine's Dock near the Tower of London.'

'Not too far to have your head chopped off.'

For Monday, he had only one bargaining chip: psychology. 'Having experienced the most recent effects from your acrobatic enterprise and ability, I leave entirely to your judgement the manner of renovation.' He watched the sudden thrill coursing her face then the immediate look of scepticism. 'All I ask is to be kept informed so we may discuss the matter like sensible adults. After all, I might just wander into the wrong bedroom.' He let suggestion roll off his lips.

Tuesday licked her fingers very slowly, seductively one by one, holding his eyes, keeping him inches apart from his food. Then so matter of fact stood and said before leaving, 'Speaking of bedrooms, your ceiling collapsed ten minutes ago.'

Monday's dark eyebrows momentarily knitted, he was not above sharing his anger and frustration with Palfrey. 'Why does she have to be so bloody superior! I should be consulted, not damn well confronted!' It took him a moment to realize Palfrey was stifling a laugh. 'Yes, ha, ha, very amusing…you see what I have to put up with? She lulls me into false security, sticks a white flag under my nose, and has the cheek to give me her bacon sandwich knowing damn well my bedroom is wrecked. I tell you, she has a sneaky way of getting one over on me, wish that I could get one over on her.'

Flour burst into a foolish giggle then waved to Palfrey to get his attention. She gestured with her hands, the medium of pantomime to which he translated. 'All is not lost, sir. It would appear there is a reading tonight in the drawing room. Men are from Mars and women are from Venus.'

'Any chance I would get an invite?'

Flour motioned again, more emphatically. 'Try to speak of Tuesday's wisdom and Monday's dark side of the moon.'

Hearing this made him feel hopeful but none the wiser. How profound would suffering have to be for a man to get close to the woman he loved?

Given the extent of this challenging undertaking, he left for a hard day's work on the drive which may or may not carry favour with Tuesday. Yet while his labour bore fruit and companionships grew to bring him fresh looks, he had come to realize the dark side of his moon was just as important as Tuesday's wisdom. Who said women are from Venus?

That evening after dining alone in his library, Monday felt the afterglow of manual labour as he scribbled his clues on paper. The big question mark was drawn against the lake for it had somehow stuck fast in his head that this held the greatest significance in order to meet the objective.

At 8.45 he looked at his watch, peeled off his glasses, lit a cigarette, and blew smoke to the side of his mouth and sat there looking at that scenic painting but was not really looking at it at all. He closed his eyes briefly to draw back the curtains on his memories, those wonderful days when the world offered hope, where his mother's arms embraced a child, how the snow engulfed the landscape and why summer smelt so fresh. Only by the absence of Gallows Humour did it all change. And then suddenly the world had rushed by and he never stopped to count the pennies in his piggy bank or what he was doing with his life.

Two raps on the door interrupted his ruminations. 'Come in,' he said and glanced round as he watched a fluffy dressing gown and slippers walk in. 'Are we off to bed?'

'Not yet,' Tuesday replied closing herself in. 'Sol, we need to talk.'

'Really? You do surprise me.' He lazed back in the chair, put his feet up on the desk and laced his hands behind his head. 'Is this where you talk and I listen?'

'Okay, I admit this morning was a little disastrous. I never calculated for your ceiling to collapse. The bedroom opposite is just as nice.'

'It overlooks the drive.'

'And what a nice drive we have.' She padded to the globe. 'Can I pour you a whisky?'

By now he certainly had her measure. 'Why don't you just come out with it?'

'Oh dear, can we wait until your mood has improved?'

'My answer is no, no to conversion of the courtroom. No to the knocking down of walls and no to anything which incorporates a lump hammer and a trowel.'

'I totally agree. Small or large whisky?'

Damn it, she's doing it again. 'Make it a small one. I understand you're doing a reading tonight. Am I invited?'

'This is partly why I am here. I thought it would be fun to go for a debate. You could put your views forward about men, the space they like to occupy, and I could put forward my views in the space women like to occupy.'

'Excuse me? I thought you occupied my space.'

'I shall ignore that infantile remark. Flour cannot speak, Bumble is still hiding in the boiler room, refuses to come out unless you join us and

Doolally is hardly in a position to put her views across since she has no preconception of twenty-first century life.'

'All the more reason you should listen to her. She might give you some tips on how to boil an egg and what pleases men most.' He grinned. 'Of course, subject to requirements.'

She tutted and sat down by the light of a candle that made her appear so vulnerable, so like a woman in need of love and protection. 'You do realize you were walking into the lake without taking a blind bit of notice. If it hadn't been for Palfrey, you would have drowned. Do you remember any of this or am I talking to a brick wall?'

'Nope and yes, you are talking to a brick wall. I woke this morning thinking it was the following day until Palfrey informed me otherwise. I must remember to thank him.'

'So do you remember anything?'

'Oh yes,' he said flippantly but had no intention of telling her, not yet. 'Are we finished then with renovating Gallows Humour?'

'If you must know I never had intentions of renovating Gallows Humour. I told you the first day we met that I wanted to install electricity. This is a wonderful home which needs a good lick of paint and preserving. I am going to install solar panels, that way we shall be independent and have all the energy we need. Do you object to any of this?'

Monday felt humble and adjusted his seating position. 'No objections whatsoever.' He then folded a piece of paper into an aeroplane shape and flew it in her direction. Well aimed. 'This must never be repeated to anyone.'

Flicking her hair to one side, she looked down and read the names of his father's executioners, and the reason why it was imperative to keep Crookshank in the dark, why he should never learn the truth, should never be made to feel accountable. She studied it for some while as though filling any vacuum of thought or intention with her mental energy and flow of ideas.

'How do you feel about your mother?'

Monday stared moodily into his glass of whisky. There was so much regret. 'Sad, very sad,' he finally admitted. 'Almost certainly, this is what she intended to tell me and I missed the opportunity to comfort her, to tell her how sorry I felt and how much I still loved her.'

'Oh, Sol, I'm sure she knows that. You never treated her badly; you just got lost in the wilderness of politics. I bet she was very proud of your achievements. Why, you could have turned out to be just like your father but here you are, risking life and limb for six poor souls. So what else can you tell me?'

At this point he wanted to say here I am, take me, rape me, do what you will but he was unable to do that. 'I was transported back to a time when this place was a courthouse. There were names on wooden crosses and I was trying to read them. Next, it all went blank.'

'Did you speak to Judge Week?'

'Yes, and he has every confidence in me meeting the objective.'

'So did he tell you anything that would help to meet the objective?'

'Not specifically. I know he sent me back to see something important. I saw the gallows and heard the bell ringing. By the way, I had a chat to Doolally this morning. She said Week had given a new ruling…a different point of the compass beckons, heed Monday's words. Did you know their graves lie at the bottom of the lake?'

'Yes.'

'Did you also know Week made a bargain, I presume after he died that they must be consigned to the lake on a Saturday?'

'Obviously it's no longer the case.' She propped her chin on her hand and leaned on the arm of the chair, accidentally presenting him with an eye-popping view of her cleavage. 'It's been one hell of a week, Sol. On Sunday night the courtroom was in session so Mike and I did a head count…thirty-four minus the six…a lot less than before. We figured they must have gone back from whence they came or not as the case may be.'

'Where else do you think they went?'

'Beyond the gates,' she assumed. 'It's not impossible so it shouldn't be ruled out. Anyhow, the interlopers that are still here, some have been very naughty. On Monday, it wasn't so bad, only a few odds and sods got broken. We thought it might have been Doolally but she claimed otherwise. On

Tuesday, Palfrey's quarters got flooded. On Wednesday, the tyres on the Rolls were slashed. On Thursday morning, we woke up to find all the furniture in Judges Chamber had been removed and placed in the dining room. But Thursday night was the worst and near catastrophic. Someone set light to the curtains in the drawing room. Thanks to Flour, Mike was able to catch it in time. Consequently, Mike went to see Hugh and it was decided we needed to act pretty fast. Hence, they left yesterday to see Nigel Friday. Anyway, Woody is consigned to you, now that you're up and running. Flour is consigned to me. And Ned is consigned to Palfrey. Doolally, Charlie and Bumble will do regular shifts in the house. That is if Bumble will leave the boiler room.'

Hell, thought Monday, that was a lot to take in. He got to his feet and poured another whisky. 'Why did Flour alert Mike?'

'Ah, hum, well…let's just say those two have found a lot in common.'

'I see.'

'I don't think you do, Sol. Mike has his head in the clouds. When we meet our objective, he's going to be absolutely devastated to lose Flour.'

'Do not understate Mike's performance. He goes through women like eating cornflakes. When the packet is empty, he will get another brand. Do you think the vandalism has been contained?'

'From midnight, only time will tell. Woody believes he has established some of the nasties. I just hope we do because so far things have not exactly gone smoothly.'

'Well Monday is here and ready to face Week's extremists.' He noted a troubled face and said, 'You look like a little worried doggie.'

She smiled and redirected her eyes. 'No, it isn't that, it's just, well, you know.'

'No, Izabo, I don't know. Unless you tell me, how can I know?'

'Don't you realize that had you died, Gallows Humour would be entirely exposed to a police enquiry and the re-emergence of Angela? As if we haven't got enough on our plate, she has it in her head I am your whore, so wouldn't she just love to destroy me. I mean, it's not as if there's the remotest possibility we are anything but business partners.'

'Tell me why not?'

'For the very reason we signed up to meet the objective. I never came here to be emotionally entangled, and likewise for you.'

'I seem to recall you telling me you're a fatalist. What will be, will be. Follow the yellow brick road and all that.'

'Well, my yellow brick road is closed to traffic.'

Monday washed a hand over his face. This is not what he wanted to hear. Feeling as though he would live with a shadow over his head where he was looking for Tuesday to shed some light, not just somebody to get him through the night, he knew he was going to have to do something about this and knelt before her, about to take the biggest gamble of his life.

'Izabo,' he said pulling the edges her dressing gown a little closer, 'whatever you wish to keep concealed I feel certain you have good reasons and I don't believe for one moment those reasons are bad. I make no apology for my darker side. It's that which makes me stalwart but I have a softer side and am not above showing it to the right woman…if only she will let me.'

Her eyes dipped. 'It would be foolish to think of me in that way.'

'I want to be foolish. Be foolish too, just this once.' He pressed his lips to hers, to her cheek, smoothing her hair, touching her skin and well on the way to his desired goal.

'Yew can finish up later.' Doolally yelled, her body unseen. 'We're waiting fer our story.'

Bollocks. It was so easy to forget the invisibles. 'Did you say Woody was confined to me and Flour to you?' he asked Tuesday getting to his feet.

'Fate rarely calls upon us at a moment of our choosing.'

'Can we not try to make our own fate?'

She hesitated at the door. 'Let me think about it.'

'Think, yes.' He liked that idea. 'But not too long, it might clog up the brain cells.'

'Sol, I do worry about you at times.' She never looked back but he could hear her titters and it made him feel good.

In the drawing room where flames trailed up the chimney, where candles lit up the walls, and where debate sounded to the topic of liberated women, Monday glowed by the hearth taking it all in. These souls, he thought, were bright as buttons, squeezed into a world that unfortunately spun in the wrong direction. Whatever would his kind make of them if not to exploit their originality? They would play their games and test Palfrey's patience yet it would only be Tuesday to take Monday from solitude to a place where his mind could journey through a world where he longed to be.

'Fifty years,' Tuesday told them, 'after the second-wave feminists smashed their way into the workplace, corporate UK is still overwhelmingly male. It is a complete scandal. Only the most exceptional women make it to the board room, yet the board room is full of men who are not in the least bit exceptional.'

'It's all humbug.' Doolally was a rebel at heart. 'Why work when a man can keep yew?'

'That is no longer the case,' Palfrey explained. 'Today, the average man on average pay would be unable to sustain a family unless the woman is prepared to make do with a tent.'

'Whazzz wrong with a tent.' Bumbled buzzed in. 'My friend Martha lived in a tent, a big tent and didn't it look the picture.'

'She wus an Injun,' Doolally scolded her. 'Injuns live in tents. Here, Woody, yew lived in a tent. Wus yew an Injun?'

Woody fed some sticks to the fire then knocked out his pipe on his leggings. 'Look to nature if yew must fer an answer. Nature has her way of setting things right.'

That seemed to kill the conversation and Tuesday turned with a sigh to Monday, wrapping her dressing gown tighter about her body. 'You have been very quiet, Sol. Care to offer your thoughts?'

'Hem,' he cleared his throat. 'Palfrey is correct. Everything is based on the ability to pay. Burning bras in the first half of the twentieth century encouraged the Treasury to make hay while the sun shone yet the dumb woman thought she was being liberated, whereas, she had unknowingly opened the doors for speculative men. They will never be taken seriously because they act like bitches on heat.' He paused to their gaping mouths.

'You wanted my opinion and I am giving it to you straight. Of course, there are exceptions, but those exceptions hold no weight in the world of economics and politics.'

'There was Mrs Thatcher,' little Charlie argued and surprised Monday. 'She took the country by the scruff of the neck a generation ago.'

'Are you into politics, Charlie?' Monday asked.

'I'm into girls,' Charlie guffawed and a bubble of laughter rose to their lips.

Monday regarded them all with pleasure, their paroxysms shook the room. For him, what started as an amusing debate swiftly deepened into something unexplainable. Even now he found it hard to believe he was in company of dead people. They were more than spirits, greater than life itself. He would do them injustice, he thought, to withhold information and was about to take another big gamble.

'You all know I spoke to Judge Week,' and stepped up his rhythm sensing their urgency. 'What I failed to mention was that his Work has been found and now in safe keeping beyond the gates. We think that night, when the book was brought here it somehow triggered off energy that opened a gateway for others to invade Gallows Humour. But there is a problem. We cannot establish your marks, and there are many, many marks, all undated.'

'Know our marks we will,' said Ned. 'I signed with a cross.'

'As did most,' informed Tuesday.

'Ask Judge Week. He will know our marks.'

'He informed me otherwise, Ned. Look, we are halfway there. Hugh Crookshank and Michael Kern are at this very point in time seeking Father Friday in the-'

'More mumbo jumbo,' Doolally interjected. 'Remember him,' she said to the others and they nodded. 'Nathanial Sunday with his heirs and graces, a puny git wishing us away…he soon got his come-uppance, had his heart taken.'

'But come back he did with a vicar to spite uzz.' Bumble reminded.

To their discontented grumbles, Tuesday rallied to Monday's side. 'There will be no mumbo jumbo or any such thing. Trust in Sol. Believe in him and remember how he risked his life for you. He will not allow anything or anyone to cause you grief, regardless of what dangers that may entail. Is that not so, Sol?'

Monday's heart glowed. 'Not that I would wish to end my life, it pleases me to think that if I did, I would be in most pleasant company. If anyone has any thoughts on the matter then speak up. Information, no matter how irrelevant could well be relevant.'

'Able Soper, his name I remember.'

'Yes, Doolally, we realize that but it's not good enough. We shall never be able to find his name in the records. If we had your name, or any of your names, we might stand a chance, a starting point in time.'

'He stole my cow and I called her Daisy.'

Monday rolled his eyes to the ceiling. Life which had been strangely merciful took on new meaning. Nothing more was said after that and he shadowed the room, picking up pieces of a broken vase which lay on a tray. He remembered now who broke it in the first place, a little restless tinker who slid away like an eel in the grass. Doolally took the blame as she often did and Doolally pieced it together again, not once, not twice but on many occasions, and he wondered why she never used glue. Probably, it was her will set against his.

'Did you know I broke this,' Monday said to Palfrey when he sidled into view. 'I think it was on my fifth birthday. I was annoyed when Mother sent me to bed early. Funny how we remember so few things and keep one or two fixed in our heads. Doolally took the blame, I remember that. And because of it, I was given another slice of cake.'

'Have you always had a sweet tooth, sir?'

Monday nodded. 'I was tall for my age but never slim. It had its advantages. No one ever bullied me at school, not even my friends were bullied. I was also picked for the rugby team though to be truthful I would have preferred cricket. Did you ever have children, Palfrey?'

'My wife had a child, grew into an adult without knowing its father. Provision has been made for you to sleep in the bedroom opposite Mr Kern's.'

'By the way, I meant to thank you for saving me. Izabo said I would have drowned had it not been for you. How bad was it?'

'Bad enough to warrant a Victoria Cross.' They smiled at each other. 'Remember Woody shall be by your side keeping vigilance.'

Monday had forgotten and glanced across the room to the dressing gown, his longing for Izabo Tuesday had just been unmercifully capped.

GOOD FRIDAY

Monday lay suspended in the warmth of the evening and marvelled how rapidly things had progressed under the supervision of Izabo Tuesday. She had stolen the hearts of the innocent as well as the guilty, opposite clans working side by side for days on end. Then he became vaguely conscious of a noise beyond the door to his bedroom, and forced himself to listen, to hear if trouble was brewing again. There was nothing, so he drifted, full of contentment to run each of the events through his mind again, wishing he could steal some moments alone with the woman he loved.

A few minutes later, about to blow out the bedside candle he caught the monolithic shadow of Woody. The temptation was there to ask, 'Any chance of asking Flour if Miss Tuesday has forgiven me?'

'Best yew look where you're going next time and walk round the bucket, not kick it out of temper to land on her head.'

Monday chuckled to the hilarious scene, one of many minor mishaps caused by a novice labourer. 'I was not angry at her, Woody. I thought if I could fill in the joints, make a good job of it, she might appreciate my artistic qualities.'

'Yew cannot lay bricks, yew cannot mix cement, yew cannot handle a simple pointing trowel so what artistic qualities were yew trying to show other than be a nuisance thirty feet high.'

Good sense told Monday not to respond. He blew out the candle and lay back in a calming gesture. 'Wake me up when someone needs me.'

'Why not wake up on the Gondola?'

'Too cold to sleep there,' Monday muffled under the sheets.

'Not if yew hev Tuesday to warm yew up.'

Monday shot out of bed, dressed fast in the dark and ran all the way, his heart going ten to the dozen. The tarpaulin, which covered the Gondola, was aglow. Why Tuesday should be there, he assumed she required privacy as he sometimes required the same, the seeking of solace in a place where danger held no fear. Having stopped short, he gathered his thoughts then gently prized himself under the cover and found her, as he expected to, supine on the cushions, a torch in her hand and a book dropped open against her knees.

'This is a surprise,' she said. 'Can't you sleep?'

'No,' he replied wriggling to her side, sharing a blanket or two. 'Carry on reading, don't mind me. What are you reading?'

'How to exterminate cockroaches.'

'Look, it was an accident. How is your head? Shall I kiss it better?'

'Sol, why are you here?'

'Fate, Izabo. There I was, ready to climb into bed when I discovered ants were crawling between the sheets, can you believe that.'

She smiled. 'Not really but do carry on.'

'They were no ordinary ants,' he said placing his arm about her. 'As I tried to brush them away, they attacked me. Woody said I best sleep in Mike's room but I said Bumble had stripped the sheets off his bed…there was only one option left, to sleep on the Gondola.'

'But sleeping here is colder than sleeping in a bed with no sheets.'

'Not true, you are here.' He took the torch out of her hand and switched it off. 'Fate, Izabo…fate we sleep this night together. Are you tired?'

It began slowly, the soft feel of her skin, the warm touch of her lips and the sharp gasp of her breath upon his face. He was swollen with desire, the need to sweep through her in waves, his hands unveiling the cloth that kept them apart. And then, suddenly a seriousness came over what they were doing, urgently, absolutely making love. He had never before felt such a deep need to move that way, carefully, inexorably, making him feel primitive, connected even to the dirt of the earth and the light of the moon.

Time passed, and his actions played in his mind as she lay silently in his arms, warm and tender. She was not asleep; he knew that but he also knew she was thinking about what they had done and wondered if she felt any regret.

'Izzy,' he spoke softly, 'tell me your thoughts?'

'You do not want to know my thoughts.'

Monday could not disguise his disappointment. 'I wish you would talk to me. Whatever you have done, it matters not. I think no less of you. Will you think no less of me?'

She never answered and he chose to let it slide, closing his eyes and holding her like a mother would hold her child that was deep in uncertainty. Whatever else, he had tasted her, had breathed in her lingering sweetness and left his mark for her to carry inside her flesh. That seemed to be as much as he could hope for and fell sleep.

He woke alone to the dawn chorus, cold and disappointed she had gone. It triggered the instinctual need to leave the Gondola and walk the estate to get his blood pumping. His eyes snaked down the long drive, a desirable access from the now renovated gates to the steps of the building when Woody emerged shouldering a scaffolding pole.

'Did yew hev a warm evening?'

'For certain I did, Woody. What's with the pole?'

'The house is done outside, all this needs to come down and returned to the builder's yard.' He pointed with his pipe. 'See that patch yonder? Ned wus thinking of laying some concrete so we could leave our handprints fer yew to remember us.'

That hit a spot in Monday's heart and he turned with cheerless eyes. He remembered the story of the artic penguin. In time after being perched atop their mother's feet for a thousand paces like a child learning to dance on its mother's shoes, the chick takes its first steps alone.

In the kitchen where breakfast came and tasted good, greasy and squeaky and crisp, Monday never said much while he was eating. He was in that faraway place wondering whether to take pictures, mount them in silver frames just like the silver frames Betty Cross had waltzing across her furniture.

'Palfrey, do you have a camera?'

Palfrey lifted his head out of the paper and smiled. 'There is a particularly nice one of Miss Tuesday emptying a bucket of cement on your trainers.'

'Why do I bother asking? Where are they?'

'Doolally took them to show Miss Tuesday who is presently in the library.'

Monday pushed back his chair. 'Bring a pot of coffee when you're ready.'

'Very well, sir.'

On the way to the library, he poked his head in the courtroom to check things out. Lately there had been a number of incidences by a few malcontents, principally to have the pleasure of disrupting the human occupants. His eyes swept from side to side, satisfied all was well then carried on with the memory of last night, his triumph and her submission, how wonderfully startled she was by his intimacy, the reaching out very slowly, kissing once, twice, fondling her and gradually allowing his curiosity to prevail. He felt she had bewitched him, this lovely creature who had made herself necessary to his life.

At the sight of Tuesday now, he stood in the doorway and watched as she ran her eyes across the photographs laid out on the desk, finding it hard to choose the best one. Then the moment was gone. She became aware of his presence and got to her feet.

'Oh Sol, look at these, there're wonderful. Palfrey takes excellent pictures. I love this one of Doolally…perhaps not, perhaps this one…or what about this one?'

'Izzy,' he murmured gently, grazing kisses on her neck. 'I missed you this morning.'

She kissed him deep. He responded, easing his hands to the small of her back and pulling her forward. It seemed strange, a miracle that the girl he had entered into contract should transmute into his lover.

'Here! No hanky-panky,' Doolally yelled. 'Night times is fer that!'

Monday picked up his rimless spectacles. 'Do we have a group photo of the tribe?'

'No!' Doolally voiced sharply. 'Charlie and Flour had a falling out and won't make up. He told her wat yew said about her fancy man. Now she's all at sixes and sevens.'

'Explain?'

'Yew said he goes through women like eating cornflakes. When the packet is empty, he will get another brand.' She stuck a finger under his nose. 'Yew better tell him to watch his step or Charlie will put him in the wringer.'

'Is Flour very upset? No, strike that. Of course she is. I am sure Mike never knew Charlie and Flour was an item.'

'No, Sol.' Tuesday enlightened him. 'They are more like siblings. But, as I tried to explain to Charlie, Mike is genuinely fond of Flour. It was your words, not his and I think he should be given the benefit of the doubt, don't you?'

From where Monday was standing, he saw Flour come into view and felt a rush of embarrassment. She signed to him, placed two hands on her heart and then to each side of her rocking head, an endearing and touching communication.

'I spoke out of turn,' he told her closing the distance between them. 'Mike has never bought a pastry brush for a woman so that must speak volumes.' The chestnut eyes flickered in confusion so he clarified. 'Remember what we talked about, men are from Mars? It was a big thing to do.'

'So why hevn't yew bought your sweetheart a trowel?'

Trust Doolally.

Palfrey, who had an original sense of timing, walked in with a tray balanced on his outstretched palm. 'Doolally, go and wash the breakfast dishes.'

'Do you want a trowel?' Monday asked Tuesday.

'Why would I want a trowel?'

'To cement our relationship,' and he grinned.

'A relationship that is two bricks short of a pack?' She laughed. 'I have a trowel, silly. Besides, all work ceases from now on. We need the professionals to wire up and they cannot come in until we can get the problem resolved. Palfrey, did the samples come?'

'I put them in the dining room, madam. Do you wish me to bring them in here?'

'Oh please.' She twisted up her hair and skewered it with a pencil. 'Sol, I think we should keep the hot air system and upgrade the boiler. It seems such a shame to pull up the floorboards and screw rads to the wall.'

Sat at the desk, he gazed at a photograph as she stood behind him. His fingers closed around her hand that lay on his shoulder, working up the courage to say two little words, two separate words to complete his dream. And just when he opened his mouth to utter gently those two little words, the door flew open and the moment had gone. Kern had come home.

For long seconds they talked over each other, smiling, excited and evidently glad to see one another. It was against such a long-established background of friendship that Tuesday offered them privacy and left them alone.

'Where is Hugh?' Monday asked pouring his friend a coffee. 'Did you manage to get hold of Nigel Friday?'

'Yes, we got hold of him. He wanted to see Week's Work so Hugh took him to his place and then he's coming here.' Kern settled down in the armchair with his coffee, crossed his legs, grinning from ear to ear. 'There we were up some bloody mountain freezing our balls off on a Yak, hardly any oxygen when this big sod covered in fur came rattling down a slope. I thought this is it, the abominable snowman.' His chuckle was infectious. 'It wasn't him. Good job too because Hugh would've paid for four seats on the plane. Anyway, we got led to a Monastery, at least it looked a bit holy and there's this guy peeping through a bloody huge telescope. Hugh said, that's the guy we need and unless you see him you will never believe he's a man of the cloth. So we told our story then all at once he grabs his bicycle clips and said time is crucial if we are to get there by Saturday.'

'Does he want to speak to Judge Week?'

Kern shrugged. 'He never mentioned a damn thing after that. How have things been?'

'Not too bad. I woke on a Saturday and unpredictably the tribe was around. Week passed a ruling and ordered them to stay. Since then, we have had a number of small fires in the court room, nothing too serious but a little unsettling.'

'I thought I could smell burnt wood. The drive looks good. How did the roofing go?'

'Izzy fitted solar panels. Want to see them?'

'Sure. So, it's Izzy now and not the Miss Know-it-all?'

Monday remained silent as he walked on.

'Did you get any backlash from Angela?'

'Not a thing.'

'George telephoned when you were in noddy land. I told him you were away on business. So has she left your flat?'

'Let sleeping dogs lie. When I'm ready I shall get Hugh on the case.'

'Did you find out who popped off your old man?'

Monday hated the deception but he had to tell Kern it was Judge Week. There was a quick exchange of glances before they ambled up the narrow staircase and set foot into a scudding swoop of cold air. Here, under the one chime bell they turned their backs to the wind, cupped their hands and lit cigarettes readying for classified conversation.

'How serious are you with Flour?' And Monday knew it was serious the moment Kern sent his eyes in another direction. 'Look, for what it's worth, I would dearly like to find a way of keeping the tribe here. If we can separate them from the interlopers there's no reason why you can't have a relationship with a ghost.'

Kern raised his brows. 'Are you off your sodding rocker or what? While I grow old, she stays the same, yeah? Apart from that little hiccup, she's sixteen years my junior.'

'You forget she is actually well over one hundred and fifty years old.'

Kern inhaled nicotine deep into his lungs and frustratingly exhaled. 'Oh man, I can't get her out of my head. On the road, in the plane, even up a sodding mountain, she did something with my brain. Once this is settled, things will get back to normal. Meanwhile, there's no harm done between the sheets.'

'Izzy would think otherwise.'

'Well, what do you think?'

'I think you're in deep shit.' And as Monday said it, he wondered if he was in deep shit too. 'Before last night I kept telling myself it doesn't matter about her past, that whatever she concealed couldn't possibly interfere with our relationship. Yet after we made love, she lay in my arms and said nothing at all. I could feel her thinking about us as though she was trying to balance some sort of loyalty. Am I making any sense?'

'I see, so you finally cracked her nut or rather she cracked yours. How did it come about?'

'Why do you ask?'

'Just being nosey, had the feeling she was beyond reach. Maybe she's got a husband and a kid. She makes out the money isn't important but maybe it is. Maybe the kid needs a major operation…loads of maybes. Unless you ask, you're never going to know, are you?'

'I have asked a couple of times but I'm afraid if I keep asking it might push her away.'

'Or afraid you won't like the truth. In my experience, there are two reasons why women keep secrets. The first, and most popular is that they're hiding a shameful past. Izabo doesn't give me that impression, so that leaves reason number two. And reason number two is not what you want to hear.' Kern flicked his cigarette to the wind and watched it travel across the roof, rolling over the eaves. 'You think she loves you but in reality, she loves someone else, so that means you're on the rebound, yeah? Did she ever mention another guy?'

Monday remained silent which in itself answered Kern's question.

'Keep it light, my man. Play it by ear. If this thing goes according to Nigel, you're going to be a very rich man, a good catch, yeah? And look at you. Lost a bit of weight, I see. Even the grey makes you look distinguished.'

'She gave me very little choice. It was either fight against her will or attach to her will. But I can't say it was unpleasant. I enjoyed working outside. We all mucked in. You know, some of the interlopers were pretty good. We just have a few nasties.'

'Is the head count still the same?'

'Yes, still the same. This Nigel Friday, what does he do exactly?'

'Not sure how he fits into the church but basically, he's a cosmologist. Damn interesting guy. Hugh reckons he has a sixth sense, literally a sixth sense. For instance, I'm squashed in the back of a taxi with the two other guys on our way from Heathrow, yeah? No two guesses as to what I'm thinking about. Mike, he said, you cannot marry a spirit. Can you believe that? Anyway, you'll like him. It's bloody cold up here. By the way the panels look good. Have you got electricity?'

To a shake of the head, Monday cuffed Kern on the shoulder and both men travelled downstairs to greet Nigel Friday, an absent-minded catholic priest and unconventional dresser. He wore a tunic of many colours under which a pair of black trousers and bicycle clips, his face was ruggedly fetching, a thick moustache hung over cherry pink lips and he smiled with a mouthful of teeth. Looking like a Christian Knight without armour, Friday's handshake was strong.

'Walk with me, Solomon Monday. I need to see the lake.'

As they fell into step, Monday asked, 'Why are you wearing bicycle clips?'

'Why do you think?'

'Because you biked here?'

'It's good you have a sense of humour; you will need it. Tell me about your past experience and leave no stone unturned.'

'Not much to tell, really. I was transported back in time. There were kids mucking about in the woods, instead of a lake there was a cemetery of sorts, lots of wooden crosses with names but I was unable to read them. I saw empty gallows and heard the bell toll.'

'Did you gather the time of day?'

'Well, that's a bit fuzzy. One minute I was by a frozen lake under a bright moon watching my Father strung up by the neck then it was daylight of sorts. I could see things very clearly but most certainly it became dark when something or someone grabbed my ankles and started to drag me down.'

'During your period of fever, did you experience any visions?'

'Yes, visions of going under. Prior to that, I spoke to Judge Week. He said no man has more confidence in another than I have in you. And no man will render more justice than I. And he also intimated he would be unable to distinguish the marks.'

'How so?'

'He spoke of his Work as a gathering of statistics rather than a morbid collection of hangings.'

'Never let your conscious override your subconscious.'

Steadily they worked through the silver grasses as the spiteful wind alternated its currents, snatching dry leaves in a merry-go-round before sinking to a pile on the ground. Then at the lake, Friday removed a pair of yellow tinted glasses from his trouser pocket and put them on his prominent nose as though the daylight was too sensitive for his screwed-up eyes. He remained quiet and still while Monday shuddered in the cold unsure if his leg was twitching with unease or if the weather was having an equally pernicious effect.

'Here is where it will happen,' announced Friday.

'What will happen?'

'The invasion of the body snatchers.' Friday roared with laughter. 'Have patience, Solomon. All is revealed by good Friday.'

Kern was right, thought Monday. This priest of many colours was certainly different, bold, charismatic and eccentric as most around him were. However, this did not explain the bicycle clips.

'So why are you wearing them?'

'Do your ankles feel cold?'

It required no reply.

Once Friday had his fill of the lake, they retired to the courtroom. As he scanned the walls, Monday scanned scorched benches, nothing that could not be rectified with a little sanding and some love.

'I would like to speak to those who require their marks,' said Friday but not directly at Monday. 'Perhaps if you care to show yourselves, we can have a nice little chat about your predicament.' His voice became mellow with reason. 'Supposing we start with Doolally…I hear you have a fondness for Solomon Monday. Would he be here to lay a trap?'

There was nothing, so Monday called out. 'Doolally, you can trust this man. His name is Nigel Friday, a descendant of Week.'

'No, my friend.' Friday quickly corrected. 'My name is to be found in the Good Friday scriptures, not in the history of Judge Week.'

'So how did Hugh come across you?'

'Why, the internet, of course.' Friday smiled and spoke into the room again. 'Solomon speaks the truth; I can be trusted.'

'Trust is to be earned,' said Ned. 'Take off your habit and let us see your trust.'

Friday removed his glasses and passed them to Monday. There was no other shredding of items or clothing, which rather surprised him. So he looked through the yellow lenses and gasped at a different perspective, a grim perspective of torment and death. But the sight of the afterlife did not disturb him. It only enhanced the magnitude of their calamity. They were a sorry sight, increasing his anxiety to make good on his promise.

When Ned manifested, the soothing talker, he paced round Friday who remained content to linger in his own spot. 'We have no faith in the church.'

Friday seized the conversational lifeline. 'Neither do I, which leaves us with another alternative, faith in the Almighty.'

While Monday settled himself on a scorched bench, he wondered why God had never been in his vocabulary much less angels and demons. He kind of slipped into a serene detachment until it seemed either forgotten or never known at all. But yes, God was a good starting point. It enabled Friday to establish a rapport and delve into their hopes and aspirations, their grievances and mishaps, and all such manner of things that might just serve more clues.

And when Friday had gained their confidence, Monday left them and went in search of Tuesday. The smell of burnt wood lessened out here. Behind him, Palfrey was catching up.

'Sir, Mr Crookshank is in the library.'

'Where is madam?'

'She went to the city to do some shopping. Mr Kern, dare I say is otherwise occupied in his room with Flour.'

Monday gave a wan smile and ducked into the library. 'Hugh,' he said closing the door. 'Good to see you. Nigel is having a chat with the tribe. Fancy a scotch?'

Crookshank held up his glass, half full. 'Palfrey tells me the courtroom has become a target for vandalism.'

'Nothing we cannot handle.'

'Never would have believed Week hung your father.'

'Life is full of surprises, Hugh. Cheers.' Monday sat behind his desk and wrenched open a drawer. 'We took some photographs of-'

'Save me the platitudes, Sol.' Crookshank floated a note, his eyes directing their challenge straight at Monday. 'Try burning incriminating evidence, not stuff it down the side of this seat.'

Alarmed, Monday spoke out in quiet emotion. 'I'm really sorry, Hugh. For fear of others overhearing, I wrote the note to Izzy. Why? Well, I suppose I wanted to share the information with my business partner. I promised her honesty and honesty was given when she asked.'

'Then offer me the same courtesy. What happened that night?'

'One boy, his mother and the sins of his Father were heaped upon his shoulders that night. To me it was just a bible, something to read, nothing important while those around were waiting for something to happen. My Father was furious, and Mother, well, she stepped in only to feel the full force of his anger. Your father and Jeremy only did what was necessary, not just for Gallows Humour but for my Mother. There was no ritual or hesitancy. He was dragged by his heels along the path towards the oaks and I watched her tie the noose round his neck. The rope was held by two decent men until the legs stopped moving. And next, I was transported further back in time to see how the gallows operated.'

'Did you see Judge Week?'

'He was not in that courtroom, not when I was a lad, but if he was, I certainly never saw him, not before or during the hanging. The only regret is to have missed Mother's last moments. I am certain she would have told me. If it's any consolation, had I been in your father's shoes I would have done no differently.'

'And neither would I.' Crookshank smiled and brought out his gold cigarette case. 'Know thyself, as the great Socrates said.'

'I am curious. This Nigel Friday, he seems to be in touch with the afterlife so why bring him here now, why not before when Jeremy was alive?'

'We never had Week's Work.'

Both men stood when Friday walked in. 'Sit, sit,' he said with considerable buoyancy and fed his nose towards the scotch. 'My, they are interesting characters. Wish that I could take them back with me.'

'Have you ever encountered anything like this before?' Monday asked.

'Many times over, my friend, many times over…I was born with a gift and diagnosed with dementia until Sister Francis decided I was touched by God.' Friday mopped sweat from his noble brow and stood looking at the window. 'This land is flat as a pancake. Remove your surrounding trees and the view becomes infinitum. There are no boundaries in this universe, Solomon. Man pats himself proudly on the back for taking a step on the moon, yet his arrogant eyes remain closed to the monsters he leaves behind.' Friday grimaced in disgust and glanced back at Monday. 'Conceit, a sense of indifference and certain self-righteousness are inbred characteristics of man. Yet if they were to stretch their minds and look at life counterbalanced with all things in our universe then what do we have?'

'A positive and negative?'

'I shall give you six out of ten for trying. No, what you have is substance and non-substance. These are two matters that coexist. Let's say a man going about his daily chores has a tingling sensation at the back of his neck, something tells him not to go to the office. Subsequently he learns the office blew up that day, but what does he say? That was a bit of luck rather than explore why he had the feeling in the first place. Are you with me so far?'

'Yes, I do believe I am.'

'Good,' Friday said returning to his view. 'Now we come to the tricky part. Sometimes substance and non-substance collide. Why? Well we can hypothesize all day and make of it as you will but the important thing to remember is that in all things there is intelligent direction.' Friday poured himself another drink and topped up two other glasses. 'We all leave our mark, Solomon, the traces of our efforts, good or bad, to be harnessed like those solar panels harness the sun. A buttercup in a field is no less important than the Pope in his refinery.'

'And where does God fit into all this?'

'Throw away your churlish thoughts, Solomon Monday. God is a word for man to bandy about and frighten people into submission for sake of themselves. The id, as I like to call it, not so much the unconscious source of primitive biological instincts and urges but Intelligent Direction. Unfortunately, man is still finding his brains. But this will never do. We have a problem to resolve and solve it we must. What is for tea?'

'Have you met Flour?'

'I have not. I have been told she bakes wonderful cakes.'

They moved quickly into the dining room and then down into the kitchen where Palfrey emerged from the larder still cloaked in his butler's uniform.

'Sir, have we adopted a disguise?'

Monday removed Friday's glasses. 'You can see another world, Palfrey. But be warned, the world is not as pretty as you think. Where is Flour?'

'Otherwise engaged with Mr Kern. Do you wish me to get her?'

Friday seated himself at the table. 'We wish to taste her cakes.'

As Palfrey brought to the table lemon meringue, jam roly-poly and the traditional fruit cake, Friday went on to explain how the glasses work. 'They absorb light in a narrow band of the spectrum, which is why I can see what is normally distorted to the naked eye. A simple idea, you may think. Not so. Impregnated into the glass is an economic element, Praseodymium. The name is derived from the Greek prasios didymos, meaning green twins. It gives glass a pure yellow colour and it is that particular purity to separate the two worlds in my mind's eye. Welders use their goggles made of this stuff but they do not see what we see. Now tell me why that is, Solomon?'

'Is it because we wear no blinkers?'

'You have it in one. People have an extraordinary curiosity for the unknown and yet they are afraid of it. Confront them with the truth and they will deny it but secretly yearn for it.'

'Nigel, do you have a greater view of our problem?' Crookshank asked.

'I most certainly do. Palfrey, let me try a slice of jam roly-poly. That's a good fellow. His Work must be returned to him, only he can administer justice.' Friday held up his hand to forestall Monday. 'He will be able to distinguish their marks.'

'Why did he not say?'

'He did not say because he did not correlate. You must try to remember, Solomon we are in the hands of greater forces. Do you think it was him to send you back to the past? No, my friend, it was that which I spoke of earlier. The likes of the dead and the likes of the living are agents that are directed for the greater good.'

Monday dropped his cake fork to the plate. 'What exactly will happen when the book is passed over? Do they return to their consigned places at the bottom of that lake? This is their home. It was promised.'

It meant little to the colourful Friday. 'Why do you think Judge Week allowed you to guard his Work all these years? For that is what you were theoretically doing when you stole it? It was you he chose to toll the bell and summon his presence. The man was falling prey to the vicissitudes of fate and the frailties of humankind when he made his deathbed promise. But nothing, however, will alter their predicted course. Six shall have their wishes fulfilled. The rest shall trade with the dark at cost to their souls. Do we have any custard?' On a single command a jug of warm custard was poured over the jam roly-poly. 'Glad you could join us, Flour. Do you wish to communicate?'

She came into view shaking her head and talk subsided.

Monday rose to his feet and went to an open barred window. He was in deep thought, the words of Friday sinking in and his own foolishness for thinking he could hold on to the tribe. 'Explain to me about the bell?'

'The bell was tolled to announce a hanging, and though you did not see a hanging it represented an action to take.'

'Presumably I ring this bell on a Saturday if I am to summon Judge Week?'

'And how fortunate today's the day.' Friday turned in his seat and glared at Monday. 'Tonight there will be a full moon. Your energy will be at its strongest. When shall I meet your Miss Tuesday?'

'When she comes back from shopping, I presume.' Monday squinted at his watch. 'Palfrey, did she say how long she would be?'

'No, sir.'

Again talk subsided then reinvigorated when Kern walked in rubbing his hands. 'Scrummy, cake for tea. Can I have a slice of lemon meringue, Flour?'

'So,' Monday threw in, 'your unconventional preaching must cause concern for your parishioners, or even the church.'

'Squeamish parishioners might prefer to put their faith in the vagaries of storytellers rather than risk being exposed to hell.'

'So this id as you call it, Intelligent Direction from where?'

'Not aliens, Solomon. The Almighty is everything, neither man nor beast but in all things.' Friday held up his plate for another helping. 'I make no apologies for intelligence. Unless one has a brain tumour, there is no defence.'

'The sea squirt eats its brain,' said Kern, smiling at the laughter he had generated. 'Palfrey took a long-winded approach to inform Sol that should he abscond from Gallows Humour without passing the pen, his heart is left behind. Makes you wonder who would have first call.'

'What do you think, Palfrey?' Monday asked. 'Do hearts go up for auction?'

'If they do, sir, no doubt Doolally would be your highest bidder.'

LEAVING FRIENDS BEHIND

On the front steps Monday checked his watch again. Darkness was half an hour away. He slipped a cigarette between his lips and lit it. Where was Izabo Tuesday? Shopping? Yes, shopping then his relief was quickly crowded by other doubts. Why was she taking so long? Was she meeting another man?

His eyes left the drive and he cocked his head sideways in Doolally's direction, emerging from the hallway. She pulled from her bag a bone china cup and saucer, except that the cup and its handle had parted company, and the saucer lay in two pieces.

'Yew can get these riveted,' she said.

'Better still, you can stop breaking things. Why do you break things, Doolally? Are you just naturally clumsy or do you enjoy it?'

'See, it's like this. The sink is higher than me elbows so when I lifts them, they slip from me hands but at least I save the pieces.'

'Why not use a box?'

'How can I wash up in a box?'

Monday chuckled. Oh he was going to miss her. She sometimes tortured his patience and exhausted his nerves but she was that edge of gold when he needed her most.

'It will do yew no good standing there.' Her head rolled to the staircase. 'Up there she is with her samples.'

'When did she return?'

'She never left.'

His stare returned to the drive. 'Do you want another week, Doolally?'

'Friday says yew must ring that bell and call Judge Week before midnight.' She hesitated but then tightened her lips. 'No good putting off what must be done.'

GALLOWS HUMOUR

As Monday wended his way to Tuesday's bedroom he tried to forget about the tribe. Why should he be sad? This is what they wanted. They were not his family, not in the true sense and although Kern's heart had been stolen by Flour it would soon return at the toll of a bell. And he, Solomon Monday, had much to be happy about. Beautiful Izabo Tuesday, Gallows Humour renovated, and a stack of money coming his way.

The four poster bed was surrounded by boxes and tools lay on the floor. Tuesday hid under a lighted candle scouring samples and lifted her head when Monday walked in.

'Izzy,' he astounded. 'Why have you kept away? And what are all these boxes doing in your bedroom?'

'That's the equipment to wire up to the solar panels.'

She rolled off the mattress placing the candle on the bedside cabinet and held out her arms towards him as he went to her.

'When was the last time I told you how beautiful you looked?'

'Never but the thought was there. Sol, what did Father Friday have to say?'

'All I have to do is ring the bell tonight for that is when I am supposed to be at my strongest, wait for Week to turn up, return his Work and he does the rest. He asked where you were. In fact he took a great interest.'

'Did he?'

'Izzy, why stay up here? He was a very interesting man to talk to. He had these special glasses. I was amazed when I looked through them.'

She moved to the window and stood there looking out to the purple sky. 'Sol,' she said. 'Now things are virtually sewn up, tomorrow I must leave.'

'Leave?' He went to her side and gently prized the head round and began to doubt he would ever see the pools of those sapphire eyes again. 'Izzy, tell me, please tell me what we did last night meant something.'

'Oh, Sol, it meant everything. I tried. I really tried to keep our relationship on a business level. It wasn't meant to happen.'

'But it did happen. Is there another man?'

'If only it was that simple.'

'Then tell me why you want to leave, put me out of my misery.'

'I would put you into your misery.' She turned into the room, rested the back of her head against the cool glass as though she had rediscovered her memories. 'It wasn't meant to happen between us, Sol. I know you find it hard to accept but I have no choice.'

'So? You want to leave because you don't think I can take the truth. Nothing you can say will alter my feelings. I can make you happy, Izzy. Marry me, or not. Are you married? No strike that. If you are, then live with me. I love-
'

'Shhh,' she uttered, placing a finger to his lips. 'Do you remember what I once said, that fate rarely calls upon us at a moment of our choosing?'

'But we can make our own fate.'

'You once asked if I was flesh or spirit. I am sorrow, my love.' Taking hold of his hand, she placed it against her unbeating heart. 'If this had a rhythm, I would gladly offer it to you. If I could cry, I would cry for eternity. I am what I am. I cannot change what I am.'

A horrible sickness swept over him. He blinked a lot, swallowed hard, his eyes felt wet and he did not want them to be nor did he want his voice to wobble when he said, 'This yellow brick road, is it for phantom traffic?'

'Sol, you really are hopeless at times. I have no future to give. You have a future to live for Gallows Humour. Another woman can bare your seeds, can make this place a happy home, everything you have ever wanted will be possible.'

'No! There is no other woman. It has to be you.' Suddenly he grew angry at himself, angry he had not seen this before and pulled away. 'You held food to your mouth but never ate, tricked me into believing you were flesh and blood! It was you all along, you who took my suitcase from the hotel, you who bought the ring, you who chose my wardrobe. It was no dream in my fevered state. You were there making love to me and do not dare to deny these things.'

'No, I cannot deny them.'

'Christ! I was suckered in by Hugh. He knew, didn't he? He tried to tell me without breaking a confidence, reality is not always quantifiable. What? So there you were, jumped out of a taxi playing your part as a runner up to Gallows Humour when you knew bloody well you couldn't have it!'

'Sol, I was-'

'Do not Sol me with that face of yours! I remember what you said on the lake, making love would only be superficial.'

'I was wrong, I was wrong. Oh, Sol I was so wrong. Please forgive me. Gallows Humour is so much more and you needed to be shown that. It wasn't meant to happen. Whatever my face reveals is how I feel and I am so, so, so very sorry.'

'But why, Izzy? Are you one of the tribe?'

She shook her head. 'Oh it's such a long story. It was an accident, just a damn stupid accident but it was fate. I know that now. My presence caused you to stay and fulfil your promise.'

He stared at her, at this woman as if she was not responsible for what she had done, this woman who had so casually picked up his life, shaken free what she wanted from it, and cast the rest aside. 'I can't handle this.' He strode to the door and stopped, running a flat hand across his forehead then through his thick black hair, willing himself to leave but wanting to stay. 'Why do you have to go if you're not one of the tribe?'

'I don't belong in your world.'

He turned round. 'Stay. Stay with me, Izzy. We can work something out.'

'Sol, I know you find this hard to comprehend, but I have no choice. I am being pulled to my grave. I felt it the moment Friday walked in. You have to let me go. There's so little time and we stand in discord rather than harmony. Please, give me your love and understanding before the bell tolls. It isn't superficial, not for me.' She held out her arms. 'Please, Sol. Give me your love. Let our parting be a happy one.'

This was the closest thing to crazy he had ever been. As he held the crying into his throat, wordlessly, he swept her up in his arms and gently lowered her to the bed. He was not a man who wept lightly, would always keep a steel grip on his emotions for fear of damaging his image but he struggled to keep the tears at bay. A rush of wetness streaked down his face. The pain was clawing at his gut as he took her passionately, almost brutally in a nightmare maze of longing, hanging on, clutching at hope. But without blood, thick and dark, hope collapsed through the skin of her light armour, reunited only in temporary happiness, as they had been last night, and yet it was a lifetime.

It was approaching midnight when she diminished in his arms, ebbing away like air escaping from a balloon, deflation until there was nothing left of Izabo Tuesday. He was in that moment now of numb acceptance, a stranger that had his arms, his legs, his eyes, a restless stranger who must keep his promise.

Silently he walked along a dark slim corridor towards the bell tower, would not be diverted, his mission, his secret. Up there he had once found a future, now he wondered if he had a future at all. He loitered, surveying the land under a full moon, the wind playing spitefully upon his face, urging him to swing that colossus above him and make it chime. Never had he felt so bereft. Nothing remained as it was. Everything came to an end.

Acceptance now, he nodded to himself and reached for the knotted cord. One, two, three, and momentum gained, the toll of the bell resonated far and wide and drowned all other sound out. And the greater the sound, the greater his physical hunger grew for a conclusion, an end to their sorrow, an end to his in the fixed belief that substance and non-substance would part friendly company and the pain would go away.

Silhouetted against the lake, Judge Culver Week appeared in his regalia and beckoned Monday to come forth with the book. Then a hand clamped firm on his shoulder.

'Be in no doubt, my friend.' Friday offered Week's Work. 'This is his time to make amends, to fulfil his promise.'

'You knew. You knew about Izabo.'

'Would it have made a difference to know sooner? Consider the anguish of putting off the inevitable, the mind searching for respite when there can be no respite. Go now, there should be no delay. Midnight opens the door to Sunday and others will try to come forth. This must not happen.'

With Week's Work, Monday continued alone, in his thoughts believing all books had a destiny, a life of their own. On his travels he passed Kern and Palfrey, said not a word and carried on in solemn silence to the open aspects of a lake which was shrouded in a grey veil, and the tribe who had gathered there. He moved among them. Some smiled, others stood confused at the prospect of liberty, their horizons and hopes confined by the limits of their haunted grounds. They inhabited a world in which there was none. Again he thought of beautiful Tuesday, felt the creeping sickness at her loss but she was not there, was not one of them.

'Be of good cheer for us, Solomon Monday.' Ned smiled. 'Better to go of our choosing than to tarry and be torn apart.'

Others drew close around him, their fragile dignities and beliefs that bad things were behind them as they listened to Judge Week, to the drifting echoes of his ecumenical words preparing a path for their departure, down deep, deep in a watery grave.

'For my judgement I am sincerely sorry.' Week continued, now in full possession of his senses, acted with an innate sense of theatre and raised his Work for the tribe to see. 'Your marks will be given to pursue your own happiness. To leave Gallows Humour, I will considerably take from my pleasure in serving here, left with Solomon Monday.'

As Week tore pages from his Work, they took their mark, and one by one they took their path into the lake, the whispers of goodbyes and the exchanging of an appreciative glance before waters engulfed them. The scene would move any mortal. Monday wept for the tribe he had lost, for the love he once shared with Izabo Tuesday and for a building that had now been consigned to the twenty-first century.

But within those pages, were guilty marks which Judge Week tore a good few out and spoke their names softly as the flames extinguished their marks, turned to ashes and ashes turned on the wind. For they were the ones already consigned to their places.

'Weep not, my kin.' Week looked up at Monday. 'You are in more need of a nurse than a wife.' He passed over his Work, a book far thinner than before. 'Not all have been consigned to their places; some have escaped Gallows Humour. Know them their marks, Solomon Monday and do as I have done should they return.' Then he opened to a page which appeared to be of considerable interest and struck a finger on that mark. 'She will return, a most foul and abhorrent woman. When the time comes, draw strength from your dark side and rid this evil. May God go with you and help you.'

The old Judge Culver Week walked into the hands of an ill-humoured lake, the waters bubbled then gradually calmed when no more could be seen of him. There was no chance that any of these souls would be seen again. But Monday could not help but feel a small sense of accomplishment, a rare moment of joy in his otherwise woeful life. They had made it.

The ravenous and freezing night lingered, seemingly without end until finally the darkness slowly retreated from the library. Monday was slumped over the desk with a photograph of Tuesday clutched firm in his hand, sadly crumpled with love. To the other side of the room, Kern was flaccid in an armchair with his own photograph to cherish and an empty rum bottle that rolled to the floor when Palfrey staggered in with a pot of coffee. His slippered feet dragged across the varnished wood and the tray clashed heavy on the desk.

Monday stirred and lifted his eyes; his mouth tasted somewhere between Gorgonzola cheese and dry biscuits. As he wiped his face from forehead to chin it was all unravelling in a hurry and directed a glance at Palfrey. 'I have a question.'

Palfrey nodded and drunk his black coffee.

'When I asked you before about Miss Tuesday, you were unable to say, not for the want of disloyalty. When I asked Hugh, he was in client confidentiality mode. Bearing in mind I have an acute hole where my heart should be, don't you think I deserve an explanation?'

Resembling not so much an efficient butler as a sorrowful body in a dressing gown, Palfrey set his empty cup aside and settled in a chair, his hands clasped, his grey head bowed. He had every reason to anticipate this question.

'My name is Cope Tuesday. Izabo was my only child. Fate, serendipity, call it what you will, at the time of making an application for this post I had not the clue of my ancestor. As Trustee to the estate, Hugh informed me in his office I would be in line to sign the register should a Monday fail to do so but I was quite content to serve Jeremy, make new friends and a life here. The tribe, as you call them had no knowledge of this. I was Palfrey, the butler and without a word of a lie, used my middle name. Hugh would occasionally give me news of my daughter, sometimes a photograph. Then one day, out of the blue she telephoned.' He looked up and smiled. 'Dad, she said, it's about time we met up.'

'Are you a builder?' Monday asked and clarified. 'Before you came here, were you a builder?'

'I was a bricklayer by trade. I have no idea why I never followed in my parent's footsteps but I built up a good business at cost to my marriage. Izabo believed I regretted having a girl but in truth she was young and loved her mother and her mother loved another man.' Palfrey heaved a sigh. Perhaps this was more difficult for him than Monday thought. 'If I had not told her about Gallows Humour, she would be alive today of that I am certain. She came here four years ago, a brief visit where we agreed with Hugh not to disclose the nature of our blood ties. Her visits became more frequent, and how she loved those poor souls. She never told me she had seen the riddle. I think she was hoping to solve the mystery so we could own Gallows Humour and work together.' Again Palfrey groaned. 'There was a terrible summer's storm last year. Lightening hit the bell tower and the quoin crashed through the roof. Water was flooding in. We thought we could weigh a tarpaulin over the ridge so we climbed on the roof. Her harness was faulty, and I was too slow to catch her fall. I held her dead body in my arms, then I glanced round thinking it was Jeremy but it was her and she said, no worries, dad, look at me, I seem to be one of them.'

The room fell terribly silent and sorrowful. Palfrey could not afford the pause, could not let the lethargy of his own sorrow pin him down.

'I took her lifeless form into my arms and together we buried the body in the woods while the ground was soaked, easy to dig. And everything changed. There were no more houses for her to build, only a plan to safeguard the secret. Unlike the others, she had the ability to go beyond the gates and went to Italy to see her mother. Izabo felt it was a good exercise in order to cut ties with her mother. Then we all know what happened upon the third day of your arrival. Hugh asked me if I would take up the pen. For obvious reasons I declined and said Izabo would like to use her persuasion in order to keep you here. Hugh was against it. He was concerned about the repercussions but in a way, he was duty bound. We all had our secrets, Sol and all of them sincere. I tried very hard to encourage her to leave this world after you refused to pass the pen but my daughter's stubbornness is comparable to your own. She heard your argument with Angela and viewed it as a God send. Every step she took, I played my part yet I did not know about that riddle. I was just as taken aback as you were.'

'Did she know about the clause in the register?'

'We both did. Aided by Woody, he slipped it in very neatly and Ned provided the impetus to make you see sense. Whatever part I played, I played with sincerity, Sol. Izabo informed me she had this feeling her accident was by design, that it had to be you to own Gallows Humour. She said her time will come when you have fulfilled your promise but such sorrow followed. She was in love with you as much as you were in love with her.'

Monday smiled to himself. 'She tried very hard to get me to pass the pen. Her capacity to understand me more than myself just makes it all the sadder. I once told her I would be grateful just to have loved and lost than not love at all. Only now do I understand the pain of losing a mate, because she was my mate in every sense of the word. It's not the same as losing a mother. Will you show me where she is buried?'

Beyond the silver grasses at the spur end of the lake, the branches of two tree species moved on the northerly breeze. It was the same gusty wind that carried the bell's toll across the land. Monday crouched down on one knee and placed a flat hand on a small mound of earth where purple clump-forming hardy perennials grew. Palfrey stooped to pick one and held it to his nose. Kern moved into position alongside.

'So much happened in a year for both of us,' Monday said. 'And there was our commonality. I would like to think she feels no pain, not where she is now.' He stood and glanced back at the house with sorrowful eyes. 'Palfrey, what am I to do? Everything feels so empty and lost.'

'I am willing to stay on and help to service your requirements.'

'This is your home, Palfrey. No, strike that. You own half the estate.'

'I did not sign the register.'

'Bollocks to signing the register. Mike, what are your plans? Do you want to finish your story here and come in on a business opportunity, the three of us, you, me and Palfrey? Let's turn the woods into a place for screaming kids with screaming parents.'

Suddenly Monday felt he had something to live for and walked on with enthusiasm leaving the others trailing behind to consider his proposition. But he had forgotten the challenging words of Judge Culver Week.

'Palfrey, where is the frying pan?' The colourful Friday had been waiting for their return. 'Hugh is at home doing what we should be doing, eating breakfast.' Clashing the pan on the range, three others were reliant on his cooking techniques. 'Tell me, my good friends, what you will do without a cook to feed your bellies?'

'We need staff.' Palfrey admitted and cracked a few eggs in a bowl. 'Are you staying?'

'I am a cosmologist not a cook. Hugh will take me to the airport to leave Monday in thoughts of Tuesday.' Friday paused for comments but Monday remained listening. 'You cannot have what is not flesh and blood.'

'To me she was flesh and blood.'

'You are not the only one who suffers with loss? Look at Michael. His heart bleeds too. Is that not so, my friend?'

'Hey, I'll get over it.'

'So bravely said, and you, Palfrey, do not blame yourself for her accident. She had a part to play as do we all. Look at their faces, Solomon Monday and find enough resolve to swallow your hurt until you hurt no more.' Friday tossed his yellow tinted glasses into Monday's lap. 'Keep them. You will be grateful one day. In this time of uncertainty, it is the teacher, not the pupil, who is master.'

Kern met his brows. 'Who made you master?'

'Let us hope not, Michael. For certain we will be good and lost. A higher authority than the likes of me guides all of us on a challenging but ultimately deeply satisfying journey. My principal hope is that as Solomon's journey progresses to the summit of understanding, he will experience the deep joy of illumination that the intelligent Almighty alone provides.'

'I was never baptized,' Kern admitted. 'The only church I ever entered was St. Paul's to test out its whispering gallery. He never picked up the receiver.'

'Perhaps you dialled the wrong number.'

All around Monday there was life but no life at all. He remembered entering the house with a fair degree of optimism but that optimism was difficult to maintain when there was so much else to remind him of his losses.

And the weather grew cold in his time of loneliness. Bare trees stuck uselessly out of the earth like stiffened arms jabbed accusingly at the sky. Sometimes he would bury himself among the electricians now forging ahead in a cruel and merciless time, and sometimes he would don on those yellow glasses. If nothing else it gave a measure of hope.

Then, for reasons only Monday knew, he sat at the dining room table with a scarf round his neck carefully arranging the broken vase like some unknown bits from an engine. Perhaps it was going to be a comprehensive exercise, one to teach him a lesson.

'Brrrrr.' Kern walked in flinging his arms back and forth. 'How long does it take to get a boiler going?'

'That boiler,' Monday left those two words hanging in the air like a cloud of cigarette smoke before adding, 'had to be manufactured. What did you make of the cook?'

'Her puff pastry sunk in the middle.'

'Perhaps you should advertise for live-in staff. Then we can go national. Or international as the case may be.'

'And where do we put them? Nine times out of ten they will have families. This bit goes there.'

Monday slapped his hand. 'I know where the pieces go. Do a collective advert, list the openings, bullet point the requirements. Single, age immaterial, sense of humour, hard working and so on…and get me a coffee.'

'Get your own. What did the guy say about Woody's drawings?'

'Five hundred and fifty-eight thousand excluding VAT.'

'You're shitting me! That's daylight robbery.'

'Know of any other company capable of doing it?'

Kern pulled out a chair. 'Sol, are you sure this is what you want? Don't get me wrong. I'm grateful to have the opportunity, but you and Palfrey don't need to work. You can both happily live off your fortune for the rest of your lives.'

'And do what all day?' He peeled off his rimless spectacles and lit a cigarette then tossed the packet at Kern. 'Here or abroad, the world has become smaller, and life is inherently unfair. We all need challenges, Mike. If nothing else it stops the brain cells from clogging up. Anyway, it's only for six months of the year and it will keep us in touch with the outside world, not that I wish to be reminded we get taxed so heavily, soon there will be nothing to tax.'

'I sort of get the feeling your heart isn't exactly in it.'

Monday let out a huge sigh. 'I miss her, Mike. I miss Doolally. I miss what we had, all of it. How do you find another life comparable?'

'You can't and that's the problem. But hell, life has to go on. Me, well, I just made a rod for my own back. Inside, yeah, I knew I was getting in deep and had this crazy notion things would get back to normal. But you, yeah…if Izabo had told you, would you have carried on?'

'Without doubt I wouldn't swap my time with her for anything. She was more real to me than any woman I had ever known. I loved her mind, her zest for life, her ability to challenge the rights and wrongs…everything really. And it must have been the same for you. Flour and Izabo were very much alike. The only difference, Flour knew how to cook.'

Kern quit smiling and bit his bottom lip then left to grieve alone.

Monday stared vacantly at those pieces, half forgotten where to place them, half forgotten his purpose and angrily knocked them to the floor. But he knew Kern was right. Life had to go on so he followed him out of the room. 'Mike,' he called out, jerking his head upstairs. 'Do you want a cup of tea?'

'Not half,' said the workers in unison.

In this now noisy, sunless shambles, Monday walked on and tripped over an empty paint can. To those who stood by, he said nothing. He just went to the kitchen, filled up the kettle and brought out the mugs. All his disquiet about messy renovations had finally come to fruition.

'This is intolerable,' Monday yelped when Palfrey showed his ruddy complexion. 'We have men crawling all over the damn place. No heating, no lighting and what's worse I can't differentiate between dry and wet walls.'

'Try using the light switches.'

'Huh?' Monday looked up. 'Damn, when did that happen?'

'Your mind is in two places.' Palfrey laid a calm hand on his arm. 'I told you, I shall handle the work. How did it go with Greenway?'

'He's taking us for a ride but as I said to Mike, no other company has the experience, especially where kids are concerned. By the way, he's having difficulty in getting local labour. I thought a national ad would draw live-in staff. We have more than enough accommodation to house them all. Are you going to take one of the bedrooms?'

'No. I rather like my quarters close to the kitchen.' Palfrey poured out the teas, his brow rising and falling in unison. 'I think Mike is making a rod for his own back. Money is not an issue but he seems reluctant to spend it.'

'Look, he feels obliged to watch the pennies. He asked me if I was sure this is what we wanted and rather than give a direct answer I veered off and spoke about the tribe…you know he hasn't done much on his manuscript.'

'And you have twice postponed returning to London to sort out the mess in your flat. Are you going to sell or let it out?'

'Well thanks to Hugh, Angela has finally left the building. Not sure. Now Mike is selling up, he would have a place to stay when he goes to London. Maggie keeps telephoning him. I think he's lost heart.'

'Perhaps you should go, take Mike with you and encourage him to work on his story.'

That sounded good to Monday. 'Are you sure you can cope?'

Palfrey smiled and picked up the tray. 'Have you forgotten, Cope is my name.'

TRICK OR TREAT

Monday turned the key in the lock to his top floor apartment and apprehensively pushed wide the door anticipating the worst of Angela's doing. Instead, a musky fragrance hit his face and the mail sat flushed on the mat.

'Phew!' Kern said brushing by with his case. 'It smells like a brothel.'

Monday paused to light up a cigarette, picked up his post then toured the fluffy cushions on the corner leather suite, a new rug upon which a glass coffee table stood and a broad leaf plant sprouting to the ceiling. In his bedroom, the intimacy of objects, a framed photograph of his mother and his dressing gown neatly folded on a rattan chair which had recently undergone restoration. Again he breathed that same musky smell and followed its source to the bathroom. There, lodge next to the sink was a small bowl of scented oil. Was Angela trying to say sorry or was it a ruse to worm her way back into his life? He did not care either way.

'Fancy a scotch?'

Kern shook his head at the patio sliders. 'I always liked this place except for the Thames. It looks so bloody dirty.'

'It is bloody dirty.' Monday went to his side and observed the efforts of enthusiastic yachtsmen in their undersized vessels. 'Mike, do you mind if I ask a personal question?'

'Sure, fire away.'

'When you made love to Flour did it seem real?'

'Yeah, course it did. Why?'

'Izabo never cried when I last held her.'

'Right, and you think it was just one merry go round for them, yeah? It was clear from the beginning that my relationship with Flour had no life outside this particular time and space. So I greedily slaked my thirst and soon discovered something, that I was conscious of nothing else except the need to possess her. I never said goodbye, not the last minute stuff. She came to me and I pushed her away.'

Monday pinched a sideways glance. 'Why?'

'Because I couldn't handle it, that's why. I couldn't face the inevitable and now I could kick myself. Sure, we knew it would happen, but what else can you say other than the obvious. Perhaps she accepted her doom without complaint, as though some giant authority had ordered her there to receive it. But you know I like to believe things happen for a reason. Maybe I gave Flour something special to take with her. Who knows? She certainly gave me a different perspective on life.'

'There was so much I wanted to say to Izabo. There again, would it have mattered? What I find difficult to accept, why she had to go. I mean, it's not as if she was part of the tribe.'

'Hell, it's a no brainer, Sol. Who would inherit Gallows Humour after you've gone, yeah?'

'We could have adopted.'

'Practicalities, my man, practicalities…little Jimmy comes into puberty and wonders why his girlfriend looks older than his mother, yeah? So, okay, it will take a while before you find another Mrs Right but it's her that can give you the 4 x 4 and taking the kids to the zoo. So, if there's one lesson to take away from all this, is that we live in a world where technology grabs your identity and shoves it on the pile marked suckers.'

While Kern tried to be philosophical, Monday got dismayed and stared sombrely into his empty glass, still living by longing. On the train, he had hardly said a word to Kern and felt every mile taken was one mile further away from Izabo Tuesday. But if any man could lead him from the doldrums, it was Kern so he turned with a dark, amused smile and said, 'Want something to eat?'

'You do the shopping. I'm in the mood to be a sucker.'

Grabbing the keys off the hall stand, Monday proceeded down the lift and passed the concierge's daughter winding a ribbon round her finger like a yellow bandage.

'Where's your father?'

'Where?' she said and looked all around her. 'I dunno.'

Among tall buildings and glass towers, Monday was distracted by all the busy people darting back and forth, some smartly dressed with glum smiles and others possessed of qualities to appal the more grandiose of recent times. He watched a couple leaning over a railing, her hand in his and huddled close in dizzy cold weather. Next, a street cleaner whirred past, brushes spinning and skidding the tarmac, grit and glass and paper skipping up into its innards. It all seemed normal but alien.

Then Monday heard his name and blinked out of his distraction, focusing upon a discreet and skilful man from The Times. Ancient eyes and bushy brows helped to serve a face as severe as that on a Roman coin.

'I thought that was you,' George spoke again. 'What's with the grey sideburns?'

'It was the worry you gave me.' Monday laughed it off.

But the Burberry coat never smiled. 'Let's have a beer.'

'How's Terrance?' Monday asked as they fell into step.

'No idea. The silly bugger got drunk and pissed off to France with his brother. You left at the wrong time, Sol. With an election in the air all the main parties are claiming to be on the side of hard working families who play by the rules. Offer a referendum on the EU membership, come out against the theory of man-made global warming, declare war on political correctness and state that there will be zero immigration and that party will sweep in with a majority. As it is, the city sees a hung parliament, which doesn't do much for my shares.'

'There is no magic bullet for Cameron.' Monday pushed wide a glass door. 'The country is looking for a strong leader and responds well under pressure.'

'I'll get these,' said George snapping his fingers. 'Word is out for a three televised leaders' debate in the election campaign.'

They talked political madness for a full ten minutes where it became increasingly easy in urban life to ignore other faces reflecting off the mirrored bar. For Monday, all details were different and had to be rediscovered.

'So come on, Sol,' George ultimately asked, 'why engage in subterfuge?'

'Has Angela been cracking your nuts?' Monday caught the flicker of his eyes and knew he had guessed correctly. With the main drama still hovering it was going to take something special to bring the focus back on reality. 'No, George, seriously, the whole thing was taken out of context. It was just a game.'

'I buy that like a buy a hole in the head.'

Monday stared at the face, a look of mocking amusement. 'Okay, what do you buy?'

'You know what struck me odd about the whole thing? Why would a woman like Angela confess to stealing in front of a fake court, unless what she said was true?'

Monday realized George had the bit between his teeth long before now and wondered if this meeting was really accidental. He also realized it was important at this moment of maintaining his composure, of keeping a straight, calm face as if it was simply routine. But he felt the heat rising from his neck upwards and looked into his beer. What could be proved? Speculation, it was all speculation.

George watched him closely. 'What's going on?'

'You tell me?'

'I can make you a rich man, Sol. Full exclusivity, name your price.'

'George,' Monday said looking him square in the eye, 'I can swear on my Mother's grave there are no ghosts at Gallows Humour. Go see for yourself. All you will find is paint cans and the start of a new business for kids. Do you honestly think I would have kids on my land if there were ghosts?'

George smiled and opened his hands. 'Sol, why didn't you say that in the first place? Let me get you another beer.'

'No. I best be off. I have to top up the larder.'

There always seemed to be a weighting inside them, things left unspoken, things not fully spoken like holding playing cards against their chests.

GALLOWS HUMOUR

As the wind blew across his face, Monday walked along the main road, the traffic steaming slowly past in fits and starts and stops. He felt like a spring was uncoiling inside him and the faster he walked the better he felt.

Armed with fresh snack supplies, Tower Bridge was suddenly visible again and, in the lift, he decided not to tell Kern. It would only complicate the matter or would it be another secret? That first time, when he had returned from the rehabilitation clinic with a thumb-sized plaster over the punctures in his arm, he told Kern there was nothing to worry about, that he simply decided to give blood. He seldom left the apartment after that and became even more hopeful that with each uneventful day Angela might just leave him alone.

Now, Monday's untroubled life proceeded quietly without interference while Kern's routine returned. For a number of days he shopped for the mundane and midnight walks around the block became a habit. Then he would slip into bed and lay awake looking at that crumpled photograph of Izabo Tuesday, remembering that awestruck Thursday morning, meeting an angel for the first time.

'Did I write that?' Kern asked on a breakfast morning and looked up. 'Damn, am I good or what.'

Monday swung the laptop round holding his mug to his lips. Two minutes later he peeled off his glasses and agreed. 'You're right, that's damn good. Did you plagiarize?'

'Hey, what do you take me for?' Then Kern leaned back and started tapping his lower lip with the end of a pen. He was showing Monday his deep thinking pose. 'Do you think I have the onset of Alzheimer?'

'There are upsides. You can see films several times over with the same amount of pleasure.' He patted him on the head like the shaggy dog he was. 'Give Palfrey a ring before you forget where you live.'

The morning paper dropped to the mat. Monday picked it up and quickly glanced over the front page. His heart stopped first, then his breathing when he read headline news:

> *There are no ghosts at Gallows Humour*
> *so who is Monday kidding?*

Beyond that, it was difficult to focus. Padding bare foot to the desk, he picked up his glasses and remained as rigid as a lamp post.

When fellow journalist, Solomon Monday inherited Gallows Humour, he found Tuesday's passion for courtroom drama much stronger and intelligent than he bargained for. As well as exposing a weird and secret collection of jury members, Miss Izabo Tuesday went on to conduct a defence for Angela Morris, model and Solomon Monday's cast-off lover. Story continues on page 6.

In a rush, Monday turned to page six and gasped at the two page spread with a picture of courtroom drama under candlelight. Alerted, Kern left his seat and slipped beside him. The transcript of the trial, virtually word for word accompanied Angela's disingenuous quotes with emphasis of ghoulish spectres and kidnapping, every line, every word of the article running back and forth in their minds like a network newsroom. It just beggared belief. At a stroke, Angela had made Gallows Humour the club house for ghosts.

'Bollocks!' Monday cursed and strode into the bedroom, stripping off his pyjama bottoms.

Kern was not far behind. 'How the hell did this come about?'

'Me and my big mouth,' Monday muffled as his head popped through a polo-neck sweater. 'I bumped into George the first day we arrived. I thought I had the whole thing sussed. Did you get hold of Palfrey?'

'No, the line was engaged. Why the hell didn't you tell me?'

'Because I'm a prat,' Monday spat out and whooshed on his jeans. His face erupted with drama. 'It's going to be all out war! I shall make that bitch wish she had never clapped eyes on me!'

'And how do you intend to do that?'

Monday was convinced that if he vilified Angela, the papers would run the story to give their readers what they wanted. But after he cooled down and looked out upon the dirty waters of the Thames, he realized retribution would only enhance her chances to earn millions. So he just stood there in profound silence, watching ripples of polished darkness break on the waves as winter clawed at the day. What he really needed to do was to end the madness that began long ago at Gallows Humour. It had dominated every action, conscripted thoughts, ruled games and ordered lives. Even now, when it was supposed to be free of conflict, doubt or dismay, it still clung to a fantasy of magic casements. And people, no matter how unscientifically proven wanted to look in those magic casements.

But the genius and wordy grace of Monday was that he always knew where his strength lay. He slowly swung his head round and smiled at Kern, for he was about to take a negative and turn it into a positive. 'I am going to give my side of the story to Harry.'

'What!' Kern astounded then brought his voice into check. 'Think this through, my man. You can't go half cock. Parents won't let their kids near the place if they think Gallows Humour is haunted.'

'But it's not and that's the irony.' Monday returned his gaze to the outside world thinking life passes by pretty quickly like smoke trapped through a keyhole. 'All my life Gallows Humour has occupied my heart. That missing piece I never really understood about myself. All my life I fought against it, even when I arrived. But what happened afterwards was indescribably phenomenal and nothing is going to put Gallows Humour on the map as a freak sideshow. Izabo said fate rarely calls upon us at a moment of our choosing.'

'So you're a fatalist now? Hell, Sol, this is madness!' At times Kern's tension and frustration burst out. 'You cannot do this to Hugh, Palfrey, and dare I say Izabo under a carpet of flowers. It's bad enough she's been mentioned.'

Monday picked up the article. 'Izabo has already been established as one of us. There is no reason to look for her body.'

'But where is she, huh? If you churn this up, reporters will be hell bent on finding her, yeah? So how long will it take to start off an enquiry and find her grave?'

'That's why I have to finish this, once and for all. Gallows Humour must be saved from media frenzy, that courtroom drama has to be turned about and viewed as a comedy. Izzy knew. She knew Angela would never let go. Now it's up to me. Angela wanted the limelight, now she's going to get it. Paradoxically, you will get free publicity for your book.'

'Come again?' Kern was lost.

'Mike, I have never asked you for anything but I'm asking you now, as a friend to ride with me on this. You're my key to make this go away.'

'And just how am I able to do that?'

'A publicity stunt, of course, how else do you think? I need to speak to Palfrey.' Monday grabbed his mobile and punched the redial button to Gallows Humour. When the line was picked up, he said, 'What's the situation?'

'Pandemonium,' Palfrey replied, a little short of breath. 'Have we by any chance a solution in mind?'

'Abso-bloody-lutely. First off, get rid of the reporters by telling them we have sold our exclusive. Second, as a precautionary measure we need a courtroom of dummies. Do you know where we could pick these up?' Monday hung on for an answer. This one time butler's ability would be tested to the fullest extent. 'Palfrey, are you still there?'

'Leave it to me.'

'Anything else I should know about?'

'Hugh is considering a move to the Himalayas.'

'Tell him not to worry. Be in touch.' While Monday redialled another number he said to Kern, 'send your synopsis to Harry and a good picture of yourself.' The line was picked up by the concierge. 'Pete, it's Sol. The woman who moved into my apartment, have you seen her around?'

'Have you read today's news?' he replied in a Dalek voice.

'Why do you think I'm asking?'

'Sure, I've seen her coming off one of the boats moored in the basin. That's where she stays, like one of your ghosts.'

Monday let that slip by. 'Do you know who owns the boat?'

'You were talking to him the other day.'

Monday smiled. Things were falling into place. 'Thanks, Pete, I owe you one.' He looked at Kern thoughtfully. 'Here's the scenario…Angela is making up to George to get me on his payroll so I can enhance her career. Obviously, word is already out on the street I'm unfit for purpose. But he looks at a sexy woman who thinks mayonnaise comes from a plant and formulates ideas of his own. Then, low and behold, I get a call from Hugh and skip off to Norfolk. And we both know what happened then. She must have contacted George after I gave her the bum's rush over the dinner table. He probably said I was back on drugs, get out with a few trinkets and stay on my boat. But nobody anticipated Doolally's intervention. Now Angela is scared. Who does she telephone? The police wouldn't take her seriously, so she thinks of George and big bucks. It's his idea to tape the case but now he has a problem. He only has Angela's word for it and a couple of sketchy pictures.'

Kern picked up. 'So he's running a fine line unless he can get your comments. They knew you would come back to the flat, made it look good to keep you calm, yeah? Then he waits to get a call from Angela when she sees us arrive. George hot foots over for some casual comments.'

'And by denying there are ghosts it gave him the ammunition he needed.'

'Now he's printed, they think they've backed you into a corner. You better have things covered, Sol, because George will take you to the cleaners.'

'George is in a big puddle of shit and hasn't got the shoes for it. The confirmation or otherwise of ghosts at Gallows Humour will be more a matter of waggish speculation than the unproven reality of an unseen world.' Monday began dialling and put the mobile to his ear. 'Mike, do us a favour and makes us a coffee.' When Harry from the Daily Express picked up, he said, 'Harry, it's Sol. Do you want my side of the story?'

'Well this is a surprise, Sol. I would have thought I was the last man you'd contact.'

'Harry, you had every right to kick me off the paper. You invested heavily and I fucked up on a big scoop. Give me a chance to make it up? You have full exclusivity with two conditions. One, my colleague, Michael Kern gets the publicity and two, I write the story.'

'Ah, Michael Kern,' Harry toned flat as though he lost interest.

'Listen, Harry this is big. It was a bizarre enactment from a scene taken out of his book. We thought it would work for a publicity stunt. Unfortunately Angela trumped us and turned it around. She was looking to make quick bucks and used George at The Times.'

'Why would George listen to your dopey girlfriend?'

'Get a reporter to St. Katherine's Dock and her dirty linen will be found on his boat. Do we have a deal?'

'Of course we have a deal. I never let business get in the way of personal grievances. Hold fast, Sol.'

With unexpected nostalgia, Monday heard the wheels of a scoop turning fast, one not to be missed or stolen. There was a time when he was grateful to be among them, surprised to have lived through a fast-tracked business where Harry's low rumbling baritone gave instructions on their handling.

Harry came back on the line. 'Okay, Sol, you have a page for tomorrow. Give me a flavour of what's to come.'

Monday could tell from Harry's strangled tone that he had the handset wedge between his chin and chest and was no doubt ready to tap into the keyboard. 'Heading, Trick or Treat? The bright scarlet of the judge's robes was the only splash of colour in the near-darkness, candlelit courtroom at Gallows Humour, a far cry from the noise and bustle of modern courts where injustice is often meted out. It was two worlds in one room, the defendant with her mobile seizing an opportunity to fool her lover at The Times, and a handful of staff playing to dummies in support of Michael Kern's new novel.'

'Uh, what was that?' Harry asked. 'Dummies?'

'Sure, dummies…mannequins if you prefer.'

'Apart from Kern and your staff, who else backs up your story?'

'My solicitor, Hugh Crookshank. I have it covered, Harry. Angela can squeal all she likes but she did this to herself, the same way she did it to me to get my contacts. But this is not about Angela. It was never supposed to be about Angela. Mike has written a good book, he just needed a break.'

'And it looks as though he's got one. So off the record, are there any ghosts at Gallows Humour?'

'Harry, if you find any you can have their exclusive.'

A hearty laugh and Harry said, 'Deadline at nine, Sol and keep it tight.'

Once Monday had struck the deal with Harry at the Daily Express, he tied a few things up in the passages of Kern's novel then rushed to Liverpool Street Station finalizing the article on the train, all niggling details to be covered by a simple explanation but certainly not that simple to do. He broke his report into two parts. The first was on his interview with Michael Kern, how the idea was struck when he saw the courtroom at Gallows Humour. The second was about Angela, how she insisted upon acting the part as a wounded lover. Izabo Tuesday was played down in a small narrative, reading her script from the book she was holding that night, as shown in the fuzzy photograph Angela had sent to George. The tribe barely got a mention since they were just Monday's staff trying to accommodate Kern's wishes. After all, it was just a publicity stunt.

And there, as steel wheels combed the lines through the shady countryside and during his pencil chewing fidgety moments, the vacant seat beside him was suddenly occupied by a nosy intruder who smelt of perfumed witchery. He turned his head slowly round and peered above his rimless spectacles keeping his emotions in check, unsure if fate had provided him with a lookalike Doolally. Her clothes were elegantly shaped around her small body, her hair tidily swept up in a bun and the smile revealed a full row of front teeth.

'Did yew miss me?' she said.

The pencil went limp in his hand, his mouth gaped.

Impelled by old habits she pinched his nose. 'Yew deaf or what?'

A collective laugh around him and Monday glanced beyond her to discover a pot of gold. Dotted about in seats was the rest of the tribe and differed in no way from other passengers. Bumble gave a little wave in her refinery forsaking her bouncy hat. Flour was positively lovely in a chequered trouser suit offering a smile like a sugar drop. And the men with their flat caps pulled down tight over their heads cut a very different dash.

'How is this possible?' Monday asked as if to himself then averted his eyes to Doolally. 'What are you doing, on this train, outside Gallows Humour?'

'Am I not the moon, yew said, look after us, yew said and yew shone that night. Kept your promise yew did, led us from darkness. Then we found us on a field so far away we got lost.'

'Lost?'

'Fer certain yew hev to be good and lost to be found by the moon, and what a time we had not that we could understand what some wus saying.' She dug into her purse and pulled out a wad of notes in various currencies. 'I never sees so much money but it don't go far. Sixty pounds, she says. Sixty pounds for a dress! A cow is worth more than a dress, I says. Would madam care to look on the bargain rail? Ned soon put paid to her manner. He takes the dress and hangs it on the rail and says, there, it's on the rail a good deal better.'

'How did you get this money?'

'We never stole it,' she was quick to say. 'Charlie saw a man turning a wheel with numbers to make everyone dizzy. See, it works like this, the man says. Put your chip on a number and if the ball lands on that number yew win. Bumble put a fried chip on his nice green table and he weren't too pleased. We didn't quite know what the matter wus, in spite of his meaning looks. But Woody soon worked it out and looked him straight in the eye. Boy, he says, if I guess the next number will yew give me a chip to play on your wheel? Yes, he says, but it comes at a high price if yew lose. What price is that, Woody says. I take the brunette home, the man says. Well, strike me down if that weren't a generous offer but Flour didn't want to leave us so Woody says how about yew take us all home.'

Monday laughed, absorbed to know more. 'So what happened?'

'Well, he never wanted us all, did he? Seeing as Flour was beating men's hearts she went over to a chap and sat on his lap while Ned pinched his black chip. He returned it after we won.'

'So you cheated.'

'Ned calls it advantaging our position. Just like yew.' She pointed to his script. 'Don't think we don't know what porkies yew told.'

'So who is better placed to get us out of the mess we're in?'

With all the excitement Doolally was capable of, she signalled to Woody and they exchanged places in a blink of an eye. Nobody noticed this sudden switch. In fact nobody showed particular interest to the world around them as the train hammered on in a hurry.

'Solomon Monday, yew are better placed to get us out of the mess we're in. Do yew still want us home or would we hinder your efforts?'

'Perhaps I never made my position clear. I never wanted you to leave in the first place. It hasn't been the same and I felt your loss greatly. We all felt your loss. But you are not tied, Woody. Now you have tasted the outside world, you may come and go as you please. You will never hinder my efforts. Gallows Humour is your home, so remember that.'

Woody dug deep into his pocket and passed over a watch. 'This is fer yew.'

Monday gazed blankly at a Donald Duck face, unlikely it would keep good time but he was deeply touched. Removing his Omega, a stark contrast to the one he had been given, others sprang up without notice and proudly showed off theirs. It would seem they had gone to Disney Land.

So as they towered above him and all around him much to the consternation of other passengers who were now aware Monday had a following, he pressed the redial button and placed the mobile to his ear. As soon as the line picked up, the happy Monday said, 'Palfrey, are you sitting down?'

'Have we further complications?'

'Depends how you view the tribe. From where I sit, they look ready to come home.' Monday expected silence not the sound of a receiver crashing to solid surface. He smiled at them. 'Give him a moment. He's just getting over the shock.'

'Where are you?' Palfrey finally voiced.

'On the train, just coming up to Diss, I think. What's the situation like with the reporters? Did you tell them we have an exclusive?'

'Most certainly I did, the consequence of which, we have a clear gate. May I expect their arrival immediate?'

'Not sure.' Monday passed his mobile to Doolally. 'Speak to Palfrey.'

'Palfrey,' she hollered down the line, 'did yew miss me?' Whatever was said in reply, it took a long while before she hollered again. 'Right yew are!' She passed back the mobile. 'We hev to go. He's missing his buns.'

A great big contended sigh wormed its way from Monday's lips as he indulgently watched them toddle down the carriage to goodness knows where, probably in search of a spot from mortal eyes so they could disappear into the ether. The advantages were too numerous to contemplate. Apart from escaping rail fares that had increased astronomically over the years, they could orbit the planet and burrow among secrets without anyone knowing.

From the station Monday grabbed a taxi after waiting outside in a shivering lump for ten minutes. Winter was lashing away at his legs and freezing the veins in his nostrils. The driver made small talk in the dark of his seat but he was no reader of The Times. Instead, he gave out knowledge in very small parcels about Gallows Humour but Monday had things on his mind, back in the thick of it where there was never enough time to meet deadlines, never enough time to be certain if all angles had been covered.

Dropped outside Gallows Humour with its ivied walls, Monday sprang out of the taxi with his case, impatient to discover the extent of the bounty within. On the steps was Palfrey in jeans and sweater, standing and listening with his head on one side.

'I was getting a bit concerned,' Palfrey said cheerily closing the front door.

'The train was held up at Diss. Did you come through with the dummies?'

'Come see for yourself.'

Monday entered the courtroom in doubt and silence. Plastic torsos and tangled arms were heaped on the floor with their heads more or less abandoned by all. Boxes brimming of theatre clothes stood on benches alongside a shambled collection of wigs. He fed a nervous look at Palfrey's grin. 'Where are the legs?'

'Since they shall be seated why are legs needed? Why are they needed at all?'

'A precaution, Palfrey. Never under estimate the ferocious appetite of the press when they get a whiff of something unusual.' Monday moved towards the library. 'I keep thinking if all eventualities are covered…what if George knows something more, you know, has an ace up his sleeve…but there again, what am I worrying about? Only nut cases believe in ghosts.'

And then for no other reason, they burst out laughing until their eyes drew tears and their stomachs ached. Yes, the whole affair was extraordinarily bizarre in so far that Gallows Humour was about to defend its case based on a plausible lie to attack an implausible truth.

Wiping his streaming eyes, Monday plugged in his lap-top and switched on. 'Palfrey, I don't think I've laughed so much in years. No strike that, probably never. By the way, where is the tribe?'

'Flour is baking cakes. Doolally is in the drawing room piecing the vase together. Bumble is doing the laundry and the men are re-painting your bedroom walls.'

'Why's that?'

'They felt it should reflect your moods. Whisky?'

Monday nodded. 'And what moods are they?'

'You are round but not always around. Sometimes you are half, sometimes whole, sometimes you are dark and sometimes you are light.' Palfrey laid the drink on the desk. 'And sometimes a slice of you is all anyone knows.'

'But Izzy knew me well, didn't she, Palfrey.'

Palfrey stared, transmitting his fondness for Monday. 'Yes, Sol. She knew you like no other. I shall leave you to it and unpack your bag.'

Monday sat back with his memories. It was all there, all within his mind, the freckles on her face, her steps through the silver grasses and so close to her grave he imagined what she must have been thinking as she carried in her basket the flask of tea and marmite sandwiches. It was all there, a memory which itself will never fade. He whispered her name like a prayer and wondered if her atoms would stay on his lips, a splutter that might set off an alarm and bring her back to him.

The sound of Doolally's shrieking laughter brought him back to his senses and he bent forward to go over the details of what he had done so far. He then took fifteen minutes to type in his script, after which he sent it by email to Harry. Only when Harry gave the thumbs up, did he travel the stairs to investigate the bedrooms.

Here, he coolly whistled at the sumptuous surrounds before gravitating to his own room, and there a silence dropped into the night. The sun had been depicted superbly on the fireplace wall, its yellowy hues diminishing towards a silvery moon that glistened against a background of blue. Yellow drapes with white nets followed through to match the covers on a four poster bed and all else remained the same, solid oak wardrobes and dresser swallowed in shadow by recessed lighting. He padded softly across the silent, spongy carpet and went into the bathroom to stand under a ceiling of melting stars. White and yellow crackle glazed tiles splashed round the Victorian porcelain furniture as it remained to be an essential part of Gallows Humour. It really left him speechless.

'I trust you like it,' Palfrey said.

'Very much so.' Monday placed his mother's photograph on the bedside cabinet then noticed another frame with a picture of Izabo Tuesday spilling cement on his foot. He picked it up, grateful for that. 'You liked this one, didn't you?'

'It rather reminds me of how you two were. After neutralizing each other with threats couched in the most diplomatic language, both proceeded without means of knowing what each other's fates would be.'

'Do you think she will return or has she gone forever?'

'Yes, it does rather beg the question now the tribe has returned.'

'Since they are here, do we still think it's right to have screaming kids on our land?'

Palfrey took a space beside Monday on the bed and let his hands fall to his lap. 'Due to current events beyond our control, we cannot keep Gallows Humour masked from the outside world but we can protect it and those within it. We need staff, and no better staff do we have than a group of people who care very deeply. Their attributes go far beyond any human resource. Their presence must be validated and we must ensure no authority higher than God can snatch their home from under their feet.'

'I'm not too sure if we should go down that route. Once their names are logged into a computer, it's going to be pretty hard to explain to the Inland Revenue where they have come from.'

'I knew a chap once, Dirty Dick but by no means dirty, and proud of his medals. Boy, he said, when you get to my age the only thing you have to worry about is losing your guns. To which I gave a terribly complacent answer whilst holding on to my wheelbarrow. The war is over, old man. I fear you will have to surrender your guns. Winston Churchill, he replied briskly, never surrendered and he had his guns till the day he died. Of course, guns being a euphemism for balls.' Palfrey stole a quick glance at Monday. 'Their guns will be far greater than any technological fiend.'

'You're right, of course, as always. Where once the distinction between the tribe appeared to revolve around Gallows Humour, now there is a different contrast. On their misguided travels, they discovered money was absolutely central to the funding of their expedition. Their one bargaining chip was gambling, quite ingenious really when you consider a roulette table was their ideal tool.'

Palfrey showed his new watch. 'I would have preferred a naked woman rather than a picture of Mickey Mouse.'

Monday showed his. 'I am never going to swap this for all the tea in China.'

'Sol, try not to get your hopes up too much. My daughter was never one of them. She had no piece of paper to give her soul a choice.'

'She said it was fate. But why did she have to die, Palfrey? We were made for each other.'

'Maybe if she had lived, all our paths would have gone in another direction, and in so doing, perhaps the tribe would still be in torment and Gallows Humour inundated with interlopers to an impossible extent. I am just grateful to have had time with her.'

'Me too.' Monday slapped his knees. 'What say we have a cup of tea then gather the tribe and put a few hours in that courtroom?'

In contrast to what had gone on before in that courtroom, the jury members soon became a structure of tight perfection with bald plastic heads. It needed the flair of an artistic hand, preferably Woody to paint in their faces and give these dummies in frocked coats a human touch. Twelve down, fifty-two spectators to go and the dawn clawed pink through the courtroom windows from their efforts.

Then the entourage of decorators in their white overalls burst into Gallows Humour and began climbing their creaky tall step ladders with a frank and fearless attitude toward the staff buzzing around them. Meanwhile, Monday stirred the teapot madly.

'Get some shut eye,' he told Palfrey who relapsed into a weary silence. 'Go on, I can take it from here.'

Palfrey just crackled and stared into space as though he had still a few cards up his sleeve. 'When are you going to tell Mike?'

'Do I need to tell him?'

'You should at least warn him before he comes home.'

'I thought it would be a nice surprise.' Monday looked at Flour who was deploying a number of sticky cherries on top of an unbaked cherry pie. 'What do you think, Flour? Do you want me to tell him or would you prefer to pounce?' He smiled as she placed a gluey finger to her lips. 'There, you see. Flour wants it to be a surprise.'

'How did you leave it with Mike?'

'He's seeing his agent this morning then hoping to be here for supper.' Monday gained the impression this was more than casual curiosity and wondered where this was leading. 'Is there something you wish to get off your chest?'

Palfrey pushed his untouched tea away and leaned earnestly towards Monday. 'Their relationship will not be sustainable.' A tap on his arm and Palfrey glanced woefully at Flour. 'Mike is not a toy to bring from a cupboard when it suits. The choice must be his and not yours.'

With those harsh words she thwacked the pie with her rolling pin and cherries shot out in all directions. Palfrey ducked as if used to her outbursts, but for Monday, a globule of cherry juice worked its way down the side of his face. She was, after all, a country girl, and perhaps too muddled for a man who was about to launch into the media limelight.

'Do you wish him to be a grateful sufferer in years to come?' Palfrey continued. 'Watch his body diminish as you lie by his side unable to age. He must be given the choice with a clear head.'

Her signing was frantic. 'Your daughter gave you no choice.'

'I was her father not her lover.'

'I shall be lover then his mother.'

'He will not wish for a mother.'

When the second wave of cherries flew through the air, this time Monday avoided the incoming. Like Mike, he would have suffered the same fate if Izabo Tuesday came back on the scene. But surely something was better than nothing. He stared into his warm mug of tea and tried to delineate the details of a complex issue. In fact it was so complex it was like filling holes in a colander.

Leaving Palfrey and Flour to argue the toss, Monday sauntered upstairs and looked around him, drumming his fingers against his trousers, anxious or agitated or just at a loss as to what to do next. Damn it, he thought, and strode into the library to telephone Kern. What will be, will be.

'Hey, I was just about to ring you,' Kern voiced. 'Great minds think alike, yeah? Maggie is wetting her knickers. She loved the piece we sketched in, and as for the publicity, well you tell me if this is not heaven. How are things your end?'

'Good, things are good. Where are you now?'

'At the flat and waiting for Pete to pick up his whisky. I should be with you-
'

'Mike,' Monday interjected. 'The tribe is here.'

'Say that again?'

'Look, I know this is probably hard to take in but try to get your head round it and consider if you want to return.'

The sound of a heavy intake of breath rushed down the line. 'Well,' Kern breathed out, 'you're right it's hard to take in, yeah? You sure this is not a wind-up?'

'No, they are here. Think about it, Mike. Think very carefully.'

'What do you think I should do?'

'You cannot look to me to be your mentor. A whole orchestra of fitness cannot protect you from old age. Palfrey tried to tell her it was your decision, so I suggest you think it through carefully before you let your heart rule your head.'

There was a brief moment of silence before Kern replied. 'Why did they come back?'

'If I was to give an honest answer, I would say there are things at work we cannot possibly understand. Doolally reckoned I was their moon and they followed the moon all around the globe until they caught up with me on the train. Have you got this morning's Daily Express?'

'Yes. It's damn good. Are you pleased with it?'

'Not read it yet. The dummies turned up so we spent the night setting up the courtroom just in case Harry comes over. You know your life is going to change from now on. Interviews, other book deals, who knows what, probably film rights but try to keep the story straight if you get interviewed.'

'Sol, I know this is an odd thing to say under the circumstance but thanks for this. I wasn't really into kids and all that, yeah?'

'I know. Keep in touch, okay?'

'Sure.'

Monday dropped the receiver onto its cradle very slowly and felt he had somehow, in a roundabout way, finally made up for his mistreatment of Kern when this friend needed him the most. Feeling a little tired, now everything had been done that could be done he slumped over his desk and fell asleep. It was a deep, dreamless patch and he never woke until the clunk of something heavy hit the desk and jolted him to life.

'Have a cup of tea and piece of fruit cake.'

Monday wiped his face, visibly surprised to see Crookshank. 'What time is it?'

'Five-thirty.' Crookshank put a cigarette in his mouth but never lit it. He sat on the arm of a chair while a small smile played on his face, but not small enough to pass Monday's notice. 'I thought you planted the seeds of a pretty convincing story.'

'What makes you happy, the story or the tribe?'

It was a few moments before Crookshank spoke again. 'Funny, for years there was this one driving force to finish what Week had started, and yet I had this emptiness after they left. They look very different.'

'But still the same.'

'Yes, still the same. How is Mike taking it?'

Monday brushed a few crumbs off his sweater. 'I think he has a different future, one that suits him. All told I think everything worked out pretty well. What do you think to the place?'

'Justice has been done to Gallows Humour but I was surprised the kitchen was untouched.'

'Palfrey liked it the way it was.' Just then Monday's mobile rang. Without his glasses he was unable to read the caller's name and responded to the mouthpiece with a hello.

'Harry here, Sol. There have been a few developments. Are you prepared to put this thing to bed?'

Monday ramrod straight. 'What developments?'

'George claims Angela is able to prove her case and suggests we meet up at your place...say in a couple of hours. Do you have a problem with that?' Harry said it in a tone that invited no choice but compliance.

'Okay, Harry, just make sure you keep them on a tight leash.'

'Another thing, Sol. Do you have electricity?'

'Harry, when are you going to learn not everything you read in the papers is true?' The disgruntled Monday hung up and looked at Crookshank. 'Relax...it's much worse than you think.'

REPUTATION AND RUMOUR

'Now chaps, reputation and rumour travels fast so tonight I play a drama of guile and mendacity. My audience must be left in no doubt that Angela is an agent of destruction.'

Monday faced a group of faithful souls, sighing and slumping within the library walls, lacking enthusiasm for his plan, gone were their customary lightness and easy laughter.

'A snake in the grass must be set ablaze.' Ned had incendiary ideas of his own. 'What's to be done cannot be remedied by words.'

Indeed not, reflected Monday. 'Gallows Humour hangs in the balance of reporters. If you show your faces, it will give Angela the ammunition she needs.'

'And how do you explain their absence?' Crookshank moved towards Palfrey. 'They will think it rather odd you have suddenly become absent of staff that had supported Mike's publicity stunt.'

'A greater explanation would be required for their attendance.' Monday argued. 'Apart from Palfrey, what credentials can they show when asked? It's easy for me to say they left my employ due to the article in The Times, that they felt persecuted and found it intolerable to stay here.'

Crookshank nodded as if Monday had scored a point. 'Do you know,' he asked Doolally, 'if Angela had access to the register?'

Doolally tried to remember, picturing her movements from the time she arrived to the time she left. 'No,' she claimed positively, 'never once did I see her in here.'

'Then we have our answer,' said Crookshank. 'She intends to challenge her persecutors. By what means her challenge is speculative. Does she know they cannot bleed or consume?'

'You substantiate my point, Hugh. All the more reason they should be absent.'

'If they are absent, it will add further speculation.' Touching Doolally's shoulder in a consoling manner, Crookshank took a seat by the window. 'If not Woody or Ned, Angela will demand the whereabouts of Doolally for it was she who threw her in that courtroom, she who caught her stealing. Sol, I can handle the background of Gallows Humour but I cannot support a fragile excuse. Doolally, at least must be shown as a staff member with Palfrey taking up his position as butler. Angela has no legal right to make any physical demands on them, and there I can tie her in knots. As for their background…why, that is easy to explain. Have they not lived here under Palfrey's supervision supporting Jeremy Sunday?'

Nothing could have prepared Monday for Angela pulling a fast one, that her dogged persistence was beyond imagination. He looked at the tribe. They offered a smile and opened their hands to show it was his choice.

'Okay,' he capitulated but warned. 'No monkey business. You will keep your presence circumspect until called upon by Palfrey. I will have any who disregard my wishes. Do I make myself clear?'

To their fiercely nodding heads, a lone voice called out making its way to the library. It was Kern, suitcase in one hand and a bunch of flowers in the other. His choice had been made. Everyone scattered immediately to greet him. He released his grip from the handle as Flour rushed into his arms and Monday felt a pinch of jealousy, wishing he could do the same with Izabo Tuesday, for sharing a love that to him was denied.

'Hugh,' Monday said. 'Fill Mike in. I need to get changed.'

In his bedroom, he quickly slipped out of his clothes and popped under a shower, confused by the planning. Which way to jump, what to do next, who to indulge in this game of deceit? He merely attempted to stay sane.

After he dried himself off, he sat on the bed for a few moments cradling that photograph of him and Tuesday, wishing he could lie back in her arms and spend a whole winter making love to her. But he shook his head and returned the picture to his bedside cabinet then pulled out clean underwear from the dresser.

'Hey, this place looks great.'

Monday glanced across at Kern entering the room. 'They want revenge but in doing so they will condemn their existence.'

'You forget they can erase memories.'

'What a good idea. All they have to do is read all about it the next day.' A clip to the ear shook Kern into reality. 'Look what happened when my memories were erased.'

'But you can't handle Angela. You were never able to. Not even I could handle her. In fact, I would go so far as to say she's the testing ground for the mafia. So we just have to play it by ear.'

'Is this what you want, here with Flour?'

'Hey, who said love was easy.' Kern poked his head in the wardrobe and pulled out a suit, giving it the once over before passing it to Monday. 'I read a book on the chaos theory, you know random events then a pattern emerges. There I am, on my lonesome and giving it great thought when there wasn't much to think about. The book is a done deal. I can write trash on my next one and still sell millions.'

'Mike, the only pattern I see emerging is the chaos in your head. You spend your whole life working to be a good writer and now you want to write trashy novels.'

'Rubbish, I don't want to write trashy novels. Listen will you? For centuries your predecessors lured Gallows Humour into a wilderness of abject misery, through cowardice, corruption and personal failings. Then you came along, yeah? You got rid of the interlopers, freed Hugh from his nightmares, gave me a future and brought back the tribe…and Angela, well, she's just part of the chaos. Here, wear this one.'

Monday took the proffered tie. 'So you think she fits in somewhere?'

'She has to. Think about it. The moment she turned up she created the chaos to cause Izabo to reveal the riddle, which in turn gave you the impetus to stay on.'

'Wrong, because Izabo had every intention of whetting my appetite with the riddle so I would stay on.'

'Are we two communicating or what? I just said that, maybe not in those words.'

'No, you were trying to justify Angela's chaos.' Monday drew close to his mirrored face and adjusted his tie. Then he stared back at Kern. 'What if I had been there at the time of my Mother's passing? Would she have told me about Gallows Humour? I think yes, she would, in which case I may have come here a lot sooner, probably met Izabo when she was alive. How's that for bloody chaos?'

Just as Kern was about to argue his point, Palfrey entered the room to announce the presence of Harry who was currently being entertained by Crookshank in the courtroom.

'Palfrey,' Monday asked slipping on his jacket. 'What was the date of Izabo's death?'

'The twenty-seventh of June last year.'

Monday stood silent and motionless for a moment. His mother had died on the twentieth of June, exactly a week earlier. Would seven days be enough to have altered her destiny? How fate could change on the throw of dice, the unspoken word of a mother, the command of the Almighty. Or it could turn on an involuntary statement Crookshank might make at a reporter's feet.

Among a courtroom of mannequins, Harry was sitting on a scorched bench wearing a blue suit and held the stub of a cigar between his teeth as he listened to Crookshank's explanation of Monday's windfall, albeit slightly divergent. At fifty-eight, bald as a coot with pale brown eyes, and skin wrinkled by a journalistic life, Harry had entry to doors that rarely opened for others, those who held similar positions to couch the news.

'This is quite a place you have here,' Harry said when Monday walked in. 'Hugh was telling me about your windfall.'

'Not so much a windfall but a battle hard fought.' He took the proffered hand. 'Please, Hugh, carry on so Harry has a clear understanding of my position here.'

'Yes, Judge Week. Since his wife bore him no children, he left Gallows Humour in Trust for my ancestor to administer. Various managers were employed to run the estate, those who fell within the terms of the Trust, explicitly their one qualification need only be in a name. Jeremy Sunday who ran the estate for sixty-two years was rather fond of Sol's political slots in your paper. When they ceased, Jeremy asked me to keep track of Sol. And here we are, a new manager to Gallows Humour.'

Harry was still curious. 'Where does this Miss Tuesday fit in?'

'That was my fault,' Monday threw in. 'Angela wanted me back on the news desk. Of course, I was not aware at the time she and George were an item. I got in touch with Hugh and told him I changed my mind so he contacted a Miss Tuesday then Mike had this bright idea and persuaded me to help him promote his book. Everyone was up for it, but things turned sour when Angela tried to pull a fast one. The whole thing got rather messy after that. Bottom line, I decided to stay on and Miss Tuesday left.'

'I was telling Hugh, my sat nav never registered this house…drove right past and turned into the Three Feathers. Odd wouldn't you say?'

'Harry, everything is odd about Norfolk. It takes a bit of getting used to but I like it here. I can forget the outside world.'

'Not any more, Sol.' Harry sparked a different conversation. 'Now the Lisbon Treaty has been enacted, the federalists are preparing for a new power grab.'

'Yes, I heard about that,' Monday said gravitating to the doors. 'But then what can you expect from the unelected President Herman Van Rompuy. Gentlemen, I suggest we proceed to the warmth of the drawing room and have a drink.'

'Take an interest in politics?' Harry asked Crookshank on the way.

'My only interest is reaching a hundred and being horrid.'

In gaiety they entered the now newly decorated drawing room where the smell of paint was at its strongest. Here, Palfrey poured sherry into three glasses, once again playing his part of butler with accustomed ease. His vacant eyes stared straight before them as he hung in the shadows like a dutiful servant.

'So, Harry, what has Angela got up her sleeve?' Monday fished, 'Ouija boards no doubt.'

Harry threw his cigar butt in the roaring fireplace and remained standing. Monday knew he was thinking about those words.

'Palfrey,' Crookshank said. 'What do we have on the menu?'

'We have cucumber sandwiches specifically to cater for the vegan, sausage rolls and Cornish pasties followed by a selection of cakes and pastries. At such short notice, the cook was unable to provide a three course meal. Do you require anything else?'

Monday glanced at Harry. 'Do you have something to ask Palfrey? If so, now's the time to do it before Angela arrives with her lap dog. Palfrey has worked here for sixteen years and only needs glasses to read.'

Harry returned Palfrey's smile. 'Sixteen years,' he said. 'So you've just settled in then?'

'No truer word spoken, sir.'

'Have you ever encountered unnatural events happening in this place?'

'Indeed I have, sir. On many occasions during the reign of Mr Sunday, I would often find my slippers under his bed. When questioned why he should prefer my slippers instead of his own he categorically denied wearing them.'

'So how did they get there?'

'The same way many things get there, by the hand of another wishing to cause mischief. Unlike the staff serving at Buckingham Palace, here they are dutifully rebellious.'

Was Harry convinced? Monday regarded him with intensity now, trying to read his reaction before going further. 'Think about it, Harry,' he finally said. 'In your life time there was never an ounce of interest taken in Gallows Humour until now. What you see is what you get and what you get is a heap of happy living away from a maddening crowd. Tonight you will eat good food served up by good people and with any luck, you will return to your desk wondering what the fuck people are doing with their lives. Britain already pays a heavy financial price for its membership in the EU and it's about to get a lot tougher. Surely there are more important issues to investigate than the ravings of a lunatic?'

'She claims she can prove this place is haunted.'

'You would have us count on her word?'

'I have been informed she can produce physical evidence.'

That alerted Monday. He set his glass down thinking things through. There was always the wrath of Angela to consider, the pride of her word at stake.

'Harry,' he said, 'be careful which side you choose. No benevolence will be shown to the likes of Angela or George if they step over the mark.'

Harry instinctively looked down to his leather worn shoes. He had been operating on goodwill and now clearly saw how little goodwill would have to do with the outcome. 'You know, it wasn't easy to let you go, Sol. You were a damn good reporter but you would make one hell of a good politician.'

The room laughed quietly as the first trickle of snow fell from the sky. Not that they noticed. As the flames threw high in the grate and time moved on while sherry warmed the dialogue, there was almost a moment where Monday believed Angela had given up, that something, somehow had veered her off course. Unfortunately that was not the case. The loud and persistent knocking on the front door drew attention to her arrival and smiles weakened as though everything was lost and thrown away.

But for the exception of Angela who gushed in her eye-popping outfit, prudence crept into male voices while introductions were made. It was an uncomfortable atmosphere, notably more for Monday who forced a civil politeness toward his challenger. The sight of her alone was enough to raise the hairs on his neck.

'Sweetie,' she said, moving crabwise, 'why has your hair gone grey at the sides?'

Monday let that slide by and instead returned to Harry's earlier remarks. 'At best the EU will prove that any country joining the euro must cede control over its tax and spending policy as well as its interest and exchange rate.'

'By God, I'd prefer to tickle an angry lion with a short stick than stay in the EU.'

There followed the customary interest among men to discuss politics much to the disappointment of Angela. She would be denied centre stage.

In the intervening time, Palfrey fulfilled his duties and kept the drink flowing. Doolally, wearing a maid's uniform, her frilly white crown slightly on the skew, drifted in with the food trolley at pains to keep her presence reckless. Next, Woody entered to top up the fire, slipping between the gathered company that was eager to remain standing. If there were others, they certainly never showed.

'Sol,' George modulated his voice, 'a word in your ear.' Moving to a quiet corner, he continued, 'listen, Sol, I just want to say this wasn't my idea.'

'Nobody twisted your arm.'

'Damn it, Sol. If you had just come clean in the first place none of this would have been necessary. I'm looking at a divorce here.'

'And I'm looking at my life.'

'All right, so now we know each other. Talk to me, this can go in your favour. She's prepared to settle this on the QT. Five hundred thousand is not a bad deal.'

Bitch! 'I do not capitulate to a blackmailer.'

George pleaded again. 'For God's sake, the money is peanuts.'

'Then you pay her.' Monday glanced across the room, his eyes to narrow slits as he picked out the strapless mini-dress talking to Kern. Things were not adding up. 'If she's looking for a settlement then there's no ace up her sleeve.'

'You're wrong, Sol. I say this as a friend. Get out now while the going is good. Pay her the money, let her have this little victory and Gallows Humour will end with your version of events.'

'Have you seen this proof?'

Whatever George said in response to this it was lost by another set of words whispered in Monday's ear.

'Solomon, the sleeper must awaken.'

The word *mother* leapt softly from his lips and he vacantly stared into the room. His heart opened to love, his mind opened to a greater possibility. With the seconds his desperation grew to fever pitch and left after making limp excuses to Harry. He stole into the library where she had come to him, where he now reached out, asking for her blessing and forgiveness.

'I'm so sorry, Mum.' Instinctively, his arms curved protectively around her, still feeling and looking exactly the same before death came knocking at her door. 'I should have been there for you at your last moments. I was wrapped up in drugs and ego-'

'There now,' she hushed him. 'Put away your silly thoughts. You have always been there, even in your transitory visits. My son, you must wake up from your ignorance. Take back what was stolen.'

'Stolen?'

'She took what she desired most, a life which was not hers to take.'

'Her?'

'Angela, who else?'

Monday stepped back in a rush, the sleeper finally awoke. How unwise it was to be trapped by the rigid confines of drugs. There was advantage to escape the outside world but there was disadvantage also. It clouded his judgement when Angela walked into his life, the insidious rise of an interloper that played her part with habitual ease.

'Why did it have to be Izabo's life?'

'There was no other to take,' his mother replied. 'It was an opportunity seized upon during a summer storm. Who would relate the incidence anything other than a tragic accident? Now you must draw upon your dark side and do what is necessary.'

'Nothing would give me greater pleasure. But her presence in the media makes that almost impossible.'

'There are other ways.' She pulled back the curtain with a modest smile. 'Look, my son. It snows and glistens with ice. Send her on a speedy journey and read her obituary in tomorrow's news.'

He could make out the diminished and broken outline of the trees, the mass that resembled nothing more than a white coat upon the landscape. Below, he looked upon the ground glittering with the night's new frost. It was the substance of magic, the nature of tragedy. 'How can I achieve this?'

'You must widen your gaze, my son. I am concerned you underestimate the gravity of coming events. You are bound on a journey that will twist the very fabric of nature, but beneath your mask of logic I sense a fragility that worries me. Steal your mind. Where is your heart, my son? You gave it to Gallows Humour, not when you signed but when you made your footsteps in its history. Nothing is beyond your reach.' A soft kiss to his cheek before leaving, she said, 'remember who you are.'

There was nothing else to look at as the room slipped back into silence. He went to his desk and pulled out a drawer. There, he brought out Week's Work, flicking through the pages until he came across a specific mark, remembered well the words of Judge Culver Week.

'Not all have been consigned to their places, some have escaped Gallows Humour. Know them their marks, Solomon Monday and do as I have done should they return.' Then the Judge opened to a page which was of considerable interest and struck a finger on that mark. *'She will return, a most foul and abhorrent woman. When the time comes, draw strength from your dark side and rid this evil. May God go with you and help you.'*

The signs had been there all along. He tore out the page, folded it once and slipped it into his trouser pocket, then left, keeping his anger in check, to swallow the hate in his throat. That pestilence, for there was no other word to describe Angela, had cruelly taken his Tuesday. As he ducked into the drawing room, a belch of flame roared up the chimney and Doolally gave a loud screech, as she always did. Slowly, he was beginning to understand the correlation between his dark side and Gallows Humour.

'Sweetie,' Angela voiced loud, her shapely legs crossed. 'Harry wondered if you had made your escape.'

Without uttering a sound he winked at Doolally and pinched a sausage roll. With his back to the fire, he studied them all, the anticipation replicated on each face. Were they waiting for him or waiting for Angela to make her move? He would test her as far as he wished.

'So, Angela did you bring your Ouija board?'

'Be patient,' she chided gently. 'We were rather enjoying Mike's version of that night.'

'Hey, don't mind me,' said Kern facing George with an air of malevolence. 'I seem to recall you found one of your own when this bloke was taping the scene.'

'Angela,' Harry spoke, calmly blowing smoke rings across the room. 'If you claim these people are ghoulish monsters, why chance your arm and come here?'

'Sweetie,' she said leaning forward to give him a bird's eye view of her cleavage. 'George is here to protect me.'

'Ah!' Monday gave a short burst of laughter. 'His bravery and nobility will prevail at last.'

Harry enjoyed his joke.

Angela glanced in Monday's direction with a look that suggested trouble. 'Amazing just how quick you've got the hang of this lying-through-your-teeth shit…think yourself so bloody clever, don't you? Where is your Miss Tuesday or should I say, where is your whore?'

'I say, Angela.' Kern objected as Monday's face glowed with anger and flames shot up the chimney again. 'There's no need to get personal. Miss Tuesday is a decent woman, was thoroughly put out by your scheming.'

'That's rich coming from you.' Angela now placed her cards on the table. 'Shall we see where Miss Tuesday lived? Perhaps it's somewhere closer to home than we think.' She glanced at Monday. 'I wouldn't worry, sweetie, too late now to move her body. What? You thought I was one step behind while you scurried about making up stories?' Her audience was now in rapt attention. 'Miss Izabo Tuesday, that slut of a woman who couldn't wait to get me out of this place, died last year, fell from this roof and has been mulling around ever since.' She turned to Palfrey. 'There is the dummy who buried her. Now ask him why?'

Palfrey kept his eyes on Monday. 'I think madam is so far removed from reality it beggar's belief. I can assure you, sir, that we have no hidden graves other than rotting corpses from centuries past.'

'No, of course not, because I removed her body which is currently in the hands of a private medical examiner.' Angela studied her nails. 'Mind you, it wasn't easy. Rather than risk the meddlesome lot that parade around like they own this place, I did it on a Saturday because that's when they disappear, back to their graves under the lake.' She looked up and reeled in Harry's wandering attention. 'So, Harry, if you care to ring the medical examiner, you might just start to believe me.'

'Sir,' Palfrey offered. 'Would you care to use the telephone in the library?'

'No,' Harry said. 'Best to do it company.'

While Angela flipped through her mobile for the number, Monday's eyes were fixed on Palfrey who seemed to be piecing things together. It was quite conceivable this intelligent man had gathered instantly the only malcontent who would have known his movements that fatal night had to be an interloper.

'Yes,' Harry made contact and the room went quiet. 'I was given your number by Angela Morris. This is Harry Webb from the Daily Express.' The intrigue of silence drew out as Harry kept his expression inscrutable, occasionally nodding, demonstrating his interest in the case. 'Are you able to give your opinion as to the source?' Harry caused further alarm to attentive listeners.

Monday was unconcerned, had every confidence in Palfrey who seemed unconcerned himself, was in that moment now of giving instructions to Doolally, requesting her to serve the sweet pastries that Flour had painstakingly baked for the men. They seemed to go down well. Even Harry had a third helping when he came off the line.

'Well?' Angela queried in his attentive pause.

'Have you any experience of human anatomy?' Harry asked. And to her puzzled expression, he explained to the room. 'It would appear Miss Morris dropped off a rocking horse.'

The room exploded into laughter which in turn exacerbated Angela's credibility. Her short-lived smugness turned quickly into seething anger. Enraged, she jumped to her feet and picked up a cake knife, ran it through Doolally. There was an intake of breath, a collective tremor of disbelief. It was the quickest of blows to give the unluckiest result. Doolally staggered with blood spills down her white apron, groaning loud then she crumbled into Monday's arms with a piteous cry. Images so vivid it held most in suspense.

Kern and Crookshank, quite predictably darted among the confusion shouting for an ambulance and then demanded Angela's arrest. For Monday, he carried Doolally upstairs in his arms showing an immense and urgent undertaking with Palfrey at his side, the fussing alarmist. All of which was an act, something he found amusing. In his bedroom, he lowered her on the bed, watched as she writhed in misery, her moans soft and persistent.

'Palfrey, do you think our dish washer will live?'

'Many times, I wager.'

Doolally opened one eye. 'How did yew know?'

'To ask you to behave is like asking ice cream not to melt in the midday sun. Am I to be enlightened on your plan?'

'Well,' she said sitting up, removing a deflated hot water bottle from under her maid's uniform. 'Charlie plays doctor and Ned is constable plod seeing as they weren't invited to the party.'

Monday sat beside her, quite happy to be coddled like an egg. 'You do realize George and Harry, especially Harry, will take quite a bit of convincing. Not least of which, Charlie is very young to play doctor and he should arrive in an ambulance. Have you made provision for one?'

'We never had ambulances in my day, lucky we had a doctor. Anyways, I'm dead.' Then she took on a mean expression. 'She should be hung. That slut is the devil. I saw it in her eyes. Who listened? Yew were wrong, now we hev a chance to put things right.'

'Do you know who she is?' Palfrey asked.

'I do,' Monday replied. 'Now is not the time for explanations. Doolally, you must curb your desire to punish Angela. I promise she will meet her demise but not here.' He squeezed her hand to make his point then glanced at Palfrey. 'Where is Izabo's body?'

'Where it always wus.' Doolally answered, her attention now drawn to Palfrey. 'How could we not know, yew silly bugger. She kept walking through doors. I says to her, if yew intend to act like yew wus alive, best yew try opening them with your mind. It's all up here, I says, in your head.' She looked at Monday. 'See it wus like this. Watch we did in the rain, surprised we did when we heard her scream. I says to her, what do yew want to do that fer, when others looking to cause mischief might take it upon themselves to dig yew up. So Woody came up with a good idea and made a pact with Judge Week so he could do it on his day off. He had to fill the hole with summat so he took your old rocking horse seeing as yew had no need of it.'

'I am amazed,' Palfrey said.

'You're amazed,' Monday echoed. 'I was down there thinking you had it covered.'

'I had it covered in my pants, Sol.'

Fate, Monday reflected, and smiled at Palfrey in paradoxical amusement. 'Doolally, who was responsible for making Angela think she had actually dug up a body?'

'Ah, best yew ask Flour. She knows more than she's telling.'

'Okay. Palfrey, make sure you stay here and look after Doolally until I give the all clear.' At the door he turned back. 'Doolally, if my heart was not already spoken for, I would give it to you.'

Before she was able to respond, Monday was shooting downstairs passing Charlie and Kern. A word out of place could be costly. At the bottom step, George sat wringing his hands looking up in a feverish state.

'How is she?'

'Alive and talking, no thanks to that vindictive parasite you brought along.'

'Sol, I swear I never knew she had that in mind.'

'What did you think she had in mind?' Acting had a particular rhythm, a wavering beat of its own. 'I swear, George, you will be held accountable for her actions. And don't think you're excluded as an accessory to blackmail.'

'This is going to ruin me, Sol.'

'Like you tried to ruin me, hmm?'

George slumped further, held his head in his hands like a defeated man, burbling nonsense. 'When we first met, she was all over me, said she wanted you to have the political slot but the position was already filled.' He looked up. 'I swear on my life, Sol, it was not meant to be personal but I got in too deep. When she telephoned, I just couldn't believe it. But the evidence was there. If only you had talked to me, told me it was a publicity stunt for Mike's new book. Instead you were asking for money.'

'I was angry. Angry she tried to pull a fast one.' Monday settled beside him feeling a little guilty he was putting George through the mill. 'Look, I know how she operates. The only person she loves is herself. That and money makes her man's worst nightmare.'

'She said she had the evidence she needed on your shelves, Sol. Something about a blank register, how Judge Week's bloodline is made to sign their hearts away and how the courtroom was used to enact past cases. God, when

I talk about it now, I sound as if I'm off my bloody rocker. The police are never going to believe me. I shall lose my wife, my job-'

'Probably your house and boat,' Monday chimed in.

'Sol, I know I've been a bastard but give me a second chance. She never told me she dug up a rocking horse. Makes you wonder why she gave Harry his number. She must have known he would spill the beans.'

'Perhaps she's in denial. Is it possible she's really mad, a schizophrenic? Not uncommon these days. I did have my suspicions when she tried to assail me in bed.'

'No truer word spoken, Sol. She did that to me. She's not right in the head, I can see that now. What can I do to make it up to you?'

'Oh, George, this goes way beyond the perfunctory tokens.' It was Monday's pleasure and George's agony. 'I have a member of my staff upstairs being attended by a doctor, and no doubt she will want to exercise her rights if she gets through this. And no doubt Harry is going to use tonight's escapades for front page news. Do you know if someone called the police?'

'Hugh, your solicitor telephoned them right away, damn nuisance. This is not going to look good for you either, Sol. I mean, you were the one who brought her here in the first place. How about some investment in your new business? Don't tell me you couldn't do with some help to get that courtroom sorted.'

Monday puffed out his cheeks. 'Well, to be truthful, I am short on funds. See, the thing is, George. You brought Angela here and-'

'No, she brought me here. We used her motor. It was her idea and Harry went along with it. If I'm to blame then so is he. Please, Sol. Does it hurt to say she was an invited guest, like Harry and me? You don't want any more publicity, do you? Parents won't want to bring their kids here if they think this is a mad house.'

Monday waited a beat to show he was softening. 'I want a retraction, not a small piece but a decent spread.'

'You shall have it.'

'And Mike gets the publicity he needs for his book.'

'He shall have it.' George offered a sweating hand. 'And I keep my reputation in tact?'

Monday nodded. He knew the score.

The doctor, videlicet Charlie, came waltzing down the stairs with his medical bag. 'Mr Monday,' he said looking quite the business with a stethoscope dangling round his neck. 'I understand the patient was stabbed with a cake knife.'

'Will she have to go to hospital?' George worriedly asked.

'She is a very, very lucky woman. The wound is not deep, painful but no real damage caused. I think we can service her needs here.'

'Oh thank God.' George shook Charlie's hand with gusto. 'Thank God for small mercies.'

'Presently she is sedated. I told your man Palfrey I will call in later. Meanwhile I suggest you let her rest.' Charlie glanced back at George. 'Did you stab her?'

'Good grief, no! It was the mad hatter in the drawing room.'

Monday looked away to conceal his amusement.

'I best be off, have other patients to attend. Goodnight.'

'Goodnight, doctor.' They said in unison.

As the front door opened for the doctor's exit, Ned walked in wearing a copper's uniform. Monday envisaged him saying hello, hello, what have we here.

'Ah, there you are,' George said. 'The assailant is in the drawing room.'

'Not so fast.' Ned brought out his notebook. 'Who might you be?'

'George Brooks, News Editor of The Times.' He poked his head outside. 'Where is your vehicle?'

Ned pointed to the bicycle clips round his ankles. 'We're not in London now, sir.'

'I am Solomon Monday.'

Ned indicated with his eyes at Monday's open jacket, the blood spots on his shirt. 'Not looking good for you, sir. I shall need that as evidence.'

It took a second for Monday to register that Ned was taking his part very seriously, the manner in which he held himself, the way he licked the end of his pencil before writing things down and how he removed his helmet tucking it under his arm.

'Right, shall we proceed to the crime scene?' Ned slowed their steps when they got close to the drawing room, as if perhaps whatever was wrong here might be contagious. 'Is the body in there?' he asked.

'No-one got killed.' Monday responded. 'The maid is alive and upstairs. The perpetrator is in there.'

Ned switched on his two-way walkie-talkie and spoke into it. 'PC Bobbins reporting in.'

An answer came back. 'Go ahead, PC Bobbins. What is the situation?'

'Tell Detective Inspector Naughty his services are not required, no-one got killed. The maid is alive and upstairs. I am proceeding inside the crime scene to interview the perpetrator and have another suspect in custody.'

'Make sure the weapon is secure and get everyone's statement. Over and out.'

Monday rolled his eyes. Whistling was a useful face-saver. He swept open the door to a trio. There was Angela sat between two men on the sofa under close arrest. Her body stiffened when she saw Ned and jumped up, but Crookshank and Kern pushed her back down. Harry smiled, a spectator leaning against the mantelpiece.

'He's not a policeman,' she contested. 'He's one of them!'

'Shut up, Angela!' Monday took control. 'Your turn will come.' He had no doubt about that and returned to the introductions. 'PC Bobbins, this is Harry Webb, Editor-in-Chief of the Daily Express. This is Hugh Crookshank, my solicitor. The woman is-'

'I know who the woman is.' Ned cut him off and took a seat opposite. 'She was in the paper claiming this place was haunted. Lucky for you Miss that I take my job very seriously. And you, sir, your face looks familiar.'

'Michael Kern, officer, the face in this morning's Daily Express.'

'I quite like that paper.' Ned looked beyond and smiled at Woody. 'Were you here when the incident took place?'

'I was outside collecting more wood fer the fire.'

'Now, who can tell me what happened?'

'See!' Angela broke in, pointing an accusing finger at Ned. 'He never asked Woody his name. That's because they know one another. Ask him, George, ask him why.'

Monday turned his head slowly in her direction and stared at her with that flat, hostile expression. 'Angela, if you don't shut up, I shall recall the doctor to shut you up! Do I make my position clear?' He watched her shrivel back into the seat followed immediately by a meek nod. The venom against him was a measure of her terror.

Crookshank spoke. 'I can tell you exactly what happened, PC Bobbins. Without any provocation whatsoever this woman became hysterical and physically attacked the maid with a cake knife. She-'

'Hold fast,' Ned broke in, 'attacked the maid with a cake knife,' he repeated whilst writing it down. He looked up. 'She?'

'She claimed the maid made her do it.'

'Now why would that be, sir?' Ned referred to his notes. 'If there was no provocation whatsoever, why would the maid make her do it?'

Good question, thought Monday.

'PC Bobbins, this woman is mentally unbalanced. No doubt you are aware of her claims in The Times, which I may add were unsupported by any credible evidence. The gentleman to your left, Harry Webb printed the substantiated truth in the Daily Express, and came here tonight, cajoled by that woman who had one thing in mind, to blackmail my client. When my client refused to concede, she then claimed Miss Tuesday's body was buried on my client's land. When-'

'Miss Tuesday,' Ned interjected. 'Was she the one who conducted a court case defending this woman?'

'Quiet so.'

'Then who murdered Miss Tuesday?'

'No one murdered anyone,' George quipped. 'It wasn't a body this mad hatter dug up but a rocking horse.' George had stunned Ned into silence. 'You heard correctly, PC Bobbins. She dug up a bloody rocking horse and sent it to a medical examiner claiming it was Miss Tuesday's body.'

'True,' Harry offered. 'I spoke to the medical examiner who appeared very concerned about Angela's mental state.'

'Hmm,' Ned hummed glancing at Angela. 'Are you currently on medication?'

Her eyes focused, her expression altered. Monday could see she was looking for a way round this. 'I demand to have a solicitor present.'

Ned flipped back his pages. 'Mr Crookshank is a solicitor.'

'Not my solicitor.'

'Then you better come down to the station.'

'Oh wouldn't that make you a happy man, Ned.'

Ned looked about and behind him then back at Angela. 'Where is Ned? Was he here when the incident took place?'

'Bastard!' She turned to George. 'I beg you, don't let him take me. He's one of them.'

'Look, my dear,' George distanced himself, 'far better you go with him and get help.'

'Why don't we all go with him, see how far he's prepared to go beyond the gates.' She tried influencing Harry. 'One last favour, Harry, just make sure I get to the police station.'

'Yes, Harry,' Monday agreed. 'PC Bobbins came on his bike. If you could give him a lift to the station with Angela then perhaps she can get medical attention.'

That forced Angela's hand. 'I would like a pee. Or do you propose I pee on the spot?'

Kern and Crookshank quickly stood up in case she did.

At last, thought Monday. He finally got her where he wanted her, knew she was bent on an escape route and he would oblige. 'Mike, see if you can find the cook to rustle up a pot of tea. I shall escort Angela to the cloakroom.'

Angela grabbed her bag in a huff, which was expected.

'Not so fast,' Ned said. 'Let me take a look in that bag.'

'Why?'

'To make sure you are not concealing a weapon.'

She slammed it into his chest. 'Next, I suppose you will ask me to strip!'

'No need for that,' Ned said poking around in her bag. 'There's not much to strip.' Satisfied with that, he handed it back with a nod.

'I want my privacy,' she demanded to Monday.

'You shall have it,' he replied hanging on the door handle.

Suddenly, Gallows Humour was placed in pitch-black darkness. Commotion broke out, exclamations of horror and heavy censure mixed with Bumble's frantic wails. Two minutes later the lights went back on. But where was Angela? Everyone fled to the front door, tracking the rear lights of a silver Mercedes.

'I left you in charge.' Ned falsely accused Monday.

'Look here, officer,' Crookshank came to his client's defence. 'Mr Monday cannot be held responsible for a black out. You searched her bag. You should have confiscated her car keys. Now get a squad car to pick her up.'

'I never took down her number plate.'

'I have it,' George said. 'CW…no, T2…err, I can't remember. Sol, you have it.'

Monday shrugged. 'Sorry, but I can't remember either.'

Ned held his head low, the helmet slipped from his fingers and bounced twice on the step for great effect. 'This is the chop for me, lose my pension I will.'

'Pull yourself together man.' The ambitious and calculating eyes of George shone bright as he gestured toward the drawing room. 'I'm sure we can work something out. What do you think, Hugh? We can make sure PC Bobbins is not held accountable for his mistake.'

Crookshank raised his brows to Monday, both secretly banking on this. 'Why not,' this solicitor said. 'Have a cup of tea and see how we can sort out this mess.'

Monday would leave them to it and moved to the library. There, he sat at his desk, pulled out the folded piece of paper from his pocket and forced that mark to reveal her true name. There was magic in Gallows Humour, he knew that now, the unexplained enchantment of a world which was still far from his understanding. He felt he had become part of its walls that had spilled their energy around him, and he also felt nothing was beyond his reach. As he looked at the name, Mary Smith coming into focus, anger and sorrow rolled into one. She had taken a life, to get a life. She had taken his Izabo, and even though Mary Smith deserved to die, he in turn would take a life by the burning of that page. It was not to be taken lightly.

'All's well that ends well.'

Monday startled and rushed the page into his pocket. It was Harry. There was no smile on his face, just a slight look of calm or maybe acquiescence.

'Sol, you and your servants were damn good. It was all I could do to stop myself from laughing. Brilliant, just bloody brilliant is all I can say.'

Monday was tongue tied. This was not how he had envisioned this happening and he was unsure how to proceed. He watched Harry light up his cigar, clenched between his teeth. No doubt he was playing it out, trying to get a rise from Monday. But Monday leaned back in his chair and said nothing.

'I'm not without some experience,' Harry said, dropping his match in the ashtray. 'I used to go fishing with my grandfather, wonderful man. Eighteen, what do we know at that age, Sol? Motorbikes and girls in hot-pants…now I am showing my age. So, there I was with the wind in my face seeing how fast I could go when this bloody big truck came whizzing round the corner. Headstone for me…I swerve, as you do, go right under his carriage, then a hand grabs my leather jacket and whisks me to the ditch. Motorbike carries on with the truck and I'm sitting there thinking what the fuck just happened. Get that mean bugger to buy you a car. That was my grandfather talking while I'm brushing myself down without a broken bone in my body. The tight sod was my Father. Now what do you make of that?'

'Amazing, truly amazing.'

'Not anywhere near as amazing to what happened tonight.'

'I'm sure I have no idea-'

'Sol, the medical examiner had a bloody rocking horse with your name scratched on it. I figured it like this. Angela thinks she's exhuming a body, leaves it on his slab none the wiser. When he walked in, he told me it was the most bizarre case he had ever come across. He telephoned Angela, asked what she was playing at. Then suddenly she comes here and she's forgotten again?'

'And the rocking horse?'

'I am going to send it to you as a Christmas present. I had a bloody good time, so know this. Your secret is safe with me. Don't forget your friends. Those were the best cakes I ever tasted.'

'Thanks, Harry. It means a lot to know you're on our side. How does it stand with George?'

Harry waved his hand. 'That man is an asshole. I watched him shitting himself over Angela. He thinks he has Hugh and your constable plod in his pocket. I suppose this is going to be the last we shall hear of Angela?'

'Trust me, Harry. She will be on her way to something far more rewarding.'

'Okay, Sol. Keep in touch.'

'Stay overnight.'

'No, best get going. The wife expects me. I shall get George out of your hair and drop him off. He can sleep on his yacht and make of it as he will.'

Monday stood and shook the proffered hand with both of his. 'Harry, I will never forget this, never.'

'And nor will I, Sol.'

Before seating again, Monday wiped a hand over his face with overwhelming relief. These last months, his most frequent companions had become doubt and near despair. He began to think idly of personal contributions others had made, new friends, and certainly old ones. His intervention had made a difference, and, better, the tribe had successfully reappeared. But there was also sorrow. Seven days, that was all, seven days to make a difference and change Izabo's fate and perhaps his fate too. But then that might have condemned the fate of others. He let out a sigh and resignedly accepted his lot. For in place of that was a bond of fellowship within Gallows Humour whose thick solid walls had something else to offer.

Palfrey entered, closing the door softly behind him. Without turning, Monday lowered his head and leaned forward, placing his forearms on the desk.

'I thought it went extremely well.' Palfrey hiked out a bottle of whisky from the globe. 'Would you care to enlighten me why Angela was left unpunished?'

'What I have to say must be said to all. Is Hugh still here?'

'Yes, somewhere around and Mike is presently with Flour.'

'We never fooled Harry but we have a good ally.' Monday held the glass to his lips and smiled. 'Ned is quite a character. Who was he speaking to?'

'Me. I am rather good on accents.'

'Do you remember the first day we met? You told me a story about a woman walking to the gallows with an umbrella.'

'So I did. That was Bumble. Like Doolally, they have their monuments. The first week of my employ I thoroughly inspected the house to discover a rather large collection of black silk umbrellas. Apparently, every time Hugh's father came when it rained, he would lose his umbrella to Bumble. One felt she could open a shop and supply the nation almost immediately it rained.'

'I suppose she hid in the boiler room.'

'Actually, she was by Doolally's side the whole time. It was her idea to fill a hot water bottle with pig's blood.'

Kern and Crookshank now emerged along with the tribe, their chattering contentment only temporary. They could afford to rest after that performance, cover amusing ground, smoke and laugh before Monday called their attention.

'First,' he opened up. 'That was a pretty spectacular performance. You all did an excellent job.' They cheered. 'Now I must tell you why I let Angela go.' He sat back and raked the room identifying Kern with his arm about Flour. In part of what he had to say would certainly go in their favour. 'You were not far off, Mike. A pattern does emerge from chaos…though sometimes that pattern is not as pretty as we think. A week after my Mother died, I met Angela at an Embassy do, as well you know. I was also in the middle of a scoop and taking drugs. Far from being in control of a situation, I was steadily losing it. What I did not know until this night is that Angela had taken a life to get a life, and that life was Izabo's.'

It held no surprise to Monday that his latter statement received quiet acceptance, for this evening's performance by Angela and what she had conveyed was like an open admission of who she really was.

'At the lake,' he continued, 'Judge Week ripped out many signatures, burnt them as he said each name. They were the ones already consigned to their places at the bottom of that lake. Not so for the tribe and I think we can guess why for are they not here and innocent. He then gave me his book, what was left of the guilty, those who had obviously absconded. He knew, as I am sure Nigel Friday knew that one day they would return for their marks. In any event, Judge Week gave me his Work, certainly not so thick and told me what to do if ever I encountered one of them. But there was a particular mark he referred me to, was no doubt aware of what this interloper had done, had taken Izabo's life in order to get a life. It is my duty to consign that interloper to her hellish resting place. Tomorrow, I have no doubt Angela will be found in one of the obituary columns. They will be able to say very little about her for not even I know her background. She picked a name, and what is in a name but not her true name.'

'How do you know their true names?' Kern asked.

'It took a little nudge in the right direction from someone I loved very much to make me see how things really worked around here. As Judge Week was Gallows Humour, so I too am Gallows Humour. I became part of Gallows Humour when I made my footsteps in its history at six years old. It's hard to explain, but my personality seems to be charged into these walls. Here is the greatest energy I can tap into, here I am able to somehow manipulate matter, know things at my most heightened times of stress or even anger.'

'Why you?' Kern asked. 'Why did Angela come after you?'

'Well that answer is very simple. What she wanted was her mark. She knew how Jeremy had taken an interest in my articles, knew I would be offered a position here and also knew that if I found her mark, I could destroy her. But I think as time grew, she felt she had me in her pocket. And let's face it, she did. She had me fooled. She certainly had you fooled.'

'I never recognized her.' Doolally said.

'Why would you? She had altered her appearance, like you Doolally. When you sat next to me on the train, I considered you were a good lookalike. It never occurred you were my one and only Doolally.' He glanced at Palfrey's stoic face. 'You blamed yourself for Izabo's death when there was no need. Angela took advantage of a summer storm and sabotaged your daughter's harness. She once said to me she believed in fate, follow the yellow brick road and see where it leads. She felt her presence caused me to stay so I could fulfil my promise but to die in order for that to be achieved, it beggars greater understanding. Perhaps Mike has the answer as to why such a sacrifice should be made, for I certainly cannot see the advantage.'

Kern made a glance at Palfrey before turning to Monday. 'The one advantage I see, if you can call it an advantage albeit an unhappy and chaotic one is that had Izabo been alive Angela would have remained an interloper. And without Angela, you might have died from your drug addiction. Sex played a pivotal role and in some small way, she kept you on your toes, driving you on. You were upset about Hilda, not being there and all that. You could have slipped deeper into the abyss after you lost the scoop, and then your job; but no, instead you cleaned yourself up then your only problem was Angela.'

Palfrey glanced at his Mickey Mouse watch. 'What seems reasonable at one in the morning might not stand up in the cold light of day.'

LADY OF THE LAKE

Monday sat pensive at his desk. The short rest, the hasty improvisation to a spectacular drama, and even the meeting afterwards seemed only to have increased his concerns.

He was afraid. What he was about to do would place him far beyond the laws of physics and humanity, the beginning of a journey into unchartered territory which could end in disaster for innocent motorists coming in contact with a careering Mercedes. It was conceivable that fate had something else in store for them, their lives mapped as surely as those who occupied Gallows Humour.

It was still snowing when he wended his wearily way to the lake that promised to consume the guilty. His breath trooped into the ether under a blackened veiled sky as he dug into his pocket for a lighter. It was a simple matter to do, a simple thing to say but not so simple when his mind raced and his shoulders hung heavy.

'Mary Smith,' he said aloud, clicking the lighter. 'You took a life to gain a life and still you craved for more. Never shall you rise again.'

Snow was the culprit that blew out the flame. Several times he clicked the lighter, and several times it refused to ignite.

'Strike, damn it! Why don't you strike! ' he voiced to himself and then went back into the house to pace agitatedly in the library while he attempted to work it out. 'Perhaps I should do it when the moon shows? No, that cannot be. Mother said tonight.' He punched his fist into his own palm. 'Yes, of course. If my mood can charge a flame in the hearth then it can charge the flame of a lighter!'

With that, he tested the theory and struck the lighter again. The flame grew wild and furious, scorched the mark then petered out. Something else was at work here. It was certainly not the mischievous Doolally or any of the tribe. For them, more than most, they required Angela's demise. So was it, Angela?

A dark impotent rage overwhelmed him. He went to his bedroom determined that she would rue her prank. She had always done all she could to obstruct his efforts, and even now it appeared she had hidden talents.

At the mirror over the sink he stared fatigued at his reflection. It had been a long day and by far the night would be even longer. After brushing his teeth, he wrenched off his blood stained shirt and dumped it in the bin. He crossed the room and sat by the fire to observe the spiralling curve of smoke drifting up the stack like a charred message. Everything was backward. Out there was the true world and in here was the true dream. Stoking the coals, his thoughts travelled to a different matter. As justice would be served for Tuesday, so justice must be served for the tribe. He called for them and they came to pay service to their master. Faced with their generosity and enthusiasm, he gathered all his courage to speak the words that had been burning on his tongue these last hours.

'There is another matter you should be aware. I know each of you hold on to your marks but you do not know your names. But I will know your names if you show me your marks.'

'Why do we want to know our names?' Charlie asked.

'I can offer you something that perhaps is due, true justice.' He paused as they came closer to listen. 'Pass me your marks and become flesh and blood.'

His statement was true and they were stunned, no doubt about that. Even Doolally was lost for words. It needed time for the information to be absorbed and passed back. So Monday kept still to their mumblings and regarded the fire burning clear with a bottle-green light. He had no intention of forcing his will upon them and felt it was their choice to either live out a natural life or remain as they were, advantaged in many respects.

'Surely not, he must be mad.'

'Are we not madder than him?'

'Ask if our marks get burnt.'

'Yes, they do.' Monday spoke. 'That is the way it must be. You cannot hold on to your marks when clearly there is no mark for the living.'

'Nozt so,' Bumble buzzed over him like a bee to a honey pot. 'That fleshy viper haz her mark still. Her wickednezz is stronger than Gallowzz Humour.'

'It is true. The flame died in my hand. But rest assured my will is far stronger than hers. Even if I have to physically strangle her, I shall keep my promise.'

Nothing escaped them, he thought. Every move he made, they saw. Every word he said, they heard. And yet they very rarely interfered unless provoked. He had the weird sensation he had become their extension, exclusively for them and wondered what strengths would be left if they chose to hand over their marks.

'Tell us what yew wish us to do?' Woody asked.

'It's for you, Woody, for all of you to make that decision. You have lived many life times among human frailties. You have travelled beyond the gates and glimpsed a life you could lead. You can find partners, fall in love and have children.' He quickly glanced at Doolally meeting her brows. 'Okay, not all can have children but certainly Flour. Charlie, you like the girls, now you can have your fill of them.'

'I can have my fill of them anyway.' He guffawed.

Flour knelt by Monday's side and placed her head on his knee. He stroked her hair knowing what was going through her mind. Freshly plonked in the limelight this week, would Kern's love for her take second place? In some quarters of the female universe, Kern's celebrity status would make him irresistible.

'Flour,' he said. 'You must make your choice wisely. Mediocrity rules and all have their prizes, lest any precious self-esteem be damaged by criticism. Top of this festering dung heap of immoral depravity is the Labour Government, whose debt-fuelled boom has now bankrupted us. Out there, in my world, it can be very hard, especially when a person is shoved in the media spotlight. Mike has already become a celebrity, like it or not. People are not always friendly, and there's so much plutocracy and bureaucracy that Gallows Humour has a lot to be thankful for. You each have the ability to do things beyond the scope of scientific explanation, things many people would give their eye teeth for, so remember that before you make your choices.'

Ned spoke, slipping silently down to his knees. 'If we choose to become like you, what happens to Gallows Humour? We are part of you, you are part of us.'

Monday tried to see Gallows Humour through their eyes, tried to understand his deep connection. Revelation could be a kind thing. His follow-up of this conversation was utterly single minded. 'I gave my heart to Gallows Humour to become Gallows Humour, but are you not Gallows Humour? Judge Week knew this, that's why he purchased the courthouse off the Crown, that's why he named it Gallows Humour for in a sense there is irony that you should have chosen to attach yourselves to the very place that took your lives. It was his deathbed promise to give you a home, because home is where the heart is.' But he trusted his mind to know what to do. 'I am reminded of the Judge's words, that no man had more confidence in another than he had in me, and no man shall render more justice than him. He told you at the lake, your marks were given to pursue your own happiness. If your decision is to walk as flesh and blood, a piece of your strength will remain in my heart and for that I will be forever grateful. My task is to guard those guilty marks, face each one as they confront me. They may wait until I am dead, but it will do them no good for I shall live on in spirit to complete my task.'

Silence followed. There could be no doubt. Their fearless faces touched upon his to show a rather simplified view. It would cost him a tormented life, and beyond infinity for who would release him of his duty?

'Solomon,' Woody smiled ruefully. 'An heir would release your burdens.'

'At what cost, my friend? Far better this way than follow in Week's footsteps. I have no inclination to spread my seeds without love.'

'Miss Tuesday took your love, no thanks to interference.'

'She wus fer him!' Doolally quickly sniped at Ned's derision. 'Her puddles weren't shallow like some I can mention.'

'Do not blame Doolally. Miss Tuesday was instrumental in my decision to stay. Both knew the odds.'

'I speak fer myself.' Woody told him. 'I do not want to become human. Man is poisoning the trees. He has no heart fer nature. Plastic bottles and bombs do not endear me to live out a human existence, grow old among those who would wish me dead. If I am as I am, and alone in my choice, will I be welcome in your spiritual company?'

As a reflex, Monday frowned though he truly could not find it in himself to disapprove of Woody's remark. 'I would hope to live a few more years, my friend. So try to put up with my human frailties.'

Woody smacked him fondly on the head. 'I tease yew, lad. Keep my mark I will, know my name as Woody.'

'Count me in.' Charlie settled his cap on his head and buttoned his overcoat to the neck as though the cold outside would affect him. 'Flour, do you want to come dancing?'

She shook her head and laid it back on Monday's knee.

'I shall come with you.' Ned volunteered. 'My mark remains with me.'

'Yew hev us fer good, Solomon Monday.' Doolally took hold of Flour's hand. 'This one needs to see that scruffy git before she makes up her mind.'

When it happened, it happened with the abruptness that would have taken another watcher by surprise. There was no warning, no sound of footsteps or voices. They just simply disappeared.

Monday sat there for a few moments then pulled himself to his feet and flopped on the bed. As he did so, a buzzing noise came from behind and he smiled. Bumble had made her choice too. How he could possibly live without them, he thought. Then sleep and dreams reasserted themselves, and he glided away under their surface until morning broke and filtered the room with ancient sunlight.

He blinked the sleep from his eyes, aware he was still in last night's trousers, and then rolled off the bed and into the bathroom. It seemed like two minutes ago he was brushing his teeth and looking at his stubbled chin. The fact that he held the guilty marks of others who escaped Gallows Humour, the business for screaming kids with screaming parents was left in serious doubt. Now it was a question of what else he could do, what business structures could be built around Gallows Humour other than return to journalism.

Slipping on a roll-neck sweater, he sauntered downstairs and went into the fug of a kitchen from which breakfast had already been served.

'Where is Mike?' Monday asked.

'Mike is having breakfast in bed. Yours is under the grill.' Palfrey kept his nose in the paper and read the stop-press column. 'Ice on the road was blamed for the accident which happened in the early hours of this morning. No other drivers were involved. The silver Mercedes spun off the road and went headlong into a tree. The woman, as yet to be identified is currently on life-support.'

Monday made no comment and poked his head in the larder. He brought out the tomato ketchup and a sliced loaf. Bacon sandwich was on the menu.

'Care to tell me why she never went up in flames?'

Monday shrugged. 'Every time I set a flame to her mark it fizzled out. Maybe my heart wasn't it in. Has Doolally informed you of my little discussion with them last night?'

'Yes. A remarkable attribute even if it was refused. It seems to me another business is on the horizon, that of finding these exiles.'

'And exactly how are we to go about it? They could be anywhere on the globe, hiding or haunting, who knows what…like trying to find a needle in a haystack. Izabo said Week's Work is an element in reaction so they will eventually come here.'

'Meanwhile, we twiddle our thumbs.'

'Palfrey,' he muffled then swallowed his half mouthful. 'I have no intention of living out of a suitcase. No, we find something else, something which doesn't involve outsiders trudging on the estate.'

'What do you suggest?'

'Erm, no idea.'

'We should ask Mike. He knows more about the chaos theory than I care to challenge. When are you considering slitting your throat?'

'I have no intention of getting married just to produce an heir. Can we now move on to something more pleasing?'

Palfrey whispered a quiet plea heavenward and returned to the paper. 'Why did my daughter feel it necessary to leave you that night? What reason did she give?'

'You know the reason so why go over old ground. It wasn't your fault. If anyone is to blame it should be me. If I had just kept clean, been alert and saw Mother another set of circumstance might have prevailed. Who really knows about these things? Mother never took me to church, never spoke about her faith, and what faith would it be if she had? Friday talks about God as the id which rather opens the door for a more scientific mind than the one that sits here.'

'It just makes me wonder why there should be no justice for my daughter.' Palfrey removed his pince-nez. 'If her life was taken for a reason then surely it should be given back.'

Monday sensed the enormity of what Palfrey had said and pushed his plate to one side. 'If a no life can take a life, then what happens in the reverse? Justice is offered for the tribe then why not for Izabo? Are we clutching at straws here, Palfrey?'

'No, you make a valid point. Question. If her life is given back, when is it given back? No doubt at the same time of Angela's death. But her mark refuses to burn, so we must ask why.'

Despite the darkness in his head, despite his desperate circumstance, he still found a bitter-sweet admiration for Angela. 'She never gives up. The tribe believes her strength for living is stronger than mine for killing.'

'Albeit her body is forced to breath, in reality she is dead.'

'So, the only other conclusion we can draw is that Izabo did return and prefers to be with the other bloke.'

'What other bloke?'

'She mentioned something about being involved with some handsome crusader for the forces of good but grew arrogant in the extent of his self-regard. Maybe she's with him swanking it up over a bottle of champagne.'

'Bumble is correct, you have gone mad.' Palfrey sat straight in his chair, invincible and indefatigable but his eyes softened at Monday's miserable face. 'She would sit in the library, by the window and read your articles to Jeremy. His eye sight had deteriorated badly in the latter two years of his life. After her unfortunate incident with which came numerous benefits, she grew curious about you, especially when there were no more articles written by the eminent Solomon Monday.'

'I'm not going to like this, am I?'

'It rather depends how you view it. There you were, overweight and unshaven when your good friend Mike telephoned trying to sound considering and measured. The implication of his last remark caused a surge of irritation no doubt, where you promptly picked up your mother's photograph and threw it at your wardrobe mirror. Oddly, the mirror never cracked but the frame did. You then, with an obvious pang of guilt picked up the pieces. To cap it, there was Angela slobbering all over you like a wet fish as you indulged in a snort of coke.'

Humiliation flooded him. He had nothing to say in response to that.

'Sol, regardless of Mike's theory, it was my daughter urging you on to take charge of your life. After you checked into the rehabilitation centre she went to Italy and there she surmounted complications. Her mother tried her damnedest to marry her off to the local baker who originated from Woking. As such, she returned a good deal wiser and readied herself for a life at Gallows Humour. Here she intended to take on a role as secretary to your not so estimable self. I said it would never work. Apart from her circumstance, what need had you for a secretary. Of course, it all became irrelevant when Doolally moved things along. And as things moved along, I think she was trying to understand what her true role should be. Often, we would talk at night in my quarters. She was very muddle-headed, torn between two worlds, the world she so desperately wanted to share with you and the world in which she had no choice. That is why I asked you what reason did she give for leaving.'

Monday could still feel the dry warmth she radiated on his body, the wet stickiness of his tears and the pain in his gut, doubting he would ever see the pools of those sapphire eyes again. 'She told me her grave was calling for her, felt it the moment Friday came on the scene. That's why she hid upstairs in her bedroom. Izabo was an intelligent woman. I think she knew my role at Gallows Humour was to safeguard the marks of the guilty and could it be done in my lifetime, who knows, perhaps not. I needed an heir, and in that event, she was unable to give me one. Even Friday knew and mentioned as such. But if she can be reborn, then where is she?'

Palfrey looked dubious, frowning as he thought about it. 'Each of us is about a hundred trillion selves. Each of our cells contains a template for our complete body. In principle, there could be many of me, you, anyone, and these clones would dominate the universe utterly. Fortunately, there are physical and biological constraints that render this fantasy impossible, but not here. Is it not reasonable to consider one cell, one viable cell has my daughter's name.'

'But that would mean I would have to wait for her to grow up.' Monday started to count in his head. 'At fifty-five, she would be twenty-two.'

'Makes you wonder, Sol. Those marks the tribe hold, you say you can turn them into flesh and blood. Flour is a borderline case. If she takes up your offer, Mike is not going to forgive you when he holds a baby in his arms.'

Monday grinned. 'This is one of your jokes.'

Palfrey picked up his paper. 'Does my face bare a resemblance of a smile?'

To get his brain in gear, Monday walked outside to taste the sparkling and motionless day. A crackling branch and the shortening sun of winter only enhanced his mood. Snow had sealed the land and when he breathed the air it smelt like needles. Having sucked a few icicles and kicked the water-butt to vent his antipathy, he stood gazing at a white blanketed lawn. It was very similar to the country's economy. There were no green shoots in sight.

'She loved yew, don't yew be forgetting that.'

He looked down at Doolally eating the air with her front teeth. 'Of course, for better or worse she loved me.'

'What we going to do about Christmas, eh? We hev no need of candles and we all like candles. Christmas won't be the same without candles.'

'Doolally, candles it shall be, lots of them.' He brought her close and rested his chin on her head. 'It will be like all the Christmases you have ever known.'

'We like lots of presents, wrapped in strings and bows.'

'Is this where I'm supposed to ask what would you like for Christmas?'

'The sink needs to be lower. Yew never did the sink.'

'What if I bought you a pair of high heels?'

That never went down too well. As she spontaneously vacated her spot, he was left holding nothing. Then Woody glided toward him, a tone of utmost politeness.

'Sorry to intrude,' he said, 'are yew thinking of doing away with my sketches?'

'Walk with me.' Monday wanted to be diplomatic not autocratic. 'I loved what you did, Woody. On the face of it, how can we have parents and their children on this land knowing what we know now? Think carefully, we would be inviting the outside world to step in and there would be those, no doubt, to take advantage, measures undertaken by desperate interlopers seeking their El Dorado.'

'If they could do it here, they can do it anywhere.'

'Point taken.'

'Yew can still hev it for screaming kids whose screaming parents wish to get rid of them.'

Monday tugged at his ear lobe. 'Well so we can…except I don't think it a very good idea. By all means, go ahead and make your dream come true, just try not to be too disappointed if only I use it. Did you make the Gondola?'

'I made your rocking horse as well.'

'That was hilarious when Harry told us she dug up a rocking horse.' Monday stopped suddenly in his tracks. 'Where did you put Izabo's body?'

'Where she could see the moon,' Woody replied and motioned to the lake. 'It was not my choice but her wishes.'

'Did you see her? When you went in after Week gave you your marks, did you see her? No, strike that. You never saw her. Why would you? You saw the moon, followed the moon round the globe, so why didn't she, unless…unless she's been here all along, waiting.' Monday was now talking to himself. 'Waiting, yes, waiting for me to get rid of Angela…helping toward that end. So why did she extinguish the flame, or did she? It had to be her, so what am I missing? Woody, what the hell am I missing?'

'What did your heart ask fer?'

'Shit! That's it!' Monday's walk became a stride, his stride a run, his run a sprint to deliver his news in wheezing panic. 'Palfrey, we're going to get Izabo!'

'Where is she?'

'In the lake and pray to God I'm not too late!'

Within seconds, Palfrey responded and both flew out of the house and into the snow covered land where it grew rapidly cold and repellent with its life so suddenly drawn.

'It was her.' Monday paused to get his breath, plucking the mark from his pocket. 'It was her, Palfrey, her to blow out the flame because I never knew she was in there, never considered the reverse could happen. I am so bloody stupid, Mother said take back what she stole.'

Already the tribe was swarming round the lake, their eyes peeled to icy waters ready to drag a floundering Tuesday back to land. As they held their positions, Palfrey found his own searching spot and nodded the all-clear.

Monday flexed fingers stiff from the cold as he stood close to the bank. He struck the lighter, his mind focused on the mark. 'Mary Smith,' he said deeply reassuring, and watched the flames take hold. 'The life you took shall be taken back, returned to Izabo Tuesday.'

At first there was nothing but the crackle and smell of burning paper, curling crisply, falling ashes to his feet. A freak gust of wind carried those remnants across the lake where the waters grumbled to take them in as though by mutual agreement. There were no rules and what followed was stranger still. She had floated just long enough for him to catch sight of her, had hovered for an instant before disappearing, leaving nothing but a faint white image.

'There!' He shouted and dived in, plummeting deep. He could imagine no world without her now, would be willing to die for her, and immersed in the murky waters with nothing but his instincts to follow. She was within his grasp, felt the wavering strands of her hair as she sank even lower. His heart was thumping wildly against his ribs. So near yet so far before another presence aided the rescue and robbed him of her arms.

It was Woody who liberated Tuesday from the icy waters while Monday was left behind, half forgotten. Did it really matter when so much was at stake? She was scarce alive, if at all, naked and pale, unmoving, couched in a blanket, but still laid in her own puddle of snowy bewilderment. Palfrey's efforts of revival were making little headway. Yet it was essential to try. Doolally pushed him aside and fed her hands through the tissues of skin and bone and massaged the heart from within. It was the substance of magic, the secret essence of witchery which brought Tuesday to life. She retched, a disgusting mass of gloop and gunk, rolled to one side with head rocking convulsions and subsequently took a huge intake of air. She coughed and spluttered and breathed again, but in spite of all this, her eyes remained closed, her resilience dwindling. Since every second counted, and denying Monday again, Woody dispatched her limp body into the house while those around followed. Events were moving.

Leaving Palfrey to accommodate his daughter's requirements, Monday's teeth chattered. Every bone in his body ached. But he had a lot to be thankful for, celebration would come later. She was no phantom but flesh and blood, his apple pie and the 4 x 4 taking the kids to the zoo. As he removed his sodden clothing and ducked under a hot shower, homing in on his future, Monday would be the man she wished him to be, the considerate lover, the husband who remembered anniversaries, the father who changed nappies and read fairytales at night. All this and more he would be. In erecting pyramids of family life there were other considerations, not least the life of a child living among ghosts. The thought barely troubled him.

In the bedroom where someone had left a cup of hot brew, Monday pulled on a vest aware of Kern cloaked in stripy pyjamas.

'I tell you, Mike. It was a near thing.'

'Yeah, I rather gathered that from Flour.'

'How do you two communicate?'

'It's like a game of charades. She mimes and I guess, although my guessing would be quicker if she stopped kissing me.'

Monday smiled. 'Soon I shall be kissing Izabo.' He watched Kern take from the wardrobe a pair of cords and it puzzled him. 'Why do you feel the need to dress me?'

'Because you're colour-blind, my man.'

'Rubbish, I have never been colour-blind.'

Not to be proved wrong, Kern rummaged in a drawer and held up two T-shirts. 'Which is pink and which is blue?'

'The right one is pink.'

'Wrong. This one is mauve.' Kern tossed over a sweater. 'I used to think you did it deliberately, just to be different or awkward, whatever. What colour is Izabo's eyes?'

'Sapphire and Flour has hazel eyes, am I right?'

'Correct. Hey, maybe Nigel was right. You do see things differently. Perhaps you only see nature's colours and not synthetics.' Kern gave him a friendly punch on the arm. 'I am pleased for you. I best get dressed. We can meet up later in the library.'

There was no doubt that Kern was in a jubilant mood, no doubt Flour had mentioned what Monday could do. Vulnerability could be removed, certainty restored. Flour may learn, may grow to understand her wider duty.

Monday retraced his steps into the bathroom, combed his hair and splashed on some potent aftershave. Satisfied with that he crept into Tuesday bedroom. The curtains were drawn, the fire was lit and roaring, and she lay there in bed like a starched dummy with Palfrey stroking her brow. It was disconcerting.

'Is this what happened to me?'

'You were feverish and talking.'

Monday took hold of her hand. 'She is warm. Perhaps she is sleeping deeply.'

'Perhaps she is held by that witch.' Doolally appeared, controversial as usual. 'Not all her evil went in that lake. She still won't let go, Solomon Monday.'

'Is Izabo not here,' Monday argued. 'Is she not alive? She wouldn't be here if Angela was not consigned to her place. I think the delay might have caused Izabo some sort of, well, dare I say, disturbance.'

'You mean her brain was left too long without oxygen?' Palfrey watched the reflex stiffening of Monday's body and shook his head. 'I will look after her if she is impaired.'

'And you think I will not!' Monday irritated. 'Call for an ambulance.'

'Is that wise?' Doolally asked.

'I don't want to be wise, I want to be happy. Here she is in a comatose state just like-' it came in a headlong rush. 'Doolally, how would you like to take the last breath of Angela?'

'Once is enough for me in that lake.'

'No, not the damn lake, but the hospital and pull the plug. Angela is being kept alive by a machine.'

'Never heard of a machine to keep yew alive.' She nudged Palfrey. 'Hev yew heard of a machine that keeps dead people alive?'

Palfrey acted swiftly. 'Come with me, Doolally and I shall show you where to go and what to do.'

'So I gets to kill her?' she said on the way.

It seemed Doolally was to get her pound of flesh after all and whichever way Monday viewed the situation, serendipity was definitely underrated.

'Here that, Izzy?' He whispered and cradled her head. 'You have been right all along. We all have a yellow brick road to follow. May I hop on yours?'

There was nothing. And while he sat and waited, head bent to her silent mouth, to him she was beautiful and smelt of freshly linen handkerchiefs. Sometimes there was a reaction, a shiver like a dying last leaf on a tree and he wondered if she was revisiting nightmares.

'Izzy,' he whispered again. 'Do not give in to bad dreams. I am here, nothing will harm you. I shall be your protectorate and love you beyond my grave, this I so swear.'

Within a short duration Palfrey entered the room in quick strides claiming any time now she would wake. He had no intention of taking second place and jostled for front line position. There he sat, holding her hand and stroking her brow.

'Come on, sweetheart…where is your fight? Open your eyes and return to the living.' The eyes fluttered open before closing again and Palfrey continued. 'That's my girl, come to Dad.'

Monday held his breath as she opened her eyes wide to glimpse what she had already appreciated. 'Dad?'

'Yes, silly old daddy.'

She struggled upright, met and answered his loving embrace. 'Oh Dad! I thought I was dead. Am I dead?'

'No, sweetheart, you are very much alive and well.'

'Dad, I had this terrible nightmare. I thought all my bones were broken and next I was buried alive and-' She paused at a stranger beside her father.

'Do you know me?' Monday asked.

'Should I?'

MISTLETOE AND CAKE

With all the agitation he was capable of, Monday stormed down the stairs feeling terribly disappointed and almost entirely cut off. He reacted poorly to Tuesday's memory loss and barked at Doolally.

'Did you ensure her body was incinerated?'

'Yew said, pull the plug!' She barked back cleaving to a bunch of candles.

'You know damn well the meaning of metaphors.'

'Tis no good getting your knickers in a twist,' she said trampling behind. 'That's not the behaviour of a man who own Gallows Humour and a fleet of heroes.'

'Ah!' He unexpectedly stopped mid-way and she brushed right through him. 'Good with the metaphors when it suits,' he said. 'And what's with the candles?'

'A happy family Christmas yew promised.'

'Yes, yes, lots of candles, a mixed selection of nut cases, presents, heroes and freeloading friends, all coming for Flour's mince pies and Christmas tree lights.'

'Yew be forgetting the mistletoe.' She puckered her lips.

'Are you going to tell me what you did with her body?'

'She wet the bed.'

An eyebrow rose. 'She turned to water?'

'I always knew yew were deaf as well as blind.'

His mood improved a little when he shut himself away in the library. He looked about him, his anxiety gone now, burned away by the need to think and act. His predicament was such that he would now live at Tuesday's mercy, what her immediate reactions would be. Her position in Gallows

Humour made it unlikely she would stay unless it had something to offer. Preferably him, he thought.

'Want a drink?' Kern walked in.

Monday turned from the window and confoundedly looked at him.

'Drink, my man. I asked if you wanted a drink.'

'Make it a double.'

'Double, hey?'

'She doesn't remember me,' Monday said returning to his view. 'The last thing she remembers is falling off the roof.'

'So, start all over again. You have the edge, remember. She likes dancing and-'

'I cannot dance.'

'Okay, try taking her out for a meal, talk about bricks and cement, you'll be well away. Buy her a trowel, yeah?' The Kern magic was working. 'Who's filling in her blanks?'

'Palfrey, though I suspect Doolally will aid in that direction.'

'There you go. Doolally is your number one fan, done deal, yeah.' There was a pause, a hesitancy and then Kern said, 'Flour wants to take up your offer, Sol.'

'Is this what she wants or what you want?'

'I tell you what I don't want. I don't want to be holding a wet nappy.'

Monday stared thoughtfully. 'Difficult to accept there are ghosts, let alone one can be brought back from the dead. If Izabo's memories are lost, I wonder what effect it would have on Flour.'

'Surely, it's a different situation. Angela had taken away Izabo's life so the reversed happened, yeah? But there was a delay, yeah? I bet in that delay, while Izabo was left in limbo, she was losing part of her. And thank Christ you worked it out before it was too late. Now in Flour's situation she's not swapping with your life, she's getting a life that was promised by Judge Week but since he's given the power to you, it's a done deal. Correct me if

I'm wrong, Sol because if this goes tits up, I'm losing a friend in exchange for a marriage on rocky foundations.'

'No, you are not wrong.' Monday could feel her presence and craned his head round. 'Flour, is this what you want?'

She had remained invisible with her back to the door listening to their conversation and now faced them with depth. Never more would she be able to hide in the shadows, to travel the globe without paying her dues or hold that young innocent look forever.

'You know what this means,' Monday told her. 'Your body will be susceptible to pain…no crossing the road without looking left and right and left again You cannot stop the aging process, a wish most women would die for. Your skin will wrinkle and if you're lucky by the time you are sixty you won't suffer from incontinence.'

'Hey! What's wrong with you?' Kern dropped his voice, making the insult more personal and intense. 'Now stop acting the prat and be serious. Can you do this or not?'

'Will you always love her, Mike?'

'Whatever emotional silt other women kicked up went away the moment I clapped eyes on Flour. I never returned to a bloodless spirit, I returned to the woman I loved, for better or worse. If you have any doubts then tell me, because life is short enough and I want to share what I have left with Flour.'

'Unfortunately, my learning curve has been steep, but I would not put Flour in any danger or give her any false hopes if I felt there was an ounce of misplaced guidance.' Monday emptied his glass and moved toward her, taking her hands in his, rubbing his thumbs over her knuckles. 'The question I must ask, if you never loved Mike, would you still opt for this?'

She placed his hands to her stomach and he understood. She wanted her fill of life, the marching of heart beats, the roses round the door and the hidden treasures which only a good man can bring. It required no other explanation.

'Mike, wait outside.'

'Why?'

'Only I know her name, only I shall ever know her name.'

'Would it be too much effort to explain why?'

'She is not meant to know her name, for knowing her name would bring meaning to her past nightmares. That is why they have never known their name, their true name. And the sooner you bugger off, the sooner I can get on with it.'

Kern begrudgingly left the room while Monday poured another drink, thirsty for the coolness of Tuesday's lips, thirsty for his own 4 x 4 and taking the kids to the zoo. And although he planned it differently, it hardly seemed worth saying.

After Flour passed him her mark, she sat down and closed her eyes. It was mere formality for him. What had once been so weak had since become so strong, unexpected, inexplicable, but he would give her life and something more. She would not see him strike the lighter. She would not see the flame grow high nor hear him whisper her name, a name no other would know but a name that once had a voice. Whoever she was before, why ever it was that she hung, she would quickly leave that behind and feel her own breathing and move into a world of sticky plasters, her imagination and excitement racing ahead.

For Monday, he had buried himself in her memories to catch the snatches of country song which had turned suddenly to the cries of dastardly rape, a sound that made him fear as only a woman could fear. There were sights which in the rarefied walls of Gallows Humour she had never encountered, extremes of filth and stench, and of pain. No voice to plead for mercy, and no mercy was given. That was her legacy, her memories scorched on his mind.

They sat in silence for a while, observing each other. Her face aglow with pinkness, flushed with blood and unwilling to trust her new voice, whereas, he was drained, and resembling a stature freed from its plinth. He emptied his glass, but the bitter taste clung. He had given her life and she had given him pain of her memories. The exchange was unequal as it was unfair.

And for selfish reasons, he asked, 'are you thinking of leaving?'

'I want to stay as a freeloader.' And he chuckled to this as she spoke with girlish smiles and giggles, too excited to hide her happiness. 'I made a cake for Izabo. One side is dark like your mood, the worst of her memories. The other side is light like your mood, the best of her memories. You can choose what memories you wish to give her. All of you, half of you or part of you, just like the moon.'

Monday grinned. It was a tempting thought to give Izabo the best of him before she knew the worst of him. He walked round his desk thinking the exchange had been fair and knelt in front of her. 'Was it you who spiked Angela's thoughts, you to blow out the flame.'

'I had to, Solomon. Izabo was so sad, had not the will to stay. She did not know her life would return. We did not know her life would return. There were many things we did not know, pacts made, secrets withheld. I withheld a secret. I was so missing Mike on our global journey. When we pin-pointed Gallows Humour, Doolally refused to see you without front teeth. She was very upset you frowned upon her appearance so we held back until the dentist made them. Without them knowing, I sneaked in and Mike was not here. Nobody was here, only Palfrey asleep and someone worse outside.'

'Yes, Angela…Angela was there digging for Izabo's body. What on earth must have gone through your mind?'

'Many confusing thoughts,' she replied shaking her head. 'Why would she want your rocking horse but did she know, I suspected not. I knew then Doolally was right to call her a devil. Her digging brought sweat to her brow, and I saw her drink orange juice from her bag. So I made my own orange juice, pure of twisted thoughts and swapped the contents. Even so, I still could not say because it would have upset Charlie. Then did it matter to say? You were best placed to sort out the mess, Woody agreed as much on the train.'

Life was funny, open to strange chance in a world he once knew very little about. Perhaps chaos had a plan after all. He took her hand to his lips, kissing her fingers gratefully. 'You better go. Mike is probably wearing out the marble.'

She hesitated, reaching out for his hair. 'You took too much of me, and now I am unable to take some back.'

'I shall cope.' He misunderstood.

'Perhaps Tuesday would prefer to see a head of black hair.'

Monday jumped to his feet and looked at his deceptive reflection in the glazed cabinet, the hair completely grey. 'Well,' he said taking a philosophical view, 'I can always dye it.' He turned round and smiled. 'These cakes you bake, obviously they alter minds. Before I signed up, I ate a couple of ginger nuts.'

'It was not my idea,' she said at the door.

'Let me guess. Miss Tuesday's wicked sense of humour.'

'No, it was Palfrey.' Then she left.

Outside he could hear Kern's euphoria and waited a beat before leaving. Alone again, he picked his way through the dining room, and down those narrow steps where the soles of his leather feet scuffed wood, a familiar melody of a time long ago. He remembered the moment half expecting breakfast, and Doolally appearing almost more passionate for its spontaneity but with the recklessness that characterized their relationship.

Here, where the kitchen smelt sweet of lemons and chocolate, Monday rattled the empty kettle and filled it up. He would take Tuesday refreshments, watch as she consumed the best of him then open her arms to welcome him. That was the plan.

Charlie showed his face, his grievance came in a rush. 'This house has gone mad. What does she want to do that for? It won't be the same.'

'Sit down, Charlie. We need to have a man to man chat.'

Charlie was no man but a mere boy on the cusp of puberty, and his eyes shone brightly, his cheeks full of bum fluff and the only thing that mattered to him was Flour.

'I know you have reservations about Mike, but he's a good chap. They will make their home here so you will still see her. But, Charlie, you must not enter her private room, their private room. You have to accept she loves Mike, and that this is what she wanted. Would you deny her this?'

'Suppose not,' he sounded unsure. 'She kept secrets from me.'

'Charlie, we all have our secrets. It's a human condition. Some keep secrets because they have wicked motives. Others keep secrets because they don't want to hurt their loved ones, and some keep secrets because they are ashamed of their mistakes. Flour kept her secret because she didn't want to upset you.'

'There should be no secrets, not among friends.'

'Oh, I quite agree, a lesson for us all to learn. Palfrey mentioned your case should have been dealt with leniency. What did you do, Charlie?'

'What didn't I do is more like.' He sniggered. 'Pressed ganged I was to serve on a sloop under mid-shipman Lord Cochrane. After he captured a Spanish frigate, I jumped ship taking with me some clothes, not mine but his which helped my journey. I wanted to serve on Nelson's ship. That's why I come to Norfolk. But I sort of got waylaid with the vicar's daughter. Here, did you know men dress up as women?'

'They are called transvestites. Another thing you should bear in mind, some bars only cater for homosexuals.'

'Cor, it's a funny ol' world. Where do they stick-'

'Yes, Charlie!' Monday interjected fast. 'It's very important to keep your views to yourself, think before you speak. There are people ready to seize upon any opportunity to make money from derogatory or racist's remarks.' Now he was looking at that lemon and chocolate cake which sat tempting on the table. 'Charlie, would you know if Miss Tuesday is alone?'

Charlie followed the eyes, was plainly in tune with Monday's thoughts and despite having no discernible appetite, he left with the memorable cake.

'Charlie!' Monday irritated. 'Come back here with that cake!'

As if that was likely to happen, Charlie had obviously taken him at his word. There should be no secrets among friends. He looked at his Donald Duck watch. The morning had gone so quickly and the nights were drawing in fast. Perhaps it was best this way. Perhaps it was time to let confluence and destiny work its magic. But he felt so drained and weak, his energy entirely spent, and pulled out a chair, sat at the table to gather his strength while the night brought its own sounds.

The door creaked open to the weight of a man, the light off the corridor coming from behind. A face appeared. It was Palfrey hanging on the handle. 'Why do you sit in the dark?'

'Did Charlie give Izabo a cake?'

'Yes.' Palfrey walked an unhurried circuit of the kitchen, was content to prolong Monday's agony. 'There is no reason why we cannot make use of the courtroom. We could give students a grounding of legal life, participate in courtroom drama.'

'Very interesting, and does the cake participate?'

'This cake,' Palfrey spoke with his head in the larder, 'is it important?'

'Hell yes. Charlie swiped it from under my nose, took my meaning of secrets too literally. Now has she eaten it all or just the worst of me?' He looked up as Palfrey came into view, and added with hope, 'or just the best of me?'

'Good gracious!' Palfrey exploded. 'What have you done?'

'In giving Flour life, as was my duty, I took on board her horrible venture to the gallows. Perhaps I should have done it another day when my mind was in first gear.'

'There is no point in complaining about the air if there is nothing left to breathe.'

'And what's that supposed to mean?'

'What do you suppose is going to happen if they all hand over their marks? There will be nothing left of you.'

'There is a complicated answer to that question.'

'In other words you have not a clue. I suggest you take up a pot of tea and be two ships roped together guided by my daughter's wisdom.'

Palfrey was an example to them all, Monday mused picking up the tray. This would be his final tribute, the last stand. He would manoeuvre with aplomb, listen to her woes, and comfort her until there was nothing else to make her feel strange to him.

But he trod jadedly up the stairs, swallowing, feeling delighted and scared. Ahead, the door was ajar and gentle light squeezed through the crack. With a stuttering heart, he padded softly across the room and found she was knelt by the fire, head buried in The Times. She could see, in the near-darkness she could see and it was only slowly that she became aware of his shadowy presence.

'Do you mind if I join you?'

'No, please do.' She held up her hands and took the tray. 'Not a very good start, is it Mr Monday.'

'Nothing we cannot remedy, Miss Tuesday.' He remembered the few times he tried to talk to her about anything serious while her face opened up, her eyes wide and her hands clasped to her chin, grasping or frustrated at his attitude.

'Did you know the Stock Market has fallen drastically?'

'We are in a deep recession.'

'No different from me. Sugar?'

Monday shook his head. 'Have you eaten the cake?'

'Not yet,' she replied passing over his tea.

'Good. No strike that. I mean it's best to eat cake in company.'

Her eyes dipped to the newsprint. 'Mr Monday, my father speaks very highly about your endeavours, but I cannot help wonder why I decimated your character in court.'

'Izabo, I hope we can dispense with the formalities.' He decided to sit squat on the floor in front of her, by the fire, the easier to converse. 'You travelled a long dark journey, mostly dark because of me, but there were lighter times.'

'Lighter times? What lighter times could there possibly be when I was murdered by your girlfriend?'

'But you did not know that at the time.'

'What else was there to know when clearly I had no life at all?' She rustled the pages portentously and then composed herself to read aloud. 'I told her it was the only way in order to get out of my commitment to Gallows Humour.' She looked up. 'Your words, not mine. My Father mentioned I signed the register over your name. Would you care to tell me why that was necessary?'

'Yes, it was combative at times, you had your way and I had the pleasure of hopping on your yellow brick road, if only for a short time.' He stirred his tea and watched her puzzle. 'Habit,' he explained. 'I used to take sugar, sweet tooth and all that.'

'Solomon,' she said folding the newspaper, exposing a small shaft of her cleavage. 'I may appear frayed around the edges but I can assure you I still have my faculties. So please, do me the courtesy of explaining what sort of relationship we had?'

'Err, bouncy. Yes, most definitely bouncy. I dropped a water bucket on your head from on high, and you retaliated by tipping the wheelbarrow at my feet, which rather cemented our relationship.' He grinned. Was he making progress? She did not reply. He waited and there was only her breathing. 'It was a two-way effort on a one-way ticket. Perhaps if you eat a piece of the lemon side, we might stand on the same platform again?'

She removed the crumpled Daily Express laid carelessly over it. His gaze travelled with hers, watched as the light from the fire danced seductively on two sides of a cake, creamy fresh lemon and mouth-watering chocolate.

'If we share, we can journey through your memories together,' he suggested.

'In sharing, you will have eaten part of my journey.'

'Ah, if I was to eat more chocolate it would make your journey less painful.'

'And no doubt make it less painful for you.'

The grin died on his mouth. 'Sharing has never been one of your defining moments. We were business partners but did you ever consult me? No, you did your own thing and presented me with a fait accompli.'

She observed him now, really observed, every detail of his face lit up by the firelight flooding back into the room. 'Strange,' she said as she pinched the thick hair of his eyebrows between her finger and thumb. 'I was a little dozy this morning but you appeared younger.'

'Yes, younger.' He tried to keep his voice level with only partial success. 'My hair went grey at the sides during the fever. Did your father tell you about that?'

'It was mentioned.'

His eyes went to her blouse, imagining the buttons scattered to the floor like fallen pennies. 'Do you want to go dancing with me?'

'Are you able to dance?'

'Not really. I would probably step on your toes and cripple you for life.'

She laughed and took the spoon from his saucer. 'It would appear you have nothing to offer me, Solomon, certainly no enthusiasm to divulge your secrets.' She scooped from two sides, choosing to take equally chocolate and lemon. 'Let us see if a memory can serve me better.'

He watched pensively as her mouth filled up with quietness. What were those memories she had consumed, he wondered. Were they the arguments in the rain? Were they equally forgiven when they made love on the Gondola? There was no way of establishing with any certainty exactly how this would go.

'Yes,' she admitted, teasing, 'the taste is superb. I quite like the two flavours.'

'Tell me what you remember?'

'Us meeting for the first time,' she said scooping up more, pausing before taking it into her mouth. 'You definitely looked a lot younger.'

Twice she emphasized his aging disposition and now it worried him. He also recalled Palfrey's concern, and it worried him further. In her spellbound silence he clawed to his feet and padded to the bathroom, locking the door behind him. And when he looked at his mirrored face, it was not the distinguished face he had seen this morning, nor the face reflecting off the glazed cabinet. It was the face of a man in his sixties. His cheeks were rough and loose around the bones, the day's stubble already itching through skin, dark points peppered with silver, and the eyes appeared shrunken in their sockets. No doubt about it, the exchange was unfair as it was unequal.

Monday sighed heavily, a rumbling gust came from somewhere far down in the sheerness of his stomach and he bent his sorrowful head wondering what fitful life he had left. It was the worst possible outcome. He turned on the tap, examined his hands, weathered and worn, the water careering into the basin, steam billowing up around his face, and he was weeping.

'Sol?' A quiet knock on the panelled wood and she said again, 'Sol?'

'Leave me alone.'

'Sol, please, something is wrong. What is it?'

'How much of the cake have you eaten?'

'A few mouthfuls. Why?'

'Do not eat your memories, Izzy. I am not the man you once knew. Leave Gallows Humour and make a fresh life without the baggage of memories.'

'But memories are what make us, Sol.'

'Your memories of me will give you heartache. I carried memories of you with such yearning and sleepless nights just for one moment in your arms. You left because you had nothing to offer me. And now I find myself in a similar position. I have nothing to offer you.'

'Explain?'

'You saw me. What other explanation do you need?'

'A man is measured by his actions, not by his looks.' The handled was tried. 'Please, Sol, unlock the door.'

He stood motionless with his eyes closed, filtering through his senses, the irony, the journey he had undertaken and it had come to this. And her voice rose and rose until it sounded almost like a simpering child, and it cracked and broke. The door was tried again.

'This is so silly, Sol. You are in my bathroom. You cannot stay in there forever.'

If needs must. 'Izzy, I never meant for this to happen. Had I known by my actions I would become aged I would not be here ordering you to leave.'

'Sol? Remember how we talked in the library about your mother, the mistakes you made. I made mistakes too. I never gave up on you because I believed in you. I still do. And you never gave up on me. Dad told me how you risked your life to save me. Sol, please? I know you are hurting. Please, please, don't give up. We can find a way round this.'

He imagined she was cleaving to the handle, her breath bouncing against the barrier between them and he gently laid his hands on the door as though to take in what he could of her. 'You once asked if I believed in fate. I do believe, Izzy. My God, I do believe. This is my yellow brick road and you have yours. We crossed briefly, the most wonderful passing, and I shall be eternally grateful. Darkness will soon draw avail over me and I will bask in that passing for eternity.'

'Oh, Sol, what did you do?'

'It matters not. Make me happy and go.'

'I will not let you die. I will not let you live in a wilderness, Sol. Whatever time you think you have left then share it with me, please, Sol. Let's sit by the fire and talk. You can have a piece of my cake if it makes you happy. You can have it all, just come to me.'

Like he once asked her to come to him? He had not expected this, the things she said, the politeness, the urgency, the thickness in her throat. Blinking back the wetness in his eyes, he turned the lock, focusing as she slowly pushed open the door.

'You are a stubborn woman, Miss Tuesday.'

'No more stubborn than you, Mr Monday.' She laughed between her coursing tears. 'Let's sit by the fire. You are no good to me or Gallows Humour if you are dead so tell me exactly what you did.'

And so he told his story. They sat entwined on the floor by the fireside with her back against his chest, his chin resting on her shoulder, both gazing into the flames. No disappointment could lessen the sense of satisfaction. He was holding her, and that was what mattered, the feel of her skin, the smell of her hair and the sound of her voice resonating through her body. Once or twice, or maybe thrice, she had taken more cake and it seemed to bring her closer to him instead of the shock and dismay.

'For every action there is a reaction,' she explained licking her fingers. 'A positive is to cancel the negative. What made you think you could give a life without consequences?'

'I have become Gallows Humour. My thoughts, my deeds are reflected within these walls, within those who serve. Judge Week said the tribe deserved their happiness, and Flour did no more than ask for hers.'

'Oh, Sol, you are such a crusader for justice. I can understand why I loved you so.'

He remained quiet at first, absorbing this. Do you still love me, he wanted to ask but instead he justified his actions. 'They were left their marks for a reason, Izzy. I cannot explain it, but I knew it could be done, had to be done. I became part of Gallows Humour when I made my footsteps in its history.'

'I too made footsteps in its history. I have always believed our lives entwine, that for whatever reason, each plays an important role in life. Sometimes we find it hard to understand why fairness is not measured equally. Yes, some do travel a more painful journey than others but in time the big picture is revealed. You just have to open your eyes to see this bigger picture.'

He grazed on her neck. 'Maybe I was a fool to consider it would alter the outcome.'

'Do you think Flour's needs were greater than yours? Where she subconsciously took with a deep hunger for life, you gave unthinkingly?'

'Whether her need was greater than my hunger, she left me her memories, horrible memories of her injustices.'

'Memories? That is illogical. Although you are best placed to receive them whilst in the act, you should not have kept them. Why was that so?'

'You ask me? I am but a novice, and still hungry.'

She turned to face him, held her hands to each side of his face, her eyes in quiet desperation. 'Sol, we can share. I too am part of Gallows Humour. I can give you some of my years and we will be equal.'

'No, out of the question.'

'Listen to me. This is why I am here, to love you, to give these walls children, to share in Gallows Humour. I signed on for the long haul too, Sol. I signed over your name, two days into one. This is the bigger picture. Would you deny it?'

'Yes, Izzy, I would deny it. What happens if one of the others seeks a life? We shall not escape death. Can you imagine our children with walking dead parents?'

'You gave too much, Sol. You should not have her memories buried deep into your heart. Next time, if there should be a next time we can be together, more measured.'

'I was measured.'

'Were you? You had done too much in one day, your emotions ran high and you were not completely in charge.'

'Izzy, I know you mean well but what you ask is out of the question. We cannot spend a few short years propping up each other's energy, and that will not bode well if we confront an interloper.'

'You know, you are absolutely right.'

'I am?'

She kissed his nose, jumped from his arms and onto her feet like a cat in search of its prey. 'Eat my cake while I get the answer.'

The cake was tempting enough, if not to fill an empty stomach. As Monday watched her bounce excitedly across the room, and leave through the door, he already felt his brain piled high with sweet nostalgia. He looked around her room, at the things that were hers and wondered if they could make love in the dark, to hide his appearance so she could remember him as he once was, strong, distinguished and hopefully still chemically potent.

'Yew is in a right pickle.' It was the turn of Doolally to battle with this curious affair. Her hunched frame settled beside him, one hand resting on his knee. 'What yew need is a gal that's not as shallow as a puddle. Did I not say that? Now swim in them.'

For a moment Monday paused, balancing a piece of cake on a teaspoon before craning his head and dropping it into his mouth.

'Cake won't solve your problem.'

'No, it will solve my hunger.' Now, glancing at Doolally, it was impossible to look into those mischievous eyes without feeling curious. 'What is going on in that head of yours?'

Doolally could not afford the pause, could not let the lethargy of his ignorance pin him down and swiftly kissed him deep, unremitting. The weariness and sadness he once felt dissipated, replaced by the heat of her strength filling his lungs, the oomph of power circulating his heart. Little would be left to chance.

'There,' she said before disappearing. 'All back to the day when yew signed on.'

It was addictive, like drugs but far more hypnotic. And while he lingered in a soporific state, Tuesday came back into the room, pulling up the folds of her skirt, kneeling in front of him. A time of uncertainty had come to an end.

'It's very simple,' she said full of glee, 'when you consider the equations.'

Monday peered at Tuesday blearily. Was he really listening or was he in wonderland. He used to imagine walking along the giddy path of a zoo, swaggering in the clarity of passion, the grasping bud and the lengthening sun of spring and the bloom of a baby inside the woman he loved. But first there was Christmas, mistletoe and cake, and Tuesday to make his dream come true.

Elsewhere below stairs in kitchen contentment was Palfrey, now in sudden conversation with Doolally.

'The sink should be lower. Who put in a sink that's too high must need their head examining.'

'It is a cold fact of nature you are the height that you are. What is wrong with the step Woody made for you?'

'None that need be spoken.'

'Well then, just because you are older does not mean to say you are right, just that you have been wrong longer.'

ALSO BY LEVITY BROWN

PHANTOM JIGSAW

WAITING FOR REVISION

Strident Cutter, owned by third-generation Tony Black, is on the brink of bankruptcy. His twin, Jason, an eminent chemist, arrives from America to help with the sale, unwittingly walking into a nightmare. What first appears to be a blank jigsaw puzzle found in the store room, the phantom riddles catapult the twins into the realms of the paranormal.

This mystery is of a soul who needs Jason's expertise to alter the course of history. There is rivalry, revenge and forbidden love; an unforgettable impact of human relationships.

BOOK OF HORTUS

A TIME FOR HEROES

Sat naked in a puddle of mud, all that he knows of himself is his name - Quercus Coccinea. Befriended by Nina, a librarian, this legendary hero will never yield - one hundred years does not make a man forgive or forget. In a world of breathtaking beauty, Quercus gathers his thousand-strong army to defeat an unbeatable enemy, gain immortality and find the lost halves of the Book of Hortus.

**Suspenseful and endlessly exciting,
this mystery is sure to thrill anyone who enjoys action,
mysticism and nature on an epic scale.**

GIDDY MIDNIGHT

THE GRAND EXIT

Warrior Queen Boudicca called upon the Goddess Andate for victory in battle against the Roman army. But what transpired gave rise to a curse inflicted upon two opposing bloodlines.

Lukas Giddy, disadvantaged by the curse, is determined to lift it.

Marcus Metellus, advantaged by the curse, is determined to stop him.

**For one woman caught between the two,
her love for Giddy and his furry companion is an act of courage.**

COMEBACK

THE LADY IN GREY

The Chief Executive

Godfrey Shilling of Fair Life Assurance is limiting the liabilities against his company. Shortly after issuing a million-pound life policy, the client drops dead of natural causes. Coincidence? With no proof, he calls upon the woman in Grey.

The woman in Grey

Enigmatic, expensive to hire, Miss Grey walks into a Norfolk Town as Godfrey Shilling's Trojan horse. With a 100% success rate as a ruthless private investigator, she is about to turn a carpenter's world upside down.

The Carpenter

Ruben Stone, hiding more than a secret or two, lives above a shop selling beautiful dollhouses and related items. No profit, no loss, no gain, no shame.

**The Black Panther writes again in this stylish mystery
murder is on the menu for those who want to die and live again.**